6-15-90

To CAPTAIN L. VON LANGEN

A MASTER MARINER IN EVERY TRADITIONAL SENSE OF LIFE WORLD.

BEST WISHES TO YOU + YOURS

AUTHOR'S NOTE

"TANKER DISASTER AT VALDEZ!!!"

"How could such a thing happen???"

And suddenly everyone has an opinion and a working hypothesis as to the "whys" and "wherefores."

Unfortunately, this country's news media are little better informed than the general public when it comes to things "Maritime." Therefore, all the reporting and investigations are failing to reveal the truth or provide the information necessary to prevent similar or worse disasters from occurring.

This abysmal lack of information and interest in the United States Merchant Marine is directly linked to America's no longer being a first-rate seafaring nation.

The U.S.S.R.'s modern merchant fleet numbers over 1,650 ships. The U.S.A. has less than 400 aging vessels.

There are fewer than 35,000 active American seamen (including licensed and unlicensed, union and nonunion, inland water and deep sea) as compared to the Soviet Union's 250,000 merchant sailors.

Ernest K. Gann, the best-selling author, (whose son, a chief mate, was lost at sea several years ago along with the captain and boatswain of a tanker on the "Valdez Run"), observed in a recent letter to me that this is not an age of sailors and that "a story about the merchant marine is much needed."

Only by knowing the past can we attempt to shape the future.

I hope my book will shed some light on the small, enigmatic fraction of society known as the "Brotherhood of the Sea" and the ships they sail.

Larry Reiner

MINUTE OF SILENCE

Publisher: INTEGRA PRESS
           1702 W. Camelback Rd., Suite 119
           Phoenix, Arizona 85015

*This is a work of fiction. The events
described here are imaginary; the settings
and characters are fictitious and not
intended to represent specific
places or living persons.*

Jacket design by Wayne Horne

Printed in the United States of America

First Printing: 1990

Library of Congress Cataloging-in-Publication Data

Reiner, Larry, 1930-
    Minute of silence / Larry Reiner.
        p.   cm.
    ISBN 0-9626148-0-7
    1. Merchant marine--United States--History--20th century--Fiction.
I. Title
PS3568.E4865M56   1990
813'.54 -- dc 20   **90-34659**

Minute
of
Silence

Larry Reiner

Integra Press
Phoenix, Arizona

Dedicated To:

The girl with the tear-filled eyes who stood watch from the window on the "tenth floor Brown."

My good friend, G. Keith Hodson, who challenged me to write this book.

And to:

Merchant Mariners the world over and those who wait for them ashore.

Special Acknowledgments

To my editor, Adam Niswander, fellow author, friend, and honest critic whose constant faith and encouragement were as invaluable in the completion of this book as was his skillful editing.

To Capt. Robert A. Beevers, master mariner and friend whose advice, guidance, and tireless efforts in providing data helped keep me on course.

Part One

1950

STATION BILL

S/T CONCORDIA

Overseas Tankers Inc.
180 Wall Street
New York City, N.Y.

WHISTLE SIGNALS -BOAT

LOWER BOATS - 1 short blast
STOP LOWERING- 2 short blasts
DISMISSAL - 3 short blasts

SIGNALS:

FIRE AND EMERGENCY-Rapid ringing of ship's bell and continuous ringing of general-alarm bells for 10 seconds.

ABANDON SHIP-More than 6 short blasts and 1 long blast on ship's whistle and same signal on general alarm.

MAN OVERBOARD-Hail and pass word "MAN OVERBOARD" to bridge.

DISMISSAL-from FIRE & EMERGENCY stations, 3 short blasts on ship's -whistle & 3 short rings on general alarm.

NO	NAME	RATING	FIRE & EMERGENCY	BOAT	Abandon Ship
		DECK DEPARTMENT			
A	Robert J. Layton	Master	On Bridge In Command		In Command opers.
1	Timothy Wilder	Chief Mate	Scene of Emergency	2,4	In Charge boats
2	Carl Finney	Second Mate	Bridge-Relieve watch	1,3	In Charge bridge
3	Michael Searles	Third Mate	Prepare launching	2,4	In Charge boats
4	Timothy Donley	Third Mate	Prepare launching	1,3	In Charge boats
5	Edward Moore	Radio Operator	Radio Room - Standby	1,3	Attend Master
6	James D. O'Malley	Boatswain	Emergency Squad-line	1,3	Fr'd gripes, falls
7	Chester Borolowski	Dayman-Deck Maint.	Emerg. S-Extra hose	2,4	Fr'd gripes, falls
8	Roland Sims, Jr.	Dayman-Deck Maint.	Emerg. S-Fire exting.	1,3	Aft. gripes, falls
9	Pedro Davila	Able Seaman 4-8	Emerg. S-Fire axe	2,4	Aft. gripes, falls
10	Robert F. Howard	Able Seaman 4-8	Emerg. S-Fresh Air App.	1,3	Release chocks
11	James Ryan	Able Seaman 8-12	Relieve Wheel (Emerg. S)	2,4	Release chocks
12	Mamud Hassan	Able Seaman 8-12	Assist 3rd Mate	1,3	Lead out painter
13	Eric Hansen	Able Seaman 12-4	Assist 3rd Mate	2,4	Lead out painter
14	William Evers	Able Seaman 12-4	Emerg. S-Fresh Air App.	1,3	Release chocks
15	Terry Cole	Ord. Seaman 4-8	Bridge-as messenger	2,4	Release chocks
16	Peter Tompkins	Ord. Seaman 8-12	Emerg. S-messenger	1,3	Secure drain cap
17	Allan Stacey	Ord. Seaman 12-4	Assist 3rd Mate	2,4	Secure drain cap
		ENGINE DEPARTMENT			
18	Fredrick Kruzic	Chief Engineer	In Charge-Engine Dep.	1,3	Assist in oper's.
19	Robert J. Pierce	First Ass't Engineer	Engine Rm. In charge	2,4	Assist in oper's.
20	John Pillars	Second Ass't Engineer	Fire Rm. In charge	1,3	Assist in oper's.
21	Henry A. Davis	Third Ass't Engineer	Steam smothering sys.	2,4	Assist in oper's.
22	Angelo Cannito	Chief Pumpman	CO_2 & Foam smothering	1,3	Turn out F. Davit
23	James Johnson	Second Pumpman	Assist Ch. Engineer	1,3	Release gripes
24	David T. Sterling	Machinist	At main panel-Eng. Rm	2,4	Turn out F. Davit
25	Spiros Dimitrios	Oiler 4-8	Fire pump-Main Eng Rm	1,3	Turn out A. Davit
26	Andre Ballou	Oiler 8-12	Assist w/ Fire pumps	2,4	Turn out A. Davit
27	Ned Carter	Oiler 12-4	Trim Ventilators	1,3	Attend F'rd falls
28	Fidel Solis	Fireman-W/T 4-8	Assist w/ Fire pumps	2,4	Attend F'rd falls
29	Paul Morgan	Fireman-W/T 8-12	Assist 2nd Engineer	1,3	Attend Aft. falls
30	Paco Hernandez	Fireman-W/T 12-4	Assist 2nd Engineer	2,4	Release gripes
31	Thomas Bender	Wiper	Engine Rm. Messenger	1,3	Release gripes
32	Frank Billet	Wiper	Emerg. S. Inhalator	1,3	Attend Aft. falls
33	Herman R. Schmidt	Wiper	Emerg. S. Fr. Air Mask	2,4	Release gripes
		STEWARDS DEPARMENT			
34	Vincent Santos	Chief Steward	In charge-Stew. Dept.	1,3	Assist in oper's
35	Samuel Diamond	Chief Cook	Secure Galley	2,4	Assist 3rd Mate
36	Robert Smith	Second Cook	Assist Chief Cook	1,3	Assist 3rd Mate
37	Waldon Reed	Night/Cook & Baker	Secure ports-midship	2,4	Ass. w/F'rd Davit
38	Andrew Talley	BR	Secure ports-port Sd.	1,3	Ass. w/Aft. Davit
39	Phillip T. Banks	Galleyman	Secure ports-St'bd Sd	2,4	Ass. w/F'rd Davit
40	James L. Dooley	Saloon Messman	Secure saloon - Aft	1,3	Standby Life Ring
41	Thomas A. Deel	Crew Messman	Secure messroom - Aft	2,4	Standby Life Ring

—ONE—

Moonless and overcast. Dead black sky and sea met without horizon. A night for fear to become reality. Knife in hand, he stood with his back to the sea peering aft. His neck and shoulders were cramped and his eyes burned from staring. Suddenly he sensed he was no longer alone on the bow. His heart slammed wildly—he couldn't breathe—THEY WERE COMING FOR HIM!

*   *   *

The *Concordia* had discharged her 117,909 barrels (4,952,178 gallons) of Venezuelan crude. In a few hours she'd sail for the Persian Gulf on a two year charter with Amarato Oil Co.

Fresh stores and potable water loaded, the tanker lay alongside the deserted dock—her 514 feet of rust-streaked hull thrusting forth like a pregnant whore. Stained, sullen, and showing her age, she was still well paid for her services. But her owners expended on her only as much as necessary to keep her afloat.

Despite the addition of steel "belly bands" running the full length of her decks and other stopgap measures, the vessel led a precarious existence—plying her trade on borrowed time.

Bill Evers dozed as the taxi sped along the deserted highway. When it slowed and turned off onto the graveled road, he sat up and leaned forward trying to catch sight of the ship he was joining. The road turned to the left and crossed over the railroad tracks as the Mississippi river came into view. A row of storage tanks appeared and a high chain-link fence, topped with barbed wire, that enclosed the refinery. The cab followed the road around to the right and stopped at the opened gate.

"Evenin'," the uniformed guard called out as he approached them, "sign in here!" He handed Evers a clipboard holding the crew list. Bill signed his name, rating, and time in as 6:00 P.M.; then handed it back.

"You can drive as far as the operations office—don't drive onto the pier," the guard cautioned the driver. He hacked up some phlegm and spit next to the fender. "It ain't too bad a hike from where he'll drop you."

The road through the refinery paralleled three big pipelines which angled around to the right and then up over a rise, giving Bill his first view of the *Concordia*. It would be the first tanker he had sailed on since the war; he disliked them, but tapped as he was and with shipping so slow, he couldn't afford to pass up the job.

As the taxi drove off, the big AB shouldered his sea bag, picked up his suitcase and started down to the ship. The long narrow pier, lined with pipes and valves, jutted out into the river, widening where it formed a "**T**" whose head stretched two hundred feet to both sides forming the main dock area.

Well old gal, we've both of us seen better times, Evers thought as he started up the long almost vertical ladder. Halfway up he paused and looked up at the T–2's rusty side. A momentary sense of foreboding made him hesitate to go on.

The second mate was in the ship's office speaking with Captain Layton when the tall, powerfully built replacement knocked on the partially opened door. The captain motioned for him to come in.

The man filled the doorway as he stepped into the room. He approached the two officers with the ease born of self-confidence. His piercing blue eyes were wide set above high prominent cheek bones; the deep lines radiating from their corners helped establish his age. His square-cut face was deeply tanned and clean shaven; the close-cropped jet black hair, thick and wiry. His nose, decidedly biased to the left and flattened at the bridge, bespoke the breaks it had sustained. A large even scar a few shades lighter than the rest of his skin ran in a neat straight line just below his right eye.

Bill placed his able-bodied seaman's document, passport, and union shipping card on the desk.

The captain recorded everything, then turned the large sheets around for the man to read. "Please sign here," he handed Evers a pen. The big AB read the **Articles**—to one or more ports in the Persian Gulf and back to one or more ports in Europe—*and such other ports and places in any part of the world as the master may direct, and back to a final port of discharge in the United States, for a term of time not exceeding (24) Twenty-Four calendar months.*

The Old Man waited till Evers completed signing the articles and filling in the other employment records. When the AB straightened up, the captain took the papers. "Only one exemption?" he inquired without looking up.

"Aye, Captain."

"Is that single—never married, or divorced, Mr. Evers?" questioned the Old Man, noting that there was no entry under "Next of Kin."

"My wife's dead, Sir. There were no children."

"Sorry, Mr. Evers." The captain was suddenly conscious of addressing the new man as "Mister"—something he never did except when speaking to a fellow officer.

Captain Layton got up and motioned towards the second mate. "This is Mr. Finney, our second officer—I think that's all I need from you now."

"Aye, Captain." Evers turned and started out of the office.

"Evers!" Mr. Finney addressed the big AB. "If you want your linen you'll find the steward working in the shelter deck."

"Aye, Second."

After getting his linen, soap, and matches, the big AB made his way aft. There was no avoiding the potent fumes wafting out of the open tank tops; he breathed as shallowly as he could till he made it into the after house.

Evers walked down the dimly lit passageway till he came to the 12 to 4 fo'c'sle. He slowly opened the door. The light from the passageway revealed an empty single berth on the inboard side. Across the room there was an upper and lower set of bunks with blue spreads serving as curtains pulled closed around them. Putting his gear down next to the empty bed, he shut the door as quietly as he could and eased himself onto the bare mattress. He was bone weary and fell asleep immediately.

The sound of a muffled scream woke Evers just seconds before the overhead light snapped on and Ryan, one of the 8 to 12 ABs, came in to call the watch.

"ALL HANDS! LET'S GO MEN—ALL HANDS—8:15!"

Ryan's voice sliced into Stacey's tortured mind. He woke violently—a portion of his brain still struggling with the vivid nightmare of being attacked on the bow.

"8:15! *Last call!* Night's cold an' black as a whore's heart. Startin' to rain again...pilot just come aboard!"

"Hey keed.... You up Keed?" Hansen's voice came from the bunk below.

Stacey had to take a few breaths before he could answer.

"Yes...thanks... I'm up." He felt the bunk stanchions lurch as his big watch partner got out of bed, and he heard him say "hello" to someone else in the room. Pushing his curtain aside, Stacey saw Hansen, still in his undershorts, on his way out to the head.

"How's it going?" asked Evers.

"Hi...okay." Stacey muttered as he lowered himself to the deck and pulled on his jeans. He hoped the new man hadn't heard him yell anything in his sleep.

—T W O—

The big AB entered the crowded, smoke-filled messroom. As usual, on sailing day, the noise level was high with men besting each other with stories and jokes, or complaining loudly about their whores or the "beach" in general. He made his way into the galley for a clean mug, came back into the messroom and poured himself a cup of coffee.

"Get squared away okay?" The question came from a heavy-set man dressed in bright new yellow oilskins.

"Yes, pretty much." Evers turned away from the coffee urn and leaned back against the bulkhead.

"How's shippin' in New Orleans?"

"Dead slow... Worse than it's been for a long time."

"Might as well take a load off." Motioning to the empty seat across from him, the man held out his hand, ham-like in size and color. "I'm Big Jim, the bosun."

"Thanks, Boats." Evers shook hands and eased himself onto the narrow bench.

The two men seated directly to the boatswain's right were laughing, rather one was laughing and the other gasping for air.

O'Malley slammed the skinny one next to him on the back. "This here's Junior," he introduced the one trying to catch his breath, "and that's Ski." He turned towards the other man... "My daymen!"

"I'm Evers," the big AB nodded at the happy pair.

"Been on the beach long?" O'Malley glanced at his watch and then up at the clock as he spoke—it was almost time to turn to.

"Damn near three months."

"Well you found yerself a home—she's a good feeder, an' as my daymen here can tell ya, we get all the fuckin' overtime we want on this scow!"

"Can use a bit of that about now."

"Should all of us get healthy this trip... We be muckin' all the way over... Everyone, black gang, steward's department—anyone wantin' to work. Tanks gotta be clean an' dry as a whistle to pass inspection at Ras Tanura."

The telephone on the after bulkhead rang.

"Standby!" Tompkins, the 8 to 12 ordinary answered. "MATE SAYS TO TURN TO, BOATS!" He shouted over the din.

"Well, 'spect it's gettin' on that time gentlemen," O'Malley addressed the three men nearest him as he hauled himself erect. "OKAY GANG! LET'S GO FORE 'N AFT!" His voice boomed out across the room.

The bosun, two daymen, and the three men of the 4 to 8 watch started for the bow—they were the "forward gang."

Evers followed his watch partners, Hansen and Stacey, Tompkins, the 8 to 12 OS, and Ryan, one of the ABs on the 8 to 12, out to the stern. Mamud Hassan, the other 8 to 12 AB, had first wheel and headed up to the bridge. The 8 to 12 and the 12 to 4 watches made up the "after gang."

Mr. Finney, the second mate, had the big steam winch in gear and turning over slowly when the after gang came out onto the fantail.

"Breast lines first! Want to take the winch, Evers?" Finney called out.

The big AB took over the winch controls as the rest of the gang began letting go the first of the lines.

Operating the winch gave Evers a chance to observe his new watch partners—Hansen, the husky AB, looked as much the typical "good sailor" as he proved to be now on deck—the young ordinary was harder to peg.

*   *   *

Outwardly, the nickname, "the Kid," did fit Stacey. He was only 5' 10", weighed 145 pounds, and although well muscled, he appeared slighter than he was. He had a pleasant face with regular features, grey-green eyes, and a mop of unruly brown hair. At twenty-two, it still looked as if he didn't shave.

Stacey's family was one of many which had to change their priorities due to the war. His father, a career officer in the army, was killed on "D day." With two sisters much younger than himself and his mother to help, Stacey's plans to go to college were ended. What he needed was a job that paid well.

Out looking for work, he found himself in front of a small office building with an unusual sign—a ship's wheel with the motto **"Brotherhood of the Sea"** around it and a pair of clasped hands below. It appealed to him.

Investigating within, it turned out that his chances for making "good money" hinged on becoming a member of the seamen's union. It was not an easy task as there were far more men than the number needed to crew the ships. To get hired on a union ship you needed experience and seniority—to get these you had to get on a union ship.

Still he persisted, returning day after day to the hall, talking to the union agents and patrolmen. After awhile they allowed him to earn a few dollars running errands, cleaning out the men's room, stacking chairs for meetings, folding union literature, and stuffing and stamping envelopes.

One day, while making coffee in the big urn for the 10:00 A.M. break, a heavy-set, dark-haired man that everyone called "Blackey" started questioning him about where he came from, why he was trying to go to sea, and what he knew about the seamen's labor movement. He didn't know much.

Stacey immediately attacked the small union library, avidly devouring all he could find relating to seafaring and unionism. He felt Blackey was the key to getting started. And he was right! Several casual conversations over coffee resulted in Blackey's inviting him to meet with "Bull" Hendricks, the overall boss, and Joe Elgin, his lieutenant.

Bull Hendricks, Joe Elgin, and Blackey Novack headed up the union's "organizers." Their toughest fight at the moment was with a tanker company that maintained a couple of fink halls to hire scabs for their ships.

The closer to the N. L. R. B. election they came, the deadlier the contest was becoming. On the disputed ships, beatings, knifings and "mysterious disappearances at sea" were becoming commonplace. And ashore, seamen suspected of being organizers were followed and attacked—sometimes killed. The body of one had been found recently stuffed in a garbage pail close to the union building.

Bull Hendricks leveled with Stacey—what he had going for him was that young as he was and with newly issued seaman's papers, the fink shipping agent would never suspect him as a union man—never mind an organizer. Against him was his small size and inexperience in defending himself in the event he was ever caught.

The "Kid," as he was now called, insisted on taking the gamble. A deal was cut—twelve months' seatime as an organizer and he'd receive his *full book* —if unlucky, the union would provide his family with the same compensation, including the death benefit, provided all full book members.

That was a long time ago. He had worked for fourteen months as ordinary seaman and wiper on several fink ships—and he had survived.

With his full book, he could choose both the ship and the department he wanted to sail in. He decided on the deck department and began completing the thirty-six months' seatime as ordinary as required to sit for his AB's ticket.

True, his days of terror at being caught as an organizer were behind him, as were the lousy meals, worn-out mattresses, and the miserable working conditions suffered by scab crews.

But now, on the *Concordia*, a "good" union ship, he was again in danger. His dilemma stemmed from his friendship with Tommy, the colored messman, and for his stand in favor of colored seamen having equal shipping rights. Many of the white crew members were from the South, and though it hadn't been voiced openly, the threat of being "taken care of," if he persisted, was as clear as if it had been shouted.

Despite the heavy rain, the work of undocking went smoothly, and in less than thirty minutes the deck gang had the tanker "singled up" waiting for the tugs to come alongside before letting go her last lines. The men of the after gang sat on the bitts or leaned against the railing waiting for orders.

Stacey looked out across the murky river. He was lost in thought. He and Tommy were both crazy to stay with the ship, especially with her no longer on the nearby foreign run to Venezuela... *Fuck the slow shipping and the time he needed for his AB's ticket.*

"LET GO THE STERN LINE!" The bull horn blared from the bridge.

"THROW HER OFF!" Finney shouted—he watched the hawser run till it bellied out in the water—"TAKE HER TO THE 'NIGGERHEAD'!"

Hansen and Stacey stepped on the line to slow and finally stop it while the others hauled the bight to the winch where Ryan took four turns on the drum.

"HEAVE 'WAY!" the second called out over the clank and screech of the old steam winch as Evers opened the valve a few more turns.

"LET'S GET HER IN!" Finney was concerned with keeping the hawser from fouling the ship's screw. "OPEN HER *ALL* THE WAY!"

"WIDE OPEN NOW, MATE!" Evers shouted back.

A few seconds later the huge eye of the mooring line squeezed shut as it passed through the chocks and onto the deck; the big AB turned the steam valve down leaving the winch drums just barely turning.

"Okay gang, we're through back here for now." The second mate started for the bridge. "Take a smoke if you want—one man stand by the tug."

"Go on," Stacey called out to the others, "I'll stand by!" He headed over to where the after tug was made fast.

Great clouds of foul smelling bottom-mud were churned up by the tanker's screw. Stacey watched the shore lights move in a slow smooth arc as her bows swung away from the long pipe-strewn pier. "Well, that's that," he said to himself—referring to his ambivalence about staying on.

When the order came, the Kid threw the tug's lines off the bitts and watched her veer off to join her sister already racing for home.

The rest of the after gang came out on deck just as Stacey started back to tell them the tug was away. They all headed for the bow to join the forward gang in securing the ship for sea.

The *Concordia* shuddered as her screw's revolutions were increased to comply with the first half ahead bell, duly recorded in the bridge bell book at 9:36 P.M. on the page dated 8/26/50.

—THREE—

Back aft, by 1:00 A.M., the messroom was deserted except for Evers, who was on standby, and "Whitey," one of the ship's three wipers.

Whitey, whose real name was Thomas Bender, had also just joined the *Concordia*. He'd caught her the day before at the two o'clock call, an hour before Evers had thrown in for the AB's job.

The wiper had staggered into the room about ten minutes earlier still dressed in his shore-side clothing. Drunk, he sat cursing and talking to himself as he tried to maneuver a half-empty bottle of gin to his mouth; another unopened bottle lay on the table wrapped in a twisted brown paper bag. His thin damp hair was plastered against his forehead and blended with his sickly colored skin.

At forty-four, with less than an eighth grade education, he was able to read—not that he was ever much motivated—and had a bare grasp of his job as wiper with no interest in knowing more.

Next to booze, he liked food. Women were only third on his list, though he enjoyed "puttin' it up some whore's ass." He would promise to go easy, but once in he'd pound and tear, her shrieks and pleas to stop driving him wild with pleasure.

Bender's career at sea began when someone at the box factory, where he was working, mentioned that a tanker company was advertising for men. He got the job because the owners were desperate for any nonunion men they could get to flesh out the crews of their recently purchased wartime T–2s. The company knew there were union organizers aboard their ships trying to sway a favorable vote for the seamen's union in the elections which were mandated under the new N.L.R.B. ruling.

A few days out of Baltimore on his first trip to sea on the *Jackson Heights*, Whitey was approached by Kruzic, the first assistant engineer, with an offer to earn extra money and time off in port. "You just find out who the union agitators are down below and which of the men sound like they may vote for the union."

Whitey became the "Bull Wiper" overnight and in short order he was supervising the efforts of the other two wipers. With a convincing line of talk, and backed with his impressive, if slovenly size, he had become a power to be reckoned with.

Kruzic kept a list of all the men who showed an interest in the seamen's union. Next to each man's name was one, two, or three check marks; one meant he was listening, two he was buying, and three that he was definitely going over to the union. A cross next to a man's name meant he was selling—a suspected organizer.

Crew members with three checks or a cross were either fired, for one reason or another, or proved to be accident prone with more than one found ashore, injured so badly that he couldn't rejoin his ship—some simply disappeared at sea.

*   *   *

The first assistant was a dark forbidding man, bear-like, both in looks and manner. He was thirty-five, just over six feet tall and weighed two hundred and fifteen pounds. None of his shipmates knew where he came from or anything about his past. Aboard ship he seldom joined in any talk with the other officers and made it clear that he intended to keep things on a strictly business basis. Even ashore he preferred to find out-of-the-way bars the others didn't frequent.

The company recognized the engineer's contempt for anything that faintly resembled communism and he soon became an important factor in its struggle with the union. Kruzic jumped at the chance to fight the "kike communists" who he felt were threatening his newly chosen career. The company provided him with funds to be used at his discretion to establish a police force throughout the tanker fleet.

The engineer's base of operations was the *Jackson Heights,* but he was also the coordinator of a traveling "goon squad" that met or joined the various ships where they were most needed to intimidate or take care of key members of the opposition.

Unknown to his employers, his expertise in dealing with problems like union organizers stemmed from his former role as an Iron Guardist. Fredrick Kruzic, born Felix Crusescu, had been a career officer in Romania's equivalent of Nazi Germany's Brownshirts. He was a leader of one of the "Death Commando" squads which slaughtered some 10,000 Romanian Jews. That was in 1940. By 1943, Kruzic was in Germany, in a town named Fichtenheim. It was a perfect place for a man like him to get ahead. He had a degree in civil engineering, and Fichtenheim was but a stone's throw from the Buchenwald concentration camp—he made a career out of designing the reduction plants that had been set up for the Final Solution of the Jewish Problem.

The clever engineer made his exit from the fatherland as soon as he felt that Germany was headed for defeat. A trip on the Underground Railroad, set up by Nazi sympathizers, saw him safely through Italy and across the seas to South America. From there it was child's play. Provided with perfectly forged papers proving he was an innocent political refugee, he entered Panama, took a short vacation, and then easily passed the examination for a Panamanian first assistant engineer's license.

In less than a month he was aboard an American owned and

operated ship sailing under Panamanian registry.

*　　　　*　　　　*

Whitey had just urinated in his pants and the smell added to his foul body odor.

Evers sat on the last bench next to the door. He had to put up fresh coffee before relieving Hansen at the wheel, but didn't relish the idea of having to be near the drunk to do so.

The wiper's big leg was planted halfway out in the narrow space between the table and the coffee urn. He slammed his closed fist on the table top in response to some conversation he was conducting with himself.

Evers delayed, hoping the messy drunk would stagger below before he had to make coffee.

"Cocksucker! COCKSUCKIN' MOTHERFUCKIN' SONOFABITCH!" The wiper took another swig of his bottle and went back to cursing aloud.

The big AB checked his time and got up, walking slowly towards the galley.

Whitey stared boldly at him as he approached.

"Watch your leg there, Mate." Evers kept his voice friendly hoping to avoid trouble.

The drunk challenged him with his stare and moved his foot out further in the aisle.

The big AB shook his head in disgust and kept his eyes locked with the wiper's as he made his way through.

"WHO THE *FUCK* YOU PUSHIN'?" Whitey yelled as Evers shoved his leg to the side.

The big AB ignored the man and went into the galley. He found a large steel pitcher with which to drain the urn and stepped back into the messroom.

"SONOFABITCH!" The wiper twisted halfway around and hurled the curse directly at him.

"Go on below and sleep it off!" Evers walked up to the urn and turned his back on the drunk. He knew there was a good chance the man would jump him, but he felt he had no choice.

Whitey's fist closed tightly around the neck of the unopened bottle. He waited till his *enemy's* hands were occupied draining the urn then rose from his seat and swung the heavy bottle in an arc calculated to smash his head.

The big AB ducked just in time—Whitey's clenched fist

slammed into his shoulder and the bottle smashed against the bulkhead. Evers had let go of the spigot the instant he sensed Whitey's move. He swung around, driving his right fist into the man's face. He caught the wiper flatfooted and felt the man's nose and teeth collapse against his knuckles.

The drunk's face split open into a bloody mess as he crashed backwards over the table and slid to the deck, his back up against the bulkhead.

Evers felt the first effects of the adrenaline pouring into his blood stream. His stomach tightened into a knot. He stood there a few seconds watching the coffee pouring out of the opened spigot, then closed the tap and picked up the fallen pitcher. The standby phone rang three times before he realized it and rushed over to answer.

"Standby!" His voice sounded unnaturally loud to himself.

"That you Evers?" Mr. Finney asked.

"Aye, Sir."

"The Old Man wants the bosun and daymen to turn to at 1:45."

"Aye, Second."

"Put a reminder on the blackboard for Hansen to call the second pumpman at 2:30...and not to forget to wake the mate when he calls the watch this morning."

"The *chief mate*, Sir?"

"Yes—thought everyone knew our fourth officer, Donley, missed the ship last night. The mate will be standing the 4 to 8."

"No, Sir...I'll put it on the board."

*　　　　*　　　　*

On the bow, the Kid walked fore and aft, first on one side of the anchor windlass, then the other. It had stopped raining but the wind was coming up and he was getting chilled. He knew there was nothing to worry about while they were still in the river—but the nightmare had been so real, he still couldn't help looking over his shoulder. The telephone under the bow apron rang.

"Lookout," Stacey answered.

"Knock off and take ten for coffee, then help the standby rig the pilot ladder."

"Aye, Second."

"Starboard side—four feet from the water."

"Aye."

"Be sure you've got a cargo lamp and a man rope."

"Yes, Sir." Stacey replaced the phone and hurried aft.

Entering the crew's messroom he saw the big AB removing the filter from the coffee urn—he also saw the unconscious wiper lying on the deck with his legs stretched straight out in front of him. The man's chin was against his chest, so Stacey couldn't see much of his face, but blood was all over his clothing and still dripped from his opened mouth. From across the room, the ordinary could hear the man's labored breathing.

Evers turned as he heard the screen door close. "Our mate relieve you?"

"Aye, told me to take a break before we rig the pilot ladder."

"Fresh coffee's ready." Evers turned and poured himself a cup.

"What's with him?" Stacey nodded towards the injured man as he went into the galley for a mug.

"Bastard jumped me from behind...with a bottle."

Stacey got his coffee and sat down across from the AB.

"Walked past him a couple of minutes ago and the son-of-a-bitch tried to brain me. You know him?"

"He's a new wiper. I saw him coming aboard yesterday." Stacey looked closely at the man. "You know...I think I did sail with him before... Sure, he was on the *Jackson Heights*—my first ship. That's four years ago."

"The *Jackson Heights!* Were you with her when Bob Allen, the chief pumpman, come up missing?"

"No. I caught her the very next trip after the accident."

"Accident..! Bob wasn't one to fall over the side. I was bosun on the *Lomar* in '43—best pumpman I ever sailed with... He had thirty years with the company and due for his pension—*It was no accident!*" Evers lit a cigarette. "Some Jew agitator for the union got his job and the same *pay-off*, if I remember rightly."

Stacey didn't answer at first, he was remembering Eddy, the man he got to like so much in the month they spent together trying to ship out from the little fink hall in New Jersey. The new AB calling Eddy an *agitator* instead of an organizer sure sounded strange coming from a union man.

"Well, like I said, I wasn't aboard when this Allen was, so all I knew is what I'd heard. But I do know my friend Eddy gave his life for the union!" He looked straight at Evers. "Jew or no Jew he was a *good* shipmate!"

"Tell the truth I never met one out here," the AB was taken aback a bit by the ordinary's retort, "but those I've run into ashore were as useless as *niggers!*"

The Kid let the comment pass.

Against his will, all that Stacey lived through on the night Eddy was killed came to mind. They were eight days out of New York bound for the Houston Shipyard for the tanker's five year inspection. That was probably the reason why he and Eddy got hired so easily at the fink hall—few seamen wanted the two weeks of filthy back-breaking work required to get a crude oil tanker gas free and clean enough for drydocking.

Being small, Stacey found it was his lot to clean the narrow spaces around the cargo pump pickup lines and under the cargo steam-heating pipes. The gas fumes burned his eyes and made him sick. Hour after hour, muscles cramped from twisting around the pipes on his knees, he scraped the stinking black tar-like sludge into the buckets passed to him through the manholes. The safety lamp, hung from a line over his head, providing more discomfort from its heat than help from its dim beam. They had been working virtually around the clock with less than four hours off in every twenty-four.

When he was finally relieved, dizzy from the fumes, he had to pause several times to hang on to the slippery rungs as he climbed up the vertical ladder.

Once out of the tank, the Kid sat on the deck with his back against the tank top. He had to catch his breath before he was able to peel off his filthy clothes and boots. As he sat there shivering in the colder air he remembered he was supposed to meet Eddy in his room when he got off work—the little pumpman had something important to tell him.

Stacey got up and went to the rail where a 55 gallon drum, top cut off and half-filled with Diesel oil, was lashed. He stripped off his undershorts, got into the makeshift tub and rubbed down with a piece of cotton waste. Then, stepping out of the barrel, he wiped himself dry with clean rags and headed for the after house. He left his rubber boots and clothing outside and hurried in to get showered and dressed before meeting Eddy.

The ordinary tapped lightly on the pumpman's door. There was no answer. He tried again; then he turned the knob. The door swung open. "Eddy?" he called out before snapping on the light switch.

There in the middle of the room, sitting in a chair with his hands tied behind his back was his friend Eddy Sommers—the 16"

Stillson wrench used to crush the pumpman's skull lay in a pool of drying blood. His head, what was left of it, hung to the side with the eyes wide open—*staring*.

The Coast Guard and two F.B.I. men came aboard when the ship tied up in Houston. Everyone was questioned, but no one had seen or heard anything. In the end only a deposition from the master was taken. The investigators went ashore and the ship was paid off.

Evers had been watching the time. "Well, let's get the ladder over." He pulled on his jacket.

The ordinary was still lost in thought and sat staring into his coffee cup. It was a moment before he looked up and saw the new AB leaving the messroom—he got up, put his cup in the galley sink, and started after him. He glanced at the man lying in the corner and was tempted to call the bridge and tell them. *That would be stupid,* he thought to himself. *Let the AB report it if he wants to—he hit him and it was on his standby.* Stacey followed Evers forward to the shelter deck where the ladder was stored. They worked well together and were done by 1:45 A.M.—it had taken them less than fifteen minutes.

It started to drizzle again as they finished up.

"Well I better get back on lookout." Stacey wasn't too happy—ordinary seamen weren't permitted to steer in a river or close to the coast—"Finney will send me back to help secure it after we drop the pilot."

"Your partner Hansen mightn't be much help to you tonight, drunk as he is," the big AB remarked as he started up the ladder to the catwalk—he hurried aft to call the bosun and the daymen before picking up the coffee for the bridge.

Stacey headed forward to resume his bow watch.

—F O U R—

Down below in the Concordia's main engine room, John Pillars, the second assistant engineer, was writing up the engine room log. He had just come back from making rounds of all the control panels and the dozens of gauges, valves, and switches he was responsible for on his watch. The chief engineer, Kruzic, was still down below following in his wake—next he'd follow Ned

Carter, the oiler, on his rounds.

No question the chief was efficient, thought Pillars, but he sure was a nasty bastard on or off watch.

In the fireroom, Paco Hernandez, the 12 to 4 fireman, stood at the large steel bench that faced the port firebox. A cool flow of air from the ventilator made his work more comfortable. He was cleaning his alternate set of fuel-oil burner tips.

The sound level was very high in the fireroom; the roar of the furnaces, rattling floorplates, and the vibrating maze of steel ladders leading up to and surrounding the massive boilers made it almost impossible to hear anything. The ever present danger of an explosion, should the boilers run dry, made it habit for most fireman-watertenders to automatically glance at the level of the boiler gauge glasses every fifteen minutes or so.

Glancing up from his work, the fireman checked his gauges. At the same time he spotted the oiler up in the fidley walking past the portside boiler. *Probably trying to lose the fuckin' chief,* Paco thought to himself. His eyes shifted to the gauges on the fireroom control panel. Steam pressures were fine and the big brass clock showed it to be 1:35 A.M. already. The watch was going fast and easy.

Carter carefully shut the steel boiler room fidley door behind him. He didn't want to awaken any of the off-watch members of the "black gang" whose rooms lined the port passageway. The oiler was out of smokes and he headed for the fo'c'sle he shared with Paco to get a fresh pack. He had one more station to check on this round, the steering engine room, where the huge engine and massive gears that turned the ship's rudder were located.

Carter glanced at his watch as he stepped out of his fo'c'sle. It was almost 1:40 A.M. *Still time to take a fast shit and get something from the night lunch,* he figured.

The chief engineer entered the main engine room.

"Should be taking departure in about an hour, Second," he spoke loud enough to be heard over the whine of the main turbine. "I'm going topside for a minute. I'll be in my room if you need me."

"Okay, Chief. Won't be much happening till we get to the pilot station."

Kruzic went up the long series of ladders leading up through the engine room fidley and stepped out into the passageway on the main deck level headed for the saloon.

Once there, the engineer paused with his hand on the refrigerator door handle. He heard sounds coming through the galley from the crew messroom. Someone said "let's get the ladder over." Then he heard the sound of a cup hitting the bottom of the galley sink, and a few seconds later, the sound of a screen door bang closed.

Opening the refrigerator, Kruzic found it devoid of anything even remotely appetizing. Neither crew nor officers openly violated each others' eating spaces or night lunches, however it was tolerated on the night watches if either side ran completely out of food.

Having heard what was obviously the 12 to 4 headed out to rig the pilot ladder, Kruzic was certain that the messroom would be deserted and thought there might be something better in the crew's night lunch left to eat. He walked through the saloon to the galley. Halfway across the thwartship passageway leading to the messroom, his eyes focused on the man folded up against the far bulkhead of the room. Continuing into the crew mess, he looked closely at the unconscious man. It was the wiper... Thomas Bender! He hadn't seen Whitey since the *Jackson Heights*.

Filthy bastard, Kruzic breathed heavily. *"The son of a bitch had to catch my ship!"* He had wished the wiper dead and gone many times over. Bender was the only one who could ever finger him for murder, but the bastard couldn't rat on him without giving himself away. The fat slob was always drunk. Some day he'd open his filthy fucking mouth by mistake!

The officers on the *Concordia* were company men, but the damned unlicensed men all belonged to one fucking seamen's union or another. There was no way he could afford to have the wiper aboard. At the very best he'd try to blackmail him into letting him ride without working and pad his overtime sheets; at the worst, he'd get them both thrown over the side with his fucking mouth!

Suddenly, Kruzic knew what to do. It was a godsend! The job was already half done. Decision made, he crossed back into the galley and grabbed the three-foot nylon line attached to the drain stopper on the edge of the sink. It would serve the purpose.

The engineer paused at the power panel recessed in the galley bulkhead. He flipped open the cover and ran his fingers down the switches, pushing the three that controlled the lights in the crew messroom, galley, and saloon to OFF.

His flashlight hung from a belt loop and he transferred it

automatically into his left hand as he hurriedly re-entered the messroom. Flashing its beam on Bender's face, he passed the line around the back of his fat neck. When he had the ends crossed in front of the man's throat, he flicked the flashlight off and returned it to his belt loop.

Whitey's eyes bulged blindly in the blackened room as the garrote flattened his windpipe; he arched backwards from the waist up, his head smashing back against the steel bulkhead. His body fought reflexively, but without oxygen, the effort couldn't last. What went on in Thomas Bender's dying brain was anyone's guess.

Kruzic had powerful hands, he held fast till the struggling ceased. The engineer's mind had already rehearsed picking up Bender's foul body and dumping it over the side. He was about to reach under the dead man's armpits when a noise startled him. Stuffing the rope back in his pocket, he straightened up. The sound of a heavy steel door closing came from the end of the passage-way.

Too late to move him, he thought as he stepped back from the body. Making his way by flashlight, he hurried into the galley, threw the three switches to ON and dropped the short piece of line, stopper still attached, into the second sink which was half-filled with cold soapy water.

Kruzic left the saloon walking as normally as he could towards his stateroom and office. His hands were bloody and he grimaced as he fumbled with the key ring on his belt. He didn't want to touch his trousers.

Opening the door to his office, he stepped in and shoved the door closed with his elbow, the latch clicked as the door locked behind him. The light had been left on as usual and he made his way, rapidly now, through his stateroom into the bathroom, tearing his soiled shirt off as he went.

Filling the wash basin, he scrubbed his face and hands, then swished his keys in the soapy water and shook them dry before hooking them back on his belt. He started to put on a fresh khaki shirt, then thinking better of it, grabbed a used one out of his laundry bag and put it on.

Home free! Kruzic breathed easier—he pulled an unopened bottle of bourbon from his desk drawer. His breath would smell of it, but he needed the liquor badly. Putting the bottle back, he gathered up the fouled shirt and towel, pulled the screen off the open porthole and threw them overboard.

The chief engineer expected all the while to hear a sound of alarm when whoever it was he heard coming discovered the body. *How lucky can you get?* He sighed with relief as he locked his office door and headed back below.

*   *   *

Carter had been halfway up the companionway to the messroom when the lights went out. He came up the remaining steps and looked around the edge of the door leading into the room.

As he started to call out to the standby, a beam of light projected a macabre image of two huge forms against the far bulkhead. Looking to the deck, he stifled the sound in his throat as he made out the men casting the shadows. One was white-haired and bloody; the other looked just like Kruzic, *the chief engineer!*

The room suddenly went black and a second later Carter heard the thump that Whitey's head made as it banged against the bulkhead. The oiler crouched in the darkened doorway, hair bristling on the back of his neck.

The clanking of a heavy steel door sounded just as the overhead lights came on. Half-blinded, he could just make out the upper torso and head of the bloody man from where he crouched. *Kruzic was gone!*

"Christ!" The oiler breathed the word as he hurriedly backed down the companionway and headed below to the steering engine room. *That fucker looked <u>dead!</u>*

Carter was still shaking when he bent over and placed his hands on the big bearing caps—they were running cool. He couldn't delay any longer. Lighting another cigarette, he inhaled deeply and decided his course of action as he left the steering engine room. He'd go back up through the fireroom, making certain that Paco saw him; then he'd make coffee in the main engine room, bring a cup to Pillars as he always did, and drink his own there with him.

If the fuckin' chief engineer came around, he'd just act natural and offer him a cup, too.

"One thing's certain," he swore to himself, "I fuckin' don't know or say *anything*... <u>No matter what!</u>"

— F I V E —

As Evers neared the after house he heard a banging sound on the well deck; he found the watertight door on the starboard side unsecured and swinging against the house. It was warped and he had to ram his shoulder against it to get it dogged down. The AB didn't want to wake anyone with the noise, but they would soon be out of the river, and the forward doors *had* to be secured at sea.

He walked down the passageway stopping at the first fo'c'sle to call O'Malley, who had his own room; then to the next one to call the daymen, who shared their's. Finally, Evers headed for the messroom hoping the drunk was gone.

No such fucking luck, he sighed as he stepped into the room. The wiper was still on the deck. He crossed over and looked down at the contorted face. It was purplish-blue and the eyes were bulged open in an obscene stare. *"Oh Christ!"* Evers exclaimed aloud. "Dead...! The bastard's dead. Must've choked on his own puke—or his heart give out." He started for the standby phone, but, by the time he reached it, rejected the idea. *My word against a dead man's — I'd be putting my head in a noose. No one seen him jump me!* Turning back to where the body lay, he glanced at the messroom clock. He had less than ten minutes to relieve the wheel.

The big AB knew he had to chance getting rid of the corpse *now*—before anyone else found it. He couldn't afford an investigation, not with his record. He'd defended himself too well too many times in his past. He walked quickly over to the body. "I'm not getting sent up for this bastard," he swore silently as he knelt down and put his arms around the wiper's chest. Straightening up, he pulled Whitey's bulk over the bench.

Goddammit! The wiper's filth covered face sagged against his chest. He balanced the heavy inert form against the table and the bulkhead, then heaved it up over his right shoulder, praying his luck held as he carried it across the room and out onto the fantail.

Evers headed for the railing where the garbage cans were lashed. Releasing the dead man's legs as he pressed the body against the upper rail, he put his foot on the lower rail and heaved himself erect. Whitey's body toppled over the side. In the darkness Evers could just see the splash as it plunged into the churning fluorescence of the tanker's wake. The thrashing screw sucked it under.

He ripped off his jacket and shirt, threw them overboard, and raced below to shower.

It was a few minutes past two when Evers stepped into the wheelhouse. Carefully shielding his flashlight, he crossed over to the after bulkhead and put the pot of fresh coffee and clean cups in the round cutouts provided for them.

"Sorry I'm late." He walked up behind Hansen.

"She's takin' a little left to hold her; ve goin' 187," said Hansen, resentment in his voice.

"187." Evers repeated as he took the wheel.

"Vheel relieved. She goes 187 Cap'n," Hansen addressed the pilot's back as he stepped away.

"Very well, wheel relieved—187," the pilot answered without turning around.

Hansen gathered up the empty pot and used cups and headed aft on standby.

The pilot swung around and faced Evers. "Are you sober, Quartermaster?" he challenged.

"Aye, Sir."

"Well your watch partner smelled like a brewery!"

Evers didn't answer. He made it a point not to say more than he had to.

"Like most squareheads," the pilot continued unabashed, "he probably held a better course drunk than he could sober!"

The second mate came in from the chartroom and walked to the coffee table. "Fresh coffee, Captain?"

"Aye, that'd be great, Second... I take it straight."

The big wooden wheel creaked as Evers turned it to the left, then eased it back to midships as soon as the bow began to swing. He wanted to keep the tanker right on the line.

The sound of three bells, rung in slow succession, came from the bow.

Finney walked back to the radar console and watched as the new target started to show. It looked more like two blips close together.

The pilot raised his binoculars. "Come right easy to 189. Nothing to the *left!*"

"Right easy to 189—nothing left!" Evers repeated.

"Let me know when you're right on." Captain Peters lowered the glasses and keyed the mike to the small two-way radio at his side. "Tug 'n tow, tug 'n tow... Tug 'n tow, this is the southbound tanker *Concordia...* Captain Peters callin'. Over."

"Aye, we hear you Captain—have you visual two miles north of us. Tug *Linda B*, Chief Mate Anders. Over."

"Thanks, Mate. How's a port to port look to you? Over."

"Red to red's fine with us, Sir. We'll start hauling over as we come 'round the bend. Over."

"Thanks again, Mate—*Concordia* over and out."

"She's 189. Right on," Evers called out the course.

"189. Very well." Captain Peters hung up the mike and swiveled around to face the radar console. "Well Second, you people will be strangers to 'our river' time we see y'all again."

"That's the truth, Captain." Mr. Finney checked his watch, then used a yellow crayon to mark the radar screen, noting the time and position of the two new targets. It was time to call the Old Man. He stepped behind Evers and tapped the voice tube— "Captain," he called softly; he waited a moment... "Capt—"

"Thank you, Second—I'm awake."

"Ten miles to go, Captain."

"Okay, I'll be right up."

Once again three bells sounded from the bow.

"That kid's got good eyes," Finney observed aloud as he went back to the radar. Sure enough, a large faint target was just starting to show up on the screen.

"I see her," the pilot had his glasses to his eyes, "plenty of time to get 'round the tug and tow before we have to worry—looks like a tanker from her lights. Ten degrees left rudder, Quartermaster!"

"Ten degrees left rudder." Evers watched the rudder angle indicator as he put the wheel over. They were closing with the tug as they turned smoothly following the curve of the river.

"See that range light comin' up?"

"Aye, Sir."

"Steady up on it and let me know your heading when you're right on."

"Aye, Pilot. Steady up on the range."

"'Mornin'," the pilot was the first to notice the Old Man entering the wheelhouse from the port wing, "get yourself a little sleep, Captain?"

"Aye, thank you, Captain Peters."

"Good morning, Sir." Carl Finney stepped back from the console. He knew Captain Layton always checked the radar first whenever he came to the bridge. "There's fresh coffee."

"Thanks, Carl, not just yet. Much traffic?" he asked peering down at the screen.

"Only the one tanker after the tow, Sir."

"Ship's steady on 177," Evers reported.

"Steady on 177, very well."

The tug was almost abeam now. The pilot stood up, stretched, and walked out onto the port wing to watch the tug and tow pass. The wind had come up considerably in just the past few minutes and it tore at his clothing.

Captain Layton stepped out onto the wing as well. He walked over to the grey wood box housing the mercurial barometer and flicked on his small penlight. It read 28.85 inches. He continued over to where the pilot stood—when the tow was past they both hurriedly re-entered the wheelhouse.

The pilot crossed to the radio and lifted the mike. "Northbound tanker... northbound tanker. This is the southbound tanker *Concordia,* three miles north of you on your port. Captain Peters callin'—Over."

The radio squawked loudly but there was no response.

"Northbound tanker, northbound tanker come in please. Over!" The pilot put the mike down and picked up the binoculars. "Take her down to half ahead, Second!"

"Half ahead," the Old Man rang the telegraph, "I've got her, Carl." He noted the time in the bell book.

"Northbound vessel come in..! *Over!!*"

Loud static.

"Northbound, I'm comin' right—givin' you all the room I can. We'll pass PORT TO PORT!! Fifteen degrees right rudder, Quartermaster!" He reached up and pulled the whistle cord.

The *Concordia's* one long blast was immediately answered.

"Well, Sir," he addressed Captain Layton who had moved to the adjoining porthole, "at least she can *hear* us... Transmitter probably on the fritz—where y'all at there, Quartermaster?"

"182....and a half...183..coming right smartly!" Evers sang out.

"HARD LEFT!" the pilot stepped out onto the port wing.

"HARD LEFT!" Evers spun the wheel over. "WHEEL'S HARD LEFT!"

"EASE TO TEN!" Captain Peters felt the *Concordia* answering her helm perfectly to swing her around the oncoming tanker.

"MIDSHIPS!" the pilot shouted from the end of the wing.

Mr. Finney stepped away from the radar and stood in the doorway to relay the pilot's orders.

"Midships! The Wheel's Midships, Second." Evers didn't shout.

"WHEEL'S MIDSHIPS!" Finney called out to Captain Peters.

"VERY WELL—TELL THE SKIPPER WE CAN COME BACK TO <u>FULL AHEAD</u>."

"Full ahead," Captain Layton responded, "I heard him, Carl."

"FULL AHEAD SHE GOES!" Finney called out above the wind.

All eyes, the big AB's included, stared fixedly at the rapidly closing lights of the oncoming tanker.

"Gonna be close!" Finney muttered.

The silence in the wheelhouse was accentuated by the click....click......click of the gyro-compass repeater as it marked the slowing arc the *Concordia* was describing—she was committed.

The heavily laden tanker slid past with less than fifty feet separating her stern from that of the *Concordia's*. Captain Peters still couldn't catch her name.

—SIX—

The *Concordia* left the flashing sea buoy on her port quarter, swung in a slow arc and steadied up on course 135. The pilot boat was less than half a mile off, her lights dancing as she made her way toward them.

The pilot shook hands with Captain Layton and Mr. Finney. He started to leave the wheelhouse, then stepped back to the wheel. "Thank you, Quartermaster." He shook hands with Evers. "You steer a *true* course, Sailor," he added as he departed out onto the wing.

The second mate picked up Captain Peter's overnight bag and followed him down to the well deck where the pilot ladder was secured. Hansen stood there shivering without a jacket.

The three men stood watching as the pilot boat crossed the tanker's bows coming around under her lee. Her searchlight came on, its intense white beam cutting across the water. The light traveled part way up the tanker's hull, then swept to the bottom few rungs of the ladder.

The small boat bobbed like a cork alongside the tanker. It took a few seconds for one of the boatmen to snare the bottom of the ladder and haul it on deck. Two other men fended off from the tanker's side as Peters climbed over the rail.

Hansen used a heaving line to lower the pilot's bag to the men waiting below.

Captain Peters, a fairly heavy man in his early sixties, went down the ladder rung by rung. Despite the lee provided by the tanker, negotiating the long vertical drop to the pitching deck of the small pilot boat was not easy. He paused a few rungs from the bottom and hung there for a second or two judging the interval between the rise and fall of the small boat. When it started on its next upward swing, he scrambled down the last few rungs and jumped to the deck as it heaved up under him. One of the boatmen reached out and grasped the pilot's arm to help steady him. They cast off and in a few moments only the boat's stern light was visible from the *Concordia's* bridge.

Captain Layton entered the wheelhouse as the small boat pulled away. He cranked the phone. "Stacey, you can go aft and help Hansen secure the ladder. Ring me when you're back on the bow." He moved the pointer on the phone to ENG.RM. and cranked the handle again.

"Engine room. Second assistant," Pillars answered.

"Morning, Second—this is the captain. We'll be getting underway shortly. Is the chief about?"

"Yes, Sir. He's around here somewhere. I'll send the oiler to look for him." Pillars looked around trying to spot Carter or the chief.

"Nothing urgent, Second. If he's busy, just let him know we'll be taking departure in a few minutes. Log it as 2:50 A.M. and be sure the second pumpman calls the bridge before he begins ballasting at 3:00."

"Aye, Captain." Pillars hung up and pressed the alert button sending out siren whoops from horns located throughout the engine room spaces.

Kruzic stiffened as the alert sounded. He had spent the last forty minutes trying to look busy as he went from station to station anticipating the discovery of Bender's body; he couldn't believe it was taking so long. Now, finally, it was happening! He steeled himself and climbed rapidly up the ladder from the lower engine room to the throttle station where the phone was located.

The sound of the siren caught Carter, the oiler, in shaft alley where he was checking the lube oil pressures and the temperatures of the massive bearings that kept the ship's shaft running true. Co-incidentally, it was a good place to stay out of Kruzic's sight. He took the series of ladders up to the throttle station two steps at a time.

Both Kruzic and Carter arrived at the throttle station within seconds of each other.

"Hi, Chief... Old Man's taking depar—" the second assistant engineer started to explain.

"WHO—DEPART—*Departure*... WHEN?" Kruzic realized his voice was too loud. The whine of the turbine on dead slow was muted and there was no need to shout.

Remembering they were still on dead slow waiting at the pilot station, Carter stood there taking it all in. *Shit, of course it's departure—that's all. Fuckin' chief looks like he's about to shit his pants. This is really something!*

"Sorry I startled you, Sir."

"NO...no. That's okay, Second." Kruzic pulled himself to-gether. "Departure...you say?"

"In about two minutes, Chief...at 2:50." Pillars turned and checked the clock on the control board. "The bastard's been at the bottle," he said to himself. "I thought I could smell it!"

Kruzic stepped over to the partially soundproofed telephone station and rang the bridge. His mind was reeling with the fact no one had yet found the body. "*Alive!* Could he be ALIVE?"

"Bridge. Second mate." Mr Finney had just gotten back up to the wheelhouse.

"Captain Layton. Is he there? This is Kruzic."

"No, Chief. Hold a second." He addressed Evers. "See the Old Man?"

"Checking out the standard, Sir."

"Chief, he'll be right with you. He's up on the flying bridge checking the standard compass."

"Yes...yes, well, nothing. We're ready down here...no need— I'll get him later." Kruzic took a deep breath. *Calm. Must stay calm. I'll find a way. If he's alive, he may never have seen me.* He stepped out of the booth and turned to Pillars. "I'll stand by the throttle, Second. Want to check on the boilers?" He was relieved that the oiler had already taken off.

"Sure, Chief." Pillars headed for the fireroom.

"Didn't hold on to his throat long enough," he agonized. "The bastard was strong! The bastard came to! No! He's dead! *DEAD!!* — and still there. Soon... Soon they'll find him. We'll be underway in a minute and I'll get up to my room and wait."

—SEVEN—

"3:20...3:20 Yentilmen." Hansen rapped lightly on the door to the 4 to 8 fo'c'sle. "3:20!" He reached in and flicked on the switch to the overhead light.

"Kill the fuckin' light," groaned Bob Howard, the AB whose bunk was the single one closest to the door; he snapped on his small shaded bunk light.

"Shit!" Terry Cole, the ordinary, pulled his curtain aside. "Where's lookout?"

"On the bow." Hansen switched off the overhead light. "Vindy and raining some—off and on... Pedro?"

"Thanks, Hansen, I'm up." Pedro Davila, the AB in the bed below Terry, turned on his light.

"Fresh coffee vating." Hansen hooked the door in the partway open position and walked on down the passageway. He rapped on the door of the fo'c'sle next to his own. "Kooky! 3:20 Kooky." He knocked again and then tried the doorknob. The door was locked. "You up, Reed?"

"Okay, Hansen... Thanks!" Waldon Reed, the ship's night cook and baker, flicked on his bunk light.

"3:20! Last call," Hansen spoke through the closed door. He went back up to the messroom where he stopped to drain the coffee through the grounds again before throwing out the filter. He was about to leave when Carter came in.

The oiler had just called the 4 to 8 black gang watch. "How's it going?" he addressed the AB as he poured himself some coffee. "Pretty quiet around here tonight, ain't it?"

"Yah, no von here, but some von fuck up the place good!" Hansen made it known.

"Anyone up and around here earlier on your standby?" Carter glanced at the corner where the bloody man had been.

"No... No von. Vell, I go call the mate."

Hansen hurried across the catwalk to the midship house with cold spray pelting in his face. He'd forgotten his rain gear in the wheelhouse. Entering the house, he paused at the bubbler for a drink before knocking on the chief mate's door.

"3:30, Mate... 3:30!" He put his ear against the door. "Vind's coming up a bit!"

"I'm up," Mr. Wilder called through the locked door. "Thanks, Hansen."

The AB went up the companionway, past the radio shack and the captain's quarters, and into the chartroom.

Mr. Finney looked up from the chart table as Hansen walked over to the door.

"I come for my coat, Sir," Hansen said in answer to the unvoiced question.

The second mate nodded his head and returned to his work.

"Starting to take some spray?" Evers watched as Hansen struggled into his rain gear.

"Yah... She be blowin' half a gale by sun up." He went out onto the starboard wing and down the ladders to the forward catwalk.

"Hi, Boats... Ski!" Hansen greeted the two as he came up onto the fo'c'slehead. "Vot happened to Yunior?"

"Well if he can get his ass in gear, we can go home." Ski grunted as he lifted another bucket of concrete and lowered it to his partner. Junior was still under the anchor windlass packing more concrete on the burlap to make a watertight seal for the chain locker.

"Do a *good* yob, Yunior," Hansen admonished as he went up to the bow.

"Nothing ahead," the Kid reported to his watch partner.

"Hokay, Keed. Maybe you betta check the mate on your vay aft!"

"I'll give everyone another call—anyone still up and about during your standby?"

"No, but I have von hell of a stinkin' mess to clean up. Some sonovabitch fuck up the whole place!"

Stacey considered telling Hansen what happened with their new watch partner and the wiper, but it was getting late. He had to hurry and check on their reliefs.

"Boats, you wanted to see me before I went aft?" Stacey called out as he approached the anchor windlass.

"Yeah, let the mate know we're 'bout done up here; anythin' else he wants tell him to ring me on the bow phone."

"Aye, Boats." Stacey hurried down the catwalk and into the

midship house. The mate was just leaving his room when Stacey got there. He gave him the bosun's message and continued aft to check the watch.

The only one still in the 4 to 8 fo'c'sle was the ordinary, Terry Cole. He was sitting on his chair pulling on his socks.

"Getting colder and plenty windy," advised Stacey.

"They still got the fuckin' lookout forward?"

"Yup, still on the bow. Not taking much spray yet, but still raining some."

Stacey headed down the passageway, checked that Reed was up and continued on to the messroom.

Both 4 to 8 ABs were seated opposite the coffee urn, half asleep. The 4 to 8 fireman-watertender and oiler sat at the table behind them playing cribbage. Stacey stripped off his rain gear, poured himself some coffee, and settled down at the after table next to the standby phone. He noticed that the mess on the deck where the wiper had lain was all cleaned up.

Save for a word or two from the cribbage players, the five men sat there silently swaying from side to side as the *Concordia* rolled along in the building seas.

Reed, the night cook and baker, brushed flour off his hands as he came in from the galley. "Sure 'nough workin' herself into a nasty blow ain't she?" He poured himself some coffee and sat down at the table opposite the passageway to the galley. "Anymore news 'bout the storm?"

"She's suppos'ta be kickin' aroun' off Cuba yet," Davila, one of the 4 to 8 ABs, yawned as he answered. He stood up and pulled on his rain jacket. As if that were a signal, all eyes went to the messroom clock. It was 3:45 A.M. and time to go. The men filed past Reed and deposited their cups in the half-filled sink in the galley passageway. The ABs left the messroom through the forward door. The two black gang members headed down the companionway leading to the engine room.

A sudden heavier than usual roll set pots and pans clattering in the galley; Reed hurried in to check things out.

Stacey sat waiting to be relieved. Since they were out of the river and the pilot gone, the 4 to 8 would be on a normal sea watch with each man taking one hour and twenty minutes standby, lookout, and wheel. Terry, the ordinary, was always late relieving the watch. The Kid waited till it was exactly four o'clock and then went to check. The ordinary was back up on his bunk fully dressed and fast asleep.

"It's 4 o'clock, Terry," Stacey called out from the doorway. There was no response.

"HEY, LET'S GET UP!" The Kid raised his voice as he stepped into the room.

"I'm up... I'm up, Goddam it," mumbled Terry. "Knock yerself the fuck off—I got first standby."

Stacey had no use for the surly ordinary. He was pretty sure that Terry was one of the crew that jumped him and Tommy back in Baytown. "Let's go, Terry." He turned and started out of the room, adding, "I'll be up in the messroom till you relieve me."

"DON'T TELL ME WHAT THE FUCK TO DO!" Terry screamed at the top of his lungs. He jumped down onto the deck.

The shout made the hair on the back of the Kid's neck stand up and his heart began to pound. "Have it your way, Terry." He tried to keep a quaver out of his voice. "But if you don't relieve me in five minutes, I call the bridge." He turned and started out of the room.

"Fuck the bridge! Get the *fuck* outta my fo'c'sle—GET THE FUCK OUT!!"

The Kid entered the passageway half expecting the enraged man to come after him. He didn't want to fight Terry even though he was sure he could take him. It would only fan the hatred against him. Terry Cole was a loud mouth drunk, but he had plenty of backing.

Stacey returned to the messroom. Hansen and Evers sat opposite each other at the aftermost table. Carter and Paco sat together at the center table. They were all drinking coffee and eating some freshly made donuts. The standby phone rang just as the Kid started to sit down—he went over to answer it.

"Standby."

"Who's this?" the chief mate asked.

"Stacey, Sir."

"Where's Terry?"

"He's around here somewhere, Mate."

"Tell him to find the second pumpman and have him call the bridge. He's probably in the after pumproom."

"Aye, Sir. I'll tell him." Stacey hung up just as Terry came into the messroom. "The mate wants you to find the second pumpman and have him call the bridge. He figures he's down in the after pumproom."

The ordinary walked past Stacey into the galley, returning momentarily with a plate full of doughnuts and a cup. He took his time adding cream and sugar to the coffee and sat down next to Carter, the oiler.

"Vell Yentilmen," Hansen stretched out his arms and yawned, "she ban rolling pretty good soon. I'm going to sleep vhile I can." He picked up his cup and plate and headed for the galley. "Good night, Kooky, an' tanks again for the doughnuts," he called out as he dumped his plate and cup in the sink.

"'Night, Hansen," the cook answered looking up from a huge steel mixing bowl—the beginnings of the breakfast biscuits. The ship's pitch and roll were not strong enough to affect Reed's work or balance, but the pots and pans were beginning to bump and slide noisily in the metal racks.

When the big AB got up and headed for the galley to drop off his cup, Stacey noticed that he was not wearing the same clothing he had on earlier in the watch.

—EIGHT—

As the *Concordia* steamed south through the early morning hours of the twenty-seventh she experienced a steadily increasing wind and wave front that met her close on the port bow. Frequent line squalls buffeted the ship with gusts up to forty miles an hour. The winds were closely followed by heavy rains that swept the decks and struck the "houses" with the staccato sound of a machine gun. When she started to take heavy spray over her bows, the lookout was changed to the flying bridge above the wheel-house.

Though the *Concordia* had been taking on ballast for several hours, she still didn't have enough aboard to lessen her 15 to 20 degree rolls. When the tanker met both wave front and storm swell at the junction of their crests and troughs, she pitched strongly enough to take light seas over her bows. And back aft, her screw lifted out of the sea, thrashing wildly till its speed was checked by the governor.

Shortly before 6:30 A.M. the required course change of several degrees to the east resulted in an easier ride. The wave front was now almost dead ahead, allowing the vessel's knife-like bow to cut through the seas, reducing her pitch and roll.

At dawn, the sun barely brightened the overcast sky. The wind had moderated to 20 mph; the air temperature was 42 degrees F. and the barometric pressure 28.70 inches and steady. A little after 7 o'clock, the radio operator entered the wheelhouse and handed the chief mate the latest weather report. It stated that the tropical disturbance had been upgraded and officially confirmed as the season's first hurricane. It was moving in a northeasterly direction at 10 miles per hour with winds of up to 90 mph. Presently off the southeastern coast of Cuba, it could pose a threat to Florida's western coast if it didn't veer off into the Atlantic.

"Coffee, Ed?" The mate crossed the wheelhouse to pour another for himself.

"No thanks, I'm heading aft for breakfast in a minute." Sparks stood looking out the porthole.

"Get everything squared away before we sailed?" The mate came back balancing a full cup.

"Yup, all taken care of." Sparks knocked on the little wooden shelf that supported the small radio set.

"Good... That's good," the mate nodded.

The cryptic exchange concerned the developing and sending off of the 8 mm movies taken of the girls at Cindy's—their joint efforts at producing a porno film.

*   *   *

Cindy's bar was less than a mile from where the *Concordia* loaded her Venezuelan crude in Puerto Arena. The town itself had been hacked out of dense jungle bordering a major branch of the Orinoco river. In fact, the tankers had to push through fetid green growth for several miles before coming to the bend in the river where the town fought to hold back the ever encroaching rain forest. Puerto Arena's old steam dredge struggled almost as vainly to keep the river deep enough for the fully laden tankers on their return to the mouth of the river.

Only the oil workers' compound and a block of newly constructed shops were supplied with electricity—yet all the Indians who worked for the Dutch oil company had American made washing machines and refrigerators set up next to their thatched huts. *Mamasitas* scrubbed their families' clothing by hand in the gleaming white machines with big bars of brown soap, and the men deposited their bottles of beer in the hot white refrigerators. The natives here were related to those up river whose sole commercial activity was the taking and shrinking of human heads. These found a ready market as souvenirs. They hung from wires in the barrooms, eateries, *farmacias,* and perhaps most incongruously in the town's tiny two chair barber shop. At $6.00 to $8.00 U.S., according to condition, they were interesting and affordable for a seaman to collect, and when he left the ship there was never a problem getting them through customs.

There were two docks in operation and a third under construction. The loading went on 24 hours a day, every day in the year. An average of three tankers a week made it in and out of Puerto Arena.

Small as the town was, it attracted all types of enterprising individuals seeking the profits made by catering to the oil workers, construction gangs, and foreign seamen.

Puerto Arena had been declared a Free Port which made it possible to buy all sorts of foreign goods tax free. The government benefitted by the resultant flow of hard currencies. "Yankee Dollahs" could buy Scotch whiskey, French wines and perfumes, Swiss watches, German cameras, Italian leather goods, and, from the States, radios, clothing, refrigerators, and washing machines. Of course the government, under the strong grip of the current dictator, extracted far more money through *mordida* than could have been realized through taxing the imported goods. In addition "the bite" was extended to the bars and whorehouses which were the main attractions for the seamen.

For a jungle jump-joint, Cindy's had real class. It was well stocked with liquor, modern music blared from new juke boxes, it was relatively clean, and it had indoor plumbing.

The place was owned by a Hungarian who had been a Nazi sympathizer. He had been wise enough to emigrate in good time and with sufficient resources to establish himself comfortably in the New World before the collapse of the Reich.

When oil started flowing out of the Puerto Arena fields, Johann Teka branched out again from his headquarters in Caracas. He established Cindy's with the same blessings and protection from the government and the police as his "houses" in Maracaibo and Puerto Piedra had received. Teka was well liked. He put money in all the right hands and was a friend to any expatriate old-worlders of like persuasion.

The girls at Cindy's were really different; all were good looking, white, and wore their hair short. Most had been deportees, their heads shaved to the scalp and thrown out of France for making life pleasant for the German soldiers during their uninvited presence in *La Patrie*.

For the right price, which wasn't really exorbitant, the girls at Cindy's would regale their clients with a full repertoire of old world perversions. There was always something new and exciting to be witnessed or experienced at Cindy's.

Tim Wilder, the *Concordia's* chief mate, and Ed Moore, the tanker's radio operator, had been going ashore together for the full year they had been shipmates. Both were in their early thirties, single, and making good money—they hit it off well. They drank fairly heavily when ashore, but back aboard ship were sober and reliable officers.

Coincidentally, they shared an avid interest in photography. Sparks had albums filled with pictures he'd taken all around the globe; some had actually won prizes in competition.

It was Wilder who had taken Sparks to visit Cindy's on the second trip to Puerto Arena. The radio operator was as much a cockhound as the mate, and this cemented their friendship. Sparks took a few pictures of the girls and gave them all copies when the tanker returned the next trip.

The first photographs were simple ones. The girls wanted to send them to friends and relatives in Europe and Caracas. Some wanted shots of themselves in sexy lingerie, "G" strings, or in the buff.

On their fourth trip to Venezuela, both men hit on the idea of doing some sex shots and selling them. It was the beginning of their porno photo business.

At first the girls did the posing for free, but when the mate started setting up his 8 mm camera and lights, they insisted on being paid for their work.

On their last trip to Puerto Arena, Sparks and the mate completed their movie.

Dedee, the girl who starred in the film, was twenty-one when she was stripped naked in the streets of Paris and marched around her neighborhood with fifteen other women accused of fraternizing with the Nazis.

She was screamed at, punched, and whipped with a belt by women who had not consorted with the enemy; then herded off to a camp where her head was shaved. After six months of internment she was deported.

Amazingly, at twenty-six, she looked as fresh as a teen-ager. Her hair was still short, but she wore it attractively with bangs across her forehead and the back curled close to her neck.

She was a striking redhead; everything about her was peaches and cream—all tones of pinks and reds. Her perfectly shaped breasts were full and heavy yet didn't need a bra to shape them. Dedee's studious avoidance of the tropic sun accented the contrast of her milk-white skin and pink nipples. Her waist was wasp-like and from it flared an ample bottom, the shape of a valentine's heart when she bent over. Her thighs and calves were flawless and she kept her legs and armpits scrupulously shaven. Her toenails and fingernails were well manicured and painted a vibrant rose-red.

It was all the two men could do to complete the movie. They could hardly walk.

"Shit, if this isn't a *classic*, nothing is!" Sparks was beside himself.

In short order their "star" came back into the room, freshly showered and dressed in a flimsy red silk robe—she had her best friend, Marie, in tow.

"You like to eat firz, Cherie?" Marie put her arms around the radio operator's neck and tried to kiss him.

Sparks avoided her lips, he had an aversion to kissing whores, especially when sober, and most especially in Cindy's where blow jobs were the house speciality.

"Zen you like zig zig now, *mon coeur?*" She reached down and put her hand on his crotch.

"I wouldn't last a minute, Baby."

"Zo... Just zo, Zweetheart," she unzipped his fly. "Ohh 'ow beeg eet is!" She slipped to her knees and started to take him into her mouth.

"Hold... Hold it!" Sparks undid his belt and struggled out of his pants.

Dedee and the mate were already on the sofa, naked and lost to the world in a mutually shared feast of their own. Tim Wilder didn't share his shipmate's delicate stomach when it came to sex.

*   *   *

"Well, I might as well head on aft," Sparks broke the silence in the wheelhouse. "You know, I've got this *bad* feeling." He glanced at Howard, the AB on the wheel, uneasy about saying too much in front of a crew member.

"You're just feeling this low coming in," the mate included the helmsman in the conversation. "What about it, Howard? You got the blues also?"

"I ain't real crazy about this fuckin' shuttle run, tell ya the truth..." the AB admitted.

The phone rang and the mate answered. "Bridge...? 86...58, thanks, First." He hung up and jotted down the rpms and sea temperature. "Look at the bright side. We won't be pissing everything away on the beach."

"Yeah... Hassan says fuckin' with A–rab women can get your *balls* cut off and sewed shut in yer mouth," the AB contributed.

"We'll have to save it for the French then," the mate answered.

"Well, I'll see ya, Tim." Sparks walked out onto the starboard wing and started down the ladder.

"Don't eat all the bacon!" The mate followed him out to check the barometer before writing up the log.

—NINE—

The remainder of the steward's department had been up and at work since 6:00 A.M. Though the seas were not all that high, the *Concordia* was still pretty light and she was rolling 10 to 15 degrees from side to side in a slow regular rhythm.

It was the occasional heavy pitch that threw a man off balance. (It usually came just as the ship reached the high spot of her roll.) Preparing and serving hot food at sea in rough weather was a difficult and usually thankless task.

Tommy Deel, the crew messman, had set his three tables and took the added precaution of pouring a goodly amount of water on the tablecloths. The wet cloths stuck to the table tops and helped prevent the dishes and silverware from sliding off as the ship rolled.

The young black was clean, courteous, and able to keep three to four orders working without mixing them up. Unless you really knew Tommy you'd think he liked his work—he did enjoy going to sea, but he didn't care very much about food. And even less the idea of preparing it. No, he didn't *ever* want to be a cook!

*　　　　*　　　　*

Tommy was twenty-three. He'd been sailing off and on for almost seven years. At seventeen he had no problem getting his seaman's papers and a ship. It was 1944 and the merchant marine was in need of men. Fewer merchant ships were falling prey to the Germans in the Atlantic. But the increasing number of convoys carrying men and munitions for the coming Allied assault on "Fortress Europa" called for all the ships and seamen the U.S. could muster.

Tommy sported a jagged scar extending from his left forehead, right at the hairline, down to the left corner of his mouth. The scar tended to pull his left eye into a permanent half closed state which he could only overcome by wrinkling up his forehead. It was a momento from a German submarine's surface attack.

His convoy had suffered eight straight days of mountainous seas off Iceland only to run smack into a pack of U-Boats that lay in wait. Separated from each other and their escorts by the storm's fury, they became easy prey. Twelve merchantmen were sent to the bottom while the enemy lost only two raiders.

Tommy Deel's vessel was one of the luckiest of the forty that originally made up the convoy. It sustained minor damage from the surface attack, and counted only three dead and five wounded in the crew. Deel, with one of the ordinary seamen from the civilian crew, was assigned to the four-inch gun on the stern of the tanker. Their job was to haul shells for the five-man Navy gun crew.

The sub surfaced directly astern of them, and its second shot made a direct hit on the four-inch gun before it could be brought into play. Two of the men killed in the attack were Navy gun crew, the third was the civilian ordinary seaman. Tommy himself was lucky to receive so minor an injury, as the others were much worse; two men lost arms, and the other lost both an arm and a leg. It was not the last convoy that Tommy sailed with, nor was it the last time his ship was hit, but it was the only injury he sustained during the war.

Tommy Deel's service during this period earned him the right to join the seamen's union. The only catch was that he could sail only in the steward's department. A year later he met and married Ellen, a girl from Baytown, Texas. It was hard to admit to her that the highest position he could hope to reach at sea was chief cook or possibly steward. It wasn't that those jobs were not important ones, it was that as a negro you accepted that type of work or went without.

He lived in constant envy of every white he met who could sail in the deck or engine department—especially the deck department. Deel would practice tying knots alone in his fo'c'sle, or on deck when no one was watching. Sometimes a friendly ordinary or AB would show him how to splice or do fancy rope work. After a while his fo'c'sle was adorned with all kinds of salty appointments. The portholes had curtains made from "small stuff" he found on deck or gleaned from the rope locker. His deck was covered with rugs woven from old heaving lines. And every swab or broom that came into his hands sported a "Turk's-head" or two.

He envied the deckhands on every vessel he sailed on, doing all the real seaman-like jobs. Taking the wheel of a ship and sharing the watch on the bridge was his constant desire. Yes, even working his way up to becoming a boatswain, or getting a third mate's ticket one day was one of his dreams. In contrast, his reality was one of dealing with the racial prejudice that sometimes flared into the open aboard ship. Then there were unavoidable fights with white crew members.

But it was the less direct bigotry that hurt Tommy Deel the most; the jokes and statements about the colored that were always bandied around, usually not right in front of you, but within easy earshot and in a casual offhand manner. They made him feel less a person than insults directed to his face.

Once in awhile, like on the *Concordia*, you did run into a white stud who was really okay, like Hansen, the 12 to 4 AB. He was a good seaman and seemed unconcerned as to what color you were. Then there was the Kid, who had become his best buddy. Al Stacey was a closer friend than anyone of his own race had ever been, especially after the fight.

It had all started when Ryan, the 8 to 12 AB, came aboard roaring drunk making it hell for Tommy to serve the watch. He tried to avoid trouble, but Ryan persisted.

"God damn your *black* ass! Get in here and take my order!" The AB hollered to him while he was in the galley getting Stacey's food. When he came back into the messroom, he set the Kid's plate down and asked the drunk what he wanted.

"What the fuck you got, *boy?*" Ryan challenged.

The Kid picked up the menu card and pushed it over to the AB.

"Hey, nigger lover, I don't need no shit from you either!" He threw the plastic card at Stacey just missing his face.

The Kid picked it up off the deck and told the AB to take it easy.

"EASY!" the drunk shouted. "That's just what's wrong on these fuckin' ships anymore! EASY MY ASS! I don't want no nigger lovin' wiseass ordinary tellin' me *nothin'*—HEAR?"

By now several more men had come into the messroom and were watching the action.

Hoping it would settle down, Tommy started over to the other table to take some orders.

"God damn you *black bastard!*" Ryan rose up from his seat and grabbed at the messman's throat. "YOU DON'T JUST WALK AWAY FROM ME *COON!*" he hollered.

"Your fight was with me!" Stacey said, getting up from the table.

Tommy would never forget it.

The AB turned around and grinned. "I'll be go to hell if it ain't!" He swung at the ordinary.

The Kid caught the blow high on his head as he ducked under the much bigger man's telegraphed haymaker. He put every one of his 145 pounds behind his own right and caught the AB flat-footed. Ryan didn't stop his backward fall till he landed on the deck.

Later that night as they left the ship on their way to visit Tommy's wife and her folks they were jumped by several men. In the unevenly matched fight, both were on their backs by the time their antagonists took off in the dark. Luckily, the sounds of the fighting brought a few dock workers and a security guard running to see what was going on. After helping them to their feet, they asked if they were all right. Though Stacey had a cut under his right eye, neither he nor Deel had been badly hurt.

"Well do we pack our gear and pile off?" Stacey was the first to speak. "Or do we go back, clean up and come ashore again?"

"Shit, man, we both been askin' for trouble hangin' 'round with each other. The chief cook an' second both been on my ass."

"What the hell for?" Stacey held his handkerchief to his cheek, pressing it against the cut.

"For the same reason we jus' got our asses whipped," Tommy explained. "They sees us as big trouble and they don't want to take no sides."

"Sometimes you got to play pat to win—I'm not throwing my hand in." The Kid started down the gravel road to the dock.

"Look man, I don' want you gettin' hurt or somethin' 'cause of me. It's you they pissed with... You knows that. Me, I'm just another no account, and they's too many of us in the steward's department to single me out." Tommy followed after him.

"You know if Hansen had been with us he'd have backed us

up," Stacey ventured.

"Ah them yeller bastards 'd never jumped us—four to three wouldna been such easy odds!"

"Fuck 'em! Let's clean up and come back. We just gotta be a lot more careful."

"Put her there, brother!" Tommy took the Kid's hand as they started up the gangway.

Later, they caught a cab at the gate and enjoyed the visit with Tommy Deel's wife and in-laws—on the northern end of the trip it was Al Stacey's mom that welcomed them home.

The two young seamen had become "brothers" in the only real sense of the word.

—TEN—

"Captain... Captain Layton! Sorry to wake you, Sir." Michael Searles, the third mate, called down the voice tube.

"Yes, what is it?" The captain sat up in bed and looked at his watch—it was after 8:00 A.M.

"Thought I'd better call you immediately. We've a man missing!"

"Searles?" Layton pulled himself out of bed—he grasped a bunk stanchion, steadying himself against the ship's roll. "What's that again?"

"First assistant called a few minutes ago. They can't find the new wiper."

"A man missing? Since when?"

"About a half hour. They've searched everywhere back aft— he never turned to this morning. The first is on the way here now."

"You have a good fix, Mike?"

"Aye, Sir, a pretty good one on Loran."

"Get Sparks on the air with it; he's probably back aft eating, the mate also. I want both of them on the bridge—I'll be right up!"

By the time the captain came into the wheelhouse, Mr. Pierce was already there. The engineer was soaking wet. He had been caught on the after catwalk as the tanker took a sea over the well deck.

"Third, get the flotation gear over the side." The Old Man turned back to Pierce. "Is Kruzic in the engine room, Bob?— Christ you're soaking wet!"

"No, Sir, I wanted to check with you first. The chief, he wasn't feeling so hot when he knocked off. He left word below not to call him this morning."

"Can we bring her all the way down?"

"Aye, Sir, I lined everything up before coming forward."

"Good!" The Old Man levered the telegraph to slow ahead. "Kruzic will be up the minute he feels us slowing, unless he's... Well, whatever—put that old jacket of mine on, First." Layton pointed to where it was hanging. "Any idea when he could have gone over the side?"

"None. Thank you, Sir." The first assistant had pulled on the heavy watch coat. "His bed was never slept in. The other two wipers said the last they saw him was around midnight. He was drunk and when they told him to knock off the noise and douse the light, he staggered out of the fo'c'sle."

"Christ! Could he have fallen or jumped overboard as far back as that?" Captain Layton shook his head.

The mate, Sparks, and Mr. Finney all came in through the chartroom door.

"'Morning, Captain," they spoke as one man.

"Good morning," Layton nodded at them. "Probably futile," he addressed everyone, "but we'll bring her about on the outside chance he went over around breakfast time."

"Flotation gear away and the light's flashing strong... Seas sure are building, Captain." Searles came in from the wing.

"Thanks, Third—Sparks, get our fix from Mike here and see if you can raise anyone close by."

Sparks and the third mate went into the chartroom.

Captain Layton crossed to the bridge phone and cranked it several times. "Standby? Who is this?"

"The bosun."

"O'Malley! Good, you're just who I wanted. We're coming about. Call all hands—I want everyone in the crew's mess. No one's to come forward till we're steadied up!"

"Aye, Sir!"

"After I speak to everyone we'll post lookouts and get our lee boat ready to lower."

"Aye, Cap'n!"

Layton hung up the phone. "Mate, I want you here on the bridge with the third. The rest of us will go aft soon as we've come about."

The tanker pitched and rolled wildly as she slowed and began to make her turn. The seas, no longer plowed aside by her knife-like bow, stormed aboard, breaking precisely at the junction of the fo'c's'lehead and the forward well deck. Great gouts of grey-white water boiled over the decks and shot massive sheets of heavy spray against the bridge.

Evers awoke as soon as the sound of the ship's turbine changed pitch. He rolled over and looked at his watch. It was almost 8:45. "They know he's missing," he said to himself. "Here goes nothing." He lay back and waited for the sound of the general alarm.

The change in the ship's speed did not awaken Kruzic. He was in an alcoholic stupor having finished a full bottle of bourbon as he waited for the discovery of Whitey's body.

*   *   *

On Half Ahead, with the sea now dead astern, the *Concordia* rode easier; the swells rolled up, lifting the stern in a rhythmic and forceful manner. Now the fantail and after house took the flying spray from the swell-borne waves as the wind, gusting to 50 miles per hour, flung them against the retreating stern of the tanker.

"Okay, let's get aft!" The Old Man pulled on his new water-proof windbreaker.

Pierce and Finney followed him into the chartroom. Captain Layton paused at the chart table and traced a finger back over the ship's course. "What are you steering, Hassan?" he called out.

"354, Captain," the AB answered from the wheelhouse.

"Make that 352!"

"Aye, Sir. 352."

"Mate, you should spot the flotation gear in a few minutes—may have to nudge her a bit more to allow for drift."

"Aye, Captain." Wilder stood at the porthole with his binoculars trained ahead trying to pick up the flashing light.

"Call me in the crew's mess if Sparks contacts anyone, Mike." Layton turned and headed down the companionway followed by the two officers. The wind held the watertight door closed; it took the joint efforts of Finney and Pierce to force it open. The three men waited till the ship rolled up to port, then pushed their way out past the heavy door, letting it slam shut as the ship rolled back to starboard. They dogged it down and stepped onto the after catwalk into an atmosphere half air and half water.

Except for the white of the spumes flashing off the waves, the sea and sky were as one. The wind wailed through the standing rigging and each stay and shroud screamed its own contribution to the cacophony.

When they made it into the after house, the Old Man advised Pierce, "Better get into some dry clothes, Bob. Then see what shape you find the chief in. I'm going to ring the general alarm in a few minutes. By now I expect O'Malley's called everyone anyhow."

*   *   *

"Well, I'm sure you're all aware we're missing a man." Layton paused and looked around the crowded room. "Anyone have any information they can give us?"

"Keep it down!" the bosun called out over the sound of small talk in the already noisy messroom.

The benches were all full. There were more men standing braced against the bulkheads and in the galley passageway leading to the saloon than there were seated. The noise and vibrations from the thrashing screw, as the swells lifted the stern out of the water, competed with the clank and clatter of pots and pans in the galley.

"As you can see, the weather isn't getting any better—our chances of spotting the man in these seas are none too good," the Old Man spoke louder.

As if to emphasize his words, the *Concordia* corkscrewed down, rolling better than 25 degrees over the following crest. The wind whipped around the house shooting heavy spray against the open portholes. Men seated at the rear of the messroom cursed and jumped up from the soaking tables to dog them down.

"So far all we know from Schmidt and Billet here," Captain Layton nodded his head at the two wipers, "is that Bender left the fo'c'sle after midnight, drunk!—Anyone see him after that?"

Stacey was seated opposite Hansen at the center table. He looked toward Evers who was standing across the room.

"Captain," the big AB stood away from the bulkhead close by the coffee urn, "about 1 o'clock, on my standby, this man you're looking for come in and staggered over to the for'd bench. He was drunk and ended up on the deck." Evers pointed to the spot across the room where Whitey had been lying when the Kid came to get him.

Stacey tensed as he listened to the big AB. "Christ, what do I say now? He's saying everything real fine—except that he hit him!" the thoughts raced through his head. "Shit!"

"Good!" The captain looked over to where Hansen and Stacey sat. "We know he was still aboard at 1:00 A.M.—now, anyone else see him then as well, or later on?"

"Aye, Sir." Stacey raised his arm.

"When was that?"

"The second knocked me off to get coffee and help the standby rig the pilot ladder. He was sitting on the deck when I came aft and was still there when we went forward around 1:30."

"Thank you... Anyone else?"

No one answered. By now a number of men had turned to look at Stacey and then at the big AB.

"Anyone have anything else at all to tell us?"

Ned Carter, the 8 to 12 oiler, sat next to Paco at the same bench as Stacey, directly opposite from him. The oiler stared at his hands and said nothing. He had looked around the room when he first came in and noted that Kruzic was not there.

"Hansen," Layton looked back to where the AB sat, "when you went on standby was there anyone in the messroom?"

"No, Captain... No von."

"Do you remember what time it was when you came down here?"

"Vell...not exactly, Sir, but it vas pass two."

"Then it looks like you two were the last to see him." Captain Layton looked at Evers and then at Stacey. "I'll need you to sign statements in the log. See me on the bridge when you come up on watch. You can get your gang started, Boats—the rest of you can go back about your business."

"Okay, Guys, 8 to 12 go forward. The mate'll tell you where he wants you; 12 to 4, one man each side of the boat deck, one on the stern—4 to 8 will relieve you in an hour." O'Malley pulled on his bright yellow slicks. "Ski, you and Junior strip the tarp and strongback off the port boat. Don't get outboard the fucker! Roll the tarp tight and see you don't go over the side with it!"

Captain Layton and the second mate got up as the deck gang started out. They made their way through the galley passageway into the saloon holding on to sinks and gratings to keep their footing.

"She still needs more ballast," Layton observed as he sat down at the head of the table. "Pierce should be back in a bit, with or without our chief engineer!"

"Coffee, Captain?" Mr. Finney went over to pour a cup.

"Aye, thank you, Carl—I see some of Reed's dandy fresh doughnuts there."

*   *   *

The first assistant changed into dry clothing and hurried over to the chief engineer's quarters. "Chief!" He knocked on the door. "Chief, sorry to call you..." he knocked louder. Just as he started to call out again, the general alarm bell resounded throughout the passageways.

For the first few seconds Kruzic's fogged mind hardly registered the ringing of the alarm, then he slowly started to come to and sat up in bed. His head ached and he could hardly focus his eyes on his watch.

The moment the bell stopped ringing, Pierce hammered on the door. "CHIEF...! Captain Layton called all hands!"

Kruzic heard the pounding on his door. He looked at his watch again to be sure. It was a minute or two past 9:00 A.M.

"Are you okay, Chief, the Old Man has—"

"Yes, yes... Who is that?" Kruzic had staggered out of the bed and braced himself in the doorway leading into his office.

"It's Pierce, Sir—are you okay?"

"Yes...yes I'm up. What's happening?" Kruzic steadied himself for the answer. "I'll be right out!"

"The captain rang the general alarm because we've a man missing. We've come about and begun a search!"

"Missing? When? Who is it?" Kruzic kept his voice controlled and kept staring at his watch trying to figure how so much time could have elapsed.

"The new wiper, Sir. The Old Man wants his locker gone through for papers, money..."

"Yes, Pierce." Kruzic's mind was whirling with a hundred conflicting thoughts. *Bender missing? Overboard? Hiding?—Or was this a ruse to grab him? Could the bastard have gone to Layton?*

"The captain's got everyone assembled in the crew's mess. I'm heading there now, Sir. Shall I tell him anything?"

"Yes, First...I... I'll be along shortly—not well, not well, but I'll be right along... Have... I'll be a few minutes."

"Okay, Chief, I'll tell him. No rush really. There's nothing for us to do right now except go through his gear." Pierce shook his head. Kruzic was dead drunk and he was happy to get away without having to go into the room.

A sudden chill shook Kruzic. He had to get himself under control. A good hot shower than a cold one. He had to stop thinking the worst. If it came, it came. Maybe his luck was still working for him. It was always there for him when he really needed it. Why not now?

When the engineer finished showering, he dressed neatly and sat down at his desk. He pulled open the bottom drawer and withdrew a fresh bottle of bourbon. *One drink just to clear my mind,* he promised himself.

If Kruzic was anything, he was methodical. He tossed the drink off and put the bottle back; then sorted things out: Who would want to throw a dead man overboard? Why...? If he was still alive, who wanted him dead besides me? Someone sure as hell must have thrown the bastard over the side—I know he was dead! Whoever beat Bender could just as easily have killed him. You kill a man to shut his mouth... *But you beat a man to get information from him!* Sweat broke out on Kruzic's forehead. He knew the seamen's union had its own goons. If they came up with information about his past operations they'd be after him.

"That's it!" he muttered aloud. *"That's it!"* He'd heard Layton speaking to the second mate at supper about the new AB who caught the ship just before they sailed. Goddamnit! It has to be! Did the union send him? Bender came aboard the same afternoon. He might have just been after him—nothing to do with *me!* The thoughts kept pounding and a throbbing migraine started to sicken him. At the very worst, the AB is a goon and knew something about Bender and me. He beat him up and got him to spill his guts... But, he can't tell anyone aboard, and he can't telegraph from the ship without putting his own head in a noose. He can't tell the union till he gets ashore—*if he gets ashore!*

The engineer got up from the desk and went over to his locker. The tanker's stern bucked and he almost lost his footing. He took the key and opened the steel door. In a moment he found what he was looking for—a small black .32 caliber Beretta. As he slipped the gun in his pocket, the realization came to him. *I heard two men in the messroom!* Kruzic knew that ordinary seamen couldn't take the wheel in the river.

"That fucking punk!" he swore under his breath. "Could be I've *two goons* out to get me. Well, we'll see now won't we—I'll be getting off this fucking ship," he patted his pocket as he started out of the room, "but not like my late friend Mr. Thomas Bender."

"Sorry to get you up Chief." Layton looked up as Kruzic stepped into the saloon. "Some great doughnuts there," he pointed to the coffee table.

Kruzic felt a sudden burst of relief. The *Old Woman* couldn't know anything. He wouldn't be able to conceal his feelings if his life depended on it. "Thank you, but I've been pretty sick, Captain."

"Yes, Mr. Pierce told me so. What do you think it is?"

"I ate ashore yesterday afternoon—food poisoning perhaps."

"If you're up to it I'd like you and Mr. Pierce to go through the man's locker with the black gang delegate—that's Ballou, I think—get his papers, any money, etc., to me and have the delegate lock up his clothes and all."

"Yes, Captain." Kruzic started to turn towards the door. "When did the man disappear, Captain?"

"Well all we know is that he was still in the crew's mess at 1:30 this morning."

"In the messroom?"

"Aye, drunk and flaked out on the deck. Both the ordinary and the new AB on the 12 to 4 saw him. By the time the last standby, Hansen, came in about 2 o'clock, he was gone."

"The new A.B. came aboard the same time as the missing man, didn't he?" asked Kruzic.

"Yes, well perhaps not the same time, but within an hour or so of each other. Why, Chief? Do you think there's some connection here?"

"No...nothing. Probably just coincidence that the last man to see him—one of the last—joined the ship right after him."

"Frankly, Chief, I never thought of it that way. Well, we better get forward, Second." Captain Layton got up from the table. "Send whatever you find to me up on the bridge." he nodded at the two engineers as they left the saloon.

"Raise anyone yet?" the Old Man called out as he and Finney got to the radio room.

"Aye, Sir. We've been lucky—the *Somerset,* a Limey tanker, is changing course to coincide with our outbound track." Sparks got up from the transmitter and handed Layton copies of the transmissions between both vessels.

The captain braced himself against the door frame as he read.

"Anyone else?"

"Not yet, Sir."

"Thanks, Sparks. I'll be in the wheelhouse—Keep trying." The Old Man and the second mate continued on up into the chartroom. "Carl, relieve the mate and have him come in here."

"Aye, Captain." Finney went into the wheelhouse. "Mate, the skipper wants you in the chartroom."

"Okay, Carl. Learn anything back there?" Wilder put the binoculars in the canvas-lined box under the porthole.

"Not much—just that he was last seen by the new AB and the ordinary on the 12 to 4." He walked over to the porthole.

"Mate!"

"Aye, Captain." Wilder stepped into the chartroom.

"Get out the river charts—we need our position at 1:30 this morning. I see you've plotted the *Somerset*."

"Aye, Sir. She'll intersect our outbound track around 10:45." Wilder pulled out the long drawer beneath the chart table. He lifted out the charts and placed them on top.

"Thanks." The Old Man reached for the log book. It only took a moment to select the right chart. He walked off their course with a pair of dividers, calculating back from the *Concordia's* 2:50 A.M. departure position. After rechecking his work he looked up and spoke to the mate. "Seem about right to you, Mike?"

"It should be, Sir. We averaged nine knots the last two hours to the pilot station."

Captain Layton put down the dividers and returned the charts to the drawer, then whistled down the voice tube to the radio shack.

"Yes?" Sparks answered immediately.

"Notify the New Orleans Coast Guard station. We were approximately parallel to the inlet of Main Pass, a mile and a half north of Pilottown, at 1:30 A.M. That was the last time the man was seen aboard."

"Aye, Captain."

"Well, Tim, we'll keep up our search till we're certain the *Somerset* is overlapping us. I'm going down to my room for a minute. The chief or the first should be up here with the wiper's papers—call me if I'm still below."

*   *   *

Captain Layton kept the crew on emergency status until 1:05

P.M. when the search was terminated. The required course change was made and the men resumed their normal sea watches.

The bosun and daymen secured the lifeboat that had been made ready to lower; the watch on deck went back to chipping and scraping the deck in the lazarette.

Sparks had spoken to a few more ships. But all were too far away or on courses too divergent to be of any assistance. The Coast Guard received the full report and description of the missing man.

The 12 to 4 was back on watch and Stacey had the first wheel. He had been on and off lookout all morning along with Hansen and Evers until they were relieved for lunch.

"Stacey," Captain Layton's voice came from the chartroom.

"Aye, Sir."

"See me here before you leave the bridge."

"Aye, Captain."

"Who's got second wheel?"

"The new AB, Sir."

"Good, I want to see him as well."

Evers looked at his watch. It was time to knock off and get ready for the wheel. He straightened up, placed his scraper and chipping hammer into an empty five-gallon can and began sweeping up the rust.

"I get her bye-an'-bye," Hansen volunteered. "Yust leave her for now." He was working several feet away and stood up to stretch his cramped legs.

"Okay." Evers pulled a clean rag out of his back pocket and wiped his face. It was hot and stuffy in the lazarette with the hatch secured. He brushed the rust off of his pants with the same rag, then used it to wipe his work boots before tossing it into the bucket. "See you," he called back to Hansen as he stepped over the high coaming leading out into the port passageway.

Ten minutes before 2:00 P.M. Evers stepped into the wheelhouse, placed the cups and coffee pot into the round cutouts in the table and walked over to the wheel.

"Course is 176, but we're all over the place—she's taking 10, 15 degrees to hold her," Stacey warned.

"176. We're working in the lazarette." The big AB took the wheel as the Kid stepped aside.

"176, Mr. Finney."

"176... Fresh coffee?" The second looked up from the radar.

Stacey ran his fingers through his hair, stepped behind Finney, and opened the door into the chartroom.

Captain Layton was stretched out on the settee. The Kid paused for a second and hesitated. He didn't know if he should wake him.

"Come in, Stacey." The Old Man spoke without getting up or moving on the settee. He was tired—more tired than he cared to admit—tired enough to promise himself that this trip was his last one.

At the end of the war he had been 62 years old and could have retired, but he felt another three years would leave him and Sally in better financial shape. Now it had been five years—not three—and he was still out here. The security excuse was wearing thin. Sally was a saver, their home was mortgage free, and their three children were all married and doing well. The idea of giving up and removing himself forever from the sea was frightening. The thought of being stranded ashore with nothing to do had kept him from going until now.

"This is really the *last* trip for me!" he thought to himself. Out loud he said, "The log is open there on the chart table—read and sign it if it's accurate... Is Evers on the wheel now?"

"Yes, Sir."

"When you're through relieve him so he can come in and sign." The captain pulled himself upright and drew the thumb and middle finger of his right hand across his closed eyes.

"Aye, Captain." The Kid walked over to the chart table and braced himself against the roll of the ship. He read the log entry. It was a short statement. At about 1:30 A.M. on the morning of August 27, 1950 he had seen the missing man lying in the corner of the crew messroom. The man appeared to be drunk and unconscious. Stacey signed it.

"Anything to add?" The Old Man looked straight into his eyes.

"No." Stacey looked down as he answered. "No, Sir. I don't think so."

"Very well then, ask the AB to come in here."

"Aye, Sir." Stacey opened the door to the wheelhouse, stepped through and closed it behind him.

Evers turned around and their eyes locked for a moment. Stacey felt lousy. He was troubled by the Old Man's asking whether he had anything to add. *Damn the AB for telling him he'd hit the man!*

"Captain wants you to go in," he said to Evers, trying to avert his eyes.

"176—I've five degrees left on her." The big AB stepped off the wooden grate.

"176." The Kid took the wheel.

"176." Mr. Finney repeated the course as Evers went into the chartroom, closing the door behind him.

"Afternoon, Captain."

"Hello, Mr. Evers. The ordinary just signed the log. I'd like you to read it and sign it if it's correct."

"Aye, Captain."

"The log is on the chart table."

Evers went to the table and braced himself against the ship's movement as he read the entry. He felt worse about lying than accidently killing the wiper. But as a realist he knew that truth was like a multifaceted gem, reflecting things differently for each person according to where they stood. He signed his name and went back to the wheel.

* * *

By ten minutes to three, quite a few men had come into the messroom for coffee. Some were still on watch, knocking off to take their twenty minute break, others were men off watch but not sleeping. No overtime was being worked on deck or down below as the weather was too rough to line anything up.

"Still taking ballast, Angelo?" the bosun called across the room to the chief pumpman.

"No, finished up a while ago."

"Well, she sure ain't riding much better—gonna have to slow this sonofabitch down. What they got her turnin', Kid?" O'Malley looked across at Stacey.

"They brought her back up to 86 just before I got off the wheel."

"Skipper still on the bridge?"

"He was when I come aft."

"You guys finished in the lazarette?" the bosun addressed both Hansen and Stacey.

"Yah, Boats, ve finish him up."

Ski and Junior came in through the after door, securing it behind them.

"Startin' to squall again." Junior stood swaying in the aisle as he pulled off the top of his two-piece rain gear and hung it by the hood from the open porthole.

The two daymen made their way down the aisle to the coffee urn, filled their cups, and sat down opposite O'Malley.

"After coffee, work with the watch on securin' in the midship locker. Get everythin' up off the deck. And them Butterworth nozzles out from under the benches so's we can get the deck scraped and primed—ain't gonna dry too damn fast in this fuckin' weather!"

"Okay, Boats, we'll get on it," Junior answered.

Schmidt and Billet, the two wipers, clambered up the companionway. They had been in shaft alley with Johnson, the second pumpman, working on a big steam-driven bilge pump. Dressed in light clothing, they were still sweating when they entered the room.

"Christ a'mighty!" Schmidt, the smaller of the two, hunched his shoulders together as he shivered in the cold air. The two men headed into the galley for cups.

"Well," O'Malley addressed the fairly full room, "we best call a special meeting after supper and get it on the minutes so we can cable the union."

"The first's got all the guy's papers out of his locker," Billet volunteered as he headed for the coffee urn.

"Engine delegate see his gear locked up?"

"Aye, Boats. The first and chief got Ballou to go through the guy's stuff with them, then locked it up," said Schmidt.

"They find his union book or card?"

"I don't know, Boats—Ballou be up for supper. Shit! I'm goin' below." Schmidt got up and maneuvered down the aisle, trying not to spill his coffee. "I'm catchin' a cold!"

*　　　　*　　　　*

After coffee, Hansen and the Kid picked up their paint and tools and headed forward. They paused as they left the after house till the ship came back level, then, struggling against the wind they started down the catwalk. Water on the well deck raced like a river below them, cascading over the sides. The *Concordia's* roll was too snappy—before they could make it across, a mountainous sea roared aboard. The two men crouched and held fast to the railing as it smashed up over them. When the tanker finally shuddered back to an even keel, they stumbled forward to the lee of the midship house.

"Sonofabitch!" the Kid was the first to speak."That one damn near took the *catwalk* with it!"

Hansen looked at his water-filled tool bucket. "Oly shit! I loose everyt'ing but da vater!" He upended the five-gallon pail then crossed to the ladder leading down to the shelter deck.

Stacey left his bucket of red lead inside the door well and went into the midship house to call the mate.

By the time he returned, Hansen and the daymen were lashing things on the shelves in the big shelter deck locker. He secured the five-gallon bucket of paint and took off his rain jacket. He would have liked to strip off his rain pants and jeans as well for they were soaked through, but it was only twenty-five minutes before they would be relieved by the 4 to 8 watch.

"Start under the bench, Kid." Junior watched as Stacey went over to the tool rack. He took a sharp scraper, a new chipping hammer and a few old rags, then crawled under the work bench. Paint and rust had built up at the bulkhead to form a solid raised mound 2 to 3 inches thick. The rest of the deck lay under a half-inch of paint over rust. He went to work in the cramped space and listened to the conversation.

"Some says the fucker had it comin' to him," Junior answered Ski.

"I never see the guy on my vatch," Hansen was explaining, "but the messroom vas all fucked up ven I come down on standby."

"Pumps says he'd sailed with the guy—he was talking to the machinist this afternoon when I went down to sharpen the scrapers." Junior's high pitched voice went on. "Seems Sterling been with him once as well. He never liked the motherfucker. Too buddy buddy with the engineers. 'Specially for a guy who acted like he run the whole fuckin' union in his spare time."

"You think someone t'row him over the side?"

"Sterling told Pumps he knew a couple of guys laying for him awhile back around the hall. Seems this Whitey beat a little Filipino ordinary half to death in his bunk—broke his fuckin' jaw all to hell and the guy like to lose an eye. The beef started 'cause this Bender was always fuckin' with the ordinary's cousin, a wiper on the same ship. He beat the guy up ashore so bad he never made it back before they sailed. But the ordinary did—ya see—and Bender caught him in the sack that night."

"Vell, he ban gone now, vedder he yump or get t'rowed over

the side."

Stacey took in all the conversation as he worked, trying to remember what he could about the wiper.

He met Whitey briefly back on the *Jackson Heights*. It was long ago and the pumpman's murder had caused him to block out everything about that trip.

Now, because of all that had happened this morning, he tried to recall what he could of the fat wiper. He remembered the first night out. Too excited to lie down before going on watch, he spent most of the time in the crew mess and out on the fantail. He remembered Bender sitting out there when he came out with a cup of coffee.

The wiper questioned him about other ships he had sailed on. Stacey told him he'd never shipped as an ordinary before, but had made several trips as galley boy on a passenger liner. It was the story that the union organizers told him to tell anyone who questioned his background.

Whitey had also asked him how he caught the *Jackson Heights* that day. Stacey told him about being registered at the little hiring hall in Hoboken. That was about the extent of his recollection.

Then as he reviewed it all in his mind, Stacey suddenly remembered something else. The next day, while calling his mom from the phone on the dry dock, he watched those who had paid off walking towards where the taxis waited. Whitey was struggling with two heavy suitcases trying to keep up with two other men. One was the chief steward, a big Greek, and the other guy... Stacey just couldn't remember... They had all nodded at him as they went by.

"YES!—For Christ-Sakes!" thought Stacey. "It was <u>Kruzic</u>, now the *Concordia's* chief engineer. I thought I *knew* him from somewhere!"

By the time his two watch partners came down into the fo'c'sle, Stacey had finished showering and was dressed in dry clothes.

He lay on his bunk with his shoes off waiting for supper. Usually he skipped the evening meal, but tonight, because of the union meeting, he had to stay up anyhow. His makeshift "jack-off" curtain was closed around his bunk and he lay back thinking.

The big, dark, hairy engineer had been on the *Jackson Heights* along with Whitey and himself—just like on here—that was a strange coincidence.

— E L E V E N —

Mike Searles finished eating, put on his rain jacket and left the saloon. Considering the weather the cooks had to contend with, it had been a damn good meal.

It was dark and he almost bumped into Bob Howard, one of the 4 to 8 ABs, as he hurried across the catwalk to the midship house. They both made it without getting too wet. The AB relieved his watch partner on the wheel and Searles, after telling the mate what the food was like, took over for him.

Wilder left the wheelhouse through the chartroom and headed down the companionway. He knocked on the door of the radio shack. "Ed, you going to supper?" He turned the knob and looked in.

Sparks was receiving; he turned slightly in his seat, nodding at the mate, and went back to writing. In a few moments he switched back to transmitting and then after receiving a final acknowledgment to his transmission, he turned around and removed his earphones. "Hi, be with you in a minute, Tim." The radio operator changed chairs, sat down at the typewriter and started to type on one of his Western Union style communique forms. "Come here and look at this," he said without looking up.

The chief mate walked over and steadied himself by gripping the back of Sparks' chair.

After a series of numbers, letters, and the time and date, the message read:

POLICE DEPARTMENT PILOTTOWN, LOUISIANA NOTIFIED THIS STATION—RECOVERY UPPER TORSO BODY FITTING DESCRIPTION WIPER THOMAS BENDER 11:00 A.M. CTZ 8/27/50—RESULT AUTOPSY INDICATES HOMICIDE—DEATH DUE TO STRANGULATION—COLLAPSED TRACHEA— SEVERE CONTUSIONS CERVICAL REGION WITH MULTIPLE LACERATIONS AND DISCOLORATION EPIDERMIS RESEMBLING ROPE BURN ENTIRE CIRCUMFERENCE VICTIM'S NECK—LACK OF WATER IN LUNGS INDICATES VICTIM EXPIRED BEFORE ENTRY IN RIVER—WRIST WATCH STILL ATTACHED TO OTHERWISE NUDE UPPER TORSO STOPPED AT 1:48—LOWER TORSO NOT RECOVERED—VICTIM SUFFERED TOTAL DISMEMBER-

MENT AT THIRD SACRAL VERTEBRAE—POLICE
CORONER REPORT FILE A8H 4521—8/27/50 TRANS-
MISSION COMPLETE—USCGS—N. O.

The mate read the message as Sparks typed it. "Well, I hate to
see the Old Man woken up, but it looks like he's going to eat
supper tonight."

"We've got a messy little murder on our first day out and a
fucking hurricane playing cat and mouse ahead of us—anything
else?" Sparks shook his head. "I told you I've got the *creeps* about
this trip, Tim."

"You better call the Skipper while I go back up and let Mike
know what's going on. Supper will have to wait."

"Okay, Tim." The radio operator pulled the message from the
typewriter, separated the original from the copy, stuck the copy in
the top drawer of his filing cabinet and locked it. He followed the
chief mate out of the radio room and headed for the captain's
quarters.

Wilder opened the chartroom door. "Mike," he called out, "let
me see you a minute." He closed the door before Searles could
answer.

The third mate crossed the wheelhouse and opened the
chartroom door. He was about to say something, but caught the
gesture from the mate indicating caution. He closed the door
behind him. "Trouble?" he asked in a low voice.

"The wiper's body—part of it anyway—was found. Sparks
just got word and took it to the Old Man. It was *murder*, no
accident and no suicide."

"How can they be sure just like that? What killed him?"

"That's all I can tell you now. I may be awhile getting back."

"What do you figure the Old Man's going to do?" Searles kept
his voice low.

"Put 'em both in irons I expect."

"In irons? *Who?*"

"Christ! The new AB of course—and the ordinary. Didn't you
read the log?"

"Yes, but I don't see where—"

"Well read it again!"

The phone in the wheelhouse rang and Wilder went in to
answer it.

"Bridge!"

"Mate?" came the Old Man's voice.

"Aye, Captain."

"Bring the log down with you. And tell Mike not a word to anyone!"

"Aye, I'm on my way." Wilder hung up the receiver and stepped back into the chartroom. The third had finished reading the log entry. "You think THEY killed the guy?" he spoke excitedly.

"Keep your voice *down*, Mike!"

"Sorry, Mate, but I don't picture the Kid committing any murder. He was on my watch a month when Carl was on vacation."

"Okay, whatever. We'll know soon enough. Not a word about this to *anyone*—you got that, Mike?"

"Of course, Mate. Sorry for talking out of turn. Just hope the Kid's not involved."

Captain Layton was dressed and seated at his desk rereading the message when Wilder tapped on the door.

"Mate?"

"Aye, Sir, it's me."

"Come in." Layton opened the door. "Sit down, Tim." He pointed to the settee and locked the door behind him. Sparks was seated on the chair next to it.

"Let me have the log."

The mate handed it to him.

Captain Layton sat back down at his desk. He read the entries signed by Evers and Stacey, then reread the Coast Guard message.

The three men sat balancing themselves against the constant roll of the ship. Layton had to make a decision. He sat, fingers drumming on the desk, as he considered his next move.

From the looks of it, the big AB seemed as guilty as Judas. By his own account the wiper wasn't in the messroom at 1:45 when he got back from putting the ladder over. He puts himself at the scene of the crime and at the probable time the wiper went into the river over the stern. The body was sliced in two and the watch he was wearing had stopped at 1:48. It was only circumstantial evidence, of course. Layton thought of the counter arguments any good defense attorney could make—the man's watch could have been set wrong to begin with, and he could have been killed anywhere on the ship, thrown overboard and washed alongside the hull till the screw caught him.

I have to make up my mind whether or not to put this Evers in

irons, or perhaps lock up both him and the young ordinary—
shouldn't take *anything* for granted—Stacey might or might not
be an accomplice.

"Christ! I must be getting too old for this job!" He spoke aloud,
though he hadn't meant to.

"Sir, if the decision was easy I'm sure you'd have already
acted on it." Wilder meant it. Despite his sometimes flippant
attitude, he admired the skipper.

The Old Man closed the log and stuffed the message in his
pocket. He pulled himself erect and held onto the edge of his desk
as the ship rolled. Crossing the office, he knelt down in front of the
ship's safe and in a few moments had it open. He pulled a set of
keys out of his pocket, unlocked a drawer in the safe and picked
up his gun—a Smith & Wesson .38 caliber revolver with a five
inch barrel. He also took out two sets of handcuffs.

"Well," he said as he closed the safe and spun the dial, "I hope
we don't have to use force." He stood up and addressed his two
officers. "I find it hard to believe the wiper was strangled. Evers
doesn't seem the type who would do a man that way." Captain
Layton was talking more to himself than to the two men who
watched him. "Okay, Tim," he continued in a much louder and
firmer voice, "take this set." He handed Wilder a pair of handcuffs.
"Put them under your shirt where they can't be seen."

"Aye, Captain."

"Sparks, you and Tim go on aft now. I'll check on Carl to see
if he's in his room. He'll come aft with me if he is—if he isn't and
you see him in the saloon have him wait there."

"Do you want us to tell anyone else, Sir?" the chief mate asked.

"No, I'll inform the rest of the officers."

"Aye, Sir." Wilder tucked the cuffs under his shirt and started
out of the room followed by the radio operator.

"Sparks, you'd best come back to the bridge as soon as you've
had supper. I'm anxious to see the next weather report."

"Aye, Captain."

"Carl!" The Old Man tapped lightly on the second mate's
door. "Mr. Finney, are you awake?"

"Yes...who is it?"

"Captain Layton. Sorry to disturb you."

"Come in, Sir." Finney opened the door; he was dressed in
flannel pajamas.

"Sorry, but it's important. Skipped supper?"

"Yes, Sir. Come in please."

Layton stepped into the room and closed the door. "Read this, Carl."

"Aye, Sir." He sat down on the edge of his bunk with the message. *"Christ!"*

"I'm going aft now. I'll want all the officers there."

"Yes, of course, Captain," Finney started to dress and mused, "tough to figure anyone I suppose."

"I find it hard as well, but with what I've got, I have to lock the man up."

"If he's capable of committing a murder like this, he may not come easy."

The Old Man held out the other pair of handcuffs. "Here, Tim has a set as well—he and Sparks are back aft waiting for us. We might as well have supper."

"We may need *more* than cuffs, Captain."

"Let's hope we don't." He patted his pocket. "I am taking a gun with me. Put the cuffs where they can't be seen, Carl."

"You know, Sir, the bosun's calling a special union meeting at 6:30, after supper. Pumps mentioned it when he came up on the bridge."

"Be the opportune time to confront them both."

"Both? You mean *the Kid* as well?"

"Stacey was the only one back there at 1:30 with the AB and the murdered man!"

"Well, I know you've got to do what you think is right, but the Kid went back on lookout after rigging the ladder—he wasn't aft at 1:45 or 1:48 when the man went over the side."

"Carl, I can't see the ordinary as a murderer either. But we don't really know if the wiper was alive at 1:45 or 1:48, or dead at 1:30!"

"Aye, that's so, Captain."

"Well, I'll decide what to do with the ordinary when the time comes." Layton looked at his watch. "It's just 5:30—we'll eat and I'll tell O'Malley I want to speak to the crew after their meeting."

"I'm ready if you are, Sir."

The Old Man put the message back in his shirt pocket and stepped out of the room in front of the second.

"Medium rare, grits, greens an' a side of spaghetti," Samuel Diamond, the chief cook, repeated Tommy's last order.

"Make that a *double* on the steak!" O'Malley's voice came

from the messroom.

It was steak night, and with the ship riding somewhat easier than it had all day, it seemed everyone who came to eat was doing so with both hands.

"Boats!" Jim Dooley, the saloon messman, stuck his head through the messroom door from the galley passageway. "The Old Man asked me to tell you to see him in the saloon when you're through eating."

"Thanks, Dooley."

Hansen and the Kid had finished eating a few minutes before and were out on the fantail enjoying a smoke in the relatively calm air. The air temperature was only 54 degrees but it was comfortable in the lee of the house.

Andre Ballou, the 8 to 12 oiler, and his partner Fred Morgan, fireman-watertender on the watch, were standing a few feet away from the forward bitts. Hansen and Stacey leaned against the starboard railing and talked.

Ballou was the engine room delegate and a fanatic union man. He lived and breathed the "contract" and could quote whole sections from it word for word. A good oiler and a hard worker, he searched out all the overtime he could for the black gang and worked much of it himself. He was neither greatly liked nor disliked by his shipmates. When ashore, he was a fairly heavy drinker and he'd have his go at a whorehouse—if it was convenient, but he was generally tight with his money. *"I'm out on these cocksuckers to make money!"* was his heated answer when questioned about his conservatism.

More men had come out onto the stern after finishing supper. Some leaned along the rail where Ballou and Morgan were standing. A few others, the two pumpmen and the machinist among them, had claimed the aftermost set of starboard bitts and the closed hatch cover to the lazarette as their perches. It was almost 6 o'clock and supper was about over. The steward's department would take a while to clean up, but the crew messroom would be ready for the meeting at 6:30.

The 8 to 12 deck watch filed out of the mess, one after another. Tompkins, the tall bony ordinary, came out rubbing his stomach. He ate like a horse but stayed skinny as a rail. He was followed by Jimmy Ryan and Mamud Hassan, the two ABs on his watch. Tompkins draped himself over the starboard winch drum while Hassan sat on the big steam cylinder. Ryan leaned against the now cold steam lines that angled around the winch's throttle control.

"Well, come mornin' they found this message all writ out fancy as can be tacked to the saloon bulletin board." The ordinary was finishing his story started at the messroom table.

"How come they never find his body?" countered Hassan.

"Well, how the fuck I know?" Tompkins' voice pitched upwards at the end of the question. "You ask anyone was on the *Sells Victory*. The crazy fucker wrote the poem and put it there for the Old Man to read. Underneath it he give his mammy's name an' address, an' a bunch of other people's names he wanted to be notified."

"Shit!" said Ryan, looking at the skinny ordinary. "After winning all that money in a poker game he just ups and jumps over the fuckin' side in the middle of Gatun lake?"

"And how come they *never* find his body?" Hassan labored the question.

"Well, how the fuck I know?" Maybe the goddam 'gators ate 'im. We get to Colon and some government guy from Panama City come aboard askin' questions and that's all."

— T W E L V E —

Evers lay on his bunk smoking a cigarette, his left arm flung across his eyes. A sardine can sat next to him functioning as an ashtray. He skipped supper and, though he would have enjoyed going out on deck for some fresh air, he didn't feel like listening to all the bullshit from the men waiting on the fantail for the meeting.

The events of the past day had brought many things into focus. Thoughts he'd hidden from since Liz's death troubled his consciousness.

What he was doing was futile—pure escape. The constant repetition, moving from ship to ship and running away. Choosing to sail in the fo'c'sle rather than getting a mate's ticket and going topside was proof of this.

"Great!" he thought, "50 years old without a future or a present."

Ever since Liz died, nothing in life held any real significance. Sailing had long since lost its appeal. All ports were the same. Leaving one ship to join another did little to relieve the monotony. And yet, when he considered going ashore, that threat was even worse. What to do? Where to begin? For what purpose?

*　　　　*　　　　*

Bill, oldest of five children, was born on February 12, 1899. His people were owners of a small but fairly successful dry goods shop in Liverpool, England.

Apprenticed to a shipwright's office at thirteen, he developed a steady hand and a keen eye for detail. Despite being a big strapping youth, in whose fists the pens and other instruments of his trade appeared inadequate, he was an accomplished draftsman by the time he was sixteen. The new designs in steam engines and boilers being invented and improved upon completely captivated him. His employer, Mr. Ditton of Ditton and Feinstein Ltd., was a second father to Bill; it was he who urged him to study marine engineering.

When the great "war to end all wars" intervened, Mr. Ditton helped Evers secure a job with the White Castle Line as a stoker on the South and East Africa run. Mr. Ditton told the young draftsman that his job would be waiting for him, and meanwhile "to become an engineer for his own good and the good of the company."

After the war, not yet twenty years old, he returned to Liverpool and went back to work for Mr. Ditton. He had earned his third assistant engineer's license in the three years he spent at sea. Mr. Ditton planned for him to begin study as a marine architect in the fall.

Two months after Bill resumed his job with the company Mr. Ditton had a falling out with the co-owner. Feinstein had been the silent partner, providing the finances while Ditton did the engineering. The split came over Ditton's refusal to cut corners in his specifications. Such cuts would have insured the firm's receipt of several important bids from companies that had become more and more cost conscious in the competitive post-war shipping industry. Ditton tried to raise enough money to buy out his partner. But lacking promotional skills, he just didn't have sufficient influence to attract the necessary capital. In the end, he was forced out and Evers left with him.

The old man was broken-hearted. It was too much for him and he took his own life a few weeks later. In the meantime, Evers had shipped out, not hearing the news till he returned to England three months later. Bill received a fairly substantial inheritance from the old shipwright. He deposited it in trust for his younger brothers and sisters so they could afford decent educations.

The loss of his friend changed Evers' goal. He went back to sea as a deckhand and rarely returned to England. He avoided the engine room, signing on only once or twice as an unlicensed black gang member during the depression years, when work of any kind was so hard to come by. He drifted away from his family. Once in a long while he'd write, but he never returned home again to visit.

Evers left a ship in New York in 1933 and spent the year ashore working on the Brooklyn docks. He applied for his American seaman's book and also applied for U.S. citizenship. He accrued the time needed to become a citizen while at sea.

When Bill started sailing American ships, making Brooklyn his home port, the conflict on the waterfront between shipping companies and the various seamen's unions was growing into an open battle waged aboard every ship he caught. He would be the first to agree that conditions aboard the average ship needed improving, but at the same time he was suspicious of the powers behind much of the unionism being preached in the fo'c'sles. For freedom loving Evers, the taint of communism that accompanied some of it was too strong to ignore.

It was tough enough to win in a beef against an individually run shipping company. It would be <u>impossible</u> to stand up against a single organization that controlled *all* work aboard *all* ships.

No, Evers decided that he'd neither fight for nor against the unions. In fact, he wanted both sides to survive—union and nonunion companies—competing in the market place. In that way a man retained the right to choose his own master and to *change* that choice as well. Human nature being what it was, Evers felt the little man would be exploited by whoever was "topside" whether union bosses or company officials. At least if neither of them got a total monopoly, a determined man could make his careful way between.

It didn't seem to matter whether a ship was union or nonunion, there were constant fights between power cliques trying to boss the less intelligent or more easily frightened men. Sometimes the cliques were tied to topside, other times they just existed below—*but always,* a man either let himself be coerced, or he had to fight to maintain his integrity.

The big AB was never coerced. If the odds were too great to exist he'd pile off. If they were reasonable he'd stay. It was like a game after a while. There was no sense trying to win against a stacked deck. Better to pass and find a game where you had a chance to win.

Winning for Bill was being left to himself. It didn't take long for shipmates to recognize that he was a loner. He was friendly, but he kept out of the politics aboard. He did his job well and had little to do with anyone topside. On those occasions, when his independence was challenged by crew members who could not accept his ways, the big AB backed his claims with his fists. He rarely lost a fight. Even when he did, nothing changed. No one who managed to best him escaped without injury. It made them think again before trying the quiet Englishman another time.

Like most men who followed the sea, as soon as the ship docked and he was off watch, he'd head for "the front," the area around the docks. It was the same in every port in the world. Here were found whiskey and women, perhaps not the best brands of either, but a man could get away from the ship for a few hours and try to make up for the weeks, sometimes months, of isolation at sea.

Evers knew that the front was not representative of the real world ashore, but the passage of years made that "real world" an abstract illusion difficult to recall.

On Christmas eve in 1938, Evers left his ship at Pier 3 Erie Basin and looked for a job ashore. He was a few months short of his 40th birthday. He had decided that life was passing him by— if he didn't take the plunge ashore now, he never would.

Bill found a good job in a small rigger's loft in Brooklyn, and—on impulse—he began attending night-time adult education classes at Erasmus Hall High School. It was there he met Elizabeth Flynn. Liz was twenty-three. She taught math in the school during the regular day sessions, and was one of the volunteer instructors for the night classes. Evers attended her geometry class twice a week, on Tuesdays and Thursdays from 7 to 9 P.M.

Toward the end of the semester, the class met on a Saturday afternoon to visit the Museum of Science and Industry in New York City. Bill became so absorbed in the working models of the latest marine steam turbines and Diesel engines that he got separated from the group.

The class had a picnic lunch at the nearby park.

Lost in thoughts of his youth and brooding over the frustration of his engineering plans, Evers had forgotten the class, the picnic and everything.

Some small sound brought him back to the present and he

became aware that he was being watched. He turned and met the eyes of his teacher.

The young woman, embarrassed at being caught studying him, avoided his eyes and spoke haltingly. "Mr. Evers...I... We missed you," her eyes returned to meet his, "for lunch."

After a few awkward seconds, Evers mumbled a thank you for her concern and by the time they left the room, he was again in full control.

Late that afternoon, as the class broke up and everyone headed their separate ways, Liz asked Bill to join her for supper. They were a few paces behind the rest of the class when she spoke and Evers was taken so completely off guard, he thought at first that he heard her wrong. When he didn't answer, she blushed and said "that was so stupid of me—you probably have other plans."

"You don't want to be wastin' your time on the likes of me, Miss Flynn." He regretted his answer the moment he said it.

Liz increased her pace and almost reached the rest of the group by the time he caught up with her. He reached out and shyly touched her shoulder. "Please let's try that again Miss Flynn. I'd be honored to have supper with you."

The relationship that developed after that night soon had Evers in a state of near shock. He and Liz had begun sleeping together. In the past, if he successfully bedded a woman he met, he always categorized her as a whore. If she successfully resisted his advances, he thought of her as an <u>untouchable</u>—like mother, sister, nun, etc. "How could an educated, young and pretty teacher like Liz take up with a base, unlearned whoremonger almost twice her age?" he asked himself in bewilderment. The only answer he could come up with tore at his heart. He began to fear that this beautiful, fair-skinned, innocent looking girl was a nymphomaniac or some other kind of sexual deviate he hadn't heard of.

When Evers met her parents—at her insistence—her father made no attempt to disguise his hostility. Bill understood that, even sympathized. But what could he do? He loved this *sick* girl with every fibre of his body. And he knew they would be married, regardless of reason or consequence. Liz asked him for a church wedding for her parents' sake even though she knew he wasn't religious. They were married June 5, 1939 in a little Catholic church near her parents' home.

The three years that followed were like a dream for Evers, he forgot the old life ever existed. He was entirely devoted to Liz, amazed at his good fortune, and finally rid himself of the idea that she had to be perverted to have wanted him.

When he realized that she was truly in love with him and that their relationship was not just some weird sex driven liaison, Bill began having difficulty expressing his own sexual desire for her. His physical need conflicted somehow with the tender and concerned feelings he had for his wife.

In February of 1940, Evers bought the small rigging company where he worked. The little business grew, and by the time the United States entered the war, they were doing well enough to put a sizeable down payment on a small two story walk-up.

It was Liz who initiated changes in their love making. First she asked that a small light be left on when they got into bed. It was she who suggested he lie back one night and let her assume the female dominant position.

Evers could hardly believe it. Here was this wonderful loving girl writhing with abandon on his organ. Liz would lower herself gently down till he penetrated, then raise up and come back down lower, again and again. She kept at it till she managed to glide up and down the full length of his erection. When she had engulfed him completely, she would move her pelvis back and forth. Liz was always very wet and as their movements increased she brought him more joy than he ever believed possible.

Often she would lean over him and kiss his nipples, an act that he found strangely pleasurable. It always strengthened his erection. Her long brown hair tented his face, and he would reach up, part it, and pull her head down to kiss her lips. Her tiny breasts were tipped with the pinkest nipples he could ever remember seeing; they were so pointed when she was aroused, especially in this position with her on top. He had to tell her to stop moving and let his need to ejaculate subside. Then he would draw her down to his chest and would take one nipple in his mouth and caress the other with his fingers. "Don't make the other one jealous," Liz would say twisting her body for him to alternate every few minutes.

When he couldn't hold back any longer he would reach over and manipulate her clitoris. They generally peaked together. The moment of release was like an explosion for Evers, especially if he had delayed his coming for a long while. He held back in order to prolong the pleasure for Liz, letting his need subside several times. When release finally came, it was so intense it was almost painful. The groans that escaped from his lips came as involuntarily as Liz's contractions.

They seldom spoke till after Liz gathered a towel up between her legs and headed for the bathroom to shower. Bill would wait a few minutes and then follow after her. Back in bed, Liz would close her eyes and drift off almost immediately. Evers would wait till her breathing became deep and regular then disengage her arm from around his shoulder. Sometimes, watching her breathing gently by his side, he would get another erection and want to take her again. It was difficult to explain. He loved and enjoyed her to the utmost, but somehow could never let his passion find full release, never experience that total falling away from himself.

He fantasized about—just for once—taking her with complete abandon in the way he would drunkenly take one of "the girls." He longed to grasp her beautiful buttocks in his hands and drive himself into her without any of the preliminaries—to pound away deeper and deeper, building to a completely uninhibited orgasmic release. He wanted to blank out the entire universe, even if for only a split second, then fall away into the total oblivion of sleep.

A few days before their first wedding anniversary, Bill found a package in the hall closet; opening it he discovered a beautifully bound copy of the *Kamasutra*. It upset him terribly, especially when he noticed the inscription on the inside cover. It was Liz's anniversary present for him. He looked through the pictures and the feeling that he wasn't satisfying Liz began to gnaw at him. He always did his utmost to please her, always holding back to be sure she was satisfied. "Perhaps she is a *nympho* after all," he thought, "or maybe I'm just *too old* for her."

He drank all that afternoon and by the time Liz arrived home he was in a black mood. She had been putting the groceries away when he threw the book on the table.

"Don't I satisfy you at all, Liz?"

"What...? Oh!" She touched the book. "Satisfy me? Bill, you've made me so happy I feel guilty for the whole world—this was a present."

"But I must not be a good lover if you have to get me a book like this." He picked it up. "Is it to excite me or teach me how to do it?"

"Oh, Bill, that's not it at all...I... Well, I thought we might look at it together and..."

"What is it I leave out?" Evers heaved himself out of the sofa and walked over to the window. He pushed the curtains apart and stared into the night—it was raining hard.

Liz crossed over to him. She slipped her hands up under his arms and clasped them across his chest. "Hon," she whispered, "you leave *yourself* out."

"Sometimes I don't think I'll ever really understand you, Liz." Evers shook his head and turned towards her. She kept her arms around him and rested her head on his chest.

"Let's go to bed now, Love," she whispered. "I want you so bad it hurts down there."

Liz came in from the bathroom wrapped only in a towel. She had taken her shower and washed her hair. Evers had showered first and lay on the bed in his bathrobe.

"You'll catch cold with your hair all wet." Bill motioned for her to get into bed.

"Wait a minute." Liz went back into the living room and returned with the *Kamasutra*.

Evers was sitting with his back against the headboard and his knees drawn up. Liz climbed into the hollow that Evers provided and began slowly turning the pages.

"Aren't you amazed at how many ways they discovered to do it?" She looked up at him.

Bill stared at the picture that Liz had turned to. Two little stone-like figures, one male and one female, were arched over each other forming a perfect oval. The artist had depicted them suspended in air with no visible support. There was no mistaking the act. The male figure had been supplied with an organ so huge that the female's mouth concealed only a small portion of it. The male was graced with a tongue of similar exaggerated size and this was stuck up into the female's vagina with much to spare. Evers studied the plate. *Did Liz really want him to do this?*

"Have you ever felt the desire to make love like in the picture?" Liz broke the silence.

"No!" Bill closed the book and placed it on the night table.

"Do you think it's wrong?"

Bill was uncomfortable. "I never gave it much thought... but it doesn't seem normal," he added. Then he asked, "Do *you* think it's right?"

"I don't know how to judge right and wrong in something like this."

"Well, you sure as hell don't make babies with your mouth!"

"But people don't make love only to make babies. Are we wrong to make love the way we do—being careful not to have a child?"

Evers didn't answer.

"Are we?" Liz persisted. "We make love because we need to, and to enjoy it. Babies are only a part of it."

"The only people who do things like in that picture are whores and queers."

"Tell me, have you never been with a woman who kissed you down here?" She touched his groin lightly. Then didn't take her hand away.

"Why do you ask that?"

"Because I want to know if I'm normal. I've wanted to kiss you here." Her hand stroked him gently.

"Yes. It's common for a guy to go ashore and pay a woman to relieve him that way." Bill felt his penis getting full and hard in her hand.

"But you certainly aren't queer. Did you feel bad having let the girl do it to you?" she asked softly.

"No... I suppose it wasn't right, but I never really felt bad about it."

"Well then, maybe it's a *natural* part of making love, Hon?"

"These were whores—girls who made their living satisfying men's needs."

"But I want to make you happy and satisfied." She closed her hand around his full and throbbing erection. "And I have a very strong desire to love you this way."

"I've never had the desire to do it to you." He reached down and took her hand away.

Liz placed her hand on his stomach and massaged gently. "Perhaps it isn't the same for everyone. I wouldn't want you to do it to me unless you want to, but it doesn't change my feelings. I feel a very real need to kiss you there." She moved her hand back to his erection.

Evers let her hand rest on him again, holding her slim wrist with the slightest pressure. He lay there trying to sort out his feelings. Was it natural for her to want to do this to him? Perhaps the prostitutes and native girls *didn't* just do it for money. But for a man to do the same to one of *the girls* he'd have to be insane or queer—to put his face in some whore's crotch, his tongue up a cunt that had fucked man after man, crew after crew—you couldn't wash that much *scum* away with an ocean.

But did he really ever think what it would be like to put his mouth on a clean girl, like Liz? Could he ever feel the same way towards her if he let her try it on him? Evers was getting very uncomfortable. He felt somehow ashamed lying there, his penis throbbing in her hand.

Liz reached up with her free hand and snapped the little bed lamp off. She gently pulled open his bathrobe and rubbed his chest. Then she sought out his nipple with her mouth. Bill lay there breathing heavily in the pitch black room while Liz gently stroked the full length of his erection. She alternated sucking and caressing his nipples with her mouth and her free hand.

Evers' back arched as he felt Liz's tongue touch the swollen tip of his penis. He started to pull away. "Please don't," her voice came to him. Then it was her soft wet lips around him.

"Liz baby," Evers groaned, no longer able to resist. He shuddered and involuntarily pushed his hips up towards her, plunging deeper into her mouth. Her fingers closed more firmly around him and her hand began to move.

"Oh, God!" The cry was as impossible to stifle as the sperm that burst forth from him.

For the first time in his life, fleeting as it was, he experienced a total escape from time, from space, from self.

In March of 1942 Evers sold his business. Liz said nothing when he signed up with the U.S. Maritime Administration. He told her the day Pearl Harbor was attacked that he would serve at sea. He sailed in April from Brooklyn, carrying munitions to England.

His ship returned to Halifax the third week in May; he had four days off and flew to New York. Liz took the time off from teaching, and they celebrated their anniversary, a little early, but filled to the last moment with happy times. On their last evening together they dined at the same little restaurant in Greenwich Village where they had their first date.

Bill wrote to her from England. His ship had been laid up for major repairs and he was assigned to another. He could not tell her the name of the vessel or where it was going, just that he was the new boatswain.

Evers didn't get the news of Liz's death till he got back to Scotland in October. He'd been flown back to pick up another tanker after surviving a disastrous convoy to Archangel. Of the three dozen vessels which sailed for Russia from Iceland that June, his ship was one of only nine that made it.

Liz had been struck down by a car driven by a drunken Negro right in front of the school.

When Bill received the news from Liz's parents, it included the information that she'd been pregnant with his child—they had been sworn to secrecy but now felt obliged to tell him. Liz had wanted to surprise him when he returned.

Evers was inconsolable. He arranged to transfer all remaining assets from their joint account at the bank together with the money realized from the sale of their house and furniture and had it divided equally between Liz's parents and his own family in Liverpool. He didn't return to New York till after the war. He never again wrote or visited Liz's family.

The big AB was so lost in thought that the hard knock on his door startled him.

"Let's go. Union meeting at 6:30!" It was Terry, the ordinary on the 4 to 8 who had knocked. The door opened. "You up?" the ordinary asked.

"Aye, thank you." Evers got up out of bed as Terry closed the door. He went over to the washstand and splashed cold water on his face. He looked into the mirror after toweling dry and stared intently at his own image.

The years showed, particularly around the eyes. They were tired eyes; eyes that had seen too much, that knew too much, that had cried too much after Liz's death.

—THIRTEEN—

Captain Layton entered the saloon with the second mate and took his seat at the head of the table. The mate and Sparks were there along with John Pillars, and Henry Davis, the second and third assistant engineers.

Jim Dooley, the saloon messman, came in and approached the table. "Can I take your order, Captain?"

"Yes. Steak, medium rare, potatoes, and some okra. And Dooley, please tell the bosun I'd like to see him when he's through eating."

"Aye, Sir." The messman turned to Mr. Finney. "Can I take your order as well, Second?"

Finney ordered a well done steak and potatoes.

As soon as Dooley left the saloon, Layton told the two engineers of the Coast Guard report and explained his plan for apprehending the suspected crew members.

Davis, the third assistant, looked at his watch. "It's time I relieved the first, Sir."

"Yes... You don't have to tell Bob anything. I'll fill him in when he gets up here."

"Yes, Sir." Davis got up and left the saloon.

Layton looked at the second assistant. "I want the chief here at 6:30 as well. When you've finished eating, would you see he's told?"

"Aye, Captain... I'd best call him now before he goes to sleep—he didn't show up for supper." Pillars snuffed out his cigarette.

"Thanks, John." The Old Man turned back to his food as the second assistant started out of the room.

"Chief!" Pillars knocked gently on the chief engineer's door. "Chief!" He knocked harder. "Chief, are you still up?" He raised his voice. "THE OLD—"

"WHAT...WHO IS IT?"

"It's Pillars, Sir."

"PILLARS...? What do you want?"

"Sorry, Chief, but Captain Layton told me to call you."

"Call me...? Wait a minute."

A moment later the door opened and Kruzic stood in the doorway.

"Come in, Pillars—come in." He stepped back to let the second enter the office.

Kruzic had been drinking heavily. His breath smelled of whiskey and his eyes were red and bloodshot.

"Come in, come in," Kruzic repeated and pointed to the chair next to his desk. "Sit down, Second. What can I do for you?"

"Sorry to bother you, Chief. The Old Man asked me to tell you he'd appreciate your staying up and coming back to the saloon at 6:30. He's got something to tell all of us."

"Something to tell all of us. What the hell's wrong with that Layton?—What is it? What does he want?"

"I don't know, Chief. I'm just telling you what he said. He's got word from the Coast Guard about the missing man. He wants all officers there when he confronts the suspect."

"The SUSPECT?" Kruzic asked in a raised voice. "The suspect of *WHAT?* I don't understand you, Pillars. You say he got a message about the wiper?"

"Aye, Chief, his body was found and indications are that he was murdered."

"Murdered? Murdered by who? *Where was he found?"*

"Chief, I don't know anymore than what I've told you."

Kruzic stared at Pillars and shook his head slowly. "Did Layton say who he suspected? Who else was in the saloon with you when he came in?"

"Well, let's see... The third assistant, the mate, the second mate, and the radio operator. The five of us were there."

"And that's all he said to all of you was he'd received a message? Did he read it to you? I don't understand."

"Frankly, Chief, neither do I. He really didn't tell us much of anything." Pillars stood up and started for the door. "Well, I'll see you back there at 6:30. I'm going to shower."

Kruzic locked the door behind him and sat down at his desk. Something was wrong. Something was *very* wrong. Could the Old Man be setting him up? Why didn't the Old Bastard tell him personally about the message? Why did he send Pillars? Kruzic began to sweat. It was possible they had something on him. But what? What could they have found on Bender to point the finger at him. "Nothing! *Nothing!"* he muttered aloud. *I've got to pull myself together.* He poured himself another drink of bourbon. He knew it would have to be his last. He'd been drinking all afternoon and didn't dare show up at 6:30 out of control.

*　　　　　*　　　　　*

Evers entered the messroom. It was almost full and sounded like the Tower of Babel. The men were talking and shouting to make themselves heard over each other and the ship's background noises.

The tanker was still pitching and rolling heavily. Occasionally a worse than usual roll resulted in spilled drinks and curses as men slid into one another on the benches. Those standing or walking grasped at anything to keep from falling.

Evers made his way into the galley for a clean cup. There were none. He washed out a used one, letting the hot water turn almost to steam from the tap before filling it. He found a tea bag, came back into the messroom and sat down at the last table in the back. Junior, Ski, and the two 8 to 12 ABs were in a noisy knot at the far end of the same table. Junior's high-pitched voice carried over the others as he wound up his contribution to the exchange.

"Shit, old Lee an' this other guy beat the fuckin' shit out of each other one night. Beat the *shit* out of each other—DRUNK!" Junior's voice rose in a screech. He was trying to tell the story without laughing as he usually did every time he told it. "The sons-a-bitches was *measurin'* their DICKS!" Again his voice leaped upwards. "To see who got the longest dick—IN THE MESS-ROOM! That LEE, he got a foreskin *that long* on his dick!" Junior held both index fingers apart on the table to show them. "So he stretched it out—an' you know old whatchacallit he's been circumcised you know, an' his ain't that long, an' he can't stretch it that long—an they got 'em layin' up on the table an' old whatchacallit—"

"LET'S GO!" O'Malley stood up and called out over the din. "KNOCK IT OFF! LET'S GET ON WITH THE MEETING!"

A few men went right on talking.

"SHUT IT DOWN—LET'S GET IT OVER WITH!" The bosun called out again and the small talk finally quit. "Okay, you guys sit down back there so the rest can get in." He gestured to those who had not filled in the tables.

Stacey and Hansen had been standing on the fantail outside the open door of the messroom along with several others. They came into the room and leaned against the after bulkhead near Evers.

"Steward." O'Malley handed a sheet of paper and a pencil to Vincent Santos, the heavy-set, middle-aged Filipino on his left. We won't chair anyone for this special meeting, but you're the recording secretary. Okay—I call this special meeting to order!" The bosun banged his fist on the table. "Ballou here has the floor," he nodded at the man sitting to his right.

"Well, I'll make this short as I can," the oiler spoke as he stood up. "The missing man joined the union after the tanker beef and got his book in March, 1948." He held it up and passed it to O'Malley.

"The first assistant got all his other papers, money, and Coast Guard discharges and give 'em to the chief to take to the Old Man." The oiler handed a folded piece of paper to O'Malley. "You'll need this, Boats. It's a list of the wiper's gear that me and the first wrote up when we went through his locker. To finish up, all I can report is the man missin' and lost at sea, so I turn the floor back to the ship's delegate." Ballou gestured towards the bosun and sat down.

O'Malley got to his feet. The talking was getting louder again. "Keep it *down!* You've heard the engine room delegate's report—what's yer pleasure?"

"Make a motion to accept!" someone called out.

"Motion to accept. Anyone second it?" asked O'Malley.

"Second the motion!" another voice called out.

"Motion made and seconded to accept the engine room delegate's report. All in favor?"

Two dozen "AYES" rang out.

"Opposed?"

Silence.

"So be it! Let the record show motion to accept the engine room delegate's report made and unanimously accepted!"

The oiler held up his hand to get O'Malley's attention.

"What is it, Ballou?"

"We can have Sparks send a short message to the hall—won't cost us that much from the ship's fund—then send a letter from the Gulf."

"Yeah, we could do it that way. Okay, the steward here will get a cable sent now and have a letter ready to go from Ras Tanura."

"We *through* yet?" A voice called out.

"Yes, that's it, but the Old Man wants a word with the crew—so just stay put after we adjourn!"

"Make a motion to adjourn!" Ski called from the back of the room.

"Seconded!" Junior sang out.

"Motion made and seconded. All in favor?"

Another chorus of Ayes.

The tanker shuddered as she rode up over a huge swell that lifted her stern out of the water. O'Malley waited until the ship resumed a more normal attitude before getting to his feet.

"Okay, let's stand a minute of silence for our departed brothers."

Stacey pushed away from the bulkhead.

The men seated at the benches got to their feet. A few lowered their heads, but most of them stared straight ahead. Several fidgeted with their pants legs, others clasped their hands behind their backs.

The Kid stood straight and closed his eyes. He thought about the men he'd sailed with who were dead and gone, the good and bad both. As *always*, he remembered Eddy Sommers.

"Okay!" The bosun rapped the table indicating the minute was up.

Immediately men began talking and moving about. Some sat back down, some stood balancing themselves by holding on to the tables.

"Okay, *hold it down!*" O'Malley called out as he saw Layton coming through the galley passageway.

Ballou and the steward stepped away from the center of the table along with O'Malley. The captain entered the room with the chief and second mate.

Surprisingly the room quieted down without anyone having to say anything.

"Thank you." The Old Man nodded his head to the assembled men. "I asked the bosun to have everyone remain here as I've information to give you—something you might want to include in your report to the union." He glanced back to the passageway where the engineers stood waiting as backups, then looked around the messroom till he spotted the suspected men.

Layton reached into his pocket and pulled out the Coast Guard message. He read in a strong, clear voice, pausing occasionally to glance around the room. When he finished reading, he looked directly at each of the men of the 12 to 4 deck watch.

The big AB had no trace of expression on his face; the Kid's registered horror at the news of the wiper's being strangled and Hansen's was completely bewildered.

Suddenly, aware that a number of men were looking at him, Stacey closed his partially opened mouth and tried to look as normal as he could. Those who weren't watching him were staring at Evers.

Captain Layton didn't miss Stacey's look, nor that of Hansen's—he had only *one* man to take.

Evers stood looking at the captain waiting for the words he knew were coming, had to come. He held no antagonism for the Old Man doing what he had to do in front of the crew. On the face of it he was the only logical suspect for the murder—a brutal and cowardly one committed on a man drunk and unable to defend himself. *Unreal. What irony!* thought Evers as he stood there without any expression showing on his face. *I didn't kill the bastard after all!*

"You can understand that I have no choice but to hold you." Captain Layton and the two mates moved down the crowded aisle toward the big AB.

Evers heard the words and knew he should respond. But his mind was racing too fast. The new information meant that the wiper had been murdered—strangled—in the short span of time between his leaving the messroom to put the ladder over and his return to get coffee for the bridge. The realization struck him. *Someone...someone in this room did for the drunken bastard but no one will believe me—no matter what I say.*

"Boats, I want you and the deck delegate to accompany me and the chief mate in getting this man's gear out of his fo'c'sle and up to the hospital room," said Captain Layton.

Evers thought, "Someone watching this is a murderin' bastard. And I got rid of the body for him! No sense tryin' to change my story—I wouldn't believe it if someone else told it to me."

In the few seconds following Captain Layton's reading of the cable the messroom turned into a Pandemonium of cursing and shoving. The men in the immediate vicinity were huddled tightly around the principal players.

Kruzic and the two assistant engineers were cut off from the scene. There was a solid block of men wedged between the galley passage and the crew messroom. The Kid and Hansen had "front row seats." They stood about three feet in back of Evers and a bit to his left. A clump of seated and standing men formed half the circle around the big AB, while a correspondingly packed group completed the remaining half behind the captain and the two mates.

Evers was hardly aware of what the Old Man had been saying. At first he didn't even feel the cuff as the chief mate slipped it over his wrist. It didn't slip on easily, however, and the pinch of it starting to close against the skin of his wrist startled him. He jerked his hand up and away from the stab of pain. In doing so his hand hit the mate, grazing his temple.

Thinking the blow was meant for the captain or himself, the mate grabbed for the AB's hand.

Evers swung around. His shoulder slammed into Wilder, knocking him backwards into the men standing behind him.

The chief mate cursed as he tried to regain his footing. "GET HOLD OF *HIM!*" he yelled.

Evers realized everyone thought he was trying to get away.

"HEY!" he yelled as several men grabbed for him. He felt a sharp, almost paralyzing pain in his right kidney as someone threw a solid punch at his back. Another man got an arm around his neck.

"Son-of-a-bitch!" he choked in rage. Now, he had no choice. Hurling himself to the side, he broke the stranglehold and grabbed the shoulders of the man behind him. The speed with which he moved caught Ryan by surprise—the 190 pound AB slammed headlong into the captain and two mates.

"GOD DAMN YOU!" Evers shouted at the four men tangled on the deck. There was a small open space around him now—he stood like a lion surrounded by jackals.

The Old Man raised himself on one knee. Putting a hand against the bulkhead to steady himself, he leveled the big chrome revolver at Evers.

"YOU DON'T NEED THAT!" The big AB looked directly into the captain's eyes.

Regaining his footing, Layton balanced himself against the ship's roll. He wasn't hurt and he sensed that Evers, though he looked like a maddened bull, was no immediate threat. The two mates and the AB had gotten to their feet as well.

"Back away from us!" Captain Layton's voice was steady as he motioned to the men behind Evers. At the same time he lowered his right hand so the gun no longer pointed at the big AB.

The chief mate stepped forward again with the set of hand-cuffs.

"MATE!" The Old Man's voice brought Mr. Wilder up short. "That *won't* be necessary!"

Evers wanted to apologize to the captain but couldn't get the words out. He had a good feeling about the man from the moment he entered the ship's office to sign on—one of those intuitions which somehow always proved accurate.

Now, he stood there feeling guilty for having had to lie to him, for knocking him down, and mostly, for breaking some unspoken and undefined trust between them.

Everyone backed away as the big AB turned without a word and walked towards the companionway. Captain Layton, the two mates, bosun, and deck delegate, followed him down.

—FOURTEEN—

The hospital room was located on the starboard side of the midships house. It had two bunks, a locker, a small desk and an adjoining head. The metal door had two heavy steel bars on the outside which could be padlocked, and the two portholes were barred.

The AB lay on his made up bunk and stared at the overhead. Except for his belt and sheath knife, which had been taken, he was fully clothed. The rest of his gear, except for his razor blades, had been deposited in the room with him.

Evers had heard the latest weather reports regarding the hurricane ahead. He wondered if the Old Man would turn back, head for some place close by or keep right on course for the Gulf— if the latter, perhaps he had time to clear himself.

The more he thought about it, the more certain he was that reporting the man's death would have had the same results. He reached for his cigarettes. *Lucky they didn't think I'd fire the ship.* He sat up and lit one. They'd have taken me ashore as the only suspect. I'd a swore I only hit him, but the autopsy would've shown he was strangled and I'd be in the same bind—except the ship and the guy who strangled the bastard would be gone. He tapped the ash off his cigarette into the little tin can at his side.

"Damn it man, you're better off aboard," he murmured aloud. Not much of a chance, but better than I'd have ashore. Whoever killed the son-of-a-bitch is still aboard. Something may come up to force his hand before the trip is over. Someone might have seen something...know something.

He finished his cigarette, snuffing it out against the side of the can, then eased himself back onto the bed and shut off the bunk light.

He tried to unwind and sleep. There was nothing he could do right now. His last thoughts before drifting off were that he must review all the possible reasons for someone to be up and about in that fifteen minutes from 1:30 to 1:45 when he'd been rigging the ladder—that, and who aboard could have had it in for the guy. He would need someone to do some poking around—perhaps the Kid. He'd have to gamble and tell him the truth.

*   *   *

Stacey lay in his bunk thinking. He felt guilt for the wiper's death. No question, if I'd have reported the man injured to the bridge he'd still be alive. Another thing to ponder was why the Old Man hadn't locked him up as well. He knew I wasn't telling the whole truth when I signed the log.

Christ! I suppose I just didn't believe he could commit murder, even after the wiper come up missing. I knew he was late getting to the wheel and I knew he'd changed clothes, but coming back, strangling the helpless guy and throwing him over the side in cold blood. *Shit....!* And I even sort of liked the prejudiced bastard.

"Hey, Keed...you asleep?" Hansen spoke quietly.

"No."

"You know, I ban thinking 'bout our vatch partner—vhy he kill dat feller dat vay."

"Yeah?" Stacey answered without enthusiasm.

"Dey both catch the ship togedder on the same day, hokay?"

"Yeah."

"You think maybe he come aboard yust to get dat feller?"

"I don't know, Hansen. Why?"

"Vell, if you vas gonna get some guy, vhy you voudn't vait till the ship vas in deep vater? Especial since dat feller vouldn't know the udder guy vas looking to get him or he vouldn't stay around the hall, huh, Keed?"

"Yeah..." Stacey was only half listening to his watch partner's labored reasoning, but suddenly he realized Hansen had a point. "So what do you think the answer is?" Stacey responded to his partner.

"I don't know, Keed, but I gotta feeling maybe somethin's fishy... And then he yust vent f'rd to the brig viddout sayin' nothing—not von vord."

"What did you think about him when he came on our watch?"

"He ban a good seaman for sure. Vat you think, Keed?"

"I don't know, Hansen... I liked him, I suppose. But Christ! Everything seems to point to him doing the guy in—don't it?" He was tempted to tell Hansen about Evers having changed his clothes, something he was certain his partner hadn't noticed. Instead he said, "We better get some sleep. It's going to be time to get up before we know it."

"Hokay, Keed." Hansen rolled over and was quiet.

*   *   *

Captain Layton sat at his desk. He'd written everything that happened as objectively as he could. The log stated that Evers had not resisted being taken to the brig and that his swinging out had been a reflex action to the pinch of the cuff on his wrist.

In fact, Layton felt that he was partly to blame for the incident since he failed to recognize that Evers was more shocked than his demeanor betrayed. By the time he did, the mate had already acted.

The Old Man looked at his watch. It was almost 9:30 and he still hadn't showered. He closed the log and got up. In the morning he'd see what the company advised him to do.

"Well that's it. But it's still hard to believe I could be so wrong about a man!" he said aloud.

Kruzic was also up at 9:30. He sat in his office drinking from a less than half-full bottle of bourbon. It was his second bottle since killing the wiper less than twenty hours ago. He was hungry and thinking about the night lunch.

He knew Layton had seen how unsteady he was when he got to the saloon. The *old woman* would report it to the company the first chance he got—unless he sobered up right now. When the scuffle occurred in the messroom, Kruzic could only barely make out what was going on. He was certain that Layton originally intended entering the messroom with all of the available mates and engineers.

"The old bastard was too cowardly to say to my face that I was drunk and not to come along, so he announces at the last minute that only the deck officers should go with him." Kruzic slammed his fist on the desk. "Well I should thank that old fool for solving the problem for me." He poured himself still another shot. "But I must be careful. The AB hasn't said a word—denied nothing— just let himself be taken. *Why...?*"

Kruzic had gone up to the bridge and carefully read the log at 4:00 P.M. when he had the excuse to speak to the pumpman and the mate about the ballasting. He knew by heart the statements made by the two 12 to 4 deck apes. "The big goon signed a statement that the last time he saw the wiper was when he and the ordinary left the messroom at 1:30. Bender's watch was stopped at 1:48, perfect timing, as the bastard said that he got back to the messroom around 1:45 and it was empty."

Kruzic got up, staggered into his bathroom and turned on the tap. He splashed cold water on his face, then reached for a towel. *I know why!* He looked at himself in the mirror. "He can't change his story without admitting he beat up the wiper and then came back and threw him overboard. The fool himself was certain he'd killed him. Who would believe he wasn't the one who strangled him?"

He straightened out his clothing. "It would have been better if

Layton had locked the ordinary up as well... Anyhow," he rationalized, "the punk isn't worth worrying about and he probably wasn't involved. Could be Bender's getting beaten had nothing to do with me—the damn AB may not even be a goon!"

Kruzic made his way back to the office and put his bottle away. He patted the automatic tucked under his shirt, locked the door behind him, and headed for the saloon.

Ned Carter lay in his bunk reading. He was trying to clear his mind of everything connected with the dead man.

He had been right next to Evers when the mate tried to put the irons on him. In fact, he almost caught the big AB's fist in his face. He had been just that close.

"It just don't make any fuckin' sense whatsoever. The fuckin' AB just stands there—don't say a fuckin' thing—and gets marched off to the fuckin' brig." The oiler closed the book, pulled his curtain back slightly and reached for cigarettes. They were in his shoes. He glanced over to his watch partner's bunk. Paco's curtain was open and the glare from the oiler's bunk light fell across the older man's face. He was sound asleep. Carter lit a cigarette and inhaled deeply. "Well, there's only one fuckin' explanation. The AB had to be in cahoots with the fuckin' chief. They must've wiped out the guy for some fuckin' reason or another. I hope that's the fuckin' end of it. But it ain't. I fuckin' well know it ain't. Why the hell didn't I pile off this cocksucker? If the Old Man turns back or we put into Cuba or Florida, I'm gone!"

—FIFTEEN—

A few minutes past 10:00 P.M. Fred Morgan, the fireman-watertender on the 8 to 12, was alarmed by a sudden increase in the heat and a change in the sound coming from the port furnace.

He ran to the main engine room where Ballou, the oiler on his watch, and Mr. Davis, the third assistant engineer, were standing at the log table next to the main engine throttle control.

"PORT FIREBOX'S COMIN' APART!" he yelled running toward them.

"WHAT'S THAT?" Davis couldn't hear Morgan's words.

"PORT FURNACE!"

Ballou stepped over to the throttle control as the engineer

raced into the fire room with Morgan.

"SHUT HER DOWN!"

"Aye, Third!" Morgan began closing off the sprayer tip valves.

Davis hurried back to the main engine room gesturing to the oiler to turn the telephone crank. He trusted the oiler at the throttle, but he preferred to handle it himself.

The bridge had already responded to the ring of the phone.

"Bridge!" Mike Searles, the third mate, called over the phone.

"Davis here," the engineer answered as he gripped the throttle control and began closing it down, "we've got an emergency—got to take her down to 40 or so!"

"What's up?"

"Port furnace come unglued—I'm calling the chief now!"

"Okay! Hate to wake the Old Man. Poor devil hasn't had much sleep since we left the dock."

"See you!" Davis hung up, moved the selector to CH. ENG. OFF. and cranked the handle. No answer. He cranked again and waited. "Cocksucker's drunk," he muttered to himself. He leaned over the table, jotted down 'Reduced to 40 rpm's, 10:04 P.M.,' flipped the lid on the voice tube and whistled. He waited a few seconds and whistled again. *Well, he could be out of his damn office* he said to himself.

"Find the chief! Look in the saloon first. If he isn't there bang on his door—he may be asleep!" The engineer spoke close to the oiler's ear so he could catch it all over the noise of the turbine.

"Okay, Third!" Ballou swung up the first of the ladders leading up out of the engine room.

"Captain Layton, Sir!" Searles called down the voice tube loud enough to arouse the Old Man without startling him.

"Yes, Mr. Searles—what is it?"

"Engine room called. Bringing her down to 40 turns! Third assistant said the port furnace is coming apart!"

"Is the chief engineer down there?"

"Don't know, Sir."

"Anyone close to us?"

"No, Sir, got it pretty much to ourselves."

"Very well, Mike. Put her on half ahead. Leave word with the engine room for the chief to get back to me as soon as possible."

"Aye, Captain. Sorry to be the one that's always calling you."

"Yes, that's alright, Mike, don't hesitate to do so. I'll be here waiting on Mr. Kruzic. Anything comes up, let me know."

"Aye, Sir." Searles rang the engine room, relayed the Old Man's message and put the telegraph on half ahead.

"Chief," Ballou spoke to the slumped form that lay across the saloon table. "Chief!" he called somewhat louder.

There was no response.

"CHIEF! YOU ALL RIGHT?"

"Huh... Whaddaya want?"

"There's trouble in the fireroom—the third told me to report it to you."

Kruzic lifted his head off the table. His lower jaw hung in a slack moronic look, complete with drool.

"Wh...whatsamatter?"

"Third sent me to find you, Sir. The port furnace broke down."

Kruzic was in an alcoholic stupor. He had come into the saloon, eaten half a bowl of cornflakes and some cheese before passing out on the table, his shirt sleeves and face smeared with milk and crumbs. The cereal bowl lay overturned in front of him.

"Okay...okay.... I'm comin'."

Ballou stood there a moment and then turned and left the saloon. He didn't have much use for the chief engineer when he was sober—drunk he wanted no part of him. He had called him; it was the third's problem now, or the skipper's. He headed down below.

"Captain Layton!"

"Yes, Mike."

"The first assistant just called—he's coming to the bridge now."

"The chief with him?"

"No, Sir."

"Where's Kruzic? I left word for him to get back to me!"

"Aye, Captain. The third assistant got your message—seems the chief's sick, Sir."

"*Sick* is he?"

"Aye, Sir. The third assistant told me he called out the first."

Captain Layton knew what Kruzic's sickness was. He found it difficult to control his anger. The chain of command below decks was in operation. The normal "cover-up" was at work. The engine room took care of its own up to a certain point according to tradition. He could not exercise his overall authority until that sometimes hard-to-define limit had been reached.

For now, all he could do was grimace and answer. "Very well, Mr. Searles, I'll be right up."

*   *   *

The *Concordia* was doing just under 11 knots till the trouble developed at 10:00 P.M.; now, a few minutes before midnight, Searles was working up the log at the end of his watch. He recorded the ship's rpm's at 40. They were making less than 6 knots. After the exchange of information with the engine room, he finished up his chart work.

It was too overcast to get a reliable star fix, but he had a good one on Loran. He penciled in the tanker's last position as Lat. 25° 45' north; Long. 87° 39' west. They were 220 nautical miles from their point of departure having steamed a little over twenty-two hours at an average 9.9 knots.

Searles noted the sky cover as 30 to 40 percent overcast, with light cirrus clouds; the wind as variable, mostly southeast to south at force 4. The sea he described as light waves, 3 to 4 feet high superimposed over heavy southeasterly swells 10 to 15 feet high. The barometric pressure was 28.90 inches and steady.

"How's she going, Mike?" Carl Finney stepped into the chartroom.

"Not bad all things being equal, Second. Hope we can get some speed up before long." He straightened up and stretched.

"How much work did they figure they've got to get her going again?"

"The first told the Old Man he should have it all together in four or five hours—barring anything unexpected. They'll probably have her going during your watch."

"Well, you might as well get some sleep before the next emergency, Mike. Some trip so far, huh? Any late news on the storm?"

"Sparks was up here when the Old Man was speaking to the first. His latest report was three hours old. Anyhow, as of 8:00 P.M. it was still 35 miles off Cuba and moving at 15 knots with winds of over 100 mph."

"Where's the report?"

"Should be with the others." The third pointed to the small box under the shelf.

Finney walked over and took out all four reports. The last gave the storm's position as Lat. 23° 20' N.; Long. 79° 30' W.

"Picked up a bit of speed," observed Searles.

"Sure has, Mike." The second traced the flattened bow-shaped arc that the four indicated positions delineated. "If it hits Cuba we're probably off the hook—not to wish it on them. But if she doesn't, we may very well have her roaring down our throats."

"We should have time to outrun it... Still a long ways off." Searles couldn't help yawning.

"Not at 6 knots."

"No, you're right, Carl... Not at any 6 knots."

"You've had the bridge for almost two full watches. You must be beat!"

"Yup...time I turned in. Good night, Carl." Searles headed for the companionway. "I'm happy the Kid on your watch wasn't involved in the mess."

"I am, too. Frankly, I still can't see the AB's doing it either. I can buy his breaking a man's neck with those paws of his in a fight—but strangling someone with a piece of line in cold blood?" Finney shook his head.

"No way of being certain about anything, I suppose. Not the weather for sure, nor what a man's capable of. See ya, Carl." He started down the ladder.

*   *   *

At midnight when Ned Carter and Paco relieved the 8 to 12 black gang watch, the first assistant engineer, the machinist, and the two wipers were still hard at work on the furnace.

The four men had to wait till the box cooled down to enter through the manhole. When they got in, they found half the bricks had come away from the steel. It wasn't going to be an easy job.

Only the machinist, Dave Sterling, and Schmidt, the skinnier of the two wipers, could get into the box. Billet, the other wiper, and Mr. Pierce, the first assistant, couldn't get through the manhole.

Pierce had gotten the first look in the box. He had squeezed his head and one shoulder in with a trouble light. The box was still too hot to work in, but he had to see the damage to give the Old Man an estimate of how long the job would take.

"Christ, the whole thing needs rebuilding!" The engineer swore as he pulled his head out. "Must be 200 degrees in there." He got up off the floor plates and headed over to the water cooler.

The first knew he had to rebrick the furnace while it was still hot. If he let it cool too much, the remaining bricks would break away as the steel shell contracted. "Okay," he wiped his face with a rag and looked at his watch, "it's almost 11. I'm going up to tell the Old Man we'll try to have her together by 4:00 A.M. Let's get started bringing up firebricks and a couple of buckets of silicate cement while we wait for her to cool down."

"The sonofabitch keeps coming down on my side!" Schmidt was breathing heavily as he got to his feet outside the box.

"Still plenty hot?" asked Billet.

"Goddam hotter'n hell!" Schmidt's face was beet-red and his clothes were soaking wet. Ash and grime trickled down his neck from the soggy rag around his head. He headed for the five gallon jug of cold water.

The machinist poked his head out of the manhole. "We'll need more bricks, short ones, First... That cement is old or something."

"What's wrong with it?"

"Too thick—not sticking good at all!" Sterling pulled himself halfway out of the firebox and reached for the bottle of water that Billet handed to him.

"Okay, come out and take a breather—we'll open a new bucket. And you best take some salt tablets." Pierce turned to the soaking wiper. "You too, Schmidt!"

During their watch, Paco, the fireman-watertender, and Ned Carter, the oiler, helped by carting off the broken bricks and dust, passed out of the firebox.

It was hot and heavy work for Schmidt and Sterling. They could not take the heat and lack of oxygen for more than ten minutes at a time before coming out for a blow and more water. Despite the prodigious amounts they drank, both men lost several pounds during the first two hours as the heat dropped from 160 to 140 degrees. Now, a little past 2:00 A. M., the temperature was around 135—still punishing to stay in the box for very long.

"Okay, hand me the new silicate as soon as I get in." Sterling pointed to the can. "Then pass those bricks to Schmidt," he spoke to Billet as he started back through the manhole. The skinny wiper followed in after him.

Schmidt removed the planks of wood he had wedged against a section of newly laid bricks.

"Cocksucker!" he swore as a number of them fell away from the steel. "Hope the whole son-of-a-bitch don't come down soon as they fire her up." He picked up a scraper and started to clean away the crumbly compound from the area.

"I didn't like the looks of this stuff soon as I saw it," Sterling said. He put his trowel down and went to the manhole. "First, a lot of it's coming back down!" he called out.

The engineer knelt down and spoke to the machinist. "How's the new compound working?"

"Don't know yet—we've got to scrape away the last section we did before going any further, Sir."

"Okay, you're doing okay, Dave. Don't stay in there too long." Pierce straightened up and wiped his forehead. "Damn boxes should've been rebuilt last year in the yard," he said to himself.

—SIXTEEN—

Stacey started forward earlier than usual to relieve the look-out. He didn't know what purpose it would serve, but he had a gut feeling the big AB was expecting him.

Evers had slept a little, but when the ship slowed he awakened and lay in bed in a state of semi-consciousness. He knew that Stacey had first standby and hoped the Kid would stop on the way up to the bow.

Sure enough Evers half-heard and half-sensed someone outside the room. He stepped over to the porthole just as the ordinary paused in front of it.

"Hi, Kid."

"How's it going?"

"Just fine, I'm happy you come by... I wanted to talk with you."

"Okay." Stacey was going to add, "I'm listening," but he stopped short, feeling it would sound antagonistic.

"You willin' to hear me out?"

"Aye, I'm willing."

"Good... There's two reasons. First, there's someone aboard who did this murder and he ain't behind these bars, and second, because I feel guilty about lying, and makin' you go along with it."

"That wasn't your doing, my not saying you told me you hit the wiper. I just didn't think it right for me to say anything more when it would appear as if I *knew* you had killed him... Before they found the guy, I mean."

"Oh?" Evers nodded his head in the dark. "And now, *after* finding the body?"

"If they were to ask me now, I'd feel right telling everything. Yes I would!"

"Makes sense, seeing as you don't have no other information... Thanks for not condemning me right off the cuff. Truth is, I did throw the bastard over the side. But I *didn't* kill him!"

Stacey started to say something, but the big AB continued before he could sort out the words.

"God's truth, I did think I'd killed him. When I got back he was lyin' there—dead! I figured his ticker give out, or he choked on his puke. Either way, dead he was and me with no witness it was self-defense, so I put him over—I'd do it again...it's only the lying that bothers me."

"Why don't you tell the Old Man the way you just told me?"

"Do you think he'd believe my story after lying and signing the log?"

"He might..." but Stacey knew he was just saying the words... "No, I suppose you're right."

"Well... Do *you* believe me?"

The Kid didn't answer immediately. He had mixed feelings about the hard-fisted, prejudiced loner.

"I...I hoped you hadn't killed the guy that way." He didn't intend to say all that.

"Well, do you?"

"Yes, I believe you, Mr. Evers."

"Thanks... That means a lot to me. Now, best watch your time—it's gettin' late."

"Still got a couple of minutes," Stacey mumbled. He felt like telling Evers about his fears for his own life on the *Concordia,* but instead he asked, "Who do you think might have killed the guy?"

"No idea, but someone sure as hell got there while we was putting the ladder over and done for the bastard."

"I'll start looking around and try to find out something."

"Be careful. I don't want you getting hurt because of me. Can you trust your partner Hansen?"

"Sure, he's an okay guy—a little slow sometimes."

"But can you *trust* him?"

"I think so—yes, I'm sure I can."

"Then ask him if he remembers anything unusual on his standby. Maybe he knows someone aboard who sailed with the wiper before, someone who might have had it in for him."

"Okay... I better go. I'll come by when I get off watch."

"Be careful!"

Stacey heard two bells sound as he hurried down the catwalk.

"Hansen?" he called out as he came up on the bow. "Sorry I'm late!"

"Dat's hokay, Keed...not too bad up here, and ve got her all to ourselves." Hansen yawned loudly and started away.

"Stay a minute, I've got something important to tell you."

"Sure, Keed, vat is it?"

Stacey rapidly recounted his conversation with Evers.

"Vell I be a sonovabitch. Vat you think, Keed?"

"I think he's telling the truth."

"Yah... Yah, Keed. I think so too...vat ve can do for him?"

"I don't know yet, we'll talk later—it's time to relieve Junior.

"Yah, I better go!"

"Not a word to anyone."

"Don't vorry, I don't say nothing!"

Hansen got to the wheelhouse and relieved the dayman on time. The ship was still slowed, and it was work to hold her. He repeatedly used 15 to 20 degrees left rudder, held it till the tanker hesitated on her run to the right, then spun the wheel midships till she began her reach again to starboard. He kept course by the rhythm of the sea, seldom looking at the compass.

The second mate closed the chartroom door behind him as he entered the wheelhouse. "Well, how's it going this morning, Hansen?"

"Yust fine, Sir."

Finney checked the radar, then crossed to the porthole and stood looking out into the night. After a few minutes, he cleared his throat. "What do you make of this business with the new AB?"

"I sure don't know, Sir."

"Seemed like a good seaman, didn't he?"

"Aye, Mate."

After what he felt was a suitable pause, Finney continued. "Ever sail with him before?"

"No, Mate...I don't think so."

"Well it's starting out to be a hell of a trip, isn't it?"

"Aye, Sir." Hansen liked Mr. Finney, he wasn't upset with the questioning, but he was being careful not to reveal anything Stacey had told him.

"Your ordinary get along with him okay?"

"Yah...seemed to, Sir."

"Know if *he* ever sailed with him before?" Finney was still fishing.

"I don't know dat, but I don't think so, Sir."

"Well, he sure was anxious to do the man in. If he'd waited awhile he'd probably got away with it clean."

"Yes, Sir."

"I wonder what was behind it—doesn't seem like a spur-of-the-moment killing. And Evers was cold sober. Must've been bad blood between them from somewhere." The second was casting about for privileged hearsay from the fo'c'sle.

"Vell I don't hear him say nothing 'bout knowin' the viper."

"What do you think made him chance killing him while we were still in the river?"

"I don't know if he ever kill dat feller, Mate."

"You don't mean you've any doubt it was *him,* do you?"

"Vell, he never say he kill him ven the skipper lock him up."

"Well, whether he confesses or not, they can still convict him on circumstantial evidence—if it's strong enough. And no one else was there but him."

Hansen nodded his head, but said nothing. He didn't know what "circumstantial" meant—he'd ask Stacey later. He glanced at the compass. The ship was fifteen degrees to the right of course. The AB looked guiltily towards where Finney stood in the dark—he turned the wheel slowly, minimizing its creaking, till he had it hard left.

The second mate watched through the porthole as the tanker's bows finally began to swing back to port.

Kruzic made his way slowly down the series of ladders, grasping the rails with both hands. The ship was not rolling more than 15 degrees, and her pitch was not pronounced, but the alcohol had affected his equilibrium to where he could not balance properly. When he finally got down on the main engine room floorplates, he looked over to the throttle station expecting to see Pierce, the first assistant—instead he recognized the slender form of Mr. Pillars.

The second assistant's back was to him, writing up the log. Kruzic looked at his watch. It was 4:42 A.M. "What the hell's going on?" he muttered to himself. Pillars was standing the first assistant's watch. He went around the ladder and started across to where the second stood.

Pillars looked up and nodded to the chief. "Good morning, Sir." He glanced back to the opened log book and laid his pencil in the fold and closed it.

"Where's Pierce?" Kruzic asked as he approached the log table.

"Still at it with the firebox," Pillars looked toward the fireroom as he spoke.

"What's that?" Kruzic hadn't fully made out what the second had said.

"Still trying to get the port firebox rebricked, Chief," he raised his voice.

"Who the *hell* turned him out to work on it? What's going on here? What happened to the box?"

"They were working on it when I came on watch at midnight, Chief. I don't know much more than that—shut her down just after 10:00 P.M." Pillars reached over and opened the log. "Davis notified the bridge at 10:04."

"Davis notified the bridge?" Kruzic's face contorted as he spoke. "Davis notified the bridge! Who in hell notified ME?"

Pillars stepped back and looked at the drunken man. He started to say something, but the chief whirled around and headed for the fireroom.

The floorplates near the opened watertight door and the three steel steps leading down from the engine room were coated with brick dust and spots of hardened silicate compound.

Kruzic slipped as he started through the doorway. *"Son-of-a-bitch,"* he cursed as his feet went out from under him. He came to a stop, still on his feet, his body arched backwards, one hand grasping the iron rail, the other thrown back, palm down against the second step.

The three men standing around the firebox were taken by surprise. They turned as they heard the chief yell.

Billet reacted first and started for the steps. "You okay, Chief?" He reached out to help Kruzic regain his footing.

"Let me be!" Kruzic snarled at the wiper. He refused the outstretched hand and pulled himself erect.

Solis, the 4 to 8 fireman-watertender and the first assistant, stood there a moment, then Solis backed away from the group, stepping over to the steel work bench to resume cleaning sprayer tips.

The awkward silence was broken by Sterling as he poked his head out of the manhole. "Let me have some more compound," he called out.

Billet jumped at the opportunity to get away. He headed for the bucket, leaving Pierce to face the chief alone.

Kruzic stared at the first assistant, his hands clenched into fists. "Get up here!" He started back into the engine room.

The first stood stock still. He was neither a formidable man, nor was he a coward. Right now, however, he was admittedly concerned with this completely out of control man.

Kruzic looked back at where the engineer still stood. "Mr. Pierce," his face wore a half-smile, "I want to speak with you!" He turned and walked a few steps into the engine room towards the main generator.

The first shook his head in resignation and started up the ladder.

Kruzic rested his arm on the railing circling the generator and watched as Pierce slowly mounted the three steps of the ladder and stepped onto the main engine room floorplates. *"I'm waiting!"* he called out.

The first looked up into the eyes of the enraged man as he started slowly toward him. "You miserable sick son-of-a-bitch," he thought, "I hope you bust a blood vessel."

"So, y...you....are running things down here now!" Kruzic croaked. *"SINCE WHEN?"* he shouted in Pierce's face.

"I was called out by the third assistant a little after 10:00 P.M. when you were reported sick."

"SICK! WHO REPORTED ME SICK!" Kruzic lifted his right hand,which was closed into a fist, and shook it in Pierce's face.

"Sir, all I know is that I was called out in your absence and I've been down here working all morning."

"ANSWER MY QUESTION!"

"I don't know—Davis only mentioned that he sent his oiler to look for you when the trouble started. When he called me down, he told me you were sick."

"LIES, ALL LIES! I WAS NEVER CALLED! *HE'LL PAY FOR THIS!*"

"Chief, if there's anyone to blame for not checking with you, it's my fault. Davis couldn't leave his station to check the oiler's report. When I came below I inspected the box and went to the bridge. The Old Man was waiting for an estimate of our down time."

"Wh...what did you tell Layton?" Kruzic's voice had become less than a shout, but it quavered menacingly over the question.

"I told him it looked like 4 or 5 hours work, Chief."

"What did you tell him was *wrong* with me?"

"Davis had already told him you weren't able to turn to—he didn't ask me anything."

"Pierce, I'm going to get to the bottom of all this, and when I do, if I find you are responsible, I'll settle with you *once and for all!*"

"Sir, I thought I was doing right to get on with the job and not disturb you. If some mistake has been made about calling you, it wasn't done on purpose."

"Very convenient. I'm reported sick and you take over in my place!"

"No, Sir, that's not it at all." The first wiped his face with a piece of rag. "We're cleaning up the box now. Should I stay with the work? I have Pillars standing my watch."

"I'm sick—remember, Pierce? Sick, so there's no need to check with me. Go to your fine friend Layton and check with *him!*" Kruzic pushed past the first and staggered down the length of the main engine turbine.

Pierce shook his head as he watched Kruzic pass behind Pillars, who stood by the log table, and start up the ladder leading out of the engine room.

The first was tempted to go over and speak with the second assistant but he wasn't sure where the man stood in regard to the chief. "I don't need that *nut* getting reports that I'm talking behind his back," he thought as he went back to the fireroom.

—SEVENTEEN—

"Yunior!" Hansen called out as he came up on the bow."

"How's it goin', Hansen?"

"Yust fine, Yunior. Yust fine."

"Well, wonder when they gonna get this old tub movin' again?"

"I don't hear nothing new."

"Nobody's out here... Unless I missed a Russki sub or two."

"You really ban vorried about them?"

"Shit!" The dayman lifted his arms off the bow apron and stretched. "I don't know... It don't look too good though, the news from Korea."

"You really think maybe ve fight vit Russia?"

"Been lots of unidentified subs sighted off the east coast of Florida this week. You read the Sunday paper?"

"No."

"Well, it looks like the fuckin' thing's blowin' up into a full-scale war!"

"Ve got enough to vorry about vit' out a voor."

"That's for sure. This break in the weather ain't gonna last. They'd better get this tub movin' before we've got that hurricane up our asses!"

"Vell, I think the skipper be knowing vat to do... I vonder vat the company vant him to do vit the AB?"

"No tellin'... I 'spect he'll be in touch with the Coast Guard and company both this mornin'. Well I'm goin' aft—see you."

"Yah, good night, Yunior... Maybe you better see the mate is up on the vay aft," Hansen called after the departing dayman.

Hansen paced the fo'c'slehead thinking about Junior's information on the trouble in Korea. He hadn't given it much thought, but now he did remember all those reports of Russian submarines following American merchant ships back in June when the fighting started.

Now, according to the dayman, it was beginning to look like the real thing again. He shuddered involuntarily as his mind swept back to the freezing cold night eight years ago when the Limey tanker he was on was sent to the bottom in a matter of minutes.

His lucky number was "7"—he was the seventh and last survivor pulled from the icy seas that night. But what of the others? The whole deck gang, except for one ordinary seaman and himself, went down with the ship—forty eight men in all lost from a crew of fifty-five.

Sometimes Hansen wished he was back in Norway, fishing perhaps, or maybe not even on the sea at all; doing God only knows what.

The seaman's life was the only one he had ever really known. His first trip was as a deck boy on a Norwegian freighter out of his home port of Oslo. He was a hard worker and in a few years he sailed steadily as an ordinary, and then at nineteen he'd accumulated enough seatime to sit for his AB's papers.

The husky seaman was twenty-six years old and sailing as boatswain the night his tanker was torpedoed. He was fished out of the freezing water by a Stateside freighter behind them in the convoy.

He worked as an "extra" in the deck gang, drawing down an ordinary's pay voucher for the rest of the trip and was given the opportunity of signing on as a regular AB for the next.

Hansen stayed with the *S/S Morristown Victory* for the remainder of the war. Then, ashore in New York, he joined the seamen's union. Five years later he became an American citizen. He rarely wrote to his family and he never returned home.

It seemed he was never able to manage to stay sober long enough between trips to put more than a couple of bucks away. The young Norwegian's life was one long series of ships, a few drunken weeks or months at most on the beach and then the need to ship out again or stay in a miserable seamen's flop house or take charity from some church mission—neither alternative sat well with the husky AB.

Though his formal education had ended with grade school, he was well read on anything related to ships, the sea, and fish. Some day he would return to Norway, meet a nice "vooman" and buy a fishing boat. *Next trip, for sure, I'll save every dime,* he would promise himself. But, invariably, he'd forget his plans after the first few drinks ashore, and it was always easy for the "girls" to get the big friendly seaman to part with his hard earned money—not just to pay for their time in bed, but for all their conniving schemes as well.

Hansen glanced at his watch; it was a quarter to four. He was supposed to be thinking of things that might help his watch partner. He reviewed what went on the morning before. He'd still been a little drunk, and he remembered the new AB had been late in relieving him on the wheel. He was angry and a little bit dizzy when he left the wheelhouse, but after that it was pretty clear to him what went on. He remembered securing the pilot ladder and he also remembered the fouled up messroom he had to clean. Then he had called the night cook and baker, Reed, the watch, and the chief mate and earlier, at 2:30, the second pumpman.

What else happened? Nothing. He sat around and played a hand or two of solitaire. No one else was around when he first came down on standby. The only one who came by was the 12 to

4 oiler. Hansen considered that a moment. The oiler had come in and looked around as if he expected to see someone—someone other than Hansen or whoever was on standby. "Vait a minute...dat feller ask me who vas 'round the place." He couldn't recall exactly what the conversation had been, but more important was the fact that the oiler had certainly been overly interested in questioning him about what was going on. "Maybe it ain't got anything to do vit it, but I tell the Keed."

—EIGHTEEN—

By 6:30 A.M. Tommy Deel had finished serving breakfast to the two wipers, the machinist, and Pillars, the second assistant engineer. Reed, the night cook and baker, had prepared the hot food for the men knocking off work on the firebox. Since he was already at work, there would be a question as to his receiving one hour of overtime. For Tommy, who was called at 5:30 A.M. to serve the men, it would be an hour and a half at the overtime rate, unless Captain Layton declared all the work performed on the box by the black gang as "safety of the vessel," which was unlikely.

Tommy finished up cleaning and resetting the forward table in the crew mess, and the one place he had set up in the saloon for the second assistant. He went out on to the fantail after completing his work. It was a few minutes past 7:00 A.M. and he would have no customers till after 7:20, when the 8 to 12 black gang and deck gang were called along with the bosun, the daymen and the two pumpmen. Regularly, the machinist and the wipers, who were also day workers would be up, but they had already been served and were not required to turn to at 8:00 A.M. this morning. They had rest periods coming to them for the hours that they had worked since being called out at 10:30 P.M. That gave them eight hours off, so they would not turn to today unless it was necessary, and then they would receive the premium overtime rate for any work performed.

Tommy sat on the aftermost set of bitts on the port side watching the dawn breaking through the grey sky. It grew rapidly lighter changing to an orange-red glow that reflected brightly off the feathery wisps of cirrus clouds. By the time the sun inched up over the horizon, the entire sky had turned a deep blood-red—beautiful but ominous. As if to lend strength to the warning, the

Concordia reared up over a long green swell and shuddered, her screw racing till the governor kicked in.

The ship was doing 12 knots at 88 rpms, good speed, considering the 15 foot swells rolling up under the keel from almost dead ahead. Her bows plowed through the crests and heavy spray broke over the well decks. But the lack of any wind and waves to accompany the swells made the vessel's increased pitch and roll seem less significant.

Unknown to the messman, these long oily-green swells were the storm's advance notices. No longer passing under the ship at the rate of one every four or five seconds, they had reduced their frequency as they increased their height and were spaced a full ten seconds apart. The changes in height, frequency and direction had a combined effect on the tanker—her responses now were more like a gigantic whale than a structure of steel. Rolling her port rail under in a graceful and confident manner, she allowed the sea to wash up over her vanished freeboard. Then she arched slowly up to starboard, seeming to bend as the water poured off her decks— her stern thrashing the sea behind her to complete the parallel.

*   *   *

"How's she going, Pedro?" Mamud Hassan stepped into the wheelhouse through the door from the starboard wing of the bridge.

"Ask me, they better slow her down," Bob Howard, the 4 to 8 AB, answered as he spun the wheel back to midships. "Taking better'n 15 degrees to hold her—course is 101."

After depositing the tote tray with the fresh coffee set-up in the nook under the table, Mamud came up behind Howard. "Okay, I got you—101."

"What's good for breakfast?" Howard stepped away from the wheel.

"They got some damn fine Canadian bacon this morning."

"A–rabs ain't supposed to eat no bacon."

"Fuck thee, Howard. I'm a converted Quaker."

"Thy ass is suckin' wind. You're a fuckin' heathen like me!"

"You damn near turned this cocksucker over about ten minutes ago." Hassan grunted as he rapidly took off almost 20 degrees left rudder. "Boy she sure runs wild when those big swells roll her up, don't she?"

"I told you." Howard had picked up the used cups and coffee

pot and switched them with the clean set-up from the tote box. "They ain't all the same size. Ever' so often a gran' daddy comes along and I'll be fucked if *you* can hold her either!"

"They doing a pretty good job serving back there, but that one big roll sure fucked up the galley. Everything came off the tables in the messroom. Kinda felt sorry for the little nigger—he sure been busy trying to keep things together."

"Take her easy." Howard walked over to the door of the chartroom. He opened it and stepped in. "She goes 101, Mate," he called out the course and started down the companionway.

"101, very well, Howard." The chief mate answered without looking up from his work.

Michael Searles, the third mate, was standing next to the chart table. He was watching Wilder make his log entries. The only significantly different data were: the direction of the swells which were now noted to be almost due east, the fact that they had increased to an average height of fifteen feet with a frequency of one every ten seconds, and the barometer was at 28.62 inches, a drop of eight hundredths of an inch in the last hour.

"I don't like the smell of things, Mike." The mate looked up and shook his head. "Hope Sparks proves me wrong with his 8:00 A.M. weather report."

"Think the Old Man will be up this morning?"

"I don't know. I hope he stays asleep awhile, but with this rolling and pitching I don't see how he can."

"Be sure you get a double order of that Canadian bacon—real good!"

"*That* was a good one! Christ!" The mate grabbed the corner of the chart table as the ship reared up over a broad swell over twenty feet high. "Don't know how much longer we can keep our speed up."

"Better go eat while you still can, Tim." The third mate had braced himself by grasping hold of one of the lower dogs on the starboard porthole next to the chart table.

Wilder waited till the ship came back to a more reasonable angle and crossed the chartroom deck in time to grasp the rails of the companionway before the *Concordia* began to roll up to the other side. He headed down the steps and paused when he got to the radio shack. The door was closed.

"Sparks!" He rapped on the door with his free hand. "You in there?"

The door opened a moment later and the radio operator

greeted the chief mate. "What the hell are you guys doing up there?"

"Not much except holding on!"

"I expect this is what you're looking for." Sparks handed the mate a freshly updated weather report.

Wilder read it as the two men stood balancing in the doorway. "Not really, old buddy. In fact, it's just what I didn't want to see."

"Still heading our way, isn't she?"

"Looks like this bitch is determined to catch us."

"And 'the condemned men ate a hearty breakfast'—let's go!" Sparks pulled the door shut behind them.

"Speaking of condemned men," the mate remarked, "I get to see our prisoner this morning when I bring him his breakfast."

"*You* bringing him his food?"

"Well, the Old Man told me to take the bosun and one dayman along when the messman delivers his grub."

"Think the *four* of you can handle the guy?"

"Hey! You're in rare form this morning, ain't you? Like a fuckin' stud horse feelin' a low comin' in." Wilder headed aft down the starboard passageway leading to the after catwalk. "I'll see what the guy wants," he spoke over his shoulder to Sparks.

"Evers," the chief mate called out before sliding back the small cover on the door's spy-hole.

"Aye," the big AB answered almost immediately.

"I'm headed aft for breakfast now and I'll get yours ordered if you'd like."

"Yes, Sir, I'd like something to eat... Eggs, anyway they can make 'em, sausage, toast, and black coffee."

"They're supposed to have a special today on Canadian bacon instead of the usual fatback—would you want some?"

"Aye, I'll have that instead of the sausage. Thank you."

"Be about twenty minutes or so." Wilder stepped away from the door leaving the small sliding panel in the open position.

Once out on the catwalk he spoke to Sparks who followed close behind him. "I'm certain that he's the coolest S.O.B. they'll ever hang for murder. Probably say—'Yes, Sir. Thank you, Sir. I'd certainly like a blindfold, Sir.'—when they march him off!"

"Now who's feeling the low?" countered Sparks.

Both men started to laugh and were still enjoying themselves as they made their way into the after house. The door got away from the mate as he held it open for Sparks. It slammed shut just barely missing the radio operator.

"Shh..Shush... You'll have Kruzic jumping all over ush." Sparks meant the words to be serious and quietly spoken, but they came out comically and loud enough to move Wilder to respond in kind.

"KRUZIC JUMP? I don't think he could stumble *ALL OVER USH* from the way he's been loading up." The mate secured the door with one dog and the two friends continued chuckling as they went down the passageway towards the saloon.

The chief engineer came out of a fitful and troubled sleep as the heavy clank of the watertight door came to him. The ship's accompanying roll made his awakening a rude one. He grasped the side of his bunk trying to lift himself out of the bed against the downward pull of gravity. For a split second his brain was filled with the sudden fear that the ship had collided with something. Then the incongruous laughter broke through to him with the mate's bold insult seemingly shouted purposely through his door.

You bastard you, he formed the words silently with his mouth. He wrenched himself up into a sitting position. "You filthy bastard, I'll pay you back. You perverted *BASTARD!*" The last word he croaked aloud. Kruzic disliked the "Old Woman Layton"—he *despised* the young chief mate, Tim Wilder, whose voice he had immediately recognized.

The ship began her opposite roll and he hung there by his arms with a sudden feeling of nausea slamming into him. He felt like lying down immediately, but he knew he'd get sick if he did. The engineer remained seated and tried to breathe deeply to hold his stomach down.

Two Kruzic's hung there. One wanted to get up *and* get out of his dirty clothes, *and* go shower, *and* perhaps go to eat breakfast, *and* face down any of the other officers who were in the saloon, including Layton *and* resume his position of authority and responsibility—the other wanted *to* escape, *to* get out, *to* get away from the ship itself, *to* never see another hated face at the saloon table, *to* get as far away from all the ignorant useless fools that he had been forced to live with for the past five years.

When he felt that he could get up, he did. First he staggered into his office and retrieved his pitcher. It was still half full. The water was tepid, but he drank almost a third of it in one long swallow. He felt the first stabs of an oncoming migraine and automatically reached for the half-empty bottle of bourbon that was in the protected rack over his desk. He drank straight from the bottle and then took another long drink of the warm water in the pitcher.

The engineer sat in the chair swaying with the ship's movements, trying to get his courage up to go and eat. The clock on the bulkhead over his head showed it to be 8:12. He still had time to get cleaned up before 8:30. "No... No, that's just what they want me to do," he said to himself. "No, I'll get something in an hour or so from the refrigerator. They can think what they want, I'm sick. Okay, I'm sick! What can Layton do to me? Log me...? I'm through with the whole filthy mess. I don't have to do anything.... I can stay sick till we get to the Gulf. That's exactly what I'll do— stay away from everybody. I don't have to step out of this room till I leave this miserable ship."

*   *   *

"What did you slow her down to, Mike?" Wilder asked as he came up the companionway into the chart room.

"I've got her at 80 as of 8:30."

"The skipper call you to slow her up?"

"No, Mate. I wasn't going to slow without calling him first, but his orders were to keep the best speed we could once both boilers were working. Sort of hated to wake him just to tell him I was following those instructions."

"That's good. Let him sleep while he can." The chief mate crossed behind Searles and spread the 8:00 A.M. weather report out on top of the chart table. "Look at this," he said, as he slipped a chart out from under their own course chart. It was the one they had been plotting the hurricane's course on. He laid it on top of theirs.

The third mate watched as Wilder plotted the storm's 8:00 A.M. position and marked it with a small cross at Lat. 23° 15' north; Long. 83°05' west. Then he extended the thin pencil line to it, connecting the previous position in a smoothly drawn arc.

"Read the rest of this." Wilder pushed the report over to Searles.

"Fifteen knots with surface winds of over 125 mph," the third read aloud.

"Closer to eighteen from our plot—here look—she's covered some 144 miles in the past eight hours." The mate walked his dividers back over the penciled line for the third to see.

"She's *moving* alright!" Searles agreed.

— N I N E T E E N —

Carl Finney woke with a start.

"11:20, Second!" The voice broke in on his confused dream. "It's 11:20!" This time the voice was accompanied with a loud knock on his door.

"Okay, thank you. I'm up!" Finney rolled over on his side and reached for his cigarettes. They had worked themselves out of the pack and lay scattered on the shelf; a few of them had fallen off and broken pieces were in the bed with him. He picked up one of the loose butts, lit it, and swung his feet over the side of his bunk. The ship was pitching heavily and from the feel of it they were not moving at any great speed.

The second mate got to his feet and went into the head. He brushed his teeth in the sink. The water was gritty and had a deep reddish discoloration from the rust being churned up in the tanks. He washed his hands and face. Then, deciding he could get away without shaving this morning, settled for a rapid brushing of his thinning hair to complete his toilet.

When Finney entered the saloon, it was deserted save for Mr. Pierce and Mr. Pillars. He took the seat opposite Pillars. "Hi, John... First!" He nodded to Mr. Pierce who, because his mouth was full, could only gesture to him from the end of the table.

"Good afternoon, Carl," the second assistant answered.

Mr. Finney ordered the roast beef, mashed potatoes, and turnip greens. The food was deftly served by Dooley, without incident, except for the spilling of some "bug juice" on the deck as he carried in a fresh pitcher of the lemon-flavored drink.

The second assistant finished eating and was now into a friendly discussion with Mr. Pierce over the relative merits of steam compared to Diesels in plants developing in excess of 10,000 horse power, and the both of these compared to proposed propulsion systems designed around nuclear fuels.

Finney had expected to find the captain in the saloon when he got there. Layton seldom left a call, but was generally in the saloon by 11:20 A.M. for lunch; he very rarely had breakfast, and he was usually there for supper right at 5:30 P.M. sharp if he was going to eat.

"Was the skipper up for breakfast this morning, First?" the second mate took advantage of a pause in the debate.

"I don't believe he was, Carl."

Finney glanced at the clock on the saloon bulkhead, it was 11:42. It was his job to see the prisoner was fed lunch, and he had forgotten to ask the AB what he wanted before coming aft for his own food. The chief mate was to take care of the chore for breakfast and supper.

Finney got up and carried his plates to the galley sink rather than chance them falling off the table before Dooley got to remove them. He then stepped into the crew's messroom. "Bosun," he addressed O'Malley who sat at the first table, "I'm going to call the bridge to find out what Evers wants for lunch. I forgot to ask him on the way aft."

"Aye, Second. You'll want me to come forward with Ski and the messman?"

"Right, Boats." Mr Finney walked to the after bulkhead and made sure that the pointer was set to BRIDGE before turning the crank.

"Bridge," came the third mate's voice.

"Mike, I forgot to find out what the AB wanted for lunch. Can you relieve the quartermaster for a minute and have him find out?"

"Okay, Carl. I'll ring you back in a minute."

"Thanks." Finney hung up and stepped out of the door onto the fantail. "How's it going?" He greeted Hansen and Stacey who were sitting on the set of bitts just outside the door.

"Afternoon, Second," Stacey answered for himself and Hansen. They had both finished their meals and were relaxing with coffee and cigarettes waiting to go on watch.

"Sure look like ve're in for more veather, Sir." Hansen nodded his head.

"I think you're right there, Hansen." The second mate balanced himself against the ship's motion by leaning against the winch drum.

The phone rang and Mr. Finney went back into the messroom. He got the information and gave it to Tommy Deel before heading back to the bridge. "Remember to let Boats and Ski know when you're ready. Boats will call me to come down from the wheelhouse and open the door for you."

"I be ready to bring the food up aroun' 12:30, Sir—that okay?"

"That's fine, Mess." Finney walked back through the empty saloon and started forward. As he passed the chief engineer's door he heard a sound that startled him. It was part laugh and part scream—difficult to describe—a somehow obscene vocalization. He paused a moment; then resisting his impulse to knock, continued on past to the watertight door.

The second mate waited till the ship started her roll down to starboard, swung the door open, stepped through and secured it behind him with a minimum of noise.

Carl Finney checked the *Concordia's* noon position as soon as he returned to the bridge. The ship had averaged ten knots on the 8 to 12 watch. But the increasing size of the swells, which seemed to grow even as he watched them, made it evident that he would soon have to reduce speed even further.

By ten minutes to 1:00 the tanker was beginning to bury her bows in heavy seas, shuddering as she reared up and voided her fo'c'slehead of the ponderous weight of water. Finney gave in to the inevitable and called the engine room, telling Mr. Pillars to reduce to 68 turns.

During the next hour, every time he tried bringing the ship's speed back up, the resulting warning vibrations which sounded through the hull forced him to relent.

The second was surprised the Old Man had not come up into the wheelhouse. He knew the captain had gotten very little sleep in the past few days, but still, it was unusual for him to miss lunch and breakfast both. And Layton was certainly concerned with the ship headed into the approaching storm. It wasn't like him to absent himself this long from the bridge. In addition there was the fact he hadn't tried to get through to the ship's agent or the company's office regarding their prisoner.

Finney checked the time. It was almost 2:00 P.M. "Stacey, try to hold her as steady as you can." He stepped out of the wheelhouse.

The wind howled and tore at his clothing as he made his way up the ladder onto the flying bridge to check the standard compass.

"How are you now?" he called down the voice tube to the ordinary.

"Three degrees left... Four left. Five left...Four left. Four left, four left, four left—"

"Very well," Finney called down and secured the lid on the voice tube. He came down the ladder and crossed under it to take the barometer reading. He hoped at first he had read it wrong. He looked at it again, wiping the tears from his wind-lashed eyes— no mistake, 28.35, down another twenty hundredths of an inch in the last hour. He closed the box, went around to the starboard wing, and stood in the lee of the bridge. The weather was getting worse by the minute and he was disturbed by a sense of impending disaster, an unnatural feeling—like being followed by someone in the dark.

The second mate came back into the wheelhouse and closed the heavy door. He hurriedly erased the compass blackboard and recorded the corrected figures, then went into the chartroom to make his log entries. When he finished, he pulled out the small atlas and the foldout chart of the area. In a few minutes he had transposed both the *Concordia's* and the hurricane's positions from the large sailing chart. The damn thing seemed to be stalking them—uncanny—as if it were able to anticipate the tanker's course and alter its own to intercept it. "Christ!" Finney muttered to himself. "I'm as jumpy as a cadet."

The discussion he once had with Captain Layton over "The Law of Probabilities" as related to natural phenomena came to mind. On impulse he opened the chart table drawer and searched around till he found the three "French curves" he was looking for. He picked up the medium-sized one first and laid its edge against the penciled-in crosses representing the various recorded positions reported for the storm. It was too small. The large one, however, fitted perfectly. He moved the long recurved arc's edge slowly upwards to where it began to intersect the various cross marks. He took a fine pencil and traced the edge of the curve; then used his set of parallel rulers to extend out the *Concordia's* intended course line. Finney picked up the French curve and carefully placed it on the chart. It was all too perfect, the lines crossed—again that eerie feeling.

The second braced himself as the tanker rode up over another huge swell. He tapped a cigarette against the chart in front of him to pack down the tobacco before lighting it.

"Well, it's the Old Man's theory and it's the Old Man's ship," he thought glancing back to the chart and his figures. "Unless we change course or that fucking storm does, there's a good chance of plowing into it dead center... And it looks to me like we're running out of time to make a decision!" Finney crushed out his cigarette. *Damn, I sure as hell hate to wake him—but I've got to.* He left the charts lying on the table and went into the wheelhouse.

"Captain Layton?" he spoke into the voice tube. "Are you up, Captain?"

Finney waited a few moments and then called down in a louder voice; he waited again, but there was still no answer. He flipped the cover closed on the voice tube, walked over to the porthole and stood watching the sea. *Probably caught him on the pot,* he thought to himself. He'd wait a few minutes and then call down again.

The big wheel creaked noisily as Stacey struggled to keep the ship on a fairly good course. He was working up a sweat as the tanker had a tendency to race to starboard as the swells rose up under her. This required his putting on twenty or more degrees left rudder. Then, as she fell off into the troughs, he had to spin the wheel back to midships.

"How's she handling?" the second broke the silence.

"Not too bad, Sir."

"Where were you working this afternoon?"

"Finishing up the scraping and painting in the bosun's locker."

"In the shelter deck?"

"Aye."

"No one's working any overtime, I suppose?"

"No, Sir—not the deck gang, anyway."

"Well," Finney yawned, "I expect I'll try again." He glanced at his watch; it was 2:26. He crossed back over to the voice tube. "Captain Layton!" he called down. "Captain!" Not getting an answer, he closed the lid and set the pointer on the nearby phone to CAPT. OFF. He turned the crank vigorously, waited a few seconds and tried again. When there was still no response, he switched the pointer to STANDBY and rang.

"Yes," came a voice.

"This is the bridge—who is that?"

"The messman, Sir." The answer came back loud enough for Stacey to recognize his friend's voice.

"Tommy?"

"Yes, Sir?"

"Look in the saloon and see if the captain's there. I want to speak with him."

"Yes, Sir. Be right back."

Mr. Finney waited till he heard the scrape of the phone as it was picked up. "Hello?"

"Sir, he ain't in the saloon!"

"Okay, Tommy, thanks. If you run into him back aft tell him to get back to me—okay?"

"Okay, Sir."

"Did you see the chief mate or the bosun around?"

"I see the bosun 'bout twenty minutes ago. You wan' me to look for him?"

"No, just thought the Old Man might have been with them—never mind now—thank you." The second hung up and turned the dial to ENG. RM.

"Engine room. This is Pillars."

"This is the bridge. We're trying to locate the Old Man."

"He hasn't been down here that I know of, Carl. If he was, I haven't seen him."

"Okay, thanks, John. The chief engineer been down there at all?"

"Haven't seen him on my watch. He wasn't to dinner either. I doubt if he's left his room today."

"Is he sick?"

"Yeah, from what I hear he's *very* sick."

"Well, okay. Anyhow, I doubt if the Old Man's there but I'll call the chief's office."

"Anything wrong?"

"No...nothing yet, but I hate to slow her down any more and it's starting to look like we may have to. Thanks!" Finney hesitated a moment, then shrugged as he turned the pointer to CH. ENG. and turned the crank. He waited a few moments and turned it again. The third time he rang it for several seconds. Still no answer. *The son-of-a-bitch is probably dead drunk.* Well at least I know the skipper's not there either. *"Where in the hell is he?"* he cursed to himself. Out loud he said, "Stacey, go on down and knock on the captain's door—good and loud—tell him I want to speak to him. If he isn't there, look in the radio shack. I don't want to call as Sparks is off duty now, probably trying to sleep. Just try the door, if it's not locked, take a look in. If it's locked, don't knock as the Old Man wouldn't be there."

"Aye, Mr. Finney." Stacey spun the rest of the angle off the wheel. "101, she's taking twenty degrees and better to hold her—wheel's midships." He stepped away from the wheel.

"101, very well." Finney stepped up onto the wooden grate as Stacey opened the chartroom door.

The Kid took the steps leading down the companionway two at a time. He was hoping to say hello to Evers, if he was up, and arrange a time to come back and talk to him. They hadn't spoken since 4:30 in the morning when he related Hansen's information about the 12 to 4 oiler.

Stacey knocked on the captain's door. He knocked again and called sharply. "Sir! *Captain Layton, Sir!*" He waited a second and then banged the door smartly with the side of his fist. "CAP-

TAIN LAYTON!"

"What the hell's going on?" the chief mate asked as he stepped into the alleyway.

Stacey jumped at the voice coming unexpectedly from behind. "I... I'm calling the captain."

"What's wrong?"

"Nothing, Sir. The second just told me to bang on his door real loud and then if he wasn't there to look in the radio shack for him."

"Well, you're *sure* following orders." Wilder turned and headed back down the companionway to the deck below where his room was. He had awakened from a sound sleep and was in pajamas, barefoot, and without a robe .

"Sorry I woke you, Sir," Stacey said to the mate's retreating back. He went to the radio shack and tried the door. It was unlocked. He opened it all the way and secured it on the hook; then crossed through the room filled with radio equipment to the door leading into Sparks' stateroom. This door was also unlocked, so he cracked it slowly and looked in—Sparks was sound asleep— he shut it quietly and went back out through the office and closed the door behind him.

Stacey gave up the idea of sneaking down to see the big AB and started back up the companionway to the chartroom. He just avoided colliding with the mate, who had pulled on a heavy bathrobe and now wore slippers. "Excuse me, Sir." Stacey stepped aside and let Wilder precede him up the steps.

The mate walked through the chartroom and into the wheel-house with Stacey right behind him.

"Well hello, Tim." Finney turned and stepped off the grate as Stacey approached. "Still 101." He looked at the ordinary.

"101—couldn't find the captain, Sir."

"Better secure those cabinet doors," Finney stepped back to the wheel, "before we trip over them." He put on more rudder angle as the Stacey found a piece of line to tie off the doors under the coffee table.

"Can't find the skipper?" Tim Wilder yawned loudly. "You see if he's down the engine room?"

"Yes, I called there, too."

"Chief's office?"

"No answer."

"Okay, Sir." The ordinary came back to the steering station.

"Thanks. She goes the same." The second mate stepped away as the Kid took the wheel. "Got a minute, Tim? Let me show you why I want the Old Man." He walked into the chartroom.

Finney laid out his plots of the storm's track and the *Concordia's* course. "See why I'm concerned?"

"What are we turning?" Wilder looked up from the chart table.

"68—and that's pushing it."

"Very neat... let's hope Sparks comes up with a report that disproves your theory."

"Hope so—I'm still anxious about Layton."

"Yeah, he really didn't look too good yesterday."

"Tim? Don't you have a spare set of keys or a master for everything."

"Yes, for the fo'c'sles, storerooms, galley, and the radio shack, I've spares. The one master I've got opens all the officers' staterooms—*except* the captain's."

"Mate, I've got a bad feeling all of a sudden—I think we'd better force that door."

"Well, you're officer of the watch. Go to it if you're *that* worried."

"No, I'm telling you I'm concerned at not being able to locate the captain. I'd of been *calling you* if you hadn't showed up."

"You're right, Carl. No sense our arguing... I'm out of sorts and half asleep yet."

"That's okay, Mate. If you think I should, I'll get the bosun to help us. Can you stand by here for me?"

"Sure, Carl... I think you're right. Go ahead."

—TWENTY—

Mr. Finney called aft and learned that the bosun had gone forward with clean rags and solvent for the men working in the shelter deck. The second put on his jacket and headed down the ladder. When he opened the watertight door he could hear the sounds of work going on. The light switch wasn't working, and he had to watch his footing as he made his way over the lines, cargo hoses, and pilot ladders, to reach the big gear locker.

"Boats, I need you to come with me. Bring a heavy maul or hammer and a big chisel," he called from the doorway.

Hansen, Junior and Ski all looked up from their work and greeted the second. They were always on good terms with him and were startled by his brusque manner.

Mr. Finney didn't look back or say anything to O'Malley as they made their way up to the captain's deck.

"Captain Layton!" Finney called out and banged on the door. "CAPTAIN, ARE YOU OKAY!" He banged on the door once again. "Well, Boats, you might as well break the lock."

"What's the matter, Sir?"

"Don't know yet—we can't find the Old Man. Just go ahead and open it!"

"Best to kick in the escape panel, ain't it, Second?"

"If you think that's easier, go ahead."

"Much better than bustin' up the door gettin' these locks broke off."

"Okay, O'Malley!"

The bosun put the chisel and hammer down and stepped back. The first kick resulted in bending the center of the panel, but the rust and paint held it from popping out. O'Malley stepped back again and kicked the top of the panel. It still held fast. He picked up the hammer and smacked the panel one solid blow at each of the four corners.

"What the *hell's* going on?" Awakened by the noise, Sparks had come out of the radio shack. "Oh Christ, something happen to the Old Man?"

"Don't know." Finney glanced at him a moment and then noticed Searles, the third mate, coming up to the door from the direction of the companionway. "Go ahead, Boats." He looked back at O'Malley who was now the center of attraction.

"Aye, Sir." The bosun stepped back and delivered a powerful kick dead center—the panel clattered into the room. He stepped back and looked at the three officers.

"Go in and open the door, Boats."

"Aye!" O'Malley laid down the hammer and crawled through the tight opening. In a moment he had the door opened and he stood aside as the second mate walked past him towards the door that separated the captain's office from the sleeping room and adjoining head.

The door was unlocked. Carl Finney opened it slowly and secured it on the hook, silently praying he'd been a fool to panic and break in. The room was dark; the portholes covered with heavy green curtains. He reached up and felt for the overhead light switch. He flicked it on, hoping desperately to find the bed empty—it was—but the room wasn't.

Captain Layton's body was sprawled on the deck, dressed in

pajamas and a robe. He was lying on his stomach with his face turned towards the door. One arm, the right, was under his body with the fingers just visible below his neck; the other was flung out in front of him.

"Oh, Christ... Is he *dead?*" The third mate stood staring over the second mate's shoulder.

Carl Finney walked closer, bent down and touched the out-stretched arm. It was cold—very cold and stiff. The captain's eyes were partially open. "Mike," he stood up, "relieve the mate so he can get down here."

"O'Malley, you and Sparks stay here with me."

Mike Searles turned and left. He hardly got a look at the body and was happy he wouldn't have to.

By the time the chief mate came into the room, Mr. Finney had found a small broken bottle of medicine and a number of tiny white pills that had rolled into the corner near the head of the bed.

Tim Wilder straightened up slowly after looking at the body. He knew enough about first aid and medicine to recognize a massive heart attack; it was obvious the skipper had been dead for several hours.

"Here." The second held out the broken bottle of nitroglycerine pills to the mate. "Poor devil must have been fighting a bad heart for some time now."

"Well, he probably would have lived a lot longer if he'd retired like he planned to... Hell, who knows, he might have preferred going out this way—still a man right to the end and not being slowly reduced to a frightened hunk of meat tucked away somewhere ashore."

"What now?" Finney asked.

"What now...? Well first off, Sparks," the mate looked over to where the radio operator stood in the doorway, "better get word to the company office that Captain Layton was found dead in his cabin." Wilder looked at his watch."Around 2:30 P.M., apparently the victim of a heart attack. And tell them we've a man in the brig suspected of killing the wiper we lost the first night out."

"Aye, Mate."

"Carl, I suppose our next move depends on the weather. There's a chance we'll be ordered to turn back. I want you to work up a few best shots—I'm thinking Tampa. Anyhow, let's have a few alternatives."

"Right away, Sir." Carl Finney headed for the doorway.

"Might as well get started, Ed." Wilder turned to the radio

operator.

"Yes, Sir." Sparks was happy to get out of the room.

"Boats, it'll be getting on coffee time soon. There isn't much we can do till we hear from the company office. Thanks for your help. You best get the word out to the crew. I'll take care of informing the engineers."

"Aye, Sir."

O'Malley turned to leave, but Wilder asked, "Do you have your third's license, Boats?"

"No, Sir."

"Know anyone else has in the fo'c'sle?"

"I hear tell Ski does."

"Okay, send him forward after coffee."

"Aye, Mate—I mean *Cap'n.*," O'Malley corrected himself. He was the first to do so.

There would be a new third mate on the 8 to 12, Mr. Borolow-ski, as Ski would henceforth be called. Mr. Searles would shift watches to the 12 to 4 and become the second mate. Mr. Finney would become chief mate and take over the 4 to 8. And Tim Wilder was the new master of the *Concordia.*

*   *   *

By coffee time everyone aboard the *Concordia*, except for Kruzic, was aware that "Old Man Layton" was dead.

There were masters whose methods of command would not invite very kind thoughts or well wishes when they took their *final departures.* Captain Layton was not one of them. The licensed members of the ship felt they had lost a fellow officer who more or less epitomized what a "Master" should be like. The unlicensed members of the crew who had been on the *Concordia* any length of time, or who had sailed with him previously on other ships were, almost to a man, deeply moved by his sudden death.

The usual loud and mostly inane small talk that accompanied a coffee break was glaringly absent. Men spoke in subdued voices and shook their heads sadly as one or another of the crew recounted some previous time when the Old Man had saved someone from going to the jug ashore. Someone else remembered a Christmas at sea when the skipper had broken out a half-dozen bottles of fine straight whiskey and several cases of beer. Another described the care he had received when stricken with a massive infection that spread up over his face and head. He spoke of how the captain visited him hour after hour giving him penicillin shots, changing dressings, cheering him up, and keeping Sparks in constant touch with the Marine Hospital for consultations with shore-side doctors. Still another told of how the *brave bastard* went below without the fresh air breathing apparatus, which had failed, and carried an ordinary, who had been gassed, up out of one of the tanks.

"That fuckin' Evers is who done for him." Ryan, the 8 to 12 AB whom Evers had thrown to the deck, was expounding to a few of the other deck hands sitting around him.

"Vell...he don't do it on purpose." Hansen disliked taking what he knew was an unpopular stand, but believing now that his watch partner was not really a murderer, he felt he had to say something in the big AB's defense.

"Maybe not, but Ryan's got a point. He did knock the Old Man down." Peter Tompkins, the ordinary on Ryan's watch, backed his partner's hand.

"I don't care about his gettin' to the wiper." Junior added fuel to the fire. "The guy probably had it comin' to him for all I know, but Christ, you ain't *ever* gonna sail with a better skipper than Old Man Layton."

"Killin's too good for the *Limey* cocksucker!" Cannito, the chief pumpman, added his opinion. It was he who had related the story about the Old Man going into the tank after the ordinary.

Evers received word of the captain's death indirectly at first. He had heard the banging and commotion from the deck above him and caught someone's words. "It's the Old Man—he's dead!"

A few minutes later, he got the news directly. Junior took the time to come up from the shelter deck before going aft, and walked up to the barred porthole. "You can add the skipper to your list."

The words were spoken as much in sorrow as in hate, and the dayman just turned away and crossed behind the house leading to the catwalk. If the man had cursed him or threatened him, the big AB wouldn't have taken it so hard. Many men kick a man when he's down—Evers could handle that—but Junior's flat, quiet statement burned deeply. He felt badly about knocking the Old Man to the deck. It added to the burden of guilt he felt for having had to lie to the captain to begin with. Realizing now that he might have actually contributed to Layton's untimely death, he was deeply affected.

Not since the news of Liz's death had he felt so emotionally drained. He lay on his bunk unable to grapple with this perverse fate. It made a mockery of the belief that a man could control, change, or effect in any manner the course laid out for him. The hope of getting a lead on the real murderer meant nothing to him now.

Stacey knew of the captain's death within minutes of discovery of the body. He was alone in the wheelhouse when he heard the third mate come running up to get the mate. He was able to hear the exchange clearly through the closed door.

He was holding as good a course as he could, alternating between watching the compass and the ship's bow as it pitched into the mountainous seas. Sheets of heavy windswept spray slammed against the face of the bridge rattling the thick glass portholes. What had already been a wild and worsening seascape suddenly transformed itself into a demented and surrealistic scene from some mad artist's canvas. The *Concordia* herself became a tiny replica of the world, tossed about like a speck of sand in a vast incomprehensible void. Time, place, and purpose were gone and all that remained was a useless rearing and plunging in a grey-green chaos.

The ordinary's mind was divided between the automatic control of his body which coordinated his actions on the wheel, and a deep trance-like state of despair brought on by the sudden knowledge of the Old Man's death. In many ways Captain Layton had reminded the Kid of his own father and the terrible feelings he'd experienced on the day he learned he had been killed came flooding back. He remembered the church service and the way his mind ad-libbed as the priest ended his sermon.

"World without end"— and without purpose—"Dust to dust"— tiny bits of matter grown conscious in a vast indifferent cosmos.

Four years of traveling the backwaters of the world had deepened Stacey's cynicism. He had seen pitiful beggar populations, miserable hovels, the lack of education and the absence of sanitation in even the crudest forms. Then there was overbreeding by millions of poor miserable little replicas of themselves who struggled and sickened and died—decimated by famines, floods, diseases and wars.

Religions—his own and all the others he'd investigated— failed to convince him that this unjust and savage world he found himself in was designed by some kindly old spirit everyone called *God*.

Take man out of the equation and the "natural world" would be a paradise. Man is the source of all that's evil. What utter *bullshit!* Where on "God's little green footstool" did these false prophets and fools who called themselves philosophers find their paradises? In the universe of the sea where the shark and the barracuda tore and slashed at any living thing, tearing away even at their own kind in a whirling frenzy of blood and gore? The same "order of the universe" dictated the less violent swallowing of the small, the weak, and the immature by the big and the strong. It was less obvious but still as horrible to Stacey.

Ashore as well, the world didn't need man and his murder, maiming and war to sicken the soul. No, the bleating of the lamb as its living, feeling body was ripped apart by the lion said it all—life feeding on breathing, pleading, agonizing life—for the young ordinary, it was the predestined end of the creature as a torn, bloody, and unrecognizable mess in the mouth of some flesh-eater that was most significant. The natural world was no more sane or kind or just than man's miserable society. How could it be expected that man should or could be any different than the stuff he sprang from?

The Kid never argued his philosophy openly with anyone. Pessimistic and cynical on the one hand, an idealist with a strong sense of morality on the other; he had trouble enough maintaining his own mental balance—never mind attempting to explain it to others. In truth, if love—real love, not merely sex—had not been vividly revealed to him, he probably would not have been able to maintain his sanity.

He had seen love in the eyes and hands of the French nuns he watched minister to the dirty, foul smelling, diseased, and horribly deformed lepers in India.

He had witnessed love one day in a deep tank when a shipmate risked certain death to grab for a man—half again his own weight—whose safety line suddenly parted. Stacey had watched helplessly, too far away to offer aid, but close enough to see the smaller man grab the man who fell. The shock was so sudden that it immediately dislocated the little man's right shoulder, but he managed to hang on with the strength of his left arm. They had dangled head down some thirty-five feet from the bottom of the steel tank till two other men made it down the ladder to pull them both to safety. The little man's legs, behind the knees where he had swung from the razor-sharp rung of the ladder, were cut so deeply it looked at first as if he had been hamstrung. *That was love—unselfish and self sacrificing—the only unknown and inexplicable factor in an equation that otherwise added up to* one big horrifying zero.

The sound of the chartroom door slamming as it got away from Mr. Searles broke Stacey out of his brooding thoughts. He turned to look at the officer.

"The skipper's dead. I suppose you heard?" Searles said as he secured the door on the hook.

"Aye, Sir." Stacey found it difficult to answer with the very real lump in his throat.

The third mate walked past the wheel and stood in front of the midship porthole looking out at the dark and wind-tossed waves cut by the steady Force 7 wind. "How are you now?" he asked without looking back.

"Three degrees right of course—104—103, 103—"

"Let me know when you're right on."

"Aye."

"Still wants to pound, doesn't she?" Mr. Searles spoke to himself aloud.

"Right on, Sir, 100. Right on—right on—one left now—two left—"

"That's fine." The third stayed at the porthole watching the swells; he was noting their interval had increased in frequency—and they were growing in length and height as well.

—TWENTY-ONE—

At 2:45 P.M. all three deck officers were on the bridge. Tim Wilder, the new captain, and Carl Finney, now chief mate, came up from Captain Layton's quarters to sign a statement in the log. Mike Searles, the newly appointed second officer, had just called the engineer on watch and had him reduce to 58 rpms.

"Mike, I need you here a while longer. I've a few things to go over with Carl, then see how Sparks is doing—hate to move Layton's body right now, but I don't want the poor devil rolling all over the deck either, and that'll be the case if this gets any worse."

"That's okay, I don't mind."

"I'm not using Layton's stateroom or his office—except for the safe. Before I forget, call aft and tell Ski to leave his gear in his fo'c'sle for now. Till things are squared away we'll all keep our own rooms."

"Aye, Sir." Searles went to the phone.

"And tell O'Malley to have the escape panel in the office repaired when the deck gang turns to."

When Captain Wilder entered the radio shack, Sparks was still trying to get through to Overseas Tankers' agent in New Orleans. There was no answer the first time and he was trying to raise the marine operator to place it again.

"Keep trying, Ed!" Wilder turned to the mate. "Come on, Carl, let's quit putting it off, we've got to do something with the Old Man's body. There's no taking it aft to the freeze-box—not in this weather."

The mate followed the new captain out of the radio shack and back to Layton's stateroom. The two men wrapped the body in clean sheets and a spread and put it on the bed. Finney went to the midship locker for some line. When he got back they put a blanket over the bunk and lashed it down securely.

"Sure going to feel strange without him."

"That's for certain... I liked him too, Carl. Let's get the hell out of here. I'm going to shower and get dressed."

Both men headed for their rooms.

When Captain Wilder came back to the bridge, Mr. Finney went out to check the barometer, air temperatures, and the standard compass. The wind was blowing half-a-gale and the waves were steadily increasing in height, their tops slashed away into broad white arcs covering the entire horizon.

Heavy spray burst over the *Concordia's* bows as she cut through the building seas. It exploded over the fo'c'slehead, flying high up over the face of the bridge and splattered against the portholes. And when the tanker fell off course to leeward or hit a bigger than usual swell she buried herself to the tank tops.

A thick layer of cirrus clouds made it seem later in the day than it was. The mate had to use his flashlight to read the temperatures and the barometer.

Except for less spread between wet and dry readings the temperatures themselves hadn't changed significantly since 2:00 P.M. They were in for rain squalls soon, no doubt. When Finney checked the barometer he was worried they might well be in for more than that. It read 28.10 inches, down another twenty-five hundreds of an inch in the last hour.

While the new chief mate was out of the chartroom, Searles worked up the ship's 3:00 P.M. position and marked it on the chart.

"Bottom's falling out of the glass!" Carl Finney remarked to Captain Wilder as he came back into the wheelhouse.

Both men went into the chartroom.

"Let me see that other chart, Mike." Finney pointed to the one partly covered by the big chart on which Searles had just marked the tanker's new position. He laid the small one with the two courses, ship and storm, up over it, then transposed the ship's new position onto it and extended the penciled course line. "Look, Captain," he turned to Wilder. "If that damn storm is still following this path," he picked up the French curve and laid it along the points marked through the last position, "we'll be smack dab in the middle of it! That assumes we maintain our course and speed and if it keeps coming on at fifteen to eighteen knots as it has been."

"I want to wait and see if Sparks' 4 o'clock weather update confirms before I make my decision. The port firebox has been trouble free—we can outrun it once we're dead certain which way it's headed." The captain glanced at his watch. It was 3:10 P.M. "Ski should be coming up on the bridge soon."

"Want to try bringing her up another five turns, Captain?" asked the new second mate.

"Go ahead, Mike."

Searles stepped into the wheelhouse and reached for the phone. He cranked it and waited. There was no answer. He cranked it again. Still no answer to the ring and the phone remained dead.

"Captain!" he called out. "The phone's on the fritz!"

"Try the messroom, Second," Wilder advised from the chartroom.

Searles switched the pointer to STANDBY and turned the crank, waited a few seconds and tried it twice more. "No soap, Captain. I think it's out—completely out. Should I try the chief engineer's office?"

Both Mr. Finney and Captain Wilder walked into the wheelhouse.

"Yes, go ahead, but it won't mean anything if you don't get an answer. He's probably still *too sick* to get to it. The S O B didn't answer a while ago when the phone was working fine."

Searles had already turned the pointer and was cranking away. "At least there's a sound now when I depress the talk button," he observed. He handed the phone to Mr. Finney and stepped back.

The chief mate cranked the phone, waited, then depressed the button. There was a slight humming sound. He switched to STANDBY, cranked the handle, waited a moment and then depressed the button. No sound. It was the same for ENG. RM.

Wilder was furious. "Damn it! They were supposed to fix the fuckin' thing yesterday! Second, relieve the wheel!" He started to speak to Stacey, then turned around and flicked the pointer to RADIO RM. and ground the crank rapidly.

"Sparks!" Ed Moore's voice came through loud and clear.

"Hi, Ed. Just checking this damn phone out... Any luck?"

"Not yet, Captain. She's got a few more ahead of us."

"Keep at it. And I want any weather news as soon as you get it." He hung up and glanced at the two mates. He might as well have said, "See, if you were thinking straight you could have checked for certain if the trouble was on this end or not." Instead, he turned to Stacey. "Go aft and tell the second assistant we've a dead line to the engine room and messroom both."

"Aye, Captain." The Kid spun off the remaining angle and stepped off the grating. He held on to the wheel till Searles took it; "100, Sir—taking mostly left rudder."

"100," Mr. Searles repeated the course.

"Stacey, tell the second assistant," Wilder grasped the door frame to the chartroom as the ship rolled heavily, "I want these phones fixed if he has to pull that goddamn chief engineer out by the ears!"—he paused—"No! I know how that'll go. Tell him to call the first and have him get on it. He can turn out the whole black gang if he has to—I want these phones working!"

"Aye, Sir." Stacey grasped hold of the opposite side of the door frame.

"Hold up! There's more."

"Yes, Sir."

"Tell the second I want her up five turns, and till the phone's working, we'll ring the telegraph once to indicate up five, twice for down five. You got that?"

"Aye, Captain."

"Leave word on the messroom blackboard that the phone is out—standby in the wheelhouse—lookout on the weather wing!"

"Yes, Captain."

"Then I want you to go to the chief's office and tell him to call me here on the bridge."

"Aye, Sir. What should I do if he doesn't answer?"

"If he doesn't, you bang on that door and make damn sure he understands I'm not asking—I'm *ordering* him to turn to. See that he answers you—in fact, tell the second assistant I want him to send the oiler up with you as a witness."

"Aye, Captain, I understand."

"Careful going aft, it's getting pretty wild out."

"Yes, Sir. Thank you." Stacey let go of the door frame and started across the chartroom.

"Captain," Mr. Finney suggested, "someone from the black gang could stay in the chief's office relaying messages between the bridge and engine room till we get the phones back."

"Good thinking, Carl. Hold up, Stacey! When he calls I'll tell *him* to stand by or assign a man. If he doesn't call or doesn't like the arrangement we'll move him out of there. Stacey, tell the second these are my orders."

"Yes, Sir." Stacey didn't relish calling the drunken engineer. He headed rapidly down the ladder.

"Thanks, Carl!" Captain Wilder was no longer angry. He walked back into the wheelhouse and grinned at his two mates. "If that drunken bastard doesn't turn to he's through on *this* ship!"

—TWENTY-TWO—

"Evers, it's me, Stacey," the Kid spoke quietly through the spy-hole.

The big AB got up off the bed and came to the door. "Hi, Kid. What's up now?"

"Phone's out to the engine room and messroom both. Wilder's out to get a piece of the chief engineer over it."

"How's that?"

"The chief hasn't answered his phone; drunk, they figure. I'll tell you later. I'm going aft to call him and tell the engineer on watch to get the phones working."

"Okay, Kid... Thanks for stopping—be careful. I've been watchin' off and on; she's been shippin' it green over the well deck."

"Right! See you later." Stacey stepped out of the midship

house. He waited till the ship began her roll up to port and then raced down the catwalk, the wind pushing him along. He made it nearly all the way aft before the tanker returned to an even keel. And by the time she started her roll to starboard he was off the catwalk and in the lee of the after house. He went down the port alleyway to the fantail. When he got to the messroom he found several men still sitting around drinking coffee.

"Ili, Keed!" Hansen greeted him as he entered.

"How's it going?" Stacey answered as be headed for the blackboard. There was a sardine can secured below it containing pieces of chalk and some cotton waste for an eraser.

"Vat's up now?"

"Standby phone's out," Stacey answered as he began chalking the message, "the one down below as well."

"Fuckin' lookout on the *weather* wing!" Terry Cole, the 4 to 8 ordinary, exclaimed as he read the message. "Wouldn't you know it. That fuckin' mate's finally got a shot at playin' Captain Bligh!"

Stacey put the chalk back and headed for the companionway to go below. "Don't go forward at 3:20 to call the mate, Hansen," he informed his watch partner. "They're all up on the bridge."

The Kid made his way down the companionway, past the black gang fo'c'sles to the boiler space fidley door. He opened it and stepped through onto the gratings. Securing the steel door behind him, he started across towards the ladder leading down to the fireroom. He waved at Paco, the fireman-watertender, who had looked up when he felt the draft as the fidley door was opened. Stacey and Paco had been on friendly terms from the start. They met and got to talking in the union hall six months earlier before they both threw in for the *Concordia*. They had even shared a cab to the dock the following day.

Stacey swung on down the ladder; it was pleasantly hot below, a nice change from the cold wet world topside.

"How she goin', Kid?" Paco had stepped over to the bottom of the ladder and spoke as Stacey came down the last few rungs.

"Not so good. Blowing like hell and we've got trouble!" Stacey answered as he stepped onto the floorplates.

"More trouble?"

"Yeah, the phone's out to the engine room and messroom. They sent me back to tell the engineer to take his signals from the telegraph. He'll be in to tell you, I expect; one ring to bring the revs up five—two to reduce five."

"That storm's gettin' bad, ain't it, Kid?"

"Doesn't look good. They're planing to change course and run for it. I've got to call the chief. The mate, I mean the new captain, is going to eat him alive if he doesn't get down here."

"That bastard's been dead drunk since we left the dock. Good luck!"

"Say, Paco, I want to ask you something."

"Okay."

"Did you notice anything strange the morning the wiper went over the side?"

"No...I don't think so. Why?"

"Just wondering. Your oiler was in the messroom around 3:30 asking my partner a lot of questions. Hansen seemed to think he was expecting to find someone besides him there on standby."

"I don't have too much to do with him, but he seems okay. Never says much—just goes on about his business."

"Okay, just thought I'd ask."

"You guys think he might have something to do with the new AB killing the wiper?"

"Paco, it isn't certain our watch partner *did* kill the guy, you know."

"No, I don't know. I thought that was pretty plain, Kid."

"Well it isn't, Paco; it isn't at all. The Old Man had to lock him up on suspicion, but that don't automatically mean he's guilty. Someone could have killed the guy while we were putting over the ladder."

"You don't think he done it then?"

"No, I really don't think so and neither does Hansen. Anyone could have come into the messroom while we were gone and done for the guy—say someone like the oiler. He could have gone topside, done it, then sneaked back without anyone the wiser."

"Hell, then I might've left the fireroom and done it, or even the engineer—no?"

"Yeah, I suppose that's possible too, but it'd be lots harder for you or the engineer to leave your stations—while the oiler has to go all over."

"Well, I can't see Carter doing anything like that, but now when I think about it, I can tell you two things... Don't you get me in no trouble now, Kid!"

"No chance, Paco; you know me better'n that."

"Okay... Carter did look upset later in the watch—going here and there where he'd just been—and there was no trouble. He was real nervous about something. He's usually not that way, goes about his job careful, but he knows his work all right. No, it wasn't his work botherin' him—had to be something else. Seemed like he was dodging the chief. The other thing is I remember looking up at 1:35 and seeing him going out the fidley door."

"Right at 1:35...? How the hell you remember something right on the minute?"

"Just do, Kid. I looked up and seen him, then I checked the water gauges and the time—habit I suppose."

"You say he was ducking the chief?"

"Seemed like it to me. I don't blame him for that—I would too, but I can't hide down here."

"The chief engineer was down below as well?"

"The son of a bitch haunted the place till after we took the departure bell at 2:50."

"Is he usually down here like that?"

"Yeah, he most time stays around long after he's needed."

"Thanks, Paco. Really, thanks a lot!" He patted the heavy-set little man's shoulder.

"Remember, don't say nothing about what I told you... I still think Carter's clean, Kid."

"No sweat, Paco. I won't say a word—so help me! I got to get moving. See you." Stacey headed for the engine room.

By the time Stacey left the throttle station, the *Concordia's* speed had been brought up 5 revolutions in compliance with the bridge's orders. Pillars didn't have to send anyone to call the first assistant as Mr. Pierce was up and working on something in the machine shop. Stacey told the first himself about the phone being out and the rest of Wilder's orders. The oiler was in the machine shop as well.

The first shut down the lathe and wiped his hands on a piece of waste. "Go ahead with him. And call both wipers when you're through," he told Carter as he exited the machine shop—the ordinary and the oiler right behind him. Mr. Pierce headed forward to the engine room, while Carter followed Stacey aft.

"Hey, hold up!" the oiler called out as they approached the watertight door to the steering engine room. "Why do you need *me* to go up with you just to give the chief a call?"

"The mate told me to have you come with me—that's all."

"Well, I don't take no orders from him!" Carter had stopped walking.

"The mate, Mr. Wilder, is captain now—I meant the captain told me."

"Look, you get someone else to do your *dirty work*. I got my rounds to do. Call one of the wipers if you need company."

"The first just told you to call the wipers *after* going with me to call the chief." Stacey stood in front of the open door and looked back at the oiler who was starting to turn back towards the direction from which they had just come. "Hey, what's gotten you so riled up?"

"Get lost!" Carter turned and started away. "You're nothin' but a goddamn trouble maker." He muttered the last under his breath.

Stacey crossed the floorplates and caught hold of the oiler's arm. "Wait a minute now, what's *that* supposed to mean?"

"Just what I said—GET LOST! You don't get on with anyone, it seems. You better watch your ass and get off *mine*!" Carter had turned around and jerked his arm away from Stacey's grasp.

"Okay, Carter, let's get something straight. I'm down here repeating only what I was ordered to by the captain. If you got something against me, that's okay, that's your business. But you're sure acting pretty strange about not wanting to do something both the captain and the first told you to."

"Get off my back, Stacey, I'm warning you!"

"Carter, you're jumping me for some reason, and it don't seem to have anything to do with this."

"I ain't alone feeling about you the way I do. The whole crew's got it in for you since the Old Man was killed."

"Since Captain Layton was *killed*? Who started that one? No one killed him. He had a heart attack—and where do you come off saying anything to me about that!"

"It was your watch partner that knocked him down. And that's what killed him!"

"I'm not my watch partner to begin with, and he didn't hit the Old Man. Ryan had no call to jump him from behind, and it was a mistake for the mate trying to put on the irons while he was just standing there shocked-like."

"Sure he ain't to blame! He didn't kill the wiper neither, I suppose?"

"Maybe he didn't kill the wiper; almost anyone could have done it. I don't remember anyone proving he did kill him. The Old Man put him in the brig for suspicion. That don't automatically make him guilty."

"It does far as *I'm* concerned—the rest of the crew, too!" Carter stuck out his lower jaw. "And there's some that thinks you got answering to do as well."

"Oh, so *that's it*, huh? Okay, my friend, you been throwing a lot of things my way—now, let me tell you something—I'm not the only one who's figured out that you could have been topside while Evers and I were putting the ladder over." Stacey kept his eyes on Carter's as he spoke. He knew he had hit home. The man looked away and Stacey could see his throat working before he answered.

"You...you're fuckin' nuts. Why the hell would *I* kill the wiper?"

"I can *prove* you were topside around the messroom about 1:30—convenient as that's when the AB and I left!" Stacey had taken a gamble. He really had nothing to go on other than that Paco had seen the oiler go out the fidley door at 1:35, but his long shot seemed to be paying off.

"You..ly...lyin' son-of-a-bitch!" Carter's voice broke.

"No, Carter, I'm not lying. I'll prove what I said when the time comes. Think Hansen didn't notice you wandering around later, asking him all kinds of questions?"

"You tryin' to pin it on *me*?"

"Just like you putting it on the AB, ain't it?"

"No, no it ain't!"

"Yes, I was up there, Evers was up there, and *you* were up there. It's exactly the same thing, and before you go around accusing anyone, you better work up your *own* excuse for being seen around the messroom."

"Shit, you said it yourself. Anyone could've been around and done it. You're nuts if you think you can put it off on me!"

"You're as good a suspect as Evers—that's all I said. Now you coming with me, or do I tell Captain Wilder you refused his direct order?"

"You don't scare me none, Stacey. I'll go, but you're gonna pay for it!"

The Kid turned and walked on through the open doorway. He was careful to keep the oiler in view, watching him start after him through the corner of his eye. He couldn't quite figure the man's actions. The oiler was as hostile and full of hate as could be, but seemed more frightened than guilty. Stacey didn't get the feeling that the oiler was capable of committing murder. He'd have to agree with Paco on that.

—TWENTY-THREE—

"Well, Ski... Excuse me, I mean Mr. Borolowski, Sir, I hope ya don't mind sharin' a fo'c'sle with one of the unwashed and unlicensed for another day or so?" Junior was rubbing it in about his partner going as third mate. The two men sat in their room drinking Junior's beer. They had left the messroom about 3:15 P.M. right after coffee time.

Since Ski had to go on watch at 8:00 P.M., he wasn't turning to after the break to work till 5 o'clock. Junior, who was Evers' replacement on the 12 to 4, was still on watch till 4:00 P.M. He was about to go back to cleaning up the bosun's locker in the shelter deck.

"You're lucky you ain't gonna be on my watch, Junior," Ski leered at his partner. "First off, I'd have to confiscate all your beer. And when we get ashore, well, I'd have to take away all your pussy as well—that stuff ain't no good for young kids like you to eat."

"Ski! Junior!" O'Malley called out and knocked on the door.

"Come on in Boats," Junior answered.

O'Malley opened the door and stepped in. "What a fuckin' day. Shit, you can't do anything on these cocksuckers the way they roll!"

"Pull up a deck and have a beer." Junior tossed the can opener to O'Malley. "They're under Ski's bed." He pointed to the double bunk against the inboard bulkhead.

"Might as well." The bosun gripped the stanchion of the double bunk as the ship's stern humped up over a swell and vibrated wildly. "Goddamn if it don't feel like they've speeded her up again. This bucket is gonna come apart at the seams one day— mark my fuckin' words on that!" O'Malley bent down and found the half-empty case of beer. Another full case was wedged alongside of it.

"We got time for another, Boats?" asked Junior.

"Yah, there's no rush going forward. You want one too, Ski?" He fished out two cans and tossed one to Junior.

"No, I'm going up to the bridge in a minute. Thanks, Boats."

"No rush, Ski. I think Wilder just wants to bullshit you a bit." The bosun opened his can and tossed the opener to Junior. He took a long swig. "Ah, that's good!" He squatted next to the bed.

"He's not so bad," Ski observed, "not for a 'Kingspoint

Special' he ain't. I've sailed with worse pricks that come up through the hawsepipe."

"He don't fuck with my gang—I'll say that for 'im." O'Malley took another swallow. By now he had eased his legs out in front of him and leaned back against the lower bunk. "He'll make a decent enough skipper some day I reckon."

"Finney's a pretty good mate. Ex-Navy, ain't he?" asked Junior.

"Yah...think so. Well, Mr. Mate... Here's to ya." O'Malley lifted his beer in Ski's direction.

"Knock it off you fuckers," Ski smiled, "I'll be back dayman soon as they get a replacement."

"How's come you don't sail on your license, Ski?" Junior became serious.

"Well, I'll tell you. That sailing topside got it's points, but I get bored staying on one run any length of time for one. For another thing, that four hours on the bridge drives me nuts. It's as bad as going quartermaster for four straight hours on a Seatrain— guess I just like day work. I don't even like sailing a watch on one of these." Ski checked the time. He got to his feet and stepped over Junior's outstretched legs. "It's almost 3:25, I better go see what Wilder wants." He looked out the porthole. "Christ! It's pitch black out and we're into a squall." The dayman pulled his rain gear off the hook and did a little jig getting the bottoms up over his pants. He carried the tops in his arms and started for the door.

"We be comin' along directly," said the bosun. "Tell the mate—I mean the captain—I'll get on reparin' that escape panel in a bit. In fact, you'll come with me." He looked at Junior. "We'll let the locker go awhile—ain't no rush." He took another drink from the can of beer. "Nothin' much we can do in this fuckin' weather anyway."

—TWENTY-FOUR—

Stacey knocked on the door to the chief engineer's office. The oiler stood a few feet away holding on to the railing at the top of the ladder leading to the lower deck.

"Chief... Mr. Kruzic!" the Kid called out and rapped on the door again.

Kruzic could barley hear his name being called or the banging on the door. He was in bed, fully clothed, having not even removed his shoes. He lay face down in a jumble of twisted linen and blankets.

"CHIEF..! MR. KRUZIC!" Stacey shouted even louder this time. "CHIEF, IT'S 3:20—THEY WANT YOU TO CALL THE BRIDGE, SIR!" The Kid hit the door soundly with the side of his fist—hard enough to make it vibrate. "THE MATE WANTS YOU TO CALL THE BRIDGE...CHIEF—THEY'VE GOT TROUBLE!"

The engineer had finished over half of his third bottle of bourbon by noon and staggered to his stateroom. Real sleep did not come and he had lain in bed hallucinating for most of the three hours.

The yelling and banging finally got through to him.

"Leave me alone." His mouth formed the words soundlessly in protest to the summons from the door.

"CHIEF, THIS IS THE LAST CALL—CAPTAIN WILDER'S COMING AFT TO GET INTO THIS ROOM IF YOU DON'T GET UP—*THEY GOT TO HAVE THIS PHONE!!*"

"Okay, I've heard your callin' the chief. I got the 4 to 8 watch to call, and the wipers as well." Carter turned and started down the companionway leading to the lower deck.

Stacey was about to pound the door again when it flew open. It caught him by surprise, his fist still in the air, "Chief, I..."

"*YOU?*" Kruzic swayed there in the doorway. *"What do you want?"*

"Mr...Mr. Wilder—Sir, he told me to call you."

"WHO?" Kruzic looked past Stacey towards the companionway where he could see someone going below.

"The captain, Sir. He gave me orders to see that you—"

"You fool!" the alcohol crazed engineer reached out and grabbed Stacey's arm. "Get in here!"

"CHIEF!" The Kid started to pull back.

"Shut up!" Kruzic snatched the gun out from under his shirt and slammed the muzzle into Stacey's ribs. *"Get in here!"* He pulled the stunned ordinary into the room, slamming the door behind him.

"Sir, I—"

Kruzic shoved the Kid back against the desk.

"Chief!" Stacey tried to keep his voice calm as he realized the state the engineer was in. "Sir, all I'm doing is trying to..."

"Shut up, you *goon!*" Kruzic's face was contorted with rage.

He reached down, picking up the chair that lay on the deck. "SIT!" he shouted, turning it around with the back facing him.

Kruzic thought he was a union goon! Suddenly, it all became clear. It was the chief! It was Kruzic who strangled the wiper. Carter, the oiler, saw it or knew it and was scared of him!

Whitey and the chief; that was the hook-up. The company spy and his contact topside on the *Jackson Heights.* Stacey's mind was in a whirl. He had to get out of there and tell the captain. Tell him it was Kruzic, not Evers. He was dead if he sat in that chair—dead as little Eddy Sommers.

"Sir, Captain Wilder just wants you to call the bridge. The phone's out to the engine room." He kept his voice steady, pretending he hadn't heard or didn't understand the engineer's reference to "goon."

"Captain Wilder. *Captain Wilder,* you say?" Kruzic stood gripping the edge of the desk with his left hand, waving the gun at the ordinary with the right.

"Sir... I've got to get back to the wheel."

"SIT!"

Stacey had no intention of sitting, but he took a step towards the chair to appear as if he was about to. He continued to talk as calmly as he could, hoping to knock the gun away and make it out of the room. "Yes, Sir. You know they found the Old Man dead in his room."

Kruzic was taken back for a moment and his eyes shifted to the phone. "Layton dead? Wilder is captain?" Kruzic spoke the words in a half daze.

"They plan to turn around and run for home," the Kid kept talking, "but they got trouble with the phones, Sir!"

Stacey took his gamble and kicked powerfully out against the chair with his right foot. The chair slammed against Kruzic knocking him backwards away from the door—but he didn't drop the gun.

"BASTARD!" The engineer staggered to keep his footing.

The ordinary lunged for the door managing to open it partway as Kruzic pulled the trigger. The sound was still hammering at his ears as the bullet slammed into his side. Stacey tried to keep his feet, but the roll of the ship added to his loss of balance. As he fell to the deck, he felt the searing pain of the second slug tearing into his back. The sound of the gun and Kruzic's insane voice shouting "BASTARD! BASTARD!" came to him. Then the door opened hitting the side of his head.

"WHAT THE HELL'S GOIN' ON!"

Stacey had almost blacked out, yet he was aware someone other than Kruzic had yelled. Another shot and he tensed for the hot tearing piece of lead, but it didn't come—instead he heard a scream from the doorway.

The third shot was for Ski. It was his voice that the ordinary heard as Kruzic shot straight into the face of the unfortunate dayman.

Ski had been on his way to the bridge. As he passed the chief engineer's office he heard shouts. The door started to open and two shots rang out. He yelled and pushed the door open to investigate. The engineer raised his gun and fired point blank. The bullet caught the newly-appointed third mate right at the bridge of his nose. He staggered backwards with only one short startled scream. Ski never had time to think—he was dead before he fell to the deck.

Kruzic never looked back. He tore out of the office like a madman and headed through the open door onto the catwalk.

It was black out and the wind slammed against him as he raced toward the midship house. The heavy rain slanted down drenching his light khakis. There was only one thought in his mind—to gain control of the ship. Kruzic pulled at the catwalk railing with his left hand, propelling himself along as fast as he could against the combined force of the wind and the pull of gravity as the ship's bows reared skyward. His right hand grasped the automatic. He had the spare clip safely tucked in his left-hand pants pocket. The engineer was in a crazed state, but he was not out of control. *First things first*, he cautioned himself as he gained the lee of the midship structure.

Kruzic hesitated a split second considering the odds of getting the other goon, right then, by shooting at him through the barred porthole; then dismissed the impulse in the light of more pressing business.

"CHRIST A'MIGHTY!" Tommy had heard the shots from the crew messroom and raced to where he thought they came from. O'Malley and Junior were right behind him. All three saw the dayman at the same moment.

"SKI! *IT'S SKI!*" Junior shouted, racing ahead of the others.

"IS HE ALIVE?" the bosun yelled as he came up to where the body lay.

The messman had let the two pass him on the way to the fallen man, and it was he who heard the ordinary's groan and noticed the partially opened chief engineer's door. Stacey had gotten to his knees, wedging his shoulder against the door for support. Tommy almost pushed the ordinary's arms out from under him as he tried to open it further. "KID! OH CHRIST! KID!"

"I think he's dead, Boats." Junior looked up at O'Malley.

"Motherfucker!" O'Malley knelt down to get a closer look when he heard Tommy's cry. *"The Kid's shot, too!"*

"Got to call the bridge...the bridge. It was the chief—not Evers." Stacey managed to draw one foot up under him. "Help me up, Tommy."

"DON'T MOVE 'IM!" O'Malley straightened up and headed for the office.

"Boats, ring the bridge now!" Stacey pulled himself erect using Tommy's shoulder.

"You betta not move, Kid!" Tommy grasped the desk to support himself against the ship's roll.

O'Malley set the pointer and cranked the phone.

"Bridge!" Captain Wilder's voice boomed out in the still room.

"Sir! This is O'Malley. Ski's been shot in the face. He's dead! We found the 12 to 4 ordinary shot in the chief's room!"

"What? *What's that?*"

"Give me!" the Kid took the phone from O'Malley.

"Captain, the AB didn't kill Whitey—it was Kruzic. He's crazy and he may be headed for the bridge!" The phone fell from his hand as the ship lurched.

"Sit down, Kid." Tommy helped Stacey into the chair.

"HELLO! HELLO! *GODDAMIT! STACEY?*" Wilder's voice came from the phone.

*   *   *

Kruzic stepped over the coaming into the midship house. He hurried past the hospital to the companionway and up the steps as rapidly and as quietly as he could. When he got to the landing next to the captain's office he paused a moment to listen, then headed aft to the radio shack.

The engineer turned the knob slowly. The door opened. Sparks sat with his back to him. He was at the transmitter, mike to his mouth.

"Marine Operator, New Orleans, this is the tanker *Concor-*

dia."

Kruzic raised his right hand and brought it down with all the force he could muster. The steel butt of the automatic thudded into the back of the radio operator's head. Ed Moore's face smashed into the set. The engineer raised his fist again, bringing the butt of the gun down against the man's exposed temple—the second blow assuring that Ed Moore's career was at an end.

"This is the marine operator, New Orleans. Hello...hello, we're ready on your call," the sexy-sounding female voice came gently from the headset.

It took Kruzic only a few moments to destroy the heart of the vessel's communications center—he worked deftly making certain no one would be calling from or to the tanker. He turned and headed out the door. *And now for you my fine friend, Captain Wilder!*

Carl Finney heard the conversation between the bosun, Stacey, and Captain Wilder. He stood balancing against the coffee table. Searles, still on the wheel, had heard it all as well.

When the phone connection had been broken, Wilder hurried into the chartroom and unlocked the cabinet next to the chart table. He pulled out the revolver, checked that it was loaded, and came back into the wheelhouse.

"Carl, you'd best stay here with Mike!" The new captain looked at Finney as he picked up the phone. "I'll have to go back—"

They all heard the footsteps. Wilder dropped the phone and grabbed the revolver from his waistband. He stepped quickly through the chartroom door and headed for the companionway.

Kruzic was halfway up the steps, his eyes glued to the top of the ladder. He fired the moment Wilder appeared at the top of the companionway. Luck was with him. His second and third shots struck the captain and the big revolver clattered down the ladder. Kruzic grabbed it and stuck it under his belt. Nothing could stop him now!

Carl Finney had come around the corner of the coffee table to follow Wilder. He got to the chartroom doorway just in time to see the wounded man slump backwards to the deck—he resisted going to his aid. The mate knew their only hope was to muster the crew and have Sparks send an SOS. He pushed Searles, who stood transfixed as he watched from the wheel, then pointed to himself and to the open door to the port wing. The dazed man started to say something, but Finney shook his head violently, finger to his lips, and backed swiftly through the open door. He ducked as he went aft past the porthole just as Kruzic reached the top of the steps to the chartroom.

Captain Wilder lay in a widening pool of blood. He rolled over and looked up at the chief engineer.

"NO ONE MAKE A MOVE!" Kruzic's voice rang through the bridge.

— T W E N T Y - F I V E —

Carl Finney never felt as alone and inadequate in his life. Captain Layton was dead; and now the mate, severely wounded and in need of immediate aid—certain to die if he didn't get it fast. The bridge was in the hands of a madman, two more of whose victims lay dead or dying back aft. And the probability of being directly in the path of a hurricane becoming a certainty. Decisions he had to make as a Navy lieutenant during convoy attacks were nothing compared to his present dilemma—the entire burden of command and responsibility for the tanker *Concordia* had suddenly and unhappily become his.

The wind howled and tore at him and he was blinded by the lashing rain. He ran in a crouched position past the chartroom and down the ladder leading to the boat deck—hardly able to catch his breath.

Finney's first impulse was to enter the house at the wooden door in front of him—it lead into the passageway where the radio shack was located. But suddenly, thinking it wiser to warn Sparks from outside rather than chance running into the madman, who might hear the door open or already be on his way down to the radio room, he continued around the after side of the house making his way to the portholes marking the location of the radio shack and Sparks' stateroom.

The mate eased himself erect at the aftermost porthole. *"Oh Christ!"* he whispered as he looked into the brightly lit radio room. Ed Moore lay sprawled in front of the transmitter. From the look of the man's caved-in temple and his unnatural position, Finney knew Sparks was beyond need or help. And it didn't take much imagination to visualize the totally ruined state of the radio equipment—enough of its destruction was clearly visible from where he stood.

In his favor, Finney figured, was that Kruzic had not seen him in the wheelhouse and wouldn't expect him to come up on watch much before 4 o'clock. He checked his watch—3:36. He still had a half hour before the engineer would be looking for him on the bridge or know that he was in hiding if he failed to show up. Whatever he could do or plan must be done now.

The wind stung his face and he shivered uncontrollably as he struggled forward along the weather side of the house. Just as he got to the face of the midship structure, the tanker buried her bows and a wall of water broke over the entire fo'c'slehead. Heavy spray flew over the bridge as he crossed to the lee side and made his way to the brig's open porthole.

"Evers!" he called hoarsely into the dark room. "*Don't* turn on your light!" His voice cracked. "It...It's me, Finney."

"Mate!" The big AB was at the porthole in a moment.

"*Listen!* The chief engineer's gone mad. He's killed Sparks and a dayman and wounded Captain Wilder and Stacey. The ordinary said it was Kruzic that murdered the wiper."

"Christ... Thought I heard shots just now! He shot the Kid?"

"He may be down here any second. I'm getting you out—stand by the door and see the passageway's clear."

"Aye!" Evers grabbed his shoes off the deck and went to the door. "It's okay, Mate," he kept his voice low.

"Keep watching!"

Finney made his way around the corner of the house and stepped into the lighted passageway. He felt horribly exposed as he stood there shivering trying to find the right key to the two big padlocks; he could hear the big AB breathing heavily through the open spy hole.

Evers balanced on one foot and then the other getting his shoes on while waiting for Finney to find the right key. He heard the lock unsnap on one of the bars just as he finished tying his laces. The AB pulled all his clothing from the hooks on the bulkhead next to his bed. The door opened. Evers stepped out of the room, closed the door quietly, and followed the mate out of the house.

"Down here!" Finney called in a low voice as he headed down the ladder to the well deck. The ship was on the top of her roll to starboard and the deck was almost dry where he stood trying to open the watertight door to the shelter deck.

The big AB grasped the two remaining dogs and pulled. The

door came open. Some of the clothing dropped on the deck. Evers picked them up and hurried after the mate, pulling the heavy steel door closed behind them. He slammed the palm of his right hand against each of the six dogs to secure them. "Here, Sir, I grabbed these." He held out the clothing to Mr. Finney.

"Got...gotta act fast, haven't got time." The mate tried to talk without shaking.

"Sir, you ain't gonna be able to do anything in the state you're in. Better get out of those clothes while you can."

Carl Finney was blue with cold and shaking uncontrollably. He knew the AB was right; the armful of clothing was really fortunate. Everything was big, but in a few moments he was in dry jeans, shirt and a jacket.

"Sir—see if one of those keys will open the bosun's locker." The big AB gestured across to the port side of the dimly lit shelter space beyond the racks of cargo hoses.

The two men crossed over and in a few seconds they had the locker opened. There was a row of beat up foul weather slicks left there for men to use on dirty jobs. The pants and jackets had tears in them and were coated with dry grease, white lead and paint; there were also several pairs of old worn-out sea boots thrown up on one of the lower shelves. By the time they were outfitted, Finney had filled the AB in on all he could tell him.

The mate looked at his watch. "It's 3:43, now pray the phone down here's still working!"

They headed for the telephone box next to the watertight door. Finney turned the crank after setting the pointer to CH. ENG.

"Mate, wouldn't it be best we get aft and work out some plan to nail the bastard?"

"No, I've got to stay on the bridge—there's no telling what this maniac will do." Finney turned the crank again. "You'll have to—*Yes!* Hello!!—*Damn!* Someone started to answer, now it's dead again." He slammed the box with the side of his fist. "Something's wrong with the SOB!"

"Sir, try the after steering station. You might catch the oiler on his last round—it's almost change of the watch."

Finney turned the dial and cranked the handle.

"Hello!" The voice came on the line almost immediately.

"THANK CHRIST!!" Finney shouted into the phone. "WHO IS THIS?"

"Carter, 12 to 4 oiler."

"This is the mate. Kruzic's gone berserk! No time to explain.

He killed Sparks and shot Captain Wilder and we know it was him who killed the wiper! I freed Evers—he's on his way aft. Get word to the first and to Boats immediately! *You got that,* Carter?"

"Yes, Sir! I'll tell them..! Good luck!"

Finney hung up the phone. "The line from the captain's office to the chief engineer's should be working—the one from the wheelhouse to the chief's was. Tell the first and O'Malley to stand by that phone!"

"Let me try for 'im now, Sir—it may be our only chance."

"No... You'd never get near him... I've got to figure a way, but I need you and boats back aft. Mr. Pierce can't handle things all alone."

"Any chance of another gun in the Old Man's office, Sir?"

"I'll check, but I don't think so. Then I have to sneak back to the wheelhouse and see what's happening with Wilder and Searles."

"You're a goner if he spots you, Mate."

"He won't! I'll call from the captain's office to let you know what I found and plan to do—one way or the other it looks like I've got to take the watch at four."

"Christ, Mate! That's just givin' 'im another prisoner!"

"I don't have a choice. If I can't get him to change course we've all had it anyway."

"The 4 to 8; you want them up on watch as well?"

"Kruzic will probably tell me, if he hasn't already called aft, when and how he wants the watch changed. He's drunk and crazy, but he isn't going to be easily fooled—whatever you do, don't try calling me in the captain's office—he might hear the phone ring."

"Aye, Mate, but I hate to see you go on back up there."

"I won't if I come up with an alternative." Finney reached up to undog the door.

"Good luck. We'll be at the phone."

"Thanks, Evers." Finney shook hands with the AB.

"Sir... It was me that threw the wiper over the side. He jumped me with a bottle and I hit him. When I come back and found him dead, I figured I'd killed 'im. But I couldn't chance goin' up against the law with no proof it was self-defense. I been in trouble before—can you understand that?"

"Well, it was wrong in a way. But yes—I do understand—if that means anything now."

"It does to *me,* Mr. Finney."

—TWENTY-SIX—

They carried the kid down to the 12 to 4 fo'c'sle and put him on Hansen's bed.

"I'll get more bandages from the medical locker." O'Malley pushed his way past Hansen and Tommy. "And send the chief cook down with them to help."

"Vot can I do, Bosun?"

"Just stand by, Hansen... They know what they're doin'. I ain't got the key to the engine room medical box, but I'll get the first to see someone brings you a shot of morphine for him."

"Reed an me's right here wid you, Kid. Now jus' you try and take it easy." Deel was more calm than Hansen, who could only watch helplessly as the messman and the cook worked over Stacey.

The big compression bandages became blood-soaked almost immediately, but they padded them over with pieces of clean sheets. Reed had once been a hospital orderly and he had worked around emergency rooms long enough to be somewhat effective in handling gunshot wounds. He poured sulfa powder into each hole after stanching the flow of blood long enough to do so. Then Tommy pressed on a compression bandage while Reed added a thickly folded piece of clean sheeting and taped it down. Afterwards they bandaged the Kid's chest and stomach with long strips of cloth cut from a clean bedspread. It wasn't the most professional looking job, but they did get the bleeding stopped. They put several blankets over the Kid, and it looked like he wasn't going to go into shock.

The one slug which struck the ordinary in the side had passed through hitting only abdominal muscle and was the least of the two wounds. The second one—in the back—had entered below the left shoulder blade and followed a rib clear around the chest coming out under his left armpit.

"The Kid's lucky as hell. Both slugs came right on through without hitting anything, it seems."

O'Malley spoke to Davis, the third assistant engineer. Davis had also heard the shots and came out of his room in time to help carry Stacey down to the 12 to 4 fo'c'sle. "Poor Ski, nothing we can do for him, though." The bosun stood a few feet in front of the sprawled body of the dayman.

"Oh for God's sakes!" Mr. Pierce closed the engine space fidley door behind him with much effort as the ship rolled down to starboard. Though informed of the shootings about five minutes before he couldn't get away till now. He had been standing by for Pillars who was working on the phone lines when Stacey left the engine room to call the chief engineer.

"He's dead, First," Davis answered the unvoiced question.

"And the ordinary?" Pierce looked up, pale and haggard.

"Looks like he'll be okay. He's down below and a couple of guys with him," O'Malley answered. "I 'spect we better take Ski somewheres."

"The phones are working from the bridge and the messroom. We had our first orders from 'Captain Kruzic'—God rot the dirty bastard!" A group of men had gathered a few feet from the bosun and the third assistant.

"Where do you think we should put Ski's body, First?" O'Malley heard what Mr. Pierce said about the phones, but he could think of nothing more pressing at the moment than caring for his dayman's body.

"I suppose you better have him carried into the room." The engineer gestured towards the chief's office. "Put him on the bed and lash it well for the moment."

"I'm gonna send the chief cook down to help with the ordinary. We might need to get a shot of morphine from you, First," O'Malley added.

Everyone looked up as the big AB stepped through the open doorway, water pouring from his paint-fouled oil skins.

"Evers!" O'Malley was the first to react, "Welcome home man!" He grasped the big AB's hand. "We been waitin' for you since Carter told us. Some mess!"

"The mate's in the middle of a worse one. The Kid!—Where is he?" Evers stared at the dead dayman as he started to take off his rain jacket.

"Down below. He's gonna be fine!" the bosun answered.

"Thank Christ!"

"Ski's dead." O'Malley shook his head as he looked back at his friend's body. "Lend a hand here! Someone tear that cocksucker's linen off his bunk and lay fresh sheets down before we put this *man* on that bed—you hear?"

Several men lifted the dayman's body and started into Kruzic's stateroom.

"Where's Mr. Finney?" Mr. Pierce addressed Evers.

"On the bridge, Sir. He wants us to stand by the phone in the chief's office."

"The chief's office?"

"Aye, he went to look for another gun. Then he's going to sneak back to see what's happening in the wheelhouse before callin' us from the captain's office."

"Here Sam!" The first handed him his key ring. "Get out two morphine syrettes and get the keys back to me."

"Yes, Sir." The chief cook started down to the engine room medical locker.

Pillars looked at his watch. "Christ, it's ten to four!" He hurried into the chief engineer's office.

Evers had stripped off the rain jacket, pants, and sea boots. "Boats!" he called out as O'Malley stepped into the office behind the first assistant.

"Yes, Evers." O'Malley didn't turn around. He was watching the dayman being lowered onto the fresh sheet that had been hastily thrown across the just-stripped mattress.

"The mate's countin' on us to put this bastard down. What say I go up on watch with the 4 to 8—maybe getting close enough before he knows it's me?"

"Christ, no, it'd never work. He's certain to check who's comin' up. Did the mate say the watch is to go forward?"

"No, not till he tells us."

The telephone rang.

"Quiet!" The first waved his hand. "Yes... Yes, I hear you. Yes, he's here. No, the son of a bitch just called down below a few minutes ago. The phones are okay. You shouldn't go back there! What...what can we do? Yes, here he is." Pierce's hand was shaking as he handed the phone to the bosun.

"Aye, Sir?"

"If I don't make it you'll have to work out something with the engineers."

"You ain't gonna do yerself or the ship any good gettin' shot up, Mate. Did you find a gun?"

"No! Nothing!"

"Maybe someone down below got one. But gun or no gun, what say we break out the fire axes and the whole gang storm the fucker?"

"No, Boats. He's two guns up there and he'll kill Searles and Wilder soon as he sees anyone coming—and kill a bunch more before we could get him down. We have to come up with a plan."

"Well, your goin' up there only gives him another ace."

"I've got to get this ship turned around or no one's going to get off it alive. We're headed straight into a hurricane! Captain Wilder was waiting for a weather update before turning away—we'll have to run from it blind now."

"Is he nuts enough to sink her?"

"Maybe... But I think he's figuring to chance the storm and get to somewhere he can get away. I've got to convince him to run first and then take her anywhere he wants."

"Aye, Mate. You want the 4 to 8 watch to start forward?"

"I'm going up now. Let him do the ordering when the watch should turn to. We'll play along and not panic him."

"Aye. Good luck, Sir."

"Let me speak to Evers."

"Aye, Mate." O'Malley handed the phone to the AB.

"Sir?"

"Evers—help O'Malley and Pierce—I'm *trusting you* to hold things together."

"Aye, Mr. Finney. We'll come up with an answer—count on that!"

"Good luck!" The phone was hung up.

The bosun and the first assistant both heard the mate's words to the big AB.

"Okay, I want the 4 to 8 standin' by in the messroom till we get word from the bridge." O'Malley spoke to Bob Howard, one of the 4 to 8 ABs who had helped carry in Ski's body. The other two members of the watch were standing outside the chief's office. "The rest of you guys might as well go on. Ain't much we can do right now. If anyone's carryin' a piece you better get it up here to me...couple of guns would sure be a blessin'. Howard, put word on the messroom blackboard and tell everyone—no one need explain why he's got it!"

"Boats, I want to lay below a minute to see the Kid."

"Okay, and check if he's got one; anyone else you see as well."

"Aye, Boats."

"Any other time there'd be a couple of pieces around, sure as shittin' there'd be—but when everythin' depends on comin' up with one—watch! There won't be any!"

The big AB went down the companionway, turned to the right at the bottom of the ladder and walked swiftly through the alleyway leading to the starboard side fo'c'sles. He paused in front of the first door, which was open.

The three members of the 8 to 12 sat there talking. They knew about the berserk engineer, the recent shootings, and that it was Kruzic who had killed the wiper. They were not prepared to see Evers.

"Gents," Evers greeted them, "the bosun's askin' anyone has a gun to get it to him, pronto! I don't have to tell you we're in bad trouble with a crazy man connin' the helm and us headed for a real blow. It might save the lot of us!"

All three shook their heads—no.

"Or if you know who might—you'll be savin' your own hides."

"Ask the Kid or his *nigger friend!* They got more need of one!" Tompkins, the tall skinny ordinary, grinned at him.

"Okay... Thank you. *I will!*" The big AB turned away from the open door. He was furious, but he concealed his anger. He didn't understand why the ordinary's referring to Tommy as "nigger" had offended him—<u>but it did</u>!

Evers didn't bother looking into the 4 to 8 fo'c'sle. The door was closed and anyhow, they had heard the bosun's request.

The AB opened the door to the 12 to 4 as quietly as he could. Tommy and another colored man were in the room.

"How's he doin'?" Evers spoke to the messman who sat next to Hansen's bunk where the Kid was lying.

"It's Mr. Evers!" Tommy rose up out of the chair. "I think he gonna be jus' fine *now!*" He sat back down slowly, eyes watering as he watched the big AB hook the door open and start towards the bed.

"I think you betta keep dat door closed—he got a fever," the other black man said.

"Sorry." Evers turned back, took the door off the hook, and closed it. The fo'c'sle smelled bad, but he realized that the man was right. "Is he awake?"

"Evers?" Stacey spoke in a dry whisper that could hardly be heard over the rumbling vibrations of the ship.

"How's it goin', Kid?" The big AB leaned over the head of the bed, supporting himself with one hand on the bunk's stanchion, the other on the back of Tommy's chair.

"Okay... I'm okay."

"Just wanted to see how you were doing...thanks for clearing me. But it won't be worth much of anythin' less you're okay."

"Tommy and Reed got me fixed up fine."

"Well then, I'm sure in debt to both of you men." Evers looked around and nodded at the silent heavy-set colored man who sat across the fo'c'sle.

"I'm da night cook 'n baker," the man informed him.

"Thank you again." Evers glanced at Tommy. "Can I see you a second outside?"

"Evers," Stacey spoke in the same weak dry voice.

"Yes, Kid?" The AB turned his attention back to the ordinary.

"Carter never told me it was the chief killed Whitey. I just figured it had to be... Be careful though. I'm pretty sure he just seen the man murdered, but he might've had a hand in it."

"Aye, I'll watch out. You better try gettin' some sleep now. Don't worry, we'll have everything under control."

"It was Kruzic who killed pumps as well—I'm sure of it. Whitey and the chief, they were the company goons on the *Jackson Heights.*"

"Okay, just lie back and don't worry none now."

"If I don't make it...."

"You're gonna be swell!"

"Yah...but if I don't...you *got* to tell Bull Hendricks and Blackey in the New York hall... Okay?"

"You'll tell 'em, Kid."

"Okay... But if I don't?"

"I'll tell 'em. Now go to sleep, Kid."

"Thanks...be careful." Stacey relaxed and closed his eyes.

Evers looked at the messman as he walked to the door. Tommy got up and followed him out.

"Yes, Mr. Evers?" the messman asked when they were both in the passageway and the door closed.

"Is the Kid dyin'?"

"No, no Sir, he jus' loss a lotta blood. He's weak as hell and Sam, that's the chief cook, jus' give him a shot."

"Well, he sure got a bunch of fine friends. Thank you, Tommy. Listen, we need a gun real bad. You any idea who might have one?"

"No, Sir, I sure don't."

"I'm not a 'Sir,' Tommy. My name's Evers. You think the Kid might have one? I know he's had trouble aboard. I didn't want to ask him—but we need it bad if he or you or anyone has one."

"I ain't and I know the Kid don't neither—not that he wouldn't be betta off with one."

"Okay, thanks, Tommy. But if you think of anyone who's got

one, tell him I need it bad. Someone's got to take this bastard out, and soon! You feel what this ship's ridin' like?"

"I'll ask all the color'd for you, Mr. Evers. That's what you means, don't you?"

"Yes—let 'em know that no one's goin' to say a thing. Let 'em give it to you if they like."

"Aye, Sir."

"Thanks for everything, Tommy—stick close to him." Evers headed down the passageway. He was looking for Hansen.

—TWENTY-SEVEN—

Carl Finney telephoned the wheelhouse before going up. He realized the possibility of being shot was high enough as it was. To come up through the inside companionway, without first calling Kruzic, might make it a certainty.

"Yes, who is this?" Kruzic spoke in a clipped voice.

"Mr. Finney."

"Yes?"

"I'm coming up on watch; I have a first aid kit with me."

"No! Take *nothing* with you."

"Chief, there's a wounded man up there. Mr. Searles can't stay on the wheel indefinitely, and we're in for it if we don't come about immediately!" He tried to keep any hint of emotion out of his voice. "We'll need Captain Wilder to help out."

"We're not turning around. When the watch comes forward there'll be all the help we need."

"Mr. Kruzic," Finney decided to gamble, "no one's going on watch unless ordered by the captain."

"I give the orders now!"

"If you're planning to head for South America, Cuba, or anywhere else you're going to want someone up there to navigate."

"I know where we are; don't fool with me. I'll kill Wilder, Searles, and *you* if I have to!" Kruzic tried to sound as confident as he could, but realized he would indeed be in trouble without a deck officer.

Finney knew Kruzic was unaware of where he was calling from. "Chief, my only concern is seeing the ship make it in one piece. Let me come forward and I'll take her wherever you wish.

And I'll guarantee you'll be able to leave her safely and unopposed as soon as we're clear of this storm."

"I see... even a guarantee. You think I'm *that* easy to fool, eh?"

"No, Chief. It's too late for games—can't you see how bad it's getting? You can study the charts and choose anywhere close enough to launch the motor lifeboat for you—a place the ship can't follow to threaten your getting away clean."

"Very interesting, Mr. Finney. Since you sound ready to co-operate I will allow your request. You can come up with the medical kit, but I *warn* you, one false move and I won't hesitate to kill everyone."

"No tricks, Mr. Kruzic. I don't know what brought all this on—but what's done is done. My job is to bring this ship and crew to port safely. Since landing you somewhere aids that purpose, I've given you my word to do so."

"I intend to search you!"

"That's fine."

"The watch will follow you *one* at a time."

"As soon as the captain calls back aft the 4 to 8 will turn to and you can tell them yourself how to come forward—so there'll be no misunderstandings." Mr. Finney was beginning to understand that Kruzic could be flattered—must be flattered—if they were to get anywhere.

"Bring me the two bottles of bourbon from my office and some dry clothing... And my heavy jacket!"

"Aye, Chief. Right away!" Finney let his breath out as he hung up the phone. The engineer was an animal, but he liked himself, if no one else, and wanted to be warm and safe and alive. True, he'd destroy himself and everyone else around him if he had to, but *only* if he had to. That was the *weak* spot—<u>the one he must work on</u>.

By the time the mate made it back and forth from the after house, it was almost 4:15. Crossing the catwalk was nearly impossible; the wind screamed and buffeted at him, almost flinging him off the grates. Massive storm swells loomed ghostly against the grey-black sky as they sped towards the *Concordia*. When they crested, they formed enormous towering mountains of water which seemed certain to engulf the ship. The wind tore the tops of the swells into long drawn-out, heavy grey-white shrouds of spume that arched up over the ponderous masses of water and blew horizontally across the weather side with staggering force.

It seemed to Finney that he would actually drown if he made the mistake of trying to breathe with his face to windward. Despite the rain gear, he was soaked through by the time he gained the lee of the midship house. Though anxious to get up to the wheelhouse, he first went to his own quarters to change his gear. He had managed to bring the items that Kruzic requested, bundled in a piece of heavy plastic drop-cloth and tied securely.

Dressed in dry clothing, his own rain gear under his arm, the mate returned to the captain's office for the first aid kit. Then, steeling himself to enter the dead man's room, he took a bottle of scotch from Layton's locker in case Wilder needed a drink.

"That's right, Mr. Finney. Turn around and lean over the settee." Kruzic reached out with his left hand and ran it slowly over the mate's arched body. He stepped back, satisfied that he had nothing concealed. "Nice and easy now—open that and put everything on the settee. Be careful not to break the bottles!"

"There's a bottle of scotch as well, Chief." Finney tried to speak as calmly as he could. "Where's Captain Wilder?"

"I'll take that here. I said sit down on the settee!" Kruzic grasped the half-full bottle of bourbon from the mate and put it in the rack over the chart table. Now he held out his hand for the other two bottles.

"Chief," Finney held them out as directed, "where's Captain Wilder?" He looked at the drying pool of blood on the deck and then at the closed door to the wheelhouse.

"There is no Captain Wilder. *There never was a Captain Wilder!*"

"The mate then. Please let me see Mr. Wilder."

"Mr. Wilder is *no longer* with us." The engineer looked straight into Carl Finney's eyes as he spoke.

The seated man gripped the edge of the settee to keep from losing control and leaping at the madman who stood before him. He suddenly felt physically sick when he realized that he had been so easily tricked by Kruzic; the engineer's wild eyes and broken grin meant Wilder was already dead while he had been pleading and reasoning with the bastard to let him bring the first aid kit.

"I buried him at sea, and I promise I'll do as much for you and Mr. Searles if you give me the least provocation."

Finney's head felt light. He sat there in a daze. What could he possibly say? *What?* The word drummed over and over inside his head. What? WHAT? *WHAT??*

"And now *you* can play captain, Mr. Finney," continued the chief, "and your first orders will be for the watch to come forward—one man to the wheel, lookout on the weather wing, and the standby back aft."

Carl Finney pulled himself together. It took all the willpower he could muster to compose his face and answer without emotion. "Okay, Chief." He rose as steadily as he could and stood facing the wheelhouse door. "I'll call now."

Kruzic closely followed the mate's movements. His eyes never shifting as he kept the revolver aimed at the man's midsection. "Hook the door open and move very slowly, Mr. Finney. Talk loud—I'll be listening!"

"Yes, Chief. The lookout won't be worth much on the weather wing, Chief. It'll be blowing a full gale soon—we've got to turn north and run for it!"

"Don't exceed your authority, *Captain*. I'll do the decision-making!"

"Very well, Sir." Finney swallowed hard at the sound of the word. He knew he had only one chance to save the ship, and he would force himself to say "Sir" to the Devil himself if it would help him do so. "After I call the watch I'd like to show you a plot of the *Concordia's* course and one of the storm's so you've all information available on which to base your decision." Mr. Finney opened the door and hooked it back as he left the chartroom. Out of the corner of his eye he watched Kruzic take his first drink from the bottle of bourbon.

The engineer crossed the chartroom to the settee. He was weary of holding onto things and balancing against the wild gyrations of the vessel. He was also cold, his clothes were not dry even though he had put the heat on in the room. He sat down, listening to Finney on the phone as he undressed.

Carl Finney glanced at Mike Searles while he made the call. The second mate was grimacing at him... Trying to tell him something.

Searles, his head turned just slightly, whispered in the mate's direction. He knew the chief engineer was watching his back from the settee in the chartroom, so he was careful to keep his position at the wheel as normal as possible as he formed the words.

The chief mate strained to catch what the man seemed so desperate to tell him.

"Murdered—*strangled poor Wilder with his own belt*—threw him over!"

Carl Finney almost retched up his mid-day meal.

—TWENTY-EIGHT—

"I fuckin' well knew it! Nothin'—not when you need one!" O'Malley gripped the table and tried to stand up as he talked with Evers and Hansen.

The two ABs sat on the opposite side of the table.

"Just finding a gun isn't gonna be our only problem," observed Evers. "It's gettin' close enough to 'im to use it—or anything else we find."

"Ve got to come up vit something soon b'for dat sonavabitch sails her under!"

Just then, Ned Carter came into the messroom, making his way towards the coffee urn.

"Hi, Boats." The oiler nodded in the direction of the three men.

Evers decided to confront the man right then. "Carter, I want to talk to you."

The oiler was halfway between the urn and the table. "One minute," he answered continuing into the galley for a clean mug. He came back out, balanced himself and poured a cup. "You want *me*?" he asked looking at the big AB.

"You were with the Kid when he called Kruzic."

"That's right. The first told me to go with him to prove the chief was called." Carter had to speak in a loud voice to be heard over the clatter and banging coming from the galley and the ship's vibrations.

"He might not have been shot if you'd stayed with him."

"Wait a minute now! I was there when he called him. I took off right after to call the watch." Carter looked around uneasily at the several other crew members sitting in the messroom.

"That's just it. You sure as hell took off fast. Did you figure something was gonna happen?"

"Fuck no! How in hell did I know he'd start shooting?"

"You damn well knew he'd already *killed* one man—didn't you?" Evers lifted himself slowly off the bench and leaned forward grabbing the edge of the table.

Carter pushed back further against the bulkhead; he didn't answer.

"Come on, man—OUT WITH IT! YOU SEEN 'IM KILL

THE WIPER!" The big AB stepped back from the table and started around towards the shaken oiler. "AND IF YOU'D TOLD THE OLD MAN NONE OF THIS WOULDA HAPPENED!"

Carter involuntarily threw his hands up in front of his face as the big AB stepped towards him—the coffee mug flew from his hands and shattered on the deck. *"OKAY!* Okay... Wait a minute, will ya?"

"I'm wantin' the truth, man, NOW!" Evers stood where he was, balancing against the ship's violent motion.

"Okay then... I wasn't sure. That's the God's truth. You see— when I got here the lights was out—then for a split-second a flashlight come on and I thought I saw the chief engineer and someone else...over there." Carter pointed across the room. "Their heads was together like. Then it was pitch dark again and I hear this thump and someone breathing hard. I didn't know what was goin' on. So help me! I just stood there at the top of the steps, in the dark—suddenly I hear a watertight door slam and a second later the lights come on blinding me some—but I see there's only this one guy, the wiper, laying up in the corner with blood all over his face."

"Then what?" Evers had stepped back and was standing next to his place at the table.

"Nothin'... I just took off."

"Why didn't you say something at the meetin'?"

"How could I?" Carter had regained his confidence. "If ya want to know the truth, I figured *you* was in on it."

The big AB nodded his head.

"You see," the oiler went on, "I knew Kruzic didn't throw the guy over the side—he was back in the main engine room when I come in from checking the steering engine. And he never left again till after we took departure. I was dead sure that you or whoever it was I heard comin' aft had helped him get rid of the guy."

The big AB had slowly sat down as the oiler finished explaining. "Okay, Carter... Makes good sense. None of it's your fault— it's all mine—mine for lyin' to the Old Man in the first place."

"I'm sorry about the Kid...I really am. See I figured maybe *he* was in on it, too!"

"Well, I've caused one hell of a mess!" Evers addressed everyone in the room. "I should've told the Old Man and took my chances."

Except for the sounds from the galley and the howl of the wind outside the opened door to the fantail, the messroom remained quiet, everyone looking at the obviously shaken man.

"Okay!" O'Malley broke the silence. "All that's by the board now. We've got to figure a way of getting Kruzic before he takes us all down to the 'locker' with 'im!"

Mr. Pillars, the second assistant engineer, Davis, the third assistant engineer, the chief pumpman and the machinist all came in from the galley.

"We've got a couple of bad leaks in the after pump room," Pillars announced to the assembled men.

"Want us?" Schmidt asked. He and Billet, the other wiper, were sitting together at the forward table.

"Yes, get your sea boots. We've got to clear the suction screens in the bilges, and rig the portable air pump."

"Must be them two wood plugs we put in last month startin' to work loose," said Billet.

"Let's hope it's only that." Pumps had gone over to the coffee urn and was balancing there trying to draw a cup.

Billet and Schmidt got up from the table and staggered past the chief pumpman on their way out. The messroom deck was fouled with water and milk from fallen cartons seeping out of the refrigerator. Soggy paperback books, swollen to twice their original size, littered the deck along with broken pieces of glass and crockery. Spilled sugar and coffee added to the mess, and the whole room had a foul, fetid stench about it.

No one was asleep. Every man not on watch had come into the crew's mess to find out what was happening. The weather was deteriorating rapidly. It was clear to everyone that the ship was in danger of breaking up if someone didn't come up with a plan to get her out of the hands of the maniac who held the bridge.

Plan after plan was proposed—everything from storming the bridge *en masse* to threatening Kruzic with stopping the ship dead in the water if he refused to come about. None of the suggestions merited the least amount of support, even from those who offered them. It was an impossible situation they faced, officers and crew alike. Nothing concrete or workable seemed to come to the fore. It seemed insane. A crazy man had killed and wounded a half-dozen men in a matter of minutes, and was now forcing his will on the rest of the crew while he drove the *Concordia* headlong into a hurricane.

—TWENTY-NINE—

Mike Searles was exhausted—it had been a long time since he'd taken a full wheel watch—and he had never steered in a sea like this. It was Howard, one of the 4 to 8 ABs, who now struggled to hold the ship on course and keep her from falling off into the cavernous troughs, while Searles kept watch at the radar and by looking out the salt-fouled portholes.

Carl Finney was in the chartroom working up the *Concordia's* position. The Loran and radio direction finder were both out. Allowing for the effects of wind and current, he did as best as he could by dead reckoning. So far, the mate had been unable to get the engineer to change course more than twenty degrees—they were now steering 80. He pleaded with Kruzic to come about to the northwest, allowing them to increase speed and get out of the storm's path.

The *Concordia* could barely maintain her course against the combined assault of wind and sea. Every time they tried to bring up her rpms, vibrations, like the death rattle of some enormous living thing, resounded through the deck plates. The tanker rose and fell four times a minute as the tremendously long twenty-foot high storm swells heaved up under her. She rolled up over them, angling first one way and then the other as the monsters raced away to the west.

Slack had developed in the port anchor cable allowing the hook to swing away on every roll to starboard and it slammed back like a gigantic bell clapper against the port bow plates as the ship reversed her direction. It was like the tolling of some great doomsday bell, sounding hollowly throughout the ship precisely once every fifteen seconds. On the bridge, it was as nerve-wracking to wait for it as it was to hear it.

The constant pounding and twisting of the ship's hull resulted in more than audible phenomena whose eerie sounds vibrated and rattled up into the superstructure; it also provided stresses to the "living" steel which could only be tolerated so long before the plates—thinned by years of rusting and punished by other storms—began to lose their resilience and harden into a dead and brittle crystalline state that must soon fail.

The forward portion of the ship's hull took the brunt of the attack, and the action below deck in the bows was the most pronounced. The anchor cables that hung down in the chain lockers slammed from side to side against the steel walls of the box-like shafts where the jumbled masses of links filled the bottom with ponderous weight. The pounding had finally broken away the cement and burlap seals from the brass plates that covered the openings below the anchor windlass. And now, each crashing sea added its measure to flood the chain lockers. These lockers were not in themselves completely watertight and they leaked water out onto the decks through which they passed. Slowly at first, and then with ever increasing volume they released more and more of their contents—adding weight to the bow. Not all the water reached the bottom to drain back into the bilges. Much of it remained to flood into rope and paint lockers.

In the paint lockers, it mixed with the contents of dozens of stove-in five gallon pails, broken loose and tumbling back and forth across the deck in a chaos of splattered colors. In the end there was only sluggish movement as jumbled cans and paint and water wedged themselves into a near-solid mass. In the flooded rope lockers, once neatly flaked out lines and coils of rope were twisted into a hopeless paint-fouled maze in the spill over from the adjacent paint lockers.

Midships, in the shelter deck, a similar mess developed. The recently cleaned and sorted bosun's locker was a shambles. Butterworth nozzles and hoses were all over the deck. The almost full barrels of Diesel oil—though covered and still lashed—had lost most of their contents—the pitching and rolling so intense that most of the oil had found its way out of the gaps in the less-than-perfect wooden lids that covered them. Well secured tools and equipment had broken loose under the constant buffeting and were now awash on the oil fouled deck along with overturned buckets of bolts and nuts, and all the rags and sawdust from their smashed containers.

In the shelter deck main area, first one cargo transfer hose, then another, broke its lashings and jumped from the steel cradles. Soon all of them were on the deck sluggishly rolling in long arcs on the rims of their steel flanges. Even moving slowly, their heavy thirty foot lengths acted as battering rams and soon pounded both pilot ladders, sailing board, wooden steps, and other lighter gear into rubbish. Dozens of burlap sacks filled with anti oil-spill compound had been torn open and the powdery white absorbent material was all over everything. In like manner, stacks of 100 pound bags of black sand, used for sandblasting, had tumbled off their pallets and many of them had broken open adding their contents to the foul mess.

—THIRTY—

Kruzic sat on the settee watching the mate as he stood hunched over the chart table. He was dressed in dry clothing and comfortable except for being hungry.

"Chief." Mr. Finney turned towards Kruzic. "Here's where I figure we're at." He pointed at the position he'd just marked on the big sailing chart and then pulled a small chart out from under the pile and spread it out on top. "And here's a plot of the storm's course through noon today."

"Stand aside, *Mr. Captain!*" Kruzic waved the revolver in Finney's face as he stood up.

"Sir..." Mr. Finney cleared his throat as he stepped away from the chart table, "I'd better go check the glass."

"Forget that! Stay where I can see you!"

"Chief... I've the wind and standard compass to check as well; if I don't, I can't navigate."

"I don't intend to have to search you every time you leave here, Mister!"

"Very well, Sir. Can Searles go?"

"Just you shut your mouth. Sit down there!" Kruzic pointed to the settee.

The engineer moved to the side of the table and looked at the work-up. "We can turn south to the Yucatan Channel and be in the lee of Cuba." He looked back at Finney.

"No, no Sir, our best bet is to come about to the northwest."

"Why... Why are you so anxious to go north?" Kruzic waved the automatic in Finney's direction. *"WHY?"*

"Not north, Sir... Northwest. We've got to keep her from falling into these troughs—as it is we're taking these seas less than two points on the starboard bow and we can hardly hold her."

"We go south!"

Finney tried his best to sound friendly. "Sir, if we head south the sea is on our beam—she could broach! If we come about to the northwest we'll have the sea on our stern, heading away from this blow, not into it."

"No turning back—we go south—with or without you, *Mr. Captain!*" Kruzic pointed the gun at the mate.

"Yes, Sir... South it'll be then... But we're going into a hurricane."

Kruzic stabbed the chart with his finger. "We'll be in the lee of Cabo San Antonio if we turn south now!"

"Chief, if the storm's where I think it is, and if it's following that curve, we'll never outrun it."

"If! If... Too many *ifs*." Kruzic grasped the bourbon from the rack and drank from the bottle. Putting it back, he upended the almost empty water pitcher and drained it.

Finney took the opportunity to change the subject. "Should I send someone for water?"

"Is there ice in the officer's lounge?"

"Yes, Sir."

"Go yourself, Mr. Captain! And bring back any food you find!"

"Sir, can I check the compass and the barometer at the same time?"

"Yes, yes, check everything. And when you come back, knock on the lee door so I can check *you!*"

"Very good, Chief." Finney held out his hand for the empty pitcher.

The winds were gusting to gale force as Carl Finney took his turn around the house. The heavy squall they were passing through made it so dark he had to use his flashlight to read the barometer. He recorded it at 28.05—down again.

Twenty foot high grey-black storm swells marched away to the west in straight undaunted ranks, seeming to ignore the *Concordia* as she twisted and plunged over their unbroken backs. One moment great sweeping crescents of white wind-torn spume arched high over the ship's superstructure, the next, solid green seas buried her well decks.

The mate braced himself at the sink in the midship deck officer's lounge. The place was a wreck! All the comfortable wood and fabric chairs were splintered. The bottom half of the newly covered long settee was still secured to the wooden platform below it, but the top half had torn loose and lay in the middle of the room, a chair leg sticking through it. Parts of their jointly owned Zenith Transoceanic Radio were all over the deck, as were books, magazines, ashtrays, broken cups and the remains of several cases of bottled soda that had tumbled out of the big storage cabinet. The deck was tacky from the contents of smashed bottles. Suitcases, some of them containing seldom used articles of clothing, were scattered about as well. They had been stored in the small closet on the port bulkhead. Now their contents were strewn around the room.

What in the hell can I do? Finney put the pitcher down in the bottom of the sink and braced himself. He opened the refrigerator; there was no food in it. It served mainly to keep beer and soda cold and as a source of ice for the midship house. He pulled out both ice trays—then thinking better about it put one back and emptied the other into the pitcher. There was no sense using all the ice since there was no way to put any more up; the water would just bounce out of the tray. "I'm sure Kruzic will want more before the day is over," he thought bitterly, "and a nice juicy steak for supper— That's it! *Supper!!* The bastard will sure as hell be asking for food to be brought forward!"

He filled the pitcher with water and started up to the captain's office. The chances of the engineer leaving the bridge were slim and he was lucky Kruzic kept the chartroom door locked on the upper landing. If he was careful not to make any noise, he could use the office to call aft without being overheard.

The rest of the plan came to him as he cranked the telephone handle.

Before Mr. Finney made it back to the wheelhouse, Kruzic ordered Searles to change course to due south and for the ship's speed to be increased to 68 revolutions. For the next few minutes both the *Concordia* and her crew suffered a plate-bending and bone-shocking ride that did more damage than was immediately apparent. The increased speed set the vessel's hull to vibrating as if a billion tiny sledge hammers were beating against the steel, killing it by crystallization. The change of course brought the storm swells in almost directly on the tanker's beam. The sea, no longer pushed aside by the bows, rode up over the decks and superstructure exerting tremendous punishing forces, first as it piled aboard when the ship went into the troughs and then again as it poured off when the *Concordia* strove mightily up over the crests.

"*SOMETHING'S LET GO, MATE!*" Davila banged on the wheelhouse door.

"WHAT IS THAT?" Kruzic's voice came from the chartroom.

"The lookout's at the starboard door. Can I open it?" called

Searles.

"Not till I'm there!" Kruzic flicked the switch and the lights came on as he entered the wheelhouse. "Open it!" He leveled the gun at the officer.

The AB stood swaying in the open doorway, water pouring off his oilskins. "Port boom's broke loose! There, you can hear it now!"

"Yes!" Searles did hear the sound of steel smashing against steel. "Can I put on the floodlights, Sir?"

"Go ahead. Tell the lookout to get back to his post!" Kruzic stepped past the AB on the wheel and crossed the deck to stand in front of the midship porthole.

The door to the starboard wing was secured and the lights from the foremast flooded the forward well deck. But they revealed little in the black driving rain squall.

"Should I shut off the lights in the wheelhouse, Chief?"

"Yes... Yes!"

Searles held on to the radar console for a moment till the ship eased in her upward roll to starboard. When it began to roll back down, he let go and moved towards the after bulkhead, grimacing to Mr. Finney as he reached into the chartroom to flick off the wheelhouse light switch.

The ship's pounding had either worked the securing lock-pin, which held the boom collared in its cradle, loose, or the collar may have broken off at the hinge. The boom itself was twisted at a crazy angle, bent from beating against the fore deck. The heavy boom had flattened the steel rails which encircled the after part of the fo'c'slehead, the ventilators, and a portion of railing on the forward catwalk. It had slammed into the starboard boom and cradle, as well as the ladder leading up on the port side from the well deck to the fo'c'slehead.

Even as Searles watched, the boom swung up again and smashed downwards in a broad arc against the already badly shattered catwalk. The rest of the beating the vessel had been taking was not really apparent, but the force of the sea had carried away over half of the steel gratings from the catwalk. Searles could see that the long shaft of the winch on the port side was bent. "Actually bent," he thought to himself. The drum at the end was twisted back at a twenty degree angle. As his eyes focused on the scene, he realized that many of the cargo transfer lines themselves had broken and were now offset to starboard.

"Are you finished with your survey?"

"She's taking a hell of a beating, Chief." Searles put the binoculars back in their box and crossed back to the chartroom door. He flicked off the deck floodlights and watched as Kruzic turned away from the porthole. The engineer made his way back into the chartroom closing the door behind him as he turned off the lights.

"Goddam nut!" Bob Howard, the AB, whispered as Searles stepped past him to take up his position at the starboard porthole.

"He's holding all the cards," the officer whispered back.

"The bastard's got to eat, shit, and sleep sometime, don't he?" The AB kept his voice barely audible.

"Maybe the liquor will put him under; let's hope so!" The new second mate shook his head wearily.

The *Concordia* reared up over a bigger than usual swell and crashed over the crest, burying her fo'c'slehead in solid sea. The wheelhouse jumped as if it had suddenly sprung free from the deck. The shock tore Howard's grip off the wheel and he smashed backwards against the after bulkhead.

The second mate was hurled to the deck and he grabbed at the closest hand-hold to avoid being tossed across the room. The binocular box which he grasped tore away from the bulkhead and the glasses flew across the wheelhouse smashing against the starboard bulkhead. Searles ended up against the door leading out to the starboard wing of the bridge. By the time Howard managed to grab the wheel, a sound like a tremendous clap of thunder reverberated through the wheelhouse and a sudden shuddering impact rocked the bridge. A scream came from somewhere outside.

"HOLY MOTHER OF GOD!" Searles yelled out as he struggled to get to his feet. "Bring her back—*HARD LEFT!!*" he yelled to the quartermaster.

The chartroom door burst open and Kruzic stood there gun in hand, braced in the door frame. "WHAT'S GOING ON HERE?" he screamed as he turned on the lights.

Howard had already recovered his position. He kept his eyes glued on the compass as he held the wheel hard left to bring the *Concordia* back to where she could live. He felt the hair on the back of his neck stand up as he sensed the rage in the lunatic behind him.

"Something hit the bridge, Sir! I've had to bring her back around. I'll go out and see, Sir." Searles prayed that Kruzic didn't challenge the course change.

The engineer, shaken himself by the violent plunge, cursed loudly but didn't rescind the change of course. He turned back into the chartroom, slamming the door behind him.

The second mate heard Mr. Finney call out from the chartroom to be careful as he unlocked the door and pushed it open. Even though it was the lee side, the wind screamed and tore at him from around the face of the bridge. As he stepped onto the wing he immediately realized what had happened. A section extending some four feet back from the tip of the starboard wing was stove in and twisted upwards. The runaway boom had finally torn loose at the gooseneck securing it to the mast and it had been hurled all the way aft against the starboard wing by the force of the ship's last plunge. The forward booms were seldom used and thus they had no running gear, no topping lifts or guys to hold them. They were only "bare sticks" secured in their cradles by steel collars. It seemed impossible for the boom to have travelled so far, but that was it all right. No sound of its thrashing came to his ears.

The lookout! The scream that Searles heard came back to him. "LOOKOUT! LOOKOUT!!" he yelled against the force of the wind. Grasping the railing that circled the house, the second mate started for the port side where the AB had been stationed. The wind tore savagely against him as he made his way around the bridge into the weather. His coat was almost blown off his back as he struggled to keep his footing and his hand hold on the steel railing. *"LOOKOUT! LOOKOUT!"* he called again as he came up parallel to the door on the port wing. There was no one on the wing—there was no lookout. It was Pedro Davila's scream he had heard as the boom smashed into the bridge. The AB couldn't stand it on the weather wing any longer and had crossed over to stand his watch on the starboard side. It had been bad enough out there on the lee side; the weather side had been impossible. The lookout had been hit by the runaway boom and carried overboard with it. This voyage of the *Concordia* had been the last trip for still another man.

—THIRTY-ONE—

The same plunge into the sea that ripped the port boom from its gooseneck had taken its toll back aft as well. The after well deck had shipped a tremendous solid river of water whose ponderous weight rose up under the catwalk with enormous force as the ship lunged back up out of the trough. Some sections of the steel gratings were bent and bowed upwards, though none had as yet been torn completely away as on the foredeck. And several of the steam and water lines running under them were broken and twisted.

"GOOD CHRIST!" O'Malley yelled as the ship pitched down into what felt like a bottomless pit. Men who were standing around the messroom braced against the tables, benches, and bulkheads, were bowled over like so many tenpins. Even those who were seated fared only slightly better. Men tumbled over each other and were slammed up against the steel bulkhead. The aftermost table wasn't able to withstand the weight of Hansen, O'Malley, Evers, and the others who tried to hold themselves to their benches by grasping it. The top broke free from the steel stanchion closest to the door and it swiveled around flinging everyone to the deck in a bruised and cursing tangle.

The big coffee urn was torn free from the steel table. Carter and another man had been bracing themselves close by and reached out instinctively to grab onto anything as the ship dropped. They had both grasped hold of the urn itself and were flung to the deck along with it and its contents. Fortunately it was almost empty and only a few men were slightly splattered with hot coffee. The broken steam line was more of a danger. It spewed live steam into the room adding to the chaos.

The destruction in the galley, which already had been considerable, was now complete. Food in preparation for the evening meal jumped the retaining racks and was strewn all over the deck. Two large clean garbage pails, used to store peeled potatoes and flour, broke loose from their lashings and added their contents to the mess. Besides the food, the deck was littered with silverware, broken dishes, pots and pans, knives, cleavers, and stove lids.

Samuel Diamond, the chief cook, was the only man seriously burned. He had been trying—against the steward's advice—to prepare a warm beef stew for the crew. Diamond was the only one next to the big iron cauldron when it was wrenched loose from the retainers, spilling out over the stove. A wave of hot stew caught him chest high and poured over him. His screams were lost in the general bedlam.

As the men in the galley and messroom tried to sort themselves out and get to their feet, a new sound of heavy runaway steel shuddered through the deck above them. The ship rolled up to port as she staggered out of the watery crevasse, then, as she sunk back down to an even keel before beginning her opposite roll—all was suddenly silent—save for the stuttering wail of her vibrations. But as the angle of her tilt up to starboard increased, another thunderous booming shock of impacting heavy steel echoed through the galley and the messroom.

Reed was the first man to notice the mixture of acid and water pouring down through the deck above. He had been caught working in the galley's thwartship passageway which connected the crew messroom and the officer's saloon.

"HEY!" he shouted as he pointed into the officer's saloon. *"Look at da overhead!"*

Streams of whitish fluid were spurting from the panelling as if a sprinkler system had been activated. The thin white painted metal rectangles were sagging down in several places, and the larger flows were coming from these areas.

The noises from the deck above increased, and by the time the ship had attained her full thirty-five degree roll up to starboard, the sound and shock thundered wildly throughout the entire after house.

O'Malley figured out what had happened. He threw his back up against the after bulkhead and grasped the phone. He cranked savagely.

"Bridge?" came Searles' voice after an exasperating delay—a delay due to Kruzic's instructions that no one make or receive a call till cleared with him.

"This is the bosun. The after house is a mess and I think we've got real trouble. Sounds like everything's come loose in the pipe-room!"

"THE WHAT?" The second mate couldn't hear over the tremendous noise.

"THE PIPE-ROOM!" O'Malley shouted. "I'M GOING UP TO CHECK! THEM DRUMS OF ACID ARE COMIN' THROUGH THE OVERHEAD!"

"OKAY, O'MALLEY, DO WHAT YOU CAN! GET HELP FROM THE BLACK GANG!"

"WHY AIN'T WE HOVE-TO, SIR?" O'Malley realized he shouldn't have said it. He knew very well what the mates were contending with up on the bridge.

Searles couldn't mention that they had indeed started to come about—not with Kruzic listening. "WE LOST DAVILA—THE

PORT BOOM CARRIED AWAY AND HIT THE WING WITH
HIM ON IT!"

"GOOD FUCKIN' CHRIST!" O'Malley stood there holding
onto the phone with one hand and gripping the dog on the porthole
next to him with the other. He felt completely drained.

The tanker's roll had eased somewhat as her bows were
headed up into the sea. The men grouped around O'Malley all
found places to stand and sit. All strained to hear the two-way
conversation.

"BOATS!"

"YES, SIR."

"THE CHIEF SAID TO HOLD OFF SENDING ANOTHER
LOOKOUT UP TILL YOU SEND FOOD FORWARD WITH
DOOLEY—AND THE RELIEF FOR THE WHEEL!"

O'Malley started to answer, but the big AB shook his head
violently till the bosun took his finger off the talk button.

Then Evers spoke rapidly. "Not Dooley! Tell him Dooley bust
his leg and a few other men in the galley's been hurt bad. Tommy
can bring it up. He's the strongest and best able to cross the
catwalk—what's left of it!"

"Sir, Dooley's broke a leg and the whole steward's department's
cut and burned. Maybe the crew messman can make it across the
catwalk, that's if there's anythin' left to eat." O'Malley had been
able to talk in less than a scream for a few moments, now the
roaring sound of steel against steel began to come again from
above. "OKAY, I'M GOIN' TO SEE WHAT I CAN DO!"

"BOATS, THE CHIEF WANTS FOOD HERE—*NOW!* LET
THEM BRING AS MUCH AS THEY CAN, EVEN IF ONLY
CANS AND BREAD. NO ONE'S GETTING RELIEVED FOR
SUPPER!"

"AYE, MATE. I UNDERSTAND. I'LL GET TOMMY
STARTED, MAYBE HE'LL MAKE IT WITH HELP." He hung
the phone up. "Sorry, I near forgot." O'Malley turned and nodded
at Evers. "Can you handle it?"

"We'll make it all right. It's got to work!" Evers looked at
Hansen. "Let's get things movin'. Tell Reed to go on down and
take care of the Kid—Tommy's to come right up!"

"Aye," Hansen answered as he started for the companionway.

The ship began another long upward ascent as O'Malley made
it to the door leading out to the fantail. He wore foul-weather gear
and his flashlight was secured to a piece of rope tied around his
waist.

"Hold up!" Junior pushed his way through the knot of men around the door. He helped the bosun open it and followed him out.

"The rest of you stay put awhile!" O'Malley called out as several other crew members started to follow him and Junior out of the room.

The *Concordia* was in the middle of another squall. It was black as night out and the stern light threw an eerie glow up against the misted air. The fantail was lifting as they secured the door behind them. A face battering wind-blown spray tore around the after part of the house from the port side and buffeted them backwards. They got firm hand-holds on the ladder leading up to the boat deck. They made it to the upper rungs just as the tanker's stern reared over a huge crest, her screw slashing vainly through as much air as water.

O'Malley let go of the rail with one hand and flicked on the long powerful, four-cell flashlight.

"Holy shit!" Junior was the first to exclaim.

The boat deck was a shambles. The pipe-room door was blocked by debris and there were steel pipes at crazy angles all over the deck. Those that had not already gone over the side were jammed between the house and the radial davits which held what was left of the port lifeboat between them. Other pipes were bent, twisted, and heaped up against a small portion of deck railing that still remained intact. It was a tangle of tons of steel just ready to break away and carry overboard on the next big plunge.

"MAKE FOR THE LEE SIDE!" O'Malley shouted out over the wind as he reached the top of the ladder. As he started on around, the stern began its downward plunge.

Junior had snapped on his own light as he struggled off the ladder onto the boat deck. The scene of destruction held his attention for a second—a fatal second that turned into eternity as the fantail dropped abruptly into the abyss.

O'Malley was less than ten feet away from the doomed man as the massive clump of twisted steel let go and slammed over the after end of the boat deck. The tangle of pipe crashed onto the fantail below, separating as it fell. Some of the pipes went right on over the side; some of them bounced like giant "pick-up sticks" off the lower deck and then went hurtling overboard. A few pieces wedged themselves between the winch, the bitts, and the hatch leading down to the lazarette.

"JUNIOR! *JUNIOR!!*" O'Malley screamed into the wind.

The dayman had been hit so fast he had no time to cry out. Even if he had, the bosun would never have heard him over the sound of the crashing steel.

O'Malley hung onto the rails, grasping them with both hands, as he stared down onto the fantail. He saw a weak shaft of light suddenly thrown from the opened watertight door below him as several men secured it in the opened position.

"CAREFUL! LOOSE STEEL ON DECK!" he warned. "TURN ON THE LIGHTS!!"

In a few seconds the fantail lights came on. They were weak, but they lit the rain-swept deck well enough for O'Malley to see that there would be no caring for the body of his second dayman— only bent piping glistened back at him.

—THIRTY-TWO—

Below in the engine room spaces, the violent gyrations of the tanker were somewhat less pronounced than up on deck. However, the stresses and strains to the hull could be seen and felt as every steel ladder and floorplate began to rattle and jump and vibrate.

Fidel Solis, the 4 to 8 fireman-watertender, had been adjusting one of the sprayer tips on the port firebox as the ship rolled down over the gigantic swell. He was hurled like a piece of wet burlap against the iron workbench behind him. The corner of the heavy table caught the little Mexican precisely at the base of the skull, all but severing the spinal cord.

"Madre de Dios!" His lips were still forming the last of the silent words as his body pitched forward face-down against the steel floorplates.

In the main engine room, the sudden shock caught Mr. Pierce making entries in the engine room log book. The first assistant was still anxiously awaiting word from the other engineers; he had to know how bad the leaks were in the after pumproom and what progress they were making to stem the encroaching flow of water. The first let go of the big ledger and grasped desperately at the table as the floorplates seemed to suddenly drop away from under him. It was like being in an elevator that had snapped its cable—

a free fall.

Part of the tabletop broke loose from the steel stanchion to which it was secured and the upper part of the engineer's heavy body was whipped around sideways before his legs and feet could follow. He was arched over the tilted tabletop with his head and shoulders turned towards the throttle station and the long, black, dial-studded main engine control panel. By the time the rest of his body started to follow suit, the top broke away completely. It was still in his hands as he was thrown forward to slam up against the panel. He fell to his knees, bruising them painfully against the unyielding steel floorplates, but was otherwise unhurt.

The engineer managed to get to his feet and grasp the handholds next to the throttle as the ship bottomed in the trough. The shock was so powerful he felt his arms extend to their very limits as his body tried to fly upward away from his desperate grip on the steel handles.

The oiler, Dimitrios, had just started down the ladder into shaft alley to check the packing glands and bearing temperatures of the main shaft. The heavy steel watertight hatch which separated shaft alley from the rest of the lower engine room spaces was secured by a locking bolt through two eyes welded to a steel partition. The descending oiler's midsection was almost parallel with the floorplates when the two-and-a-half by three-foot hatch slammed down. The tip of the locking pin had somehow worked its way into the straight position and the sudden plunge of the ship let the pin ride on out of the eyes through which it passed. If he had been one rung lower on the ladder when the hatch dropped, it would have taken his head off at the neck or smashed his skull like an egg.

Dimitrios was lucky. The lip of the hatch caught him on the upper arm and spun him face upwards, his back striking against the sharp hatch coaming. The edge of the hatch itself slammed into his chest, knocking the wind out of him as he hollered out. His left foot had caught between two of the rungs as he was thrown backwards over the coaming and he felt a sharp burning sensation as the wall of his lower stomach ruptured at the groin.

The oiler also felt several of his ribs crack when the hatch lid smashed down; he tried to lift the weight from his chest, but couldn't budge it. He knew he was hurt, but thankful it hadn't been worse. Dimitrios managed to get his hands up on the coaming and braced himself by exerting as much upward force as possible. By doing so, he prevented the heavy weight from crushing him when the ship bottomed in the trough.

"Help!" he called out weakly to the empty space around him. He was about to try again, when—as if in a dream—he saw faces swimming over him.

"GET A WRECKING BAR!" the machinist yelled to Schmidt, then knelt down and grasped the heavy hatch cover. He didn't try to lift it off the stricken man; he just relieved as much of the weight as he could by balancing backwards against it.

The wiper hurried towards the tool storage area in the machine shop and was back in a moment with the bar and a two-foot length of steel pipe.

"Christ! My nuts are tore!" Dimitrios groaned.

"Up we go!" Sterling grunted as Schmidt wedged the end of the heavy bar under the hatch cover. "Good! Hold what we've got!" The ship had reversed her roll and the force of gravity was acting against them.

"Wedge the fucker!" The wiper nodded towards the hinges.

The machinist jammed the short length of pipe in-between the cover and the coaming; the weight was now off the oiler. He reached down and grasped the man's shoulders to pull him out.

"NO! *Don't!* My foot's caught!" The pain in his chest suddenly became knife-like and the oiler gasped as the broken ribs expanded. Talking and being able to breathe more freely with the weight off him allowed the broken ribs to shift and cut into the surrounding muscles.

"Get a half-inch hardened bolt and nut," said Sterling. "We've got to secure it upright."

When Schmidt returned with the bolt, the machinist barred the hatch cover back far enough to pull out the pipe they had wedged between the cover and coaming. They forced the cover up and put the bolt where the locking pin was supposed to be.

"Hold it now." Sterling stepped over the oiler and went down the ladder to release the man's foot while Schmidt helped ease him down to a seated position on one of the rungs.

"Boy, am I happy you guys came along." Dimitrios shivered as he spoke.

"Take hold around my neck as tight as you can." Sterling bent over the seated man. "We got to get you off the ladder." The machinist knew the oiler was going into shock and wanted to get him topside before he blacked out.

It was painful for Dimitrios to raise his arms over his head, but he managed to do so and held fast. Sterling raised up and locked one arm under the injured man's buttocks while he gripped the rail with his free hand. The wiper grabbed hold of Dimitrios' shoulders as they came up parallel to the top of the ladder and helped take a part of the weight off the machinist.

"Here—can you balance on your good leg a second?" Sterling asked as he made it up onto the floorplates.

The oiler nodded and stood as well as he could on both legs, supported from behind by Schmidt. "My legs are okay. I tore something in my balls and my ribs are busted." He took only shallow breaths to minimize the searing pain in his chest.

"Should I get the stretcher?" asked Schmidt.

"I can walk up better," Dimitrios said.

"Okay, then let's try it." The machinist put his left arm around the oiler's waist, and Schmidt let go and circled around behind. The passageway was too narrow for three to walk abreast. Getting up the ladders was a slow and painful trip for Dimitrios and they had to adjust their progress to coincide with the ship's motion.

The oiler was secured in his bunk much as Stacey had been lashed into his. Sterling wrapped several long strips of sheet around the man's chest to prevent him from dislodging the broken ribs as he breathed.

"Your nuts are okay," Sterling reassured the stricken man. "You got a hernia; a rupture—that's all. They can tuck you in and sew it up easy."

"Should I stay with him?" asked Schmidt. He put a second blanket on top of the injured man.

"Yeah, I'll head back and let the first know where you are." The machinist headed for the door. "You'll be fine, Dimitrios. Don't worry about anything."

"Thanks, but who's gonna stand my watch?"

"I just said don't worry about anything!"

"Wait!" Dimitrios looked at Schmidt. "I'm okay for now, you better go on. The first will probably have Solis cover for me, and he'll need you in the fireroom."

"You sure?" Sterling asked.

"Yah, I feel okay right now."

"Okay," the wiper nodded, straightening up. "I got you tied in pretty good. I'll tell Reed and Tommy to look in on you. They been watching the ordinary what got shot."

Sterling and Schmidt had left the after pumproom to report to the first just before the tanker plunged over the damaging crest. The portable air-driven pump had been working well and, along with the less-healthy main steam pump, they were finally gaining on the leaks. They had been starting down the alleyway from the steering engine room when they had heard Dimitrios groaning for help.

Now, some ten minutes later, both retraced their steps past the hatch to shaft alley where the oiler had nearly been killed. The ship was still pitching and rolling in the storm-tossed seas, but not with the murderous abandon she displayed before her suicidal course had been changed.

"Paco?" Sterling was the first to recognize the 12 to 4 fireman-watertender as he and Schmidt entered the fireroom. "Holy Christ!" he stared past Paco at the sprawled body of the dead Solis. *"What happened?"*

"First assistant found him after we hit that big swell."

"Is he dead?" the wiper asked as he came up closer.

"Must've broken his neck," Paco continued, "probably went out like a light... No one's seen the oiler."

"Dimitrios? We just brought him topside; busted a few ribs. Where's the first?" Sterling asked.

"At the throttle. He's okay; Carter turned to with me."

"And that fuckin' Kruzic?" asked Schmidt.

"Still holding the winning hand." Paco shook his head in resignation as he glanced up at the water gages.

"Let's go!" Sterling looked again at the small dead man who lay off to the side of the steel work bench. "Poor bastard!" He started up the ladder into the main engine room with the wiper right behind him.

The dead man seemed to be trying alternately to stretch out as the ship rolled down to starboard, or get back up on his legs as the roll was reversed; the body arched upward because Paco had lashed the feet to the bottom of the steel bench.

Mr. Pierce had already put the entire black gang on emergency status. There was no longer a "watch below"—the same conditions prevailed in the deck and steward's departments.

The after pumproom was filling with water again. The big steam-driven bilge pump had dropped back down to less than fifty percent efficiency, and the small air-driven pump was damaged when it broke loose and fell through the opened floorplates. It came to a stop inches from Johnson, the second pumpman, and

Billet, the other wiper, when the big swell hit; both were knocked off their feet and submerged in the flooded bilges. Aside from that and a few other bruises suffered by the chief pumpman and the third assistant, all four men had survived the sudden plunge to the bottom of the trough in surprisingly good shape. They were now ready to kick over the auxiliary steam pump and to start repairing the main and the portable.

*　　　*　　　*

O'Malley and several men were still trying to secure what they could up in the pipe-room which was awash in acid and water. All ten of the 55 gallon drums of deck-cleaning acid had broken away and poured out their contents as they were stove-in and punctured by the heavy steel valves and pipes wreaking havoc in the large enclosure.

When the tanker reached the top of her roll, the acid-water mix was over two feet deep at the low end. Men, dressed in sea boots and oilskins, worked in a series of hit and run sorties. Securing long heavy lengths of pipe and huge gate valves—some weighing several hundred pounds apiece—was a deadly and death-defying task. The added factors of slippery decks and the continuously shifting noxious body of diluted acid made it almost impossible.

It was the big valves that made the terrible thunderous sounds that echoed down into the galley and messroom. They were rounded on their bottoms and, once loosed, rolled along with complete abandon. They smashed into the drums of acid, against the pipe racks, and bounced off the bulkheads hitting each one in turn like a monstrous game of billiards. Eight men—some from the deck department and some from the black gang—spaced themselves about the room or right outside the open doors on either side. As the ship's roll favored one side or the other, the men nearest that area attacked one runaway valve or length of pipe after another. Wrecking bars, "bull ropes," two- and three-foot lengths of 4" x 4" lumber, wedges, and sheer guts were their only weapons.

The trapped acid-water mix raced back and forth from roll to roll. Some poured up over the high coamings of the opened watertight doors on each trip, but most was still contained in the room and continued to drain down through the holed and rust-rotted deck to the saloon and galley overheads. For some reason the deck over the messroom didn't let go and it escaped the deluge.

The wreckage to the boat deck on the starboard side was not

as severe as that on the port, but the starboard lifeboat was stove in. A large valve had bounced out of the pipe-room when the watertight door had been smashed open and bounded up into the boat. The thin steel hull had a four-foot-long tear. It looked like a sloppily opened tin can. The valve itself had continued over the side taking a portion of railing with it; the ends of the rails were bent outboard in smooth half arcs.

Two men were injured securing the pipe-room. Andre Ballou, the 8 to 12 oiler, had his left foot pinned against a bulkhead by a short length of 4" diameter pipe. It slammed into his ankle and almost severed the foot at the joint. He hobbled alone across the boat deck and down the ladder leading to the crew messroom. Robert Smith, the second cook, saw him at the open door and helped him over the coaming; he led the injured man to the same corner of the room where Whitey had been strangled and had him sit on the deck. Ballou braced himself against the bulkhead and held onto the bench as the cook cut the sea boot away with a butcher knife. He gave Ballou a half full bottle of gin to drink from, then poured most of what remained into the deep ugly wound. He wrapped the foot as best he could with clean dish towels and twisted one below the knee into a tourniquet.

With the help from the galleyman, Ballou was taken below to his fo'c's'le and lashed into bed with his foot raised. They went to the Kid's fo'c's'le to alert Reed, telling him what they had done. Reed told the second cook to stay with Stacey as he left with the first aid kit. Thankfully, he still had sulfa powder left.

Big Jim O'Malley's wrist was broken. He had jammed a heavy pinch bar up under a half dozen 20 foot lengths of 6" pipe. Another man, trying to get a piece of heavy line passed around them, lost his balance and skidded away. The pipes began to break free from the stack and the bosun—unwilling to jump free and let the pipes loose upon the fallen man—held what he could till help arrived. The strain had been enormous as the ship went through her full arc of 70 degrees; O'Malley felt his left wrist snap as he held the bar up against the weight.

"Fuckin' wrist is broke!" he cursed as the fallen man got back to the heavy bull rope and managed to get his turns around the still nestled pipes. As soon as the line was secured, they drove wedges under the pile.

"Better go below, Boats," Jimmy Ryan advised O'Malley.

"I'm okay—get that one before it gets away!" O'Malley indicated a huge valve which had begun to roll. It had come free again from the heavy stanchion and was held now only by the lashings around its three-foot diameter wheel.

—THIRTY-THREE—

"Bridge!" Searles answered the phone.

"This is the bosun." O'Malley stood with his back braced against the bulkhead in the chief engineer's office. He held the phone in his right hand. His left arm rested in a cloth sling around his neck. "We've got a couple more injured back here and not much left in our medical kit or the one down below."

"Yes, O'Malley... Is the chief's supper on the way?"

"Aye, the messman's startin' forward now. Can he bring some stuff from the bridge medical kit aft?"

"Good, Boats...Good. I'll see what we can send back with him."

"Hansen's comin' with the messman to help him get it there. He'll go to the wheel and Ryan, the 8 to 12 AB, will be takin' lookout 'stead of the 4 to 8 ordinary—Cole's been hurt."

"Okay, Boats—I'll tell the chief. And the pipe-room?"

"Secured as best we could."

"The lifeboats?"

"Port side's done for. Starb'd one's holed bad, but—"

"O'Malley—I've got to hang up!"

The phone went dead, but not before the several men gathered around the bosun heard the heavy pound of Kruzic's fist smacking the chart table and his guttural drink-slurred voice call out *"THAT'S ENOUGH!"*

"Well, I suppose this is it!" O'Malley hung up the phone.

"Don' you vorry, Bosun. Ve gonna do a good yob on him."

"I hope he don't spot you." O'Malley turned to Evers.

The big AB was dressed in slicks with a hood and had a towel around his neck pulled up over the lower part of his face. Many men wore a towel as an added measure against the wind and rain on lookout. Evers was counting on it to hide his face. They had told the bridge that Ryan was going up on lookout instead of the 4 to 8 ordinary, as he was closer to the big AB in size.

Tommy Deel was visibly shaking. It wasn't so much the fear of coming face to face with the crazy engineer that had him at loose ends; it was the fact that everything seemed to depend on him now.

"You goin' to be okay, Tommy?" Evers still doubted the Negro messman could come through with the plan.

"I gotta be, Mr. Evers." Tommy breathed deeply and pulled himself erect. There was a heavy wooden tray suspended around his neck by a piece of line. It was an open box-like affair 16 inches wide and 22 inches long with a 3 inch high lip running all around it. In the tray were several plates of food. One platter had slices of white turkey, another, diced pieces of Australian roast beef, still another held potato salad; they were all prepared foods from cans. There was a bowl of lettuce and tomato salad, glass jars of mustard and hot peppers, and salt and pepper shakers; all the platters were covered with waxed paper. A heavy clean bath towel lay over the entire tray. It hung over the sides about 5 inches below the bottom like a skirting, secured on the front side with a number of small broad headed nails that the bosun had driven in. Down the sides and in the back there were only three nails; one at each end, and one in the middle. The last three had smaller heads and the towel could be pulled away from the tray to reveal its contents.

Hansen carried a cardboard box filled with plates, silverware, napkins, two loaves of bread and several cans of fruit and juice. The coffee tote-tray was slung over his left shoulder.

"Okay, chances are he'll only let one at a time come into the chartroom. He'll search whoever goes first before letting the next one up the companionway." O'Malley looked at Hansen and Tommy. "As for you, Evers—I don't know—you're goin' up the outside ladder to the weather wing. He mightn't search you till after he gets the food. Or he may forget it since he has both wing doors closed and locked from inside—anyhow, you'll just have to play it by ear." O'Malley grimaced as he bumped his bad arm against the desk.

"Well," said Evers, "if everyone's ready let's get started." The big AB pulled the towel up higher on his face and stepped back so the messman could get by with the tray.

Tommy stepped out into the alleyway headed for the opened watertight door.

"Good luck, all of you!" the bosun called after them.

Evers was the last man to step out on the deck leading to the catwalk. The wind tore across the after well deck whipping a stinging spray high up over the mainmast; the range light showed weakly through the gloom. It was about 5:30 P.M. and the little remaining daylight was dulled down to a dark grey by the overcast skies. The tanker began to roll over a swell topped with a huge breaking wave; it seemed to curl up almost on top of them before she lifted up over its shoulder. Evers looked at the sky as the ship rose. The wind blasted the salt spray into his smarting eyes, but not before he saw an ominous sight. He almost called out to the two men ahead of him who struggled along the battered catwalk.

"The fool!" he swore to himself. *He's done for the lot of us!* There was no mistaking the long pitch-black line spread across the eastern horizon. It was the bar of the hurricane; massive dense black cumulonimbus clouds marking its outer rim. "No sense upsetting 'em any more than they are," he thought as he pushed on after them.

The ship rolled back down to port just as the messman made it to the opened starboard door of the midship house. The well deck shipped the heavy sea like a reef at high tide, without resistance; the tank tops scarcely hindered or parted the water as it washed green across the deck. Tommy slipped and clutched wildly at the door frame with his free hand. Hansen came up behind and grabbed hold of the frame. He shoved up against the little messman, supporting him as he started to swing backwards. Tommy recovered his balance and stepped over the high coaming.

Evers, a few steps behind them, was caught in the heavy spray that burst up over the catwalk.

"You all right?" The big AB hung on to the open door frame and addressed himself to Tommy.

"Yes, Sir, I'm okay, Mr. Evers." The messman was breathing deeply as he braced himself against the bulkhead, one hand gripping the steel bar on the locked hospital door.

"He gonna do yust fine!" Hansen nodded confidently.

"Okay, I'm startin' on up to the port wing. Remember, Hansen, if anything goes wrong, you or someone got to get to the lee door and *unlock it*—or it's all over!"

"It's gonna vork, don' vorry!"

"Good luck!" Evers turned away into the wind and started around the house.

"Well, sounds like food finally got here!" Kruzic had just finished taking another drink; he put the almost empty bottle back as he heard Hansen call out.

"Mate, ve bring up the stuff?" Hansen called out again.

"Get up and unlock the door, *Mr. Captain*." Kruzic pointed the revolver at the mate.

Finney stood up—he almost collapsed; the past half-hour had

been an agony of suspense and soul-searching. Now, his plan was to be tested; the curtain was going up whether the players were ready or not.

"You don't look so good, Captain." Kruzic smiled at his captive. He enjoyed the frustration and rage visible on the man's face. *Just a younger version of "Old Woman Layton"* thought the engineer. "What has happened to your so quiet, confident, salty manner now, Mr. Captain?"

Carl Finney crossed the chartroom and went down the companionway. At the bottom he turned and looked back up at the engineer.

"One man at a time. He's to put down his things and turn around with his hands flat against the bulkhead over the settee— you know the position very well by now, do you not, Captain?"

"Yes, Mr. Kruzic." The mate's voice was flat and resigned as he spoke to the two men through the closed door, relaying the engineer's instructions.

"Very good, Captain, very well. Now unlock the door and secure it open on the latch... That's fine—now back into your corner!" Kruzic moved away from the landing as Finney came back up the stairs.

Carl Finney started past the engineer, who stood with his back to the chart table, he hesitated for a split second as he passed between his antagonist and the settee. The mate's mind whirled with a sudden feeling of despair; his plan was doomed to fail, he should chance lunging for the miserable bastard right now. Then the sudden upward thrust of the *Concordia's* bows threw him towards the settee and he had to grab it to prevent being thrown to the deck. It seemed like a sign—he must hold to the plan. Righting himself, the mate stepped to the side of the settee and stood back against the bulkhead; he grasped the edge of the big porthole for support.

Kruzic caught the momentary hesitation in the mate's movements. His eyes narrowed as the man turned towards him from the corner of the room. *"Turn around and face the other way!"* he shouted, suddenly feeling that the dog might yet have some teeth. "Well, we'll pull the rest of those soon enough," he promised himself as he made for the open door.

Hansen and Tommy stood at the bottom of the companionway waiting for the order to come up. They were both sweating profusely in their oilskins, partly from standing in the relatively warm passageway, partly from tension and excitement.

"You first! Hansen, isn't it?" Kruzic called down to them. His hand held the revolver steady in front of him.

"Aye, it's me, Chief."

"Slow and easy, now. Come on up!"

"Aye, Sir." Hansen began the climb up the stairs. The ship's roll made him swing up against the side of the companionway bulkhead and he gripped the rail with his free right hand.

"Over to the settee now." Kruzic backed away from the entrance as the husky AB approached the head of the ladder. Now he stood once again with his back against the chart table.

"Put the box down and steady it with your foot."

Hansen put it down and straightened up slowly, one hand on the settee, his leg wedged against the carton.

"Hold out the coffee tray!"

"Aye."

Kruzic looked at the coffee pot and three cups. "Take the tray from him, my silent friend in the corner." He gestured towards Carl Finney.

"Yes, Sir."

"See you don't upset it, *Captain*... Now, Hansen, the box... Open it!"

"Aye." Hansen knelt down holding onto the settee with one hand, opening the carton with the other.

Kruzic could only see the two loaves of bread. "Take the bread out and put it on the settee!"

"Aye, Sir." The AB lifted each loaf out, one at a time, and placed them well back against the backboard.

"Now tip the box up!"

Hansen did as he was instructed.

Satisfied the box contained what it was supposed to, Kruzic had the AB remove his bulky rain gear and searched him as he stood spread-eagled over the settee with his hands against the bulkhead, one foot still jamming the box of food against the base.

"That's fine, Hansen." The engineer stepped back. "Now unlock the door to the wheelhouse and go in."

"Aye." Hansen's voice was little more than a rasping grunt. He had been clamping his jaws together so hard that his neck was throbbing painfully, he could scarcely open his mouth. The disgusting sensation of the engineer's hand running over his body had almost made him lose control. He had locked his muscles so rigidly that he was as yet unable to relax.

"Go on now!"

Hansen forced himself to move. He unlocked the door and swung it open.

"The man you're relieving stays in the wheelhouse till I tell him to go aft!" Kruzic called out. *"Do you hear me?"*

"Aye," Howard, the AB on the wheel, answered.

"Close it!" Kruzic walked over and locked the door as soon as it was shut. He balanced against the ship's shuddering downward pitch. The unattended box of canned food slid across the deck towards him. He reached down, lifted it to the chart table, and stacked the cans in the rack alongside the bottles of liquor. The rest of the box, with its paper napkins and silverware, he wedged in the corner below the table. Glancing briefly at Mr. Finney, Kruzic started back towards the top of the companionway.

Tommy tried to gulp down his fear as he saw the head of the stairwell suddenly fill with the dark bulk of the chief engineer's body. He stood there staring at the big hairy fist which held the gun pointing down at him. He found it almost impossible to look up past it into that mad face. *You gotta get him for the Kid—you gotta. Look at him! You gotta look at him, you weak black bastard!* he agonized.

"Well, well...if it isn't 'Little Black Sambo'," Kruzic sneered. "Come on up slow and easy."

Tommy couldn't seem to get started up the ladder. He was rooted to the deck, left hand grasping the rail, the right grasping the corner of the tray. He couldn't take his eyes off the gun.

"MOVE, DAMN YOU!"

Tommy barely heard the engineer's voice. He was in a state of almost total mental paralysis. His mind rejected the grim reality that faced him. He felt exactly the same as when the concussion of a German sub's perfect hit on the after gun had sent him reeling to the deck to lie trance-like, hypnotized amid the horror of broken dead bodies and screaming wounded.

"MOVE, NIGGER!" Despite his shouting, Kruzic wasn't in the least angry with the terrified little messman. He was, in fact, immensely gratified hurling abuse at the scared man and felt relieved and safe with his entry into the chartroom. Hansen, on the other hand, had kept him worried and on edge till he was locked into the wheelhouse.

"Sorry...Sir. Yes, Sir." Tommy started slowly up the steps. He looked down away from the gun, staring straight ahead as he passed each rung. As his head came up level to the chartroom deck, his eyes focused on the shoes of the engineer who had stepped back against the chart table. By the time he stood at the entrance of the room, he was looking again at the gun.

"Well now, little man," Kruzic was obviously enjoying himself, "let's see what you've got for me?"

"Food, Sir... Good food, Sir." The messman swayed there balancing the covered tray with his left hand, grasping the edge of the settee with the right. He forced himself to look up slowly past the gun, past the bulky jacketed body and up into the broad face of the madman. By the time his eyes locked with those of the engineer's, Tommy Deel had pulled himself together.

"Stay where you're at and take off the towel. Open it!"

The messman felt the ship shudder as she bottomed in the trough; he hesitated a moment as he felt her begin to lift and roll back up to starboard. "The towel's nailed down, Sir," Tommy explained as he let go the back of the settee and grasped the right hand corner of the tray. He started to lift the back of the towel free with the other hand. "Dere you are!" He grimaced, working the rest of the towel off.

"Roast beef!" Kruzic was genuinely pleased as he got a whiff of his favorite food.

The towel had not completely cleared the tray when the ear-shattering blast of an explosion filled the room. The next smell that came to the engineer was of burning flesh and hair—not unfamiliar to the ex-crematorium expert—but this time it was his own. Before the sound of the explosion reached full volume in the enclosed chartroom, Kruzic's piercing scream crystallized the bizarre scene.

The powerful recoil from the flare launcher threw Tommy backwards into the settee—the wooden tray and its contents just missing his face as the tray flipped over his head, striking the bulkhead behind him. Tommy threw his hands up instinctively to ward off the plates and bottles. The empty tray came to rest in the middle of the room, face down on the deck; the towel, still attached securely to the front edge, was in flames from the muzzle blast. The big Very pistol signal launcher, which O'Malley had so carefully wired to the bottom, remained in place. It lay exposed with its full inch and a half bore lined up dead center at the edge of the tray—the trip-wire from the trigger through the three tiny eye bolts leading to the right hand corner still intact.

Carl Finney stood frozen in the corner. He was the only one in a position to fully witness the gruesome spectacle. A moment before, his heart had been thumping painfully in his tensed throat as the little Negro messman struggled with the towel. Then, as he prayed and waited for his plan to unfold, the madman in front of him suddenly flung out his arms and flew backward against the chart table.

The flare plowed into Kruzic catching him low in the stomach. The tip of the missile passed through the outer clothing, driving itself into his flesh, while the main portion of the fiery charge spread out across his midsection. The fierce heat of the burning magnesium ignited hair, flesh and fabric with equal ease.

To the mate, it looked as if a red ball of fire had suddenly burst forth from the middle of the engineer's body. Streamers of brilliant burning magnesium alloy shot out in a great incandescent halo enveloping his upper torso; a mixture of blue and black smoke filled the air. Carl Finney's mind was so completely transfixed by the visual impact that he never heard the report of the shot or Kruzic's scream.

In the wheelhouse, the explosion and outcry seemed to come simultaneously. Bob Howard was standing braced at the porthole about a foot or so away from the door leading out onto the starboard wing. Hansen, while relieving him at the wheel, had given him the word to be ready to open the door as soon as he was told to.

"OPEN!" Hansen yelled out as the roar of the explosion and Kruzic's scream came to them.

Howard hesitated—the noise was greater than he anticipated; he hadn't known what to expect. Hansen hadn't dared to do more than whisper hurried instructions about standing by to open the door when he heard something in the chartroom.

"OPEN! *OPEN FAST!!*" Hansen yelled again to Howard.

Mr. Searles had as little knowledge of the plan as did Howard. He stood glued to the radar console waiting, as Hansen had told him, for the chartroom door to be opened by Mr. Finney or Tommy. The officer had been completely stunned by the tremendous explosion and had forgotten he was supposed to relieve Hansen at the wheel when things started happening.

"MATE! DA VHEEL! *TAKE DA VHEEL!!*" Hansen let go with his left hand; he reached out, and pulled Searles towards him from the radar set.

Evers had stationed himself at the corner of the bridge on the starboard side, ready to move either way; to the port wing if Kruzic had decided to check the lookout before letting the food into the chartroom; to the starboard wing if that door was thrown open. In either case, he would have to try his luck with the second of the two Very pistols which he and O'Malley had taken from the lifeboats. Captain Finney's plan included Evers as the back-up man if Tommy failed to get a shot off or if he missed. The door on the starboard side was to be flung open to admit the big AB. Hansen was to hurl himself against the locked chartroom door while Evers came behind him to try to take the engineer out. If Kruzic had first checked on the lookout and ordered him to come around to the starboard door to be searched, then Evers was to try for him before the engineer recognized him.

Hansen had expected the chartroom door to be opened immediately after the explosion. Since it hadn't, he was certain the plan had not met with success. He started to put the emergency plan into operation.

In the chartroom, Tommy Deel struggled to his feet as the *Concordia's* bows reared upward; he staggered backwards again, almost falling onto the settee. A fiercely burning torch came rushing towards the messman, propelled by the same force that had nearly thrown him down. Only the engineer's legs were still recognizable—from the waist up he was completely ablaze. The first hellish scream was reduced to a moaning wail seeming to come from far away—something difficult to associate with the thing which lurched by him and went hurtling down the companionway to the landing on the deck below.

Just as Captain Finney started towards the chartroom door leading to the wheelhouse, it slammed open and Hansen stumbled into the room with Evers close behind.

"CAPT'N!" Hansen yelled as he just avoided colliding with him.

"*WHERE IS HE?*" shouted Evers, the Very pistol clenched in his right fist.

The chart table was burning as was the shelf right above it.

"Down...down the stairwell," the captain gestured. "I don't think he's going to get very far." Finney reached for the fire extinguisher secured near the top of the companionway. "Get the other one from the wheelhouse!" he called out.

Captain Finney pointed the cone-shaped nozzle at the chart table and pulled the lever. The fire was out by the time Howard rushed in with the big brass water-soda extinguisher.

Evers had gone over to the head of the companionway with Hansen. They stood there watching the now silent corpse being consumed. Kruzic had landed head down in the corner up against the opened door—flames rapidly devouring his legs which stretched upwards resting on the rungs of the ladder. The paint on the companionway was blackened a third of the way up to the top and little flashes of flame played on the bulkheads.

"*Yeesus* Christ vot a vay ta go!"

Tommy moved over to look and Hansen stepped back with his fingers on his nose. "Vot a stink!"

"Better get that fire out!" Finney handed the extinguisher to the big AB.

"Aye, Sir!" Evers handed the flare launcher to Tommy and took the extinguisher.

"*CAPTAIN! CAPTAIN FINNEY!*" Searle's terror-filled voice came as Evers turned the nozzle on what remained of Chief Engineer Fredrick Kruzic

Carl Finney and the four men in the chartroom were immediately aware that something was very wrong. Searle's voice came to them as the ship began to climb steeply up out of the last trough—this time however, no countering force seemed to hold her from swinging off. As the ship rode up over the steep shoulder of the swell she started to slip away to starboard, lurching and shuddering, her angle continuing well beyond the 25 to 30 degrees she had regularly been assuming.

"SHE'S NOT RESPONDING!" the officer's panicked voice rang out from the wheelhouse.

Howard dropped the unused fire extinguisher and grabbed the corner of the chart table as the brass cylinder flew across the room. It narrowly missed Captain Finney, who was struggling to keep his footing as he clutched at the door. Hansen and Evers held onto the railing heading down the companionway. The big AB had been forced to let go of the extinguisher to keep from following it headlong down the stairs. Tommy spun around backwards, landing up against the settee. He sat there holding onto its back till it gave way and threw him to the far corner of the room.

"WHEEL'S ALL SLACK!" Searles shouted as he hung onto the useless wheel with his left hand, his right arm wrapped around the binnacle.

"SWITCH TO ELECTRIC!" Finney prayed it was a hydraulic line break that rendered the telemotor inoperative.

Searles spun the big wooden wheel six times around to the right, then held it midships as he struggled to reach around the front of the telemotor to shut off the hydraulic valve.

Finney pulled himself into the wheelhouse. He grabbed the "Iron Mike" and turned the control to MANUAL from the OFF position; he looked up at the rudder indicator as he turned the small electric steering wheel to the left. *Nothing!* He turned it faster till it was hard over, then spun it back all the way to the right. No change in the indicator—it just swung slowly through a five degree arc—there wasn't any feeling beneath his feet of the ship responding. "My God...*The rudder's carried away!*" Finney lunged for the telegraph. He swung the lever to STOP and almost pulled the General Alarm switch, but held back as he envisioned men trying to get forward to man their emergency stations or to the bridge to begin clearing away the midship boats.

There was no chance of launching a boat in the massive seas which trapped them aboard the stricken vessel. Their only chance was that the ship herself might withstand the storm. It would be a miracle if the tanker survived intact. More probable was the prospect of her splitting in two and, if that happened, only the buoyant stern section would have a chance of floating for any length of time. What happened to everything forward of the after house would depend on where she split. Carl Finney ordered everyone off the bridge and back across the catwalk to the after house.

The *Concordia* heeled over at an angle of almost 45 degrees, dipping her port wing into the sea. Then she slid back down to starboard and buried her bows deep into the following trough. It seemed an eternity as the entire fo'c'slehead flooded over. The forward well deck was covered all the way aft to the face of the midship structure—the tank tops invisible from the bridge.

—THIRTY-FOUR—

The captain completed his phone conversation with the first assistant engineer. He had informed Mr. Pierce about the state of things on the bridge and cautioned him to be ready to secure all watertight doors and hatches. Finney was encouraged to learn in return from Pierce that the main steam pump was back in service and they were gaining on the water in the after pumproom.

There was not much more he could do. Not even the emergency radio had been spared to them. Kruzic had seen to that, smashing the small two-way set in the wheelhouse as well.

O'Malley was still speaking with Captain Finney on the standby phone when Mike Searles and the four men who came aft with him lurched into the messroom.

"Aye! They just come in, Sir!" The bosun nodded at the successful team.

"Get your starboard boat patched as best you can, Boats—but we'll stay with the ship till it's certain she can't stay afloat."

"Aye, I understand...you coming aft, Sir?"

"I'm getting the log book and—"

The *Concordia* rolled violently onto her starboard beam as she lifted over the crest of a huge swell. The first of the savage cyclonic winds marking the fringe of the hurricane struck the broad expanse of her exposed hull on the up-lifted port side. And the wind, howling with a new and demoniac voice, overcame all other sound. The tanker had entered another dimension—no longer under control—the once powerful and capable vessel was an insignificant piece of buoyant scrap tossing about in an alien environment.

Most of the men in the messroom were thrown against the starboard bulkhead in a cursing, thrashing heap. O'Malley was one of the few who maintained his stance, but his broken wrist slammed painfully against the telephone box. He kept the receiver wedged under his chin as he held onto one of the porthole dogs with his good right hand.

The tanker kept her list so long it seemed certain the next massive wall of water would roll her over on her stack.

"BOATS!!" Carl Finney's voice came back over the phone.

"Aye, I'm here!"

"She can't take too many more like that!"

"You best start aft, Sir! Now!!"

"Right away. Get to work on that boat, O'Malley." Finney hung up and started for the chartroom.

The ship had come back to an almost even keel as she finally rolled sluggishly down. The wind tore insanely at every piece of standing rigging. Even with the doors closed in the chartroom the scream of the vibrating steel cables made it almost impossible to think.

The captain picked up the log book and found the revolver where it had come to rest under the back of the broken settee. He felt the ship starting to heel over on her starboard beam and the deck began to cant up to port once more. Finney went back into the wheelhouse planning to leave from the starboard wing, then re-enter the house from the boat deck to get to the captain's office—he couldn't stomach going down the companionway where he'd have to step over Kruzic's stinking corpse.

"Think someone should see he makes it okay?" Evers asked as O'Malley hung the phone back in the box.

"Maybe so." The bosun looked around and glanced at the only officer in the room.

"I should have stayed forward," Searles spoke. "I better—"

"Best let Evers go!" O'Malley winced. The pain in his wrist was starting to make him feel sick to the stomach. "We gotta get started on the starb'd boat."

The big AB didn't wait for the officer's consent; undogging the watertight door he stepped out onto the fantail. Towering masses of black clouds obscured the sky; he could scarcely move against the wind whipping around the stern. Struggling from one hand hold to another he gained the lee of the starboard side. Then, pausing a moment to catch his breath, he started forward.

The *Concordia* buried her starboard rail in the sea as he rounded the face of the after house. The wind, momentarily blocked by the rearing port side of the hull, could not bring its full fury against him as he hurried toward the catwalk.

The catwalk itself was no longer intact. Many of the steel-mesh gratings had been torn away and those remaining were buckled and loose under foot. Getting back from the bridge with Searles and the others had been bad—now it was almost impossible. When he got to sections where the gratings were gone, he faced the handrail and moved sideway across the bare steel frame that once supported them.

Out in the middle of the catwalk the wind buffeted at him with incredible force. He was still thirty feet from the midship house when the tanker began her opposite roll. A mountainous comber towered over the ship—its top shearing off into a huge elongated grey-white mass. The water smashed into him like a solid wall inundating his two-piece oilskins. Evers lost his footing and was swept off the catwalk. Grasping wildly, he caught hold of the lower railing and struggled desperately to pull his feet back to the frame. The AB wrapped his right arm around the rail and tore away at his jacket with the other to free his left arm and shoulder. Managing to do so, he locked his freed left arm around the rail and released his right—the water-filled top tore away.

The tanker started to shudder violently as she strained to lift her buried deck. The AB turned his efforts to shedding his rain pants and sea boots. A solid mass of water surged up under the catwalk. Evers had just gotten rid of the rest of his gear when the sea struck the lower part of his body—he held on—both arms straining at their limit.

As the AB struggled back up onto the catwalk, he realized the *Concordia* had lost the battle. The port side of the tanker rose from the sea with an odd angle between the midship house and the well deck. Instead of forming a smooth arc at the junction of the superstructure and the rake of the hull, the house slanted away awkwardly.

"Her back's broken!" Evers spoke the words aloud. He licked the salt from his lips. *Where in the Christ is he?* he thought as he looked toward the bridge.

The big AB knew the ship had only minutes to live, perhaps seconds; the next wave could do for her—he visualized the bent and torn horizontal and vertical frames in the hull beneath the canted deck—the inner bulkheads separating the three cargo tanks just aft of the house were certainly buckled as well.

The next punishing assault would collapse what little support remained within the web of steel. And when that happened, the hull plates themselves would shear, splitting the tanker in two— the only chance a man had of survival lay back aft.

"What in the hell's keepin' 'im?" he swore as he tried to decide whether to go on or start back to the safety of the stern.

Evers struggled forward to the end of the catwalk. Sudden heavy rain swept horizontally across the deck as he entered the house. The tanker had rolled her starboard side back up and hung there close to 45 degrees. The AB went down the passageway as fast as he could. The angle of list was so great that he was walking in the juncture of the port bulkhead and the deck. He pulled himself up the companionway, reaching the captain's office just as the ship fell drunkenly back into the trough. The door was closed. He tried the handle and shouted. The knob turned, but the door was jammed.

About to turn away and look up in the chartroom, Evers thought he heard someone call out. He backed up against the bulkhead and threw his shoulder into the door. It slammed open. "CAPTAIN?" he called into the empty office as he latched the door against the bulkhead.

"Here!" a voice came faintly from the adjoining stateroom.

The AB crossed over and opened the door. Captain Layton's blanket covered body was lashed to his bunk. Captain Finney was on the deck; one leg bent at the knee, the other stretched out at an odd angle.

"Must of blacked out." Finney shook his head and started to try and pull himself erect. He grasped the edge of the desk with his left hand and pushed against the bulkhead behind him with the palm of the right. *"Damn it!"* He groaned and slipped back to the deck.

"Let me help you."

"Leg's broken!"

"Aye, hold on." Evers lifted the captain's right arm across his shoulder as he stooped down. "She's breakin' up. We got to get aft." He straightened up holding on to the injured man's belt.

"The log book... It's probably under the bed—got away from me." Finney balanced on his one good leg.

The AB had to grasp hold of the desk to keep them both from being thrown to the deck. "Forget it! *Forget everything!!"* He put his right arm around Finney's waist and started across the room.

"Evers, the Old Man's papers." The officer pointed to a big manila just in front of the captain's bed.

The ship shuddered and the room shifted suddenly, seeming to rock off the very deck.

"Hold fast!" Evers kept moving for the door. "Probably wont make it as it is!"

Carl Finney fell silent. The pain in his broken right leg was heightened every time it came in contact with the AB. He hobbled along on his left foot as Evers helped him down the companionway and through the passageways leading out.

When they got to the open watertight door, Evers supported the captain against the frame; the two men looked out at the wild scene.

"Goin' to have to carry you...And I need your boots," the AB pointed at his stockinged feet, "most of the grates are gone—we can't make it side by side."

"I'm pretty heavy—you wont make it with me on your back." Finney grasped the door frame as the AB eased the boot off his injured leg. "Get aft before it's too late!"

"Stow that!" Evers pulled off the other boot and put it on as well. "There now." He helped the injured man over the coaming.

The ship was lifting her port side again as Evers turned and bent down to take Mr. Finney on his back. The wind and rain were momentarily cut off by the lee of the hull, but even in the dark, both men could see the unnatural angle the house had assumed; it was starting to take on a direction of its own. As the tanker's roll increased, the structure seemed to be canting to the opposite side— it was beginning to tear away along with the entire forward end of the ship.

"*HOLD FAST!*" Evers yelled as he started across to the catwalk.

Captain Finney bit through his lower lip to keep from screaming. His broken leg was slammed time and time again as the big AB forged ahead. Evers grasped the steel railing with his right hand, his left arm locked up under Mr. Finney's left thigh. The *Concordia* had attained the top of her roll as he reached the short ladder from the main deck level to the catwalk.

"*SHE'S GOING!*" Carl Finney hollered out as Evers stepped up on the first rung.

The officer was looking down to his right when the well deck below them suddenly parted in a long ragged furrow, the shorn edge below them turning back like a hastily opened tin can. The scream of the ripping steel was almost beyond human tolerance. He couldn't believe what he was witnessing. Even in the dark, with the rain beating down, the white sparks from the rending steel lit the gaping void.

The two men felt themselves suddenly hurled skyward as the massive weight of the forward half of the vessel broke away. The AB's knees were buckling under him and Finney's weight was increased threefold by the sudden upward leap of the after section. Though the shorn edge of the *Concordia* was arching up, the ladder on which they stood was sagging beneath them. *There was nothing supporting it any longer from below!*

The big AB fought to hold on. The captain's arms nearly choked him as he threw his remaining strength into climbing the last two rungs.

Several men had rushed out of the after house as the shuddering vibrations and the thunderous report of the rupturing hull echoed throughout the stern section. Those in the messroom had gone around the starboard side and forward along the alleyway. They stood in the lee of the house staring out into the driving rain. Others, who had been around the chief engineer's office, stood in the portal trying to see forward into the darkness.

O'Malley was among those who had come from the fantail. "SWITCH ON THE CARGO LIGHTS!" he called out to the group of men clustered at door.

"YEESUS CHRIST! SHE'S SPLIT!!" Hansen's voice could just be heard over the wind. He was standing next to O'Malley and had seen the ghostly white of the midship house loom off to starboard, already well away from the stern section of the bisected ship.

The cargo lights came on, but did little to disperse the gloom. The roar of the hurricane obliterated all other sounds as the broken hull rolled back to level in the trough.

The pounding force of the sea now drove unhindered across the ragged forward edge of the well deck. It came as more of a concussion than an audible sound.

"DEY'VE HAD IT, BOATS!" Hansen was the first to put words to what everyone was thinking as they looked forward.

"MAYBE. I'M GONNA SEE!" O'Malley started to pull himself around the house, bending over into the driving rain.

"NO—I VILL!" Hansen grabbed hold of the forward railing on the face of the house and came up alongside O'Malley. *"You von't make it, Boats!"*

"GO BACK, O'MALLEY—I'M GOING WITH HIM!" Mike Searles ordered as he stepped through the portal. He had a flashlight in his hand and waved it momentarily in the bosun's direction.

The bosun stepped back; he knew Hansen was right. He couldn't make it—not with one arm. "CAREFUL!" he called out after the two men.

The young officer disappeared into the darkness. Hansen followed after him, groping for hand-holds and turning his face to the right every other step in order to breathe.

The beam of the mate's flashlight suddenly disappeared from up ahead. Then it flashed again below off to his right. A scream rose higher than the roar of the wind that blasted against Hansen's ears. The AB felt the sea burst up around him and the grate he stood on suddenly pivoted away from underfoot. He locked his arms around the railing and pulled himself up, legs dangling in the swirling water, till he made contact with the steel side support of the missing section of catwalk. As he hung there, he heard another sharp cry of terror from below. The well deck under him was a solid sheet of water. Hansen scrambled up onto the section of catwalk behind him. He was about thirty-five feet from the after house—the grey-white bulk loomed securely behind him in the dim cargo light—ahead there was nothing but blackness.

"MATE!!" he screamed out into the watery void below, but he knew he was alone on the catwalk and that calling to Mr. Searles was useless—useless as trying to go any further along the torn and twisted catwalk. The two missing men must still have been on the bridge when it carried away. Hansen looked again into the dark, then started to back away from the empty section when he stopped. His eyes had picked up a movement ahead of him. "Evers... Yesus Christ...it's *him!*" Hansen formed the words without saying them. "EVERS!" he was finally able to scream out "HOLD UP—CATVALK'S GONE!!"

The two men came on soundlessly. Hansen pulled himself out onto the frame and struggled forward against the wind. They came together half way across the open section. Evers faced the starboard rail and hauled his feet sideways step by step on the steel angle below him. Hansen reached out and grasped the captain's back with his left hand and turned in the same direction as Evers. He tried to relieve as much of the big AB's burden as he could. It was awkward. When they got to the intact portion of the catwalk, Hansen dropped behind and followed after them, his left hand supporting Captain Finney's right thigh.

"HELP!" Hansen called out as they approached within a few feet of the house.

Several men quickly came forward and eased the injured man off the big AB's back. They carried him into the first assistant's room and put him on the bed. Someone went below to get Reed.

*   *   *

The stern section pitched and rolled violently for the first few minutes after separating from the forward part of the vessel. Then, instead of wallowing beam end into the trough as the vessel had while intact, she began to come about and rode more or less stern first against the sea. As the water flooded the open set of No. 5 cargo tanks, the forward part of the hulk rode lower—the entire length of the well deck now acting as a great sea anchor, trailing behind the stern and keeping them hove-to.

To the men, the pitching and rolling were routine. But the incessant shrieking of the raging wind, blasting the hulk at over 125 mph, was impossible to ignore.

Captain Finney lay back in the bed sweating from the pain. He had refused to take more than one big swallow of whiskey from the bottle before Reed began pulling and twisting his leg; finally managing to set it. Now it was splinted with mop handles, padded and secured to his right leg with sheeting and small pieces of line. The leg had broken above the knee and taken unimaginable punishment on the trip from the midship house. It was a miracle that the broken bone had not severed any major veins or the artery.

"Where's Pumps?" Finney handed O'Malley the cup used to wash down the three aspirin he had prescribed for himself.

"Should be back in a minute or two with the first assistant." O'Malley took the cup and got up. "I'm goin' back and help with the boat soon as Howard or the ordinary on his watch gets here."

"What does it look like?"

"Should be okay—got the plates cut and ready to stitch her together. Damn lucky the davits missed gettin' bent!"

"Good...be careful up there!"

"Aye, it's still a wild ride. I've got safety lines for the men and we're workin' mostly inside the pipe-room."

"Stay off those decks till the last minute."

"Aye... If she keeps her ass to the weather like she is we'll make it without the boat."

"Captain Finney." Howard, the 4 to 8 AB knocked on the open door. "We're ready!"

"Okay, I'm comin'." The bosun got up. "Well, Sir, I'll be up on the boat deck if you need me."

"Thanks, O'Malley." Captain Finney nodded and lay back in the bed.

—THIRTY-FIVE—

When Mr. Pierce and the chief pumpman got back to the captain, they were almost in a state of collapse. But the news they brought was encouraging. The release of bunker oil that Finney ordered was working well in stopping the seas from breaking over the hulk. In addition, the pumps were all operating.

"Good, that's real good!" Captain Finney answered after getting the full report. "Now if we can keep her trimmed as she is we've an even chance of staying afloat."

"All the beating she's taken could split her again right across the after collision bulkhead, especially if the front end of this thing gets too heavy for the stern." Mr. Pierce hated to be negative at a time like this, but he felt the new captain should be completely informed.

"You mean if the inner bulkheads go between No. 5 and 6 tanks, the stern will ride *too high* in the water?"

"Yes, and the bulkheads could go on crumpling clear back through No. 8 and 9. That could lift the stern high enough to break her up again," Pierce explained. "The plates are thinned out pretty bad under the stern section—that's why we're still springing leaks."

"Well, we've got to try to keep her riding like she is. If we don't I think she'll turn turtle, Bob. I suppose we don't have too many options."

"No, Sir... It's ride or get off."

"Getting off is not really an option right now—more like suicide. The chance of clearing away the lifeboat without smashing it alongside the hull is less than 1 out of 10, and the probability of it surviving this hurricane is a hell of a lot less."

Pumps and Mr. Pierce nodded agreement with the captain's assessment.

"I'm afraid the boat's not going to be of much value till the worst of this has blown over. If we have to, I'd rather chance gradually flooding the engine room spaces to keep her trim. There's more chance of surviving on a dead hulk that's hove to than getting into that boat in this storm."

"How long do you think before it passes?" asked Pierce.

"Depends on its diameter and how fast it's still traveling, First."

"What's your best estimate? Can you even make one?"

"Not too easily, but since she was moving so fast—18 knots —I sort of feel she's still tight—maybe 100 to 150 miles in diameter."

"The eye?"

"No, the whole storm. The eye of a tight storm would be about a fourth of its diameter."

"So at 18 knots, it could still be 6 to 8 hours till we were out of it?"

"Yes, assuming we were dead center. Less if we only cut a corner of it."

"It's almost 6:30 now." Mr. Pierce looked at his watch. "If we're estimating anywhere close, we've another couple of hours of this, then maybe two hours of calm before the wind comes around from the other side."

"And we get it just as bad again?" Cannito, the chief pumpman, questioned.

"I'm afraid so," Captain Finney answered. "It's the same storm, just the rear end of it."

"Well, it will sure as heck be a night to remember." Mr. Pierce got up from the chair.

"This is your room, Bob. Could I be moved to the empty daymen's fo'c'sle?"

"I won't be getting much of a chance to sleep, and I heard the bosun tell the deck gang to sew bags for Ski and Solis. O'Malley asked if I'd read over them. It's a cruel night to bury a man, but he's right."

"Aye. Still, it's more than we could do for the Old Man—and all the others." Finney winced as he shifted his leg. "I'll ask to be moved into the chief engineer's office when you're through."

"Aye, Captain Finney." Mr. Pierce left the room with the pumpman.

*　　　　　*　　　　　*

It was 9:30 P.M. when most of the crew gathered in the messroom.

The bodies of Ski and Solis had been sewn up in bags made from new canvas. Inside each bag, at the foot, was a sack filled with heavy steel shackles. They both rested on a wide plank made from four eight-foot-long pieces of staging—a new flag was neatly draped over the makeshift bier.

Mr. Pierce balanced against the after bulkhead self-consciously thumbing his small worn Bible.

O'Malley started to say something when Evers came through the forward door into the room.

The wind's quit! The big AB looked around at the men standing near the flag-draped forms.

Several of the crew members stood up listening—those closest to the watertight door rushed to open it. When it swung back, the lack of wind was beyond comprehension. The sky was clear and they could see the stars. Except for the heaving motion of the hulk as it rode the massive swells, the sea had lost its fury. What made the lull ominous was the weird distant roaring sound of the winds which still encircled them.

"The eye!" Howard exclaimed to the cluster of men who spread out onto the fantail. "We're right smack dab in the middle!"

"Okay, okay, let's get on with it!" O'Malley's voice was strangely hoarse. He turned away from the open door and headed back to where the bodies lay.

The men assembled on the stern with the bier resting on the after set of bitts. The house lights were on and a cargo lamp had been rigged to the after railing. The first assistant braced himself against the rail and cleared his throat.

"We gather here to pay our last respects to two fellow sea-farers, Ski and Solis..." Pierce looked around the fantail, "young men...good men who will be missed by their families and friends..." The engineer cleared his throat again. "Fidel was on my watch. I really didn't know that much about him till today when I had to go through his personal things. Do you know he was a decorated hero? Yes...That's right... Fidel Solis earned a Silver Star as a soldier in the Battle of Okinawa. He had a half a dozen battle stars and a Purple Heart with Cluster. He was married to a Japanese girl. Strange, all I knew after six months he was on my watch was I didn't have to worry about the boilers. I know he was a Catholic and I'm no substitute for a priest, but I don't think he'd object to my saying a few words from the Bible."

The first looked over at O'Malley. "From what the bosun and others informed me, as rough and tough as Ski was known to be on this ship, he was a man of compassion; one who was always willing to help a man down on his luck. We all knew he was a hard worker and a fine seaman. But there was something Ski knew, that we should all bear in mind. In time we all depart this world, and if there is a judgement day, our worth to our Maker won't hinge on what we ended up with, but what we gave. Our charity and love and good works will be what's tallied on that day. Ski was single —no children—yet he has donated a monthly allotment to a home for orphans for a number of years now, and his will names this home as his sole beneficiary.

Mr. Pierce held the Bible up under the light and read from Psalm 42, emphasizing verses 7 and 8.

"DEEP CALLETH UNTO DEEP AT THE NOISE OF THY WATERSPOUTS:

ALL THY WAVES AND THY BILLOWS ARE GONE OVER ME.

YET THE LORD WILL COMMAND HIS LOVING KIND-NESS IN THE DAYTIME, AND IN THE NIGHT HIS SONG

SHALL BE WITH ME. AND MY PRAYER UNTO THE GOD OF MY LIFE..."

Looking up, O'Malley nodded to the four men who stood, two on each side of the bodies. They picked up a corner of the staging and moved to the after railing.

"We therefore commend the bodies of Fidel Solis and Chester Borolowski to the deep." The engineer made the sign of the cross.

The four men held tight to the sides of the staging as the weighted canvas bags slipped silently out from under the flag and disappeared into the swell that rolled up under the stern.

Mr. Pierce looked up at the gaunt, disheveled group as he closed the Bible. "Lord, you've seen fit to take our captain and several members of our crew this trip. Some of our shipmates lie gravely injured in their fo'c'sles. Why we have been chosen to suffer all that has befallen us these past few days is not easy for us to understand. We who are still in the midst of the tempest ask your mercy. Thy will be done... Let us stand a minute of silence in memory of our departed brothers."

*   *   *

MIAMI BEACH TRIBUNE: Sunday, September 1, 1950
TANKER SPLITS IN TWO
15 MEN SAVED AS STERN SINKS

USCG station Key West, Florida reported the rescue of fifteen men from the sinking stern section of the tanker S/T Concordia. Lights from the battered hulk were first spotted some 200 miles from Key West at 11:00 P.M., Thursday by a U.S. Weather Bureau Service Hurricane Hunter aircraft. The S/S Coral Victory en route from Veracruz to Miami, responding to Coast Guard emergency broadcasts, altered course and arrived at the scene of the disaster at 6:00 A.M., Friday. Two of the seventeen men still aboard the rapidly sinking stern went down with it before they could be taken off. Survivors told rescuers that the tanker broke in two around 6 P.M. the previous evening when the vessel lost her rudder while battling 50 to 60 foot seas thrown against her by the hurricane. Second

Mate Carl Finney, the only surviving deck officer, revealed that the ill-fated vessel had been the scene of several killings in addition to the accidental loss of men during the storm. The officer informed authorities that fourteen crew members had chosen to take their chances in the one remaining lifeboat and that they left the hulk shortly after 10:00 P.M. Thursday against his advice. Captain Dennis Havermill USCG, in charge of the Coast Guard's Air-Sea Rescue branch at Key West, stated that while the search for the missing crew members of the lifeboat was continuing there was little chance of their surviving the storm. Names of the dead and missing are being withheld pending notification of next of kin.

*   *   *

MIAMI BEACH TRIBUNE: Monday, September 11, 1950
SURVIVORS OF ILL-FATED OIL TANKER
REVEAL TALE OF MURDER AND HEROISM
ON HIGH SEAS

A bizarre tale of murder and heroism on the high seas is coming to light following the Coast Guard investigation into the loss of the S/T Concordia and twenty-six of her forty-one crew members. Fifteen survivors were rescued from the sinking stern of the tanker in the Gulf of Mexico. Incomplete disclosures by the Coast Guard Board of Inquiry reveal that a number of the men killed and missing were victims of murder and not the storm. Five of the fifteen who survived the trip are still hospitalized, one as the result of gun shot wounds. It was learned that one AB (Able-Bodied Seaman) William Evers, age 50, lost his life while making a third trip below to carry wounded and injured men up to the deck of the sinking hulk. The other man lost during the rescue operation was Samuel Diamond, the severely burned chief cook. Search for the missing lifeboat and its fourteen occupants was abandoned last week following the recovery of a piece of shark-bitten oar and a shredded life preserver stenciled with the tanker Concordia's name. The floating debris was found by the crew of a shrimp boat and turned over to the authorities. Survivors: Carl Finney, Second Mate; Robert J. Pierce, First Assistant Engineer; John Pillars, Second Assistant Engineer; James D. O'Malley, Boatswain; Robert F. Howard, AB; Eric Hansen, AB; Allan Stacey, OS; David T. Sterling, Machinist; Spiros P. Dimitrios, Oiler; Andre Ballou, Oiler; Paco Hernandez, Fireman-watertender; Herman R. Schmidt, Wiper; Waldon Reed, Night Cook and Baker; Phillip T. Banks, Galleyman; Thomas A. Deel, Messman.

Dead or Missing: Robert J. Layton, Captain; Timothy Wilder, Chief Mate; Michael Searles, Third Mate; Fredrick Kruzic, Chief Engineer; Henry A. Davis, Third Assistant Engineer; Edward Moore, Radio Operator; Roland Sims, Jr., Dayman; Chester Borolowski, Dayman; Pedro Davila, AB; James Ryan, AB; Mamud Hassan, AB; William Evers, AB; Peter Tompkins, OS; Terry Cole, OS; Angelo Cannito, Chief Pumpman; James Johnson, Second Pumpman; Ned Carter, Oiler; Fidel Solis, Fireman-Watertender; Paul Morgan, Fireman-Watertender; Frank Billet, Wiper; Thomas Bender, Wiper; Vincent Santos, Chief Steward; Samuel Diamond, Chief Cook; Robert Smith, Second Cook; James L. Dooley, Saloon Messman; Andrew Talley, BR.

Part Two

1984

—THIRTY-SIX—

The bumpy ride on Air Alaska came to a blessed end for Al Stacey. Despite a lifetime of flying around the world to catch new or rejoin old ships, he still disliked flying. The trip to Anchorage on the big jet was bad enough. The part he really dreaded lay ahead—up over the snow-capped mountains and glaciers in a tiny charter plane trying to find Valdez!

"Not a happy homecoming," mused Stacey. "Tommy was probably back aboard by now. Thank Christ, he'd taken his relief trip off as well. But Thompson, his chief mate and good friend, he—"

"Hope you enjoyed the flight, Sir." The lilting voice of the tiny redheaded flight attendant followed him out the door.

"Yes, thanks." Stacey hitched his shoulder to let the heavy flight bag ride easier as he made his way down the ramp, still thinking about the loss of the chief mate. Not just Jack, who'd taken over as relief captain, but the young second mate, Williams, who went chief. And Tommy's relief, Golden. Abe Golden— fitting name, Abe, for a really able seaman... If I'd been out there —maybe it never would have happened. If I'd been aboard... *"NUTS!"* he exclaimed aloud.

"Hey, man!! Who da hell you shovin'?" The big black man he'd collided with on the ramp took a hop and a skip to keep from falling as he regained his balance.

"Sorry, mister," Stacey muttered, "didn't see you." *Nuts! Nuts! Nuts!—that's what you'll be if you keep thinking this way.*

"Tha's a'right, man." The young black fell in stride with Stacey. He had an army surplus duffel bag draped across his shoulder—too big for carry-aboard had it been full. "Say, man, you knows this place?"

"Not much to know," Stacey answered. "Where you heading?"

"Valdaaz. I got me a ship to catch!"

"Valdez," Stacey corrected him. "If you want to follow along, I've got to catch one there as well."

"No shit, man... You a seaman?" The man stopped and shifted the bag to his other shoulder. "What ship *you* on?" he asked as he caught up again.

"The *Alaskan Seas.*"

"Hey, man! That's *my* ship, too!"

"Oh!" Stacey was starting to enjoy the exchange. "Well, I'm certain there's room for both of us aboard. What job did you make, Mister..? I didn't catch your name."

"Mike, Mike Whaler—and I'm ta be the ord'nr'y seaman—what job you got, man?"

"Captain." Stacey turned away as the young black took a double take. He couldn't help smiling.

"Oh shit....CAP'N?—you *jivin'* me, man... *Ain't you?*"

"No." Stacey stopped walking and turned around. He put out his hand. "Pleased to meet you, Mr. Whaler, I'm Captain Stacey."

"SHIT! I mean *DAMN*, SIR... I sure didn't—"

"No problem, Mike. That's where we sign in for the charter flight." Stacey motioned across the terminal. "I've another bag to pick up first. You, too?"

"No, Sir."

"Is that all the gear you've got?"

"Yes, Sir."

"Well, the company used to provide insulated jumpsuits, parkas, and boots, but no more. You'll be issued a 'Survival Suit' —that's all."

"Savaaval suit! I *wears* a Savaa—?"

"No! No, it's not something you wear—only for an emergency —to keep you warm and afloat. You understand?"

"Yes, Sir, now I unnerstans." Mike looked down at his frayed coat sleeves. "Suppose I gotta get sumthin betta."

"I have to get out to the ship as early as possible. Here, put that bag down and let's check your ticket."

Mike searched his pockets till he came up with it.

"See!" The captain pointed out the time. "4:35 P.M. to Valdez. You've got over three hours to kill and you get to go in a Convair, not in the *flea* I'm taking. You're paid straight on through and you've plenty of time to go shopping."

"I'm 'bout tapped, Sir—hafta make do till I gets some bread." He folded the ticket and put it back in his thin wallet.

"Mr. Whaler," Captain Stacey cleared his throat, "is this your first ship?"

The black's pained expression was enough of an answer.

"Look, you've got the job." Stacey said it as fast as he could; unless he was mistaken, he saw a slight glisten start to show in the man's eyes. "But you're going to need the proper gear—you can have an *advance* on your wages, money... so you can go shopping.

Okay?"

"Yes, Sir." Mike looked away. "It *is* my first job, Cap'n an' I—"

"No problem." Stacey reached into his jacket pocket and pulled out a long blue zippered trucker's wallet. "Will three hundred dollars do...? Better make it four—damn clothing isn't cheap up here."

"Fo... Fo hunnred dollas an' you jus' *handin'* it ta me?"

"No, not just handing it to you. I'll need to see your seaman's papers and your shipping card. There," said Stacey as the man handed them over, "just sign this." He hurriedly wrote out an IOU with Whaler's name and seaman's "Z" number on it.

"Sir, I wanta th—"

"You don't have to thank me, Mike. It's an advance—it'll come out of your wages. And you'll *earn* every penny of it on my ship. Better get a move on. Here's your papers and be sure you're aboard an hour before sailing—SOBER!"

—THIRTY-SEVEN—

Survival Suits... SURVIVAL! That's the name of the game all right, thought Stacey. The means to prevent hypothermia at sea had been common knowledge for years. Three years before, two ships went down in the North Atlantic within weeks of each other. Perhaps it was the newspaper pictures of the frozen corpses stacked like mackerel on the decks of the rescue vessels that finally forced the companies to provide the suits, however, covered self-righting lifeboats were *still* not a requirement on American merchant ships.

He'd gotten a momentary lift from the encounter with the young black, but even that turned sour when he had sensed the man's discomfort.

The little Cessna droned on through the grayness. Rain or condensation—Stacey couldn't decide which—streaked the windows. There wasn't anything much to see.

"Sure shook me when I heard 'bout Captain Thompson and the others...didn't know 'em—only Captain Jack!" The pilot turned his head towards Stacey. "Flew *him* in lottsa times. Nice guy... Really nice guy. Just fate I 'spect!"

"Just fate?"

"How's that?" The pilot didn't catch Stacey's rejoinder.

"No, NOT JUST FATE!" Stacey spoke over the sound of the engine. *"GREED!!"*

"There we are!" the pilot announced as they broke through the clouds and skimmed over the ghostly peaks ringing the huge Valdez oil terminal. "Why greed?"

Stacey pointed down at his ship—boldly highlighted by the powerful floodlights. "Look at her *stern!"*

"No savvy, Captain Stacey."

"Neither did the people who designed her!"

The pilot banked to the right and crossed over the ominously craggy mountains heading towards the airport.

"What do you mean about the stern, Sir?" the pilot asked as the *Alaskan Seas* came back into full view.

"Just that she hasn't got one... Not one to speak of," Stacey explained. "A following sea or a sudden course change—a chopped stern can be awash in a flash! Look over at Dock #1, Smitty!" The captain gestured at the old stretched T-2 tanker berthed there, her empty hull high in the water. "Look at the fantail on her! The stern... How broad and round her bottom is! Sea comes up under her she'll ride it up—not bury herself under it!"

"Aha! Okay..." Smitty started his turn and thumbed the mike to raise Valdez and confirm their approach to the tower.

Stacey listened to the exchange.

"Why the different design?" the pilot asked as he brought the plane over to the new heading.

"Why...? Well you can't haul oil in her ass—so they cut it off—that allows bigger tanks for the same tonnage!"

"Great..! Just great! So *money* is the bottom line! And it don't matter if guys like Thompson 'buy the farm'."

"That's about right," Captain Stacey nodded in agreement, "and it's usually the 'good guys' that buy it. Out on the stern securing deck acid—three men for a dozen 55 gallon drums of degreaser!"

"Motherfuckers!!" Smitty snapped on the landing lights as he nursed the plane through the crosswinds. "How do the *bastards* get away with it?"

Stacey watched the double row of blue lights on the snow-lined runway coming up at them and squeezed the St. Christopher medal that Keiko insisted he wear every time he had to fly. Actually, he thought, it *did* make him feel better—even if he didn't believe in such nonsense.

*   *   *

The captain stepped out of the taxi and handed the driver twenty-seven dollars. The fare was twenty-two dollars for one passenger. He thought of Mike Whaler and hoped the man would run into someone heading back to the docks so they could split the fare.

The jetty led out from the tree-lined shore. The tall pines looked like ghostly gray tepees. A bitter wind blew as he made his way down the wide spotless concrete pier. There were no exceptions. You walked to and from the ship, unless you went off in an ambulance—captains and ordinary seaman alike. Stacey was thankful his two pieces of luggage balanced each other and were not that heavy. He left most of his gear aboard when he took his vacations.

It was cold, and the gloomy gray-black September sky made the snow look that much colder. The jetties, docks, and ships were all well lighted, however. The red lights atop the surrounding peaks and storage tanks along with the blue lights from several different spots in the sprawling complex gave the port a somewhat festive—even if sterile—air.

During the summer, Valdez was magnificent. Stacey had yet to meet a seaman who didn't gape at the wonder of it: dazzling white mountain tops with the varied greens of trees and grasses springing from their lower flanks; the reds, pinks, and yellows of wild flowers pushing their way up out of the dark-gray slate—the absolutely unexpected crystalline-clear blue of the ancient glaciers.

The water around the docks was a subdued pastel gray-blue; in the narrow ship channel it was greener and clearer, and in Prince William sound, on a sunny day, it surpassed the color of the finest emerald.

Fish and wildlife abounded. Sea otters cavorted, usually in pairs, thumping mussels and clams against their chests to break them open; then rinsing them in the water before eating them. Seals, spoiled by the easy life and safety of the docks, clambered up onto the tankers' sternposts when they rode high out of the water. And ashore, seaman learned not to get between "Mama Bear" and her cubs on the way back to their ships.

Stacey came to a halt, put down his suitcase and let the flight bag slip off his shoulder. *"SURVIVAL!"* —he thought—"I'll be lucky to survive *this!"* He was sweating and short of breath and the damn ship was still a long way off. He glanced towards the shoreline. It was at least a quarter mile back and he had that or more yet to go. "Everything has to struggle to survive," he mused. "When you stop, you're an endangered species—that was true for men (seamen in particular!) as well as bears."

A light snow was starting to fall. "Seamen are *definitely* on the list," he thought as he hefted his gear and continued on his way. "Like the bears, except for mothers with cubs, we've also been spoiled by the scraps thrown our way and are less wary or able to fend for ourselves."

"When ya stop fightin', ya start dyin"—the words of the bull-headed boss of the seamen's union when Stacey had first sailed as an organizer came back to him.

"The old bastard was right!" Stacey spoke to himself aloud as he stopped again to rest. From where he stood the huge empty hull of the *Alaskan Seas* filled his whole horizon.

Over the years, Stacey rarely thought of his earlier days sailing in the fo'c'sle. But the loss of three men and the heightening tension between his union and the consortium of tanker companies allowed nightmarish flashbacks and a host of other long suppressed ugly memories to come flooding back.

Golden, the "Golden Jew" or the "Golden AB,"whatever the hell it was he'd named himself, had reminded Stacey of his friend Eddy, the plucky little pumpman—gone these many years—killed fighting for a seaman's right to decent working conditions. Strange, you found only a few Jews out here then, or now for that matter. But those you *did* find were the exact opposite of the stereotype of their brethren ashore.

"Left-handed SOB's is what we are!" Pumps would explain.

Explain..?? How would you explain to a fighter like Eddy what had become of the proud union they'd fought for? What would the "Great White Chief" (their red-neck, renegade leader) himself say if he knew what had followed in his wake? Union officials whittling away at the agreements to accommodate the demands of the shipowners—backing down from every conflict with the "powers that be" in and out of government, under-selling their own membership to grab another union or nonunion contract. The results were disastrous. Idiocy was the industry norm. Chief pumpmen worked 15 to 18 hour shifts without relief because compromise and acquiescence had dispensed with the second pumpman.

The licensed deck officers' union was just as guilty. The chief mate allowed to work the same way—round-the-clock.

One man to discharge or load a tanker carrying 1,500,000 barrels of oil—more oil than 12 of the old T–2s could haul. One man, whose shifts often as not turned into 24 hour stints or more when the inevitable breakdowns occurred.

"How do the *bastards* get away with it?" Smitty, the pilot, had asked. No one ashore would believe what was going down out here. No one, of course, but the shipowners, whose <u>bottom line myopia</u> clouded their common sense. They claimed automation allowed, and foreign competition demanded the crew reductions. What was that? *Ignorance and greed?* Or only *GREED??*

Never mind the philosophical question of whether "man was made for work or work was made for man." Despite the hundreds of thousands of inner-city youths without jobs, the quest for any means of reducing labor-intensive industries went marching on.

At sea the result was ONE SHIP, with a crew of 25 men, carrying the *same* amount of oil it once took *a dozen T-2 tankers,* each with a crew of 41 or 42 men, to haul—<u>500 men replaced by 25</u>! How much better off would this country be if hundreds of thousands of Mike Whalers were entering the Merchant Marine or similar trades instead of ending up on the dole; wasting their lives and society's resources?

But even this was not enough—not by a long shot. A new Coast Guard approved manning scale for the *Alaskan Seas* was on Stacey's desk now. As of January 1, the deck gang was to be reduced to six men. No daymen. No Bosun. No ordinary seamen. One of the ABs was to be designated as AB/Boatswain. SIX MEN ON DECK! As it was now, with 10 deckhands and only 15 other men aboard, he dreaded an emergency that might require fighting a fire or launching a lifeboat. Lifeboats, except for Coast Guard drills in a sheltered harbor, seldom saw service in good weather. Rescue operations were generally performed in heavy seas and under the worst of circumstances. If the six men you sent out got into trouble, how many trained men did you have left to send out in another boat to aid them and the people they'd gone out to rescue?

And just what does the wording of the Coast Guard manning requirements mean? After specifying three Able Seamen and three Maintenance Persons holding the endorsement for Able Seaman, it goes on to say that up to two <u>Specially Trained Ordinary Seamen</u> may be substituted for two of these Able Seamen.

"What in the hell is a *'SPECIALLY TRAINED* ORDINARY

SEAMAN?'" the captain swore aloud. "And if they're not going to ship any more ordinary seamen on these tankers, where are rated deckhands going to come from?" All of a sudden it became clear to him. "GOOD CHRIST!—They plan to do away with the ABs! THEY'RE CRAZY!!" He dropped the suitcase and let his shoulder bag fall alongside it in the snow.

Opening his coat, he stood there looking ahead at the tanker's bulk. He was aware of vessels three times her capacity, but the *Alaskan Seas'* size still amazed him: 990 feet from stem to stern, 90 feet from keel to well deck, 180 foot in beam. Over 16 million cubic feet of mass—the equivalent of 1,333 average-sized single story houses.

"No... No sense at all," Stacey muttered aloud. No way could they begin to justify it. Even if inflation since the '50's had been twice the actual rate, they would still have to admit that they had made good money even then—with a dozen tankers and a dozen crews—and oil at $2.00 a barrel!

12 hulls and plants to maintain in order to haul 12 cargoes (each worth about $250,000) meant $3,000,000 divided by 500 men— $6,000 a head. Compare that with the *Alaskan Seas'* cargo of 1.5 Million barrels of crude at $20.00 a barrel. That made $30,000,000 divided by 25 men or $1,200,000 a head. The difference was a factor of 200 to 1.

The price of a house, like that of gold and oil, had gone up 10 to 1—wages not even that. What was the justification for profits 20 times that amount? And there were Ultra-Large-Crude-Carriers that factored out at 75 *times higher!!*

Yet, despite profits one could only describe as obscene, Stacey's crew would soon be reduced to 21 men. There wasn't enough profit to allow the Mike Whalers of the world to learn the trade and earn a living—not when you could get 6 men to burn themselves out on overtime, instead of paying 10 men their regular wages and funding their health and retirement plans.

Stacey angrily brushed the snow off his head and picked up his gear. "Bastards!" he cursed aloud. "And the damn Coast Guard lets them get away with it! *Power!* POWER and GREED!"

It wasn't the ratings and the officers. The captain knew them —good men most of them, conscientious and hard working for the most part. At sea they were brave and able in their missions. No! it was higher up where the "Power Brokers" played that the deals were cut!

Too soft... he thought, *all of us too soft.* It wasn't one union, but all of them: unlicensed, deck officers, engineers. Their memberships cutting each other's throats while their leaders cut deals—deals with the companies—deals with the government—all under the guise of honest trade unionism.

"And we've only ourselves to blame." Stacey shook his head. "We've become gutless rank and filers going along with any immorality our leaders propose. Under-cutting each other's contracts, back-stabbing the men working next to us, anything—just so long as it is presented to us as necessary to save our jobs.

"GREED at the top! FEAR at the bottom! *INTEGRITY NOWHERE!!* A sociological 'food chain,' a 'FEEDING FRENZY,' a—"

"Cap'n!"

Tommy's greeting took Stacey by surprise.

"You shoulda called the dock from Valdaaz."

The captain put his gear down. "Vald<u>e</u>z," he corrected, grasping the bosun's calloused hand.

"Sure good ta see you, Sir!"

"Everything okay at home? Ellen? The kids...?" Stacey released his hand and tapped Tommy's shoulder with the side of his fist.

"Yes, Sir... Everyone's jus' fine—not kids no more," Tommy picked up the suitcase, "but more gran' kids 'n I can handle... How's Keiko?"

"Good...real good. She's found her another horse to feed." The captain lifted his flight bag and fell in step with the bosun. "Start loading yet?"

"No, Sir. Jus' now finishin' with ballast... Sure gonna miss Golden."

"We all will—Thompson, and Williams, too."

The two friends fell silent as they made their way through the falling snow.

The dock's operations office loomed eerily in the semi-darkness as they drew closer to the end of the jetty. The numerous pipelines that ran underneath the 12 foot wide dock were suddenly visible as they arched upright and crossed the spotlessly clean steel-grated loading platform.

A complex of pipes carried water (fresh and salt) steam, electric cables, fire-fighting chemicals, etc., above, around, and below the dock—each finding the valve, connector or piece of equipment intended for it.

But it was the four huge pipelines—which had just off-loaded the *Alaskan Seas'* 200,000 barrels of dirty ballast and would soon fill her 13 enormous cargo tanks with 1,500,000 barrels of heated crude (at 100,000 barrels per hour)—that dominated the surrealistic scene.

The lines were linked to towering "Chicksans" that soared high above the ship; colossal praying mantises whose gigantic arms were long jointed pipes that plunged down to the tanker's manifold.

"Ahoy below!" a female voice hailed them from the tanker's well deck. "I've a heaving line tied off there for your gear, Sir."

"Thank you, Angela!" Stacey resisted the temptation to tell her to have someone help her with his things.

One at a time, the bosun took a few turns around each piece of luggage before calling to the AB to haul away. Captain Stacey had already started the climb up the steep 75 foot gangway.

"Tha's it!" Tommy called out as the last bag was hauled up. "Toss the line down," he yelled up to Angela, "an' I'll tie 'er back off!"

—THIRTY-EIGHT—

Stacey entered the wheelhouse from the port wing of the bridge as the eye of the stern line hit the water. Two huge tugboats backed and pushed to turn the tanker away from the dock. The third mate logged "last line away" at 10:18 P.M. on the page dated 9/9/84.

It was no longer snowing, but it was cold and windy. The well decks glistened wetly in the reflected shore lights. They were mostly snow-free due to heat from the crude oil (which came aboard at 105 degrees F.) but here and there patches of ice persisted.

The pilot gave his orders from the bridge to the tug captains and they repeated each command before executing it, as did the third mate at the telegraph and the AB on the wheel—*the timeless litany of the sea.*

The *Alaskan Seas'* huge wheelhouse contained an array of navigational equipment and monitoring systems that rivaled those aboard Star Trek's "Enterprise." The main console, sporting myriad gauges and digital readouts, sparkled and glowed in different colors like precious stones.

In addition to the RDF (radio direction finder) Loran, satellite navigation system, standard steering compass, two gyro compasses, two fathometers, two radar sets (3 cm. and 10 cm.) there was a collision avoidance radar and twin Doppler systems. Rudder angle and rate–of–turn indicators mechanically displayed overhead on the forward bulkhead were repeated in digital readouts on the steering station console.

"The equipment is first class," thought Stacey, "two of everything—as it should be—except for the main propulsion unit. Like all of the huge modern merchant vessels being built these days, the *Alaskan Seas* had no back up for her single Diesel engine. If she lost her plant in a storm, along the coast, or maneuvering to avoid a collision, she was in *God's* hands not his. What a gamble for the people who make these decisions to take! A few decades ago, no naval architect would have dreamed of designing a ship with a *single* boiler or Diesel. Personnel required for operation of these ships were being reduced to 'zero redundancy' as well. But there were already too few people aboard to allow even one to get sick or miss a sailing without taxing the remaining crew.

"The time required as an apprentice should have been increased, not decreased as it had. Special courses for quartermasters provided by the union and nonunion schools were fine, but they were no substitute for the three years at sea originally required of an ordinary seaman before he could sit for his AB's papers. Simulation exercises and book answers could never replace time and experience. Exotic electronics could break down like anything else. And when that happened, the only margin of safety you had were people who could 'fly by the seat of their pants.'

"*The industry, unrestrained by government, the Coast Guard or the unions, had set a course for disaster!*"

"Well, Captain," the pilot pulled his stool closer to the porthole, "looks like it's clearing finally."

"How's that?" Stacey hadn't heard the remark.

"Clearing!"

"Yes... Yes, it is."

"We can bring her up to full ahead." The pilot glanced over to where the officer of the watch stood.

"Full ahead!" The third mate rang the telegraph and recorded the time in the bell book.

"Left easy to 245, Quartermaster."

"Left easy to 245," the old AB repeated.

"Any more news on your contract negotiations, Captain?" the pilot spoke as he raised his binoculars.

"No, nothing."

"It's obvious this consortium of tanker companies don't really want a contract. There's been no negotiating or bargaining—just demands."

"I hope that isn't the case." Stacey glanced up from the radar screen.

"They can't justify a 25% reduction in wages and cutting vacation days in half when they're earning more than ever."

"245—right on!"

"245. Very well!"

"What's your theory, then?"

"Well... I'll tell you, Captain." The pilot crushed out his cigarette. "From what I see this has been in the plannin' since your last contract."

"How do you mean?" asked Stacey.

"Who pays the overtime for tank cleanin', maintenance, and the like on these chartered haulers?"

"Well...the oil companies do, but I don't see what you're driving at."

"Simply this. It's 'Big Oil' that's calling all the shots. When they reduce their overhead to these tanker outfits they increase their profits. And they're starting this plan by painting you—O U T—out!"

"Coffee?" Stacey asked as he went to the set-up and poured himself a cup.

"No, thanks," the pilot answered, then continued. "And when they've gotten rid of you union deck officers they'll be able to make these companies roll back the engineers' wages and benefits as well—'Divide and conquer'!"

"That wasn't new," thought Stacey, "'Big Oil' trying to get the chartered haulers to cut down expenses. But pressuring them to refuse to bargain in good faith with the union was new—in fact, it was downright scary!"

"Cat got your tongue?" the pilot challenged.

"Just thinking..." Stacey came back to the porthole. "Only flaw in your reasoning is it's Big Oil that'll lose the most if these tankers are tied up for any length of time. And I don't see how these tanker companies can replace masters and mates on five or six dozen tankers all at once."

"You can't, huh! Take it from me, they've had it planned for a couple of years—it'll be done overnight!"

Stacey knew the older man's background and respected his knowledge of the oil industry, but this much intrigue was a little hard to believe. "Well, Sir, I really don't see how. They can't fill all these jobs with people fresh out of maritime colleges, and—"

"Bring her to 255," the pilot interrupted.

"255!"

"No, Captain," the pilot agreed, "they can't. But they sure as hell can replace 'em with the deck officers the oil companies been givin' early retirement to these past few years!"

"You really believe they planned this so far in advance?"

"Yes, Sir! And these tanker companies have got themselves another source of deck officers—right out of one of the engineers union's locals. Hell, they been secretly meeting with 'em and offerin' a 'sweetheart deal' for over a year!"

"255 she goes, Pilot." The old AB was taking in the whole conversation, but he felt curiously remote.

"255. Thank you, Quartermaster."

A beam of light momentarily cut the darkness as Angela entered the wheelhouse. She stood near the steering station a few moments letting her eyes adjust to the dark before stepping behind the helmsman.

"Going 255. Only takin' a spoke or two to hold her." The old AB turned the small wheel back to midships and stepped off the grate. "Where we workin'?"

"Wheel relieved—255." Angela's voice was barely audible in the huge room. "The gang's about through forward. Boats said for you to take coffce, then meet him in the pumproom with the ordinary to swing the blank."

"255." The pilot glanced back at the pleasant young face just visible in the light from the steering station. "And how goes it with you tonight, young lady?"

"Fine, Sir."

The pilot stood up, stretched, then turned back to the porthole and picked up his binoculars. "Do you think your union will strike, Captain?"

"I don't know. We've been riding high on gains won a long time ago... Most of them thanks to the old boss of the unlicensed seamen's union."

The captain remembered well the charismatic "Man from Dixie"—the boss of the organizers.

Bull Hendricks became the new leader of the seamen's union when his predecessor, the fearless old Scandinavian (whose white-visored cap had become every union seaman's symbol of strength and solidarity) died in 1957.

A few weeks later Stacey stood at the massive mahogany bar in the union operated tavern and told the newly elected president about his decision to try sailing topside. He had passed the Coast Guard exams, gotten his original second mate's license, and was joining the deck officers' union as an "applicant"—Stacey was retiring his seamen's union book.

"Wish ya luck? Course I wish ya luck!" Stacey could see the scene as if it were yesterday. The old organizer boss slammed his ham-like fist on the bar hard enough to make their beer mugs bounce. "You'll be needin' all the fuckin' luck ya can get not to *starve* with them fuckers. 'Sides, I don't think you'll be able ta tolerate them finky cocksuckers very long!"

Knowing how the man felt about the weaker company-oriented deck officers' union, it was as good a send-off as he could expect from the crusty old warrior.

"Put her on half ahead, Third."

"Half ahead... Sir," the young third mate, who hadn't said a word till now except to repeat a command, addressed the two master mariners. "You're a retired skipper from an oil company, working as a pilot for the state of Alaska."

"That's so," the pilot answered.

"And Captain Stacey, Commodore of this tanker company's fleet, with 15 years seniority, has got almost 30 years invested with the union. Tell me, if you were both starting out again today—as I am—would you go company or union?"

"Union," Stacey was the first to respond, "but I can't honestly say the choice would be as easy today as it was years ago."

"Company!" The pilot surprised everyone in the wheelhouse. "But *this time* I'd keep my nose up out of the soup and into where *decisions* are made—just complaining about these damn oil companies isn't going to change them!"

"Well...! Gee..! And thanks...! You've both been a *real great help* in making up my mind!"

Everyone, including Angela, laughed in response to the young officer's rejoinder.

When the mirth subsided the pilot turned around on his stool and looked again at the pretty girl. "Bring her right easy to 270. Let me know when you're right on, Quartermaster... Or should that be...Mistress?"

"Right easy to 270—MASTER is fine! *Sir!!*" Angela was not amused.

The captain knew the old pilot was only joking with the girl—Angela was very capable at the wheel. Still, he chuckled inwardly when the pilot continued to dig.

"Or should that be helmswoman...or person?"

"Right on, *Sir*. 270!" Angela called out.

"270. Very well."

Captain Stacey couldn't help sharing the pilot's misgivings when it came to women at sea.

On modern vessels, like the *Alaskan Seas,* where each person had a large comfortable room with adjoining bath, there was no problem for both sexes to live aboard in privacy. And there were amenities undreamed of a decade ago. All accommodation spaces were air-conditioned. Officers and crew had their own reading rooms, TV lounges, exercise facilities (complete with saunas and showers) and there was an Olympic-style swimming pool complete with private dressing rooms for the entire ship's company.

But the fact remained that the presence of women aboard ship was not without its challenges. Whether they were loose or proper, fights over them were frequent and sometimes deadly.

As for the work, reasonable men, and most were, usually "cut some slack" for the lady sailors. But now, with the gangs being reduced further, that wouldn't be possible. Everyone would have to carry their own load; whether mucking or hauling buckets when tank cleaning, manhandling the heavy cargo line reducers, or swinging blanks in the pumproom.

Admittedly, thought Stacey, the women that opted for this way of life were generally gutty and willing workers. He admired them. It was just that there were so many routine jobs, never mind emergencies, that demanded an upper body strength that females were just not endowed with.

"10 degrees left rudder." The pilot stood up and walked over to the radar. "Put her on slow ahead."

Angela and the third mate repeated and complied with the commands.

A few moments passed as the tanker began her turn to the left.

"Where are you now, Quartermaster?"

"241—coming left."

"Midships...steady up on 225." The pilot walked back to the porthole as Angela repeated the order and eased the wheel.

The ship swung slowly in line with the approach to the ship channel.

"225. Right on!"

"225. Very well." The pilot flipped on his hand-held radio and reported the *Alaskan Seas'* speed and position to the Coast Guard station; they were entering the "narrows."

—THIRTY-NINE—

The *Alaskan Seas* logged arrival at Puerto Armuello, Panama at 6:30 A.M., September 24, and by 8:00 A.M. she was at the dock preparing to discharge her cargo of North Slope crude.

The trip was without incident—but tension from the threatened job action had divided the crew. Telex messages from the three unions—licensed deck officers, engineers, and unlicensed seamen—each gave different versions of the issues involved and how their members should react.

Many of the engineers and seamen argued against their union officials and called for solidarity with the licensed deck officers, but there were too many crossed interests. Both unions harbored hopes of cutting down their unemployment by supplying the companies with deck officers should the LDO union lose its contract.

*   *   *

The concrete bridge linking the port and the town had collapsed in recent torrential rains. Since that was the only way into the little city with its duty-free stores, hotels, bars, and whorehouses, the crew would have to be content with the few establishments within walking distance of the ship, or find a way across the river on foot. Repairs could not be made until the river subsided.

Having the afternoon off, Mike Whaler went ashore. It was overcast and a light drizzle made walking around looking at the lush scenery less pleasurable than he had anticipated. He finally wandered into a small *cantina* that catered to native dock workers.

He sat staring unhappily at his beer; it was warm and tasteless, and he was being hassled by a taxi driver who had left his cab on the other side of the river. The drivers crossed over makeshift bridges of felled trees, bringing girls, the usual assortment of cheap jewelry, and narcotics with them.

"No, man, I done tol' you to let me be!" Whaler turned away from the persistent salesman.

"*Si, Senior...* Okay... okay." The unhappy man closed the little ring box. "Perhaps a good watch, *amigo?*" He reached into his pocket and came out with a handful.

"Shit, man! I wants to relax and you jus' keeps at it. I gotta watch an' I don' wants no ring, no junk, no nothin'! All's I'm takin' back wid me is a couple a beers."

"But you like the womans? No?" The driver's almost imperceptible nod alerted the skinny mini-skirted girl across the room. She hurried over and sat down, her knee pressed against Mike's, one hand resting on his thigh.

The screen door opened and Angela came into the dimly lit room, followed by Henry, the old AB on his watch, and the bosun.

"That you, Mike?" Angela called out.

"Hell, it ain't that dark in here!" Tommy quipped.

Mike waved to the three, then turned back to the driver. "Look, man, I jus don' wants nuthin'—my friends is here."

"This Rosa, she's new... Almost like a virgin!"

"No, man! I says no!" Mike pushed the girl's hand away from his groin.

"Okay... Maybe later? Okay?" The driver persisted.

"Go on now!" Mike warned. "I means it!"

The pair got up from the table.

"What was that all about?" Angela chuckled as she and the others pulled up chairs.

"Man! That dude's got somethin' in every pocket!" Mike shook his head at the retreating figures.

"*Cerveza?*" The barefooted wife of the *patron* came over as they sat down.

"*Si, Senora.*" Angela opened her wallet. "*Cuatro.*" She held up four fingers. "*Quanto?*"

"No!" Whaler pushed her money back. "I'm buyin'."

"Well, thanks, Mike—better go easy on your spending though. We may all be getting off up north," she reminded him.

"You really thinks we'll hafta?" Mike's voice reflected his unhappy feelings.

The fifteen days at sea had become the most significant "happening" in the young black's life. As soon they were away from the coast, Angela and old Henry had started teaching him to steer. He worked overtime every day with pneumatic chipping guns and wire brushes on tank tops and cargo lines, then primed and painted them. He was learning how to operate winches, tie proper knots, and how to make up and toss a heaving line. Everything, even the first night's struggle in the pumproom securing the huge cargo line blank now seemed pretty neat. And he was making real money for the *first* time! He had already earned enough to cover his $400 advance from the Old Man and had plenty left over.

The *Senora* was back with the drinks. She put down the little round tray and turned four almost clean glasses right side up. *"Limas...?"* she asked.

"Si, por favor." Angela smiled, continuing to practice her Spanish.

"Thanks, Mike." Henry picked up one of the beers. "What do you think, Boats?"

"No telling... Ain't no one wants to be outa work... But if all of us keeps backing off from these companies we gonna be right back where we started."

"Yeah, but topside been gettin' the lion's share of everything. Twenty, twenty-five years back an AB workin' overtime made more than any third mate—now look at our wages!" the old AB exclaimed.

"That's so... But it ain't their fault. Our pay should've been getting higher—you know we been falling behind every agreement. Hell, we ain't even got a real contract right now."

"What do you mean by that, Boats?" asked Angela.

"Thought we renewed the 'tanker agreement' a couple of months ago," Henry added.

"No, Sir. We still workin' on a 15 day 'reopener' clause is all —no new 3 year contract. The companies is jus' keeping the unlicensed on ice till they deals with the officers."

"Well, I can't get teary-eyed 'bout these fuckin' officers— 'scuse me, Angela. They been in bed with the companies for years. Now, all of a sudden, they're 'gung-ho' union men looking for us to help 'em."

"What do you think we should do, Boats?" asked the girl.

"I feel we gotta back 'em. They've made mistakes, like not supporting the oil dock workers strike las' year—and it's true they ain't always helped us stand up to the companies... But we hafta start stickin' together somewheres."

"Ah, you might as well stick with *scabs* as throwin' in with them!" the old AB snorted.

"Union and nonunion, they—" Angela started to speak.

"SCABS!" Henry interjected.

"Shouldn't fight," she continued, "and that's terrible to call someone *that* just because they think differently. My grandad sailed his whole life for a nonunion oil company. He felt they treated him right—it was his choice! He believed that was what America and *freedom* was all about!"

"You right, Angela," the bosun agreed. "You got good an' bad on both sides, and everyone should have the choice like you says. Standin' up to the bad in a union or a company is the only *good* fight. But if you union, then you gotta support other union brothers when they right!"

"Shit! It'll never happen! You got mates shipping out of the engineers' hall and ours both, Boats...! And—*hell!*—the deck officers' union is supplyin' their own cruise ship with unlicensed!" The old AB finished his beer and gestured to the barefoot woman.

"No denyin' that, Henry. All of us been fightin' each other for what few jobs is left, even though we belongs to the same Labor Federation—and that's jus' what the companies is countin' on. If this raiding and not supportin' each other don' stop, there ain't gonna be no more unions!"

The *Senora* came back with four more beers and wiped the table. When she left, the conversation did not immediately pick up again; the four sat quietly drinking their beer.

"How many ships would be tied up if we all went on strike?" Angela broke the ice.

"Figure about fifty, maybe sixty," the old AB volunteered. "That about right, Boats?"

"Yep... One helluva lot—considerin' we less than four hundred American-flag ships left."

Mike hadn't said a word since the discussion began. He knew little about the issues and his feelings where in turmoil. It was his first real job; far better than anything he had ever found ashore—the thought of losing it overwhelmed him.

The ordinary was starting to show the effects of a mixture of sad thoughts and warm beer. He finished two more in rapid succession while the others nursed their last round.

"Ain't none of my business, Mike," advised Henry, "but if

you're plannin' on takin' beer back to the ship, you best not come aboard weavin'."

"Hey, man... I ain't gonna get drunk!"

"Didn't say you was. But if you even *look* drunk this Old Man'll have your booze. And if you're loaded when you turn to, you best pack your gear."

"That's so, Mike." The Bosun lent support to the old AB's advice. "He's one way on that."

"He's sure got himself a reputation at the hall," Angela added. "Lot's of people wont throw in for a ship if they know *he's* skipper."

"Well," Tommy answered her, "you'll find it's the 'performers,' as runs him down. It's true, they don't las' but one trip with him. He's hard—no denyin' that—Angela, but he's straight, and speakin' for myself, I'd rather have it that way... You can *sleep* nights knowin' this Old Man's on the bridge!"

"He musta come out of the Navy," Henry joined the discussion again, "or maybe Kingspoint!"

"No, Sir... He come outta the fo'c'sle." Tommy glanced at his watch. "He organized for the union, and he retired a full book."

"Well... There's still got to be a limit to interfering with people's life styles—even out here," observed Angela.

"No...! Not when it come to the safety of the ship. Put yo'self in his shoes. He gotta be on top of everything and everyone—officers and crew alike."

"But he's *not* hired by the company to police people's morals."

"Look, Angela... I don't know nothin' 'bout that. But I do know there jus' ain't no slack running a ship like this. One bad judgment—one wrong turn of the wheel—one mistake at the manifold, in the tanks or in the pumproom and you got yo'self a spill or a collision—or you blows sky high!"

Tommy bought the next round of beer.

A few mariachis showed up, alerted there were seamen stranded on this side of the river. The music was good and it was loud enough to attract other crew members from the *Alaskan Seas*, and more taxi drivers with their girls.

"Well, you guys have a good time." Tommy got up and slipped the leader of the little combo a ten dollar bill. "I gotta get back and square some things away... Cheer up, there's a chance it'll all be settled."

*   *   *

The deck gang turned to at 4:15 the following morning, and by 7:00 A.M. the tanker was secured for sea, outbound for Long Beach to bunker and take stores on her way back to Valdez.

After supper, the unlicensed crew held a special union meeting, and to the bosun's surprise, all hands, including Angela, old Henry and the new ordinary, voted to back the deck officers. The final resolution was to paint a huge canvas sign declaring their sympathies—to be hung over the tanker's side should the deck officers strike.

The seven-day trip to Long Beach was to be a pleasant one for the deck gang. The plans to muck No. 2 wing tanks were cancelled and, since it had stopped raining the second day out of Panama, the mate had the bosun turn out everyone in the deck gang who wanted overtime painting the boat deck and the stack."

"Mike...! You working overtime today?" Angela knocked again on the ordinary's door. "12:45, MIKE!"

"Yeah! Thank you, Angela. I be there."

She continued down to old Henry's fo'c'sle and after getting an affirmative response, headed for the bosun's locker.

Tommy was checking a long gantline when the girl came in. He glanced at his watch. "You early. Rest of the 8 to 12 all turnin' to?"

"Aye, Bosun!"

"You got a good partner in that Henry, and the new ordinary seem real willin'."

"You said it. They're both great guys... Boats, can I paint on the stack today?"

"We got the 4 to 8 comin' out, so there's more hands than we needs aloft. I'd like for you to tend lines and mix paint with me." Tommy started pulling another gantline through his hands, twisting it every so often to open the lay and check for rot or broken strands.

"Look, Bosun, it's a beautiful warm clear day out. I *want* to go aloft."

"Jus' ain't necessary, Angela. We got plenty—"

"Damn it , Boats! Is it *the captain* giving you orders?"

"Hold on there now, Missy!"

"Okay, Boats... Okay...I'm sorry. But I know he's against women out here—period! *That's* what I meant by <u>interfering with</u>

<u>people</u>!"

"This one ain't gonna be no good." Tommy dropped the line and held out his key ring. "When we turns to, cut me forty fathom offa the new reel and put me a good whippin' on both ends."

Angela took the keys and started out of the locker, then turned back. "Boats... I'm not turning to for overtime today—or any day!" She handed the keys back to Tommy.

"That's foolish!"

"And I'm paying off in Long Beach." There were tears in her eyes. "I'm a *green ticket AB,* Bosun! THREE LONG YEARS!" she shouted. *"THAT DAMN CAPTAIN CAN'T—"*

"ANGELA!" Tommy quieted her. "Angela... Don't be like that. He ain't against you... He say the other day he rather have *you* on the wheel than anybody."

"Anyone can steer!"

"You know that ain't so... Look...a gal on a ship of his a couple years back come off a stage—they was paintin' the face of the bridge, an—"

"Oh come *off* it, Boats. Accidents happen!"

"Her hand jus' weren't able to marry the gantlin' long enough to ties off her end. The other AB try to grab her, he fall 60 feet head first. The gal come down tangled wid the line—it save her life— but the rope burn most her face away."

The story made an impression on the girl, but she managed to conceal it.

"So...no more women can go aloft?" Angela shook her head.

"Where we workin', Boats?" The old AB looked into the bosun's locker.

Tommy handed the keys back to the girl. "Angela's gonna make you up a new gantlin'. When the ordinary get here you two carry the stages up to the boat deck."

*   *   *

At 2:30 A.M. on October 3 the *Alaskan Seas* anchored off Long Beach. Thirty minutes later she was hooked-up and receiving her fuel from a Diesel oil barge secured alongside.

The first launch from shore brought a few newspapers and the ship's mail. A few minutes later it left with those off-watch crew members wanting to go ashore.

The deck gang handled stores throughout the day as the various ship chandlers delivering food, clean linen, deck and engine room supplies arrived with their tugs and barges.

By the time the 3:00 P.M. break came around, the last thing left to come aboard was a new ninety-foot aluminum gangway. It was to be dropped off for another of the company's ships on their return trip to Panama. After coffee it was lifted aboard and made fast on the starboard side of the well deck, lashed to the tank tops with wire slings and chain-binders.

The tanker was secured for sea by 4:30 P.M. and the bosun and the chief mate went forward to weigh anchor. Mike Whaler and Henry, the old AB, went with them to rig a fire hose to blast the mud off the cable and hook as it came up. There were automatic wash-down nozzles in the hawsepipes but they never seemed to do a good job.

At supper, the saloon and messroom were almost deserted; most of the officers and crew who were off watch had eaten ashore. Only one man missed ship, the chief pumpman. He would have to pay his own air fare to Valdez to catch the tanker and probably a fine to pay the seamen's union as well.

—FORTY—

Captain Stacey paced back and forth on the starboard wing. The wind was picking up and the sea grew choppy as the *Alaskan Seas* left the sheltered bay. The lights along the coast twinkled brightly in the growing darkness as they seemed to grow smaller.

"Sir!" the radio operator called out as he stepped from the wheelhouse and approached the captain. "This just came in." Stacey was handed a fluttering piece of paper.

"Thanks, Sparks." Shielding his penlight, he read the communication.

TELEX ASN 03 OCT 84, 2118Z
1604312 KFDA X
VIA COMSAT
10/03 2015 Z
WU
1604312 KFDA X

EASYLINK 4070416A002 3 OCT 21:50/21:53 EST
FROM: TLX 762711 L D O BAL. MD.

LICENSED DECK OFFICERS UNION
TO: 7135041350 &
M/T ALASKAN SEAS
OCTOBER 3, 1984

TO ALL CONTRACTED VESSELS:
DUE TO ACTIONS OF TANKER COMPANIES ALL MASTERS AND MATES ARE TO IMMEDIATELY CEASE ALL WORK NOT NECESSARY FOR SECURITY OF VESSEL AND SAFETY OF CREW.

SPECIFICALLY: NO UNDOCKING, SHIFTING, LOADING, DISCHARGING, TANK CLEANING, TRANSFER OF CARGO, BALLASTING, DEBALLASTING, OR ADMINISTRATIVE AND CLERICAL WORK.

ALL DECK OFFICERS SHOULD REMAIN ABOARD VESSELS TO PROTECT THEIR JOBS AND SHOULD DEMONSTRATE THEIR COURAGE AND WILLINGNESS TO FOLLOW THESE INSTRUCTIONS AND REFUSE TO LEAVE THEIR SHIPS VOLUNTARILY.

OUR JOB ACTION IS NECESSARY TO PROTECT NOT ONLY OUR WAGES AND BENEFITS, BUT ULTIMATELY THOSE OF ALL OFFICERS AND CREW MEMBERS.

COMPANIES' ACTIONS AGAINST LDO UNION MASTERS, MATES, AND PILOTS IS THE OPENING WEDGE THAT WILL FINALLY DESTROY ALL OTHER HARD WON UNION CONTRACT CONDITIONS AT SEA. ENGINEERS AND UNLICENSED CREW MEMBERS SHOULD BE ADVISED OF THIS AND THEIR SUPPORT REQUESTED.

SINCE THE COMPANIES HAVE REFUSED TO BARGAIN IN GOOD FAITH, THE MEMBERSHIP MUST STAND UNITED IN THIS JOB ACTION IF WE ARE TO PREVAIL IN PROTECTING OUR FUTURE.

ANY LDO OFFICER NOT SUPPORTING THIS JOB ACTION SHOULD BE REPORTED TO HEADQUARTERS. PLEASE ACKNOWLEDGE NEXT PORT AND ETA.

PRESIDENT
LICENSED DECK OFFICERS UNION

"Well, that's it!" Stacey folded the telex. "If we'd received this an hour ago we'd be caught swinging from the hook."

"It seems strange that they haven't been able to reach some sort of an agreement."

"Do me a favor, Sparks; make duplicates." Stacey handed the message back. "And post them in the saloon and crew's mess."

"Aye, Sir. It's getting cold out here—I'll see to it now." The radio operator started back towards the wheelhouse.

"Thanks." Stacey rubbed the back of his neck and stretched his arms over his head. "Now for the company's version," he said to himself.

It wasn't long coming.

"Captain." The radio operator tapped gently on the office door. "You still up, Sir?"

"Aye, come in." Stacey was reading. He put the book down as the door opened.

"From the company office this time, Captain." Sparks put the message on the desk and waited while the Old Man read it. "Want me to post copies like before?"

"Might as well." Stacey shook his head. "I'm turning in now. Anything else you receive can wait till morning—unless you feel it's urgent."

"Aye. Goodnight, Sir." The radio operator closed the door and headed for the copy machine in the officer's dayroom.

"Shit!" The young third mate read the latest telex. It was 7:45 P.M. and he was drinking coffee, waiting to go on watch. Sparks came in and tacked the new telex up next to the first one.

TELEX ASN 03 OCT 84, 2054Z
1604312 KFDA X
VIA COMSAT
10/03 2146Z

22:30 EDT OCT 3/84
FROM: TRANSEAS N.Y. N.Y.
TO: MASTER M/T ALASKAN SEAS

   MESSAGES HAVE BEEN SENT BY LDO UNION INCITING OUR MASTERS AND MATES TO ILLE-GAL ACTS. ANY DECK OFFICER WHO REFUSES

TO OBEY LEGAL COMMANDS, OR PERFORM AS-
SIGNED DUTIES, OR REFUSES TO LEAVE A SHIP
WHEN SO ORDERED SHALL BE FIRED AND PER-
MANENTLY BARRED FROM REEMPLOYMENT.
APPROPRIATE CRIMINAL, CIVIL, AND LI-
CENSE PROCEEDINGS WILL BE TAKEN.

VIOLATION OF OBLIGATIONS WHILE UNDER
FOREIGN ARTICLES IN A NON-CONTIGUOUS
UNITED STATES OR FOREIGN PORT CONSTITUTES
A MUTINOUS ACT.

WE EXPECT THE SUPPORT OF OUR LOYAL
DECK OFFICERS.

PORT CAPTAIN
TRANSEAS N.Y. N.Y.

"'A pox on *both* your houses!'" The young officer shook his
fist at the bulletin board.

*   *   *

The bosun knocked on the chief mate's door. "It's 7:20!"
"Come on in, Boats."
Tommy opened the door. "Mornin', Sir."
"Come in—sit down." The officer was just out of the shower
and had a towel wrapped around his waist. He was in his late
thirties, a tankerman and LDO union member for almost twenty
years. The man was well over 6 feet tall and had the build of a
weight lifter—his upper body tattooed from neck to wrists. His
hair appeared longer than it was due to his heavy full black beard.
Though sailing as mate, he was a master mariner, with over
ten years in the company as chief mate and relief captain.
"Didn't know if you was wantin' to be called this mornin' or
not, Sir."
"Yeah... Some heavy shit coming down." The mate towelled
himself dry as he spoke. "I'm not turning to, Boats, but there's no
sense you people not working O.T. till this shit gets resolved."
"Well, we havin' another meeting at coffee time... Most of the
unlicensed crew is for supportin' the LDO's job action."
"That's a help—might still have a chance to beat these

assholes. It'll be interesting to see how the engineers aboard swing." The officer went into his bedroom and pulled on his trousers.

"If the 'rank and file' don't make themselves heard out here, there's ain't gonna be no unions," Tommy remarked as the mate came back into the office.

"Might as well finish painting the tank tops and cargo lines we primed last week—while we still got the weather!"

"Only the watch on deck, Mate?"

"Fuck no...turn out anyone wanting to work—I can still sign the overtime sheets!"

"Aye, Mate... Good luck." Tommy left the office and headed below to call the gang.

*   *   *

"This gonna be short," the bosun addressed the crew members gathered in the messroom. "Angela here wrote out this for anyone wantin' to sign." He held up the paper, then put it down on the table. "She'll take it up to Sparks and find out how many ships we can send to. We'll pay from the ship's fund like we all agreed. Anyone got somethin' to add?"

No one spoke.

"Then this meetin's adjourned. Let the deck gang sign first so they can get back to work."

The long sheet of yellow paper was neatly printed with a message to be transmitted to the headquarters of the seamen's union and a crew's list with room for signatures.

FROM: CREW MEMBERS OF M/T ALASKAN SEAS.

TO: PRESIDENT OF THE SEAMENS' UNION.
BROOKLYN, N.Y.

AND CREW MEMBERS OF THE FOLLOWING SHIPS:
....
....
....
....
....

10/4/84

DEAR SIR AND BROTHER,

WE THE UNDERSIGNED UNLICENSED CREW
MEMBERS OF THE M/T ALASKAN SEAS THINK
YOU SHOULD KNOW WE ARE UNANIMOUS IN
OUR OPINION THAT THE CONSORTIUM OF
TANKER COMPANIES HAS NOT BARGAINED IN
GOOD FAITH WITH THE LICENSED DECK OFFI-
CERS' UNION.

AS SUCH WE FEEL OUR UNION SHOULD EMPLOY
ANY AND ALL MEANS AT ITS DISPOSAL TO COME
TO THE AID OF THIS FEDERATION AFFILIATED
MARITIME UNION IN ITS "BEEF" WITH THE
TANKER COMPANIES.

FRATERNALLY YOURS,

BOATSWAIN......................
8 X 12 ABLE-BODIED SEAMAN..........
8 X 12 ABLE-BODIED SEAMAN..........
12 X 4 ABLE-BODIED SEAMAN..........
12 X 4 ABLE-BODIED SEAMAN..........
4 X 8   ABLE-BODIED SEAMAN..........
4 X 8   ABLE-BODIED SEAMAN..........
8 X 12 ORDINARY SEAMAN............
12 X 4 ORDINARY SEAMAN............
4 X 8   ORDINARY SEAMAN............
CHIEF PUMPMAN..........
QUALIFIED MEMBER ENGINE DEPT. ....
QUALIFIED MEMBER ENGINE DEPT. ....
WIPER..........
CHIEF STEWARD/CHIEF COOK..........
GENERAL STEWARD UTILITY..........

Angela picked up the paper after the last crew member left the
messroom. Other than the chief pumpman—who had missed the
ship—*everyone* had signed.

*   *   *

The following morning the captain asked the radio operator to routinely post all incoming telexes pertaining to the job action in both the saloon and the messroom.

By coffee time that afternoon the bulletin boards were covered with ships reporting their status:

"ANCHORED MISSISSIPI RIVER—NO WORK—NO BOARDING PERMITTED."

"AT CHORPUS CHRISTI—NO WORK—REFUSED TO LEAVE VESSEL—EXPECTING ARMED GUARDS TO ARRIVE SOON."

"AT KEY WEST—NO WORK."

"ANCHORED OFF ENGLAND—NO WORK."

"SUBIC BAY, PHILLIPINES—NO WORK—RESISTING BOARDING."

"ANCHORED OFF STATEN ISLAND—AWAITING WORD."

"ENROUTE DIEGO GARCIA—NO WORK—STAND FAST BROTHERS!"

"AT ANCHOR—LONG BEACH—NO WORK—NO BOARDING."

"ANCHORED—CHIRIQUI GRANDE—EXPECT TO BE FORCED OFF LATER TODAY—SISTER SHIP ARRIVED TWO HOURS BEFORE WE DID SO THEY GOT HONOR OF BEING FIRED FIRST. STAND STRONG AND BEST WISHES TO ALL STANDING FIRM FOR SOLIDARITY."

The following day, October 6, the unlicensed crew of the *Alaskan Seas* got an answer from the headquarters of the seamen's union. Sparks posted it just before for the 10:00 A.M. break.

TO: SHIP CHAIRMAN AND CREW MEMBERS OF
   M/T ALASKAN SEAS.

I RECEIVED YOUR WIRE OF OCTOBER 4, 1984
ADDRESSED TO HEADQUARTERS REGARDING
THE STATUS OF LDO UNION ON TRANSEAS
VESSELS. WE ARE NOT AWARE OF ANY LABOR
DISPUTE. THEREFORE NO ACTION IS NOW BEING
CONSIDERED BY THE SEAMEN'S UNION. ALL
CREWS ARE TO REMAIN ABOARD SHIP AND
CONTINUE TO OPERATE THEIR VESSELS, AND
PERFORM ALL ASSIGNED DUTIES. WE WILL
ATTEMPT TO HAVE A PATROLMAN MEET YOUR
VESSEL AT THE NEXT PORT OF CALL OF THE
SHIP AT OR NEAR A SEAMEN'S UNION HALL. IF
YOU HAVE ANY FURTHER QUESTIONS CONTACT
HEADQUARTERS COLLECT BY PHONE.

PRESIDENT
SEAMEN'S UNION

"CHICKEN SHIT BASTARDS!" The old AB stood looking at
the answer from headquarters.

Tommy came into the messroom and walked over to the
board. "You talkin' to yo'self again there, Henry?"

"CHICKEN SHIT...! This fuckin' union is turning into nothin'
but a bunch of *goddam scabs!*"

Tommy read the message.

"The cocksuckers *'are not aware of any labor dispute',*"
Henry quoted headquarters in a high falsetto. "I ain't got no love
for topside...but this is too much! Boats, if our goddam officials
are that stupid—or that rotten a bunch of hypocrites—then we
ain't got a union worth a *shit!*"

"We been takin' the easy path. You know what old Abe
Golden used to say: 'Clean the shithouse or learn to like the
smell!'"

"He was a stand-up guy all right!" I was AB with him on the
East Coast the winter of '78-'79 when the oil companies were
saying there was no fuel oil. That's what we was hauling!" Henry
slammed the table top. *"Shit..!* They run us up and down the coast
for a month before they let us off-load."

"Which ship was that?" asked Tommy.

"Remember the *Transeas Express*?"

"Yeah, she was a scow."

Mike Whaler, Angela, and the two 4 to 8 ABs came in headed for the coffee pot.

"We anchors off Staten Island covered with 300 hundred ton of ice and the Coast Guard pulls a fuckin' fire drill! It's 15 degrees above zero. Naturally every leaking connection's making for more ice and we're already slipping all over them goddam decks."

The others in the room had pulled up chairs at various tables and were listening to the old AB—none had gone over to see if there was any new messages posted.

"Golden had a fit. He was yelling and cussin' and this Coast Guard captain threatened to take his papers.

"'Go ahead try for 'em. I'd love a day in court to point out this ship's violations.'

"'WHAT VIOLATIONS?' The officer yells.

"Abe pointed at the pumproom. 'A pumproom with <u>one</u> <u>fuckin' door</u>—*look at the sonofabitch!* An explosion or anything and you can't get in or out. There ain't even a goddam <u>kill switch</u> on deck to shut down the cargo pumps. If you've a spill or a fire, you gotta call the engine room on the phone!! But you guys *pass* this SOB every inspection! And how come we ain't got a wind-shield wiper that works? Some way to run a ship—opening a porthole to scrape ice with a knife to see where you're going...! *Shit!'* says Abe and he just turns around and walks away."

"They ever rig another door to the pumproom?" asked the bosun.

"Naw... Anyhow she wasn't around that much longer. Month after Golden and I piled off the fucker blew up! Peeled the fuckin' well deck like a sardine can from the after pumproom clear to the midships house. Later they come to find they was using a hose to transfer dirty ballast through an open tank top—with welding goin' on! They got a damage estimate at better'n 20 million so they just scrapped her."

"Coulda been worse—as I remembers there weren't no one killed or hurt."

"That's true, Boats... Just blind luck. Not a soul on deck and the explosion never touched either house."

Tommy went to get coffee, then came back to sit at the table nearest the bulletin board. "Yep, that Golden was all man! He'd stand up to the company, union, anyone."

Henry sat down opposite the bosun and lit a cigarette.

"Abe an' me went back a long way," continued Tommy. "In '72 I took me an AB's job on one of them converted T–2s they rigged out to be a Container Ship. She was the *Intercoastal Trader,* runnin' from Jacksonville through the Canal on up to Long Beach. That's where I met him. We was watch partners six or seven months."

Angela got up and walked over to the bulletin board. She had liked Abe Golden very much. *"Damn them!"* She read the telex from headquarters.

Tommy went on. "Those converted T–2s had air-conditioning but there were containers stacked on the well deck blockin' the air to the fo'c'sles. The company didn't have no fans or wind-scoops for the portholes, so when the air-conditioning broke down, it was a major problem. Me an' Golden had the 12 to 4 fo'c'sle with them steam lines runnin' overhead. The temperature got to 130 degrees an—"

"You have any cots?" Henry interrupted.

"None... Rest of the fo'c'sles and the officers' rooms two decks up weren't much better. Everyone took to sleepin' on the boat decks. Even they was too hot to lie on. Sheets an' spreads were always black with soot from the stack."

Angela sat down at the table and gestured to the old AB for one of his cigarettes.

"The bosun was the ship's union delegate, but he wouldn't do nuthin'," Tommy recounted. "Bein' I was deck delegate, the gang asks me to get the union to tie the ship up for repairs. I tried, but nuthin come of it. We lives that way for two months till we paid off in New York."

By now the others had gone over to the bulletin board and read the telex from the union. They also stood or sat closer to the bosun's table to listen.

"The crew all put in for the subsistence accordin' to the contract for havin' no fans, scoops, or cots.

"Well, here come the patrolman an' a couple of goons soon as we ties up. He knew all about the beef and he knew who made all the phone calls. Everyone was madder'n hell. He said Headquarters wanted the ship paid off and we'd get the extra money due us later on.

"He give a whole bunch of excuses for the company not gettin' the air-conditioning fixed or providin' fans and cots for us. This go on for about an hour and he don't get nowheres. Finally he blew up.

"'CLEAR THIS GODDAM ROOM!' he shouted. 'EVERY-ONE...! EXCEPT *YOU!*' he pointed at me. And sure enough each an' every man what swore they was gonna stand fast got out in a hurry. All but Golden.

"'*YOU DEAF OR SOMETHIN'?*' he shouted at Abe.

"'No, Sir.'

"'WALK THEN—*WHILE YOU STILL CAN!*'

"'No, Sir. Not unless the deck delegate here tells me he wants to speak private about something.'

"'*Give me your book!*'

"The patrolman's face was red as a beet, an he keep clenching' his fist an' lookin' over at his two goons. But he knew he couldn't do nuthin'—*not with two of us.* One man can have a bad accident real easy an they'd gets away with it, but it ain't so easy explainin' two.

"Abe, he jus' smiles, walks over and puts his book down in front of the guy.

"'Get out of here—*the two of you!*' The patrolman shoves the book back at Golden."

"Ever collect the subsistence?" someone asked.

"Naw... We knowed we wouldn't once they got the crew to go along with the pay off. That were about the beginning, tell you the truth. Only a few years before, the union would have tied that ship up till we'd *got* our money. The deal makers was just gettin' started then. One excuse after another for the companies and the contract always gettin' bent more'n more... A union, or anythin' else can't be no better than the people as makes it up!"

The unliscensed crew members, furious with headquarter's reply to their telex, voted to stop working all overtime in protest and just stand their sea watches.

*   *   *

The afternoon of October 7 found Sparks busily posting dozens of communications received throughout the previous night and that morning.

The deck gang had turned to at 1:00 P.M. to prepare the ship for docking. The first thing they did was to hang the huge canvas sign over the side for all the world to see as the *Alaskan Seas* entered Prince William Sound. The tanker was scheduled to dock "starboard side to"—securing the sign was tricky as that was the weather side.

At the 3:00 P.M. break, everyone gathered around the bulletin board.

"COMPANIES HAD SOME EARLY SUCCESS WITH SWIFT POLICE ACTION AND REPLACEMENT CREWS OR FINKING MEMBERS OF OUR UNION ON SEVERAL OF THE TANKER CONSORTIUMS' VESSELS IN THE GULF, BUT RESISTANCE STIFF-ENING EVERYWHERE INCLUDING STRONG SUP-PORT OF ENGINEERS AND UNLICENSED CREW ON SOME SHIPS INDICATING OUR MOMENTUM GAINING STRENGTH."

"VALDEZ PIPELINE IS SHUTTING DOWN AS NO SHIPS WILL LOAD AT VALDEZ. ALTA STAR SHUT DOWN ON ARRIVAL AT DOCK. ENGINEERS AND CREW VOWED TO SUPPORT DECK OFFI-CERS IN JOB ACTION. AKENTA AND NASTAR DUE NEXT IN VALDEZ COMMITED TO SHUT DOWN. ENGINEERS ON AKENTA IN SUPPORT OF LDO'S. ALASKAN SEAS NO WORK—COMMIT-TED TO SHUT DOWN IN VALDEZ."

"Well, there *we* are!" Angela pointed out the message. It had been underlined by the radio operator. "I suppose the Old Man is already packing his bags."

"That suppos' ta be funny?" Mike Whaler asked from where he stood behind the girl.

"No, Mike. And to tell you the truth, the more I see of this mess, the more I hope we can do *more* than hang a sign."

"Go on. Read da rest."

Angela turned back to the board and continued reading aloud to Mike Whaler and the group clustered around them.

REC'D THIS A.M. FROM TRANSEAS OHIO: "RECEIVED YOUR TELEX. WE ARE AT ANCHOR THE LOOP SINCE 0000 10/7 PLAQUEMINE PARISH POLICE TO TAKE US OFF IN IRONS. KEEP THE FAITH. WE ARE BEHIND YOU."

"TRANSEAS WASHINGTON, TRANSEAS AR-

TIC SHUT DOWN AT PANAMA ON BOTH COASTS. TRANSEAS OREGON SHUT DOWN AT LOOP OUTSIDE NEW ORLEANS AND TRANSEAS NATALIE COMMITTED TO SHUT DOWN ON ARRIVAL."

"CORONASUN SHUT DOWN INSIDE MISSISSIPPI RIVER ENTRANCE. CORONASEA SHUT DOWN AT ANCHORAGE ST. THOMAS. CORONASTAR COMMITTED TO SHUT DOWN."

"CAPROCK CANYON AND CAPROCK GORGE COMMITTED TO SHUT DOWN."

"HOLIDAY LINES' PRINCESS MARIA STOPPED FRIDAY IN LOS ANGELES BY WORK STOPPAGE."

"OCEAN LIFT BERING SEA SHUT DOWN IN KEY WEST UNTIL MATES REMOVED BY U.S. MARSHALL."

"TRANSEAS ALICE AND TRANSEAS VIVIAN NOTIFIED COMMANDER SUBIC BAY THEY ARE OBSERVING JOB ACTION AND WILL NOT MOVE FROM ANCHORAGE."

"CAPTAIN OF THE PORT'S OFFICE IN NEW ORLEANS HAS RECOGNIZED OUR ACTION AS A BONA FIDE LABOR DISPUTE AND IS INSTRUCTING ITS PERSONNEL NOT TO INVOLVE THEMSELVES OR HARASS OUR LDO'S IN ANY WAY."

"FIRED LDO OFFICERS REPORT OIL COMPANIES SUPPLYING CORPORATE JETS TO FLY SCABS OUT TO REPLACE THEM ON STRIKING VESSELS."

"FINKS AND SCABS WEARING MASKS TO CONCEAL THEIR IDENTITIES BOARD TANKERS AS LDO OFFICERS ARE REMOVED BY ARMED GUARDS."

"STRIKE COMMITTEES IN BALTIMORE, BOS-

TON, PORTLAND AND LOS ANGELES PREPARING CHARGES AGAINST FINKING MEMBERS OF LDO UNION WITH DAILY FINES."

"Listen to this!" Angela read the message that the *Alaskan Seas'* engineers sent to their union headquarters. Sparks had underlined it as well.

"DEMISE OF LDO UNION REPRESENTATION CAN ONLY LEAD TO FUTURE LOSS AND/OR REVISION OF OTHER EXISTING MARITIME CONTRACTS (ENGINEERS' UNION NEXT???)

"WE FEEL ACTION IN SUPPORT OF LDO IS APPROPRIATE AND WE ARE PREPARED TO STAND WITH OUR UNION BROTHERS. WE REQUEST COMMUNICATION FROM HEADQUARTERS FOR ACCURATE INFORMATION AS TO WHAT IS HAPPENING AND WHAT COURSE OF ACTION WILL BE?"

RESPECTFULLY,
ENGINEERING OFFICERS
M/T ALASKAN SEAS

"Guarantee ya," Henry predicted, "they'll get a bullshit answer from their bosses just like we got from ours!"

After coffee the gang went back on deck. It was cold and the wind whipped an icy spray over them as they worked.

By 4:30 P.M. most of the docking preparations were complete. While some deckhands secured the last of the scupper plugs on the well deck, others readied the six Fire-Fighting Foam Stations—training the gun-shaped barrels at the inshore manifold. Several fire hoses were run out on deck, and the ship's two dozen life preservers were placed in their racks.

As planned, no work was performed in preparation of deballasting or loading.

*   *   *

"Cap'n Stacey." Tommy knocked on the Old Man's door. "That you, Boats?"

"Aye, Sir."

"Be with you in a minute." Stacey finished stuffing the last few pieces of clothing in his flight bag and walked over to open the door. "Come in and set awhile."

"Everythin's ready on deck. It'll be an hour or so fore we're alongside the dock... I see you're all packed there, Cap'n." Tommy looked at the luggage against the bulkhead as he went over to the settee.

"Yeah. Ready to go." Stacey turned his chair and sat down facing the bosun.

"I know you ain't gonna jus' agree to get off."

"No, they'll have to fire me and force me off."

"If they start strong armin', you got a crew behind ya!"

"Thanks, Tommy. It wont come to that. And I don't want any of the crew to overreact and get in trouble."

"They will if anyone puts a paw on you. I'll see to that!"

"These are different times, Tommy. They do their dirty work with a lot of class."

"No possible chance of a settlement?"

"I don't know, Boats. It seems this was all planned a while ago."

"From the look of all them cables, I don't see the companies bein' able not to come to terms. Looks like you people got plenty of support—even the engineers!"

"Union officials, ours included, don't always respond to their membership's wishes. Sometimes it takes more than just asking to change things."

"Sad, but true. If there gonna be anything left out here worth fightin' for we better get started."

"Well, I think it's late in the game for me... Sort of feel Keiko'll have her way this time."

"Meanin'?"

"I'm old enough to retire."

"Heck, you younger'n me. You ain't but what...? fifty-six, fifty-seven? That ain't old enough for the rockin' chair."

"If I'm not old enough, I'm sure tired enough!"

"Bein' commodore of this fleet makes it sorta necessary for you to speak out, don't it, Cap'n?"

"Well, I wrote this out as starters." Stacey handed the paper to the bosun.

"THE HONESTY AND COURAGE OF THE ENGI-NEERS AND CREW OF THE ALASKAN SEAS IN SUPPORTING THE LDO IS PROOF THE 'AMERI-CAN WAY' IS NOT AS DEAD AS THE CYNICS WOULD HAVE US BELIEVE. UNFORTUNATELY, THESE VIRTUES ARE RARE, SO MUCH SO THAT 'BOSSES'—IN AND OUT OF GOVERNMENT—OFTEN IGNORE THEM.

"WE LEARNED (OR SHOULD HAVE) DURING WATERGATE THAT WHEN OUR LEADERS ARE WRONG, AND WE KNOW IT, THEN WE MUST NOT FOLLOW THEIR ORDERS.

"MAN IS A 'SOCIAL ANIMAL' BY AGREE-MENT— NOT BY NATURE. THE AGREEMENTS ARE TOO OFTEN VIOLATED AND THE RESULTS ARE WARS AND HOLOCAUSTS. WE STILL HAVE A LONG WAY TO GO.

"BUT WHO WOULD WANT A RETURN TO CHAOS? CIVILIZED PEOPLE MAKE AGREEMENTS BECAUSE THEY ELECT TO TRUST THEIR FEL-LOWS. SHIPS SIGNAL THEIR INTENT TO PASS EACH OTHER IN SAFETY BY THIS PRINCIPLE— WE KNOW WHAT HAPPENS WHEN IT IS VIO-LATED.

"THERE'S ROOM FOR ALL PEOPLE OF GOOD-WILL OUT HERE, AND FOR ALL PHILOSOPHIES OF LABOR.

"UNION OR NONUNION IS NOT AT ISSUE IN THIS 'BEEF'—WHAT IS AT ISSUE IS INTEGRITY.

"COMPANIES AND SEAMEN ENTER INTO AGREEMENTS BECAUSE BOTH SIDES BENEFIT. THESE CONTRACTS CONTINUE AS LONG AS THAT STAYS TRUE, BUT THEY ARE SUBJECT TO CHANGE OR CANCELLATION—THE ONLY THING THAT CAN'T CHANGE IS INTEGRITY!

"UNFORTUNATELY, THIS IS EXACTLY THE CASE HERE. THE TANKER CONSORTIUM HAS NOT BARGAINED IN GOOD FAITH. THEY HAVE DEALT IN SUBTERFUGE AND VIOLATED THE SOCIAL CONTRACT—<u>WHILE SIGNALING TO PASS SAFELY THEY CROSSED OUR BOWS</u>.

"VICTORY IN THE 'GOOD' FIGHT IS NOT AL--

WAYS IMMEDIATE. TYRANNIES AND ABUSES CONTINUALLY THREATEN, BUT THEY ARE ALWAYS OVERCOME, RELEGATED TO DARK CHAPTERS IN OUR PAST.

"JUST REMEMBER THAT <u>HONESTY</u>, <u>CHARITY</u>, AND <u>INTEGRITY</u>—ATTRIBUTES THAT APPEAR THE WEAKEST AND MOST FRAGILE—ARE ACTUALLY THE STRONGEST AND MOST PREVAILING FORCES IN MANKIND'S ASCENT."

—FORTY-ONE—

"Good throw, Mike!" Angela shouted her approval to the ordinary as the heaving line arched high in the air.

The weighted "monkey's fist" landed with a thud on the concrete dock well over a hundred feet from the tanker's side. Within seconds linemen ashore had a messenger bent to it, and Mike and Henry hauled it aboard. The ordinary held the slack as the old AB untied the heaving line and secured the end of the messenger to the wire eye.

Angela had the winch out of gear and as soon as Henry was through she let it slack off.

The old AB watched the heavy steel mooring wire run through the chocks, sinking into the water. He waited till enough wire was out for the dock's winch to haul it ashore to the bollard. "That's enough!" he shouted. "Put her in gear!"

Mike had already coiled his heaving line and hurried aft to throw it again for the next messenger.

The ship's powerful whistle echoed against the operations building as she answered the signals from the tugs. It was dark and cold and a strong offshore wind fought to hold the vessel away from the dock. The tanker's winches heaved the slack out of the mooring wires as the tugs strained to push her alongside, her manifold in line with the waiting Chicksans.

The *Alaskan Seas* had been secured for 30 minutes, and a fine sleet-like rain whipped at her empty decks. The absence of the usual sound and bustle at the manifold lent an eerie feeling to the deserted scene.

Captain Stacey placed the remaining payroll records and files on top of his desk, then went to the safe and withdrew two large manila envelopes. He emptied them on the desk and recounted the money, recording the totals in a small ledger. Satisfied that all was in order he returned the envelopes to the safe, spun the dial and left the office. He went back to the stateroom, got a book and settled down in his recliner to wait.

After supper, the crew messroom was still full of people waiting around—no one was working, except for a deckhand on security watch at the gangway. The room buzzed with small talk and speculations.

The report of a ship exploding in San Francisco bay had just been received and it also was posted on the bulletin board. It stated the tanker had been refused escort to the dock by inland pilots sympathetic to the LDO, then stranded in the Oakland Estuary when longshoremen, also in sympathy, refused to dock her. A couple of men were dead or missing and several badly burned and injured in the massive explosion that peeled back over 50 feet of her well deck. The FBI was investigating the possibility of there having been a bomb planted aboard her due to the ongoing labor dispute.

*   *   *

At 6:30 P.M a Valdez Oil Terminal security van drove down the jetty and stopped next to the operations office. Three men got out of the vehicle and climbed the steep gangway, identifying themselves to the watchman as the tanker company's port captain, port engineer and agent. Crossing the deserted decks, they entered the after house and took the elevator up to the captain's deck. They walked down the passageway to Captain Stacey's office.

"Best wait till I've spoken to him," the young port captain advised. "I know him and there's a chance he'll listen to reason."

The port engineer and the company agent nodded and moved away from the door.

Stacey had dozed off over his book and it was a moment or two before he heard the knock.

"Commodore!" the young captain called out again.

"One moment!" Stacey stood up and walked into his office. He put the novel down on top of his flight bag and went over to open the door.

"Commodore Stacey." The young captain held out his hand.

"Captain." Stacey accepted the brief formal hand shake.

"May I come in, Sir?"

Stacey stepped aside allowing the port captain to enter.

"You're certainly looking fit, Commodore," his attempt at bonhomie registering zero. "Sorry I'm late getting here," he went on when the silence started to be unnerving, "our car broke down."

"Then you're not alone, Captain?"

"No, Sir." The young man was thankful for any answer. "The agent and port engineer are here. I asked them to wait outside till I spoke with you."

"That wasn't necessary, but go ahead Captain, I'm listening."

"I noticed there was no one at the manifold. Are you waiting for the shore gang?"

"No, Captain. I didn't let them board."

"I see... Have your mates refused to deballast the vessel?"

"No, Sir. The decision not to off-load is mine."

"Well, Sir, as port captain I must order you to proceed immediately with deballasting... I sincerely hope you'll remain loyal to the fleet and comply."

"There'll be no off-loading or loading so long as I'm master of this ship."

"If this is your position, Sir, than I ask you to voluntarily relinquish your command at this time. Hopefully later you'll reconsider and return to the company."

"No, Captain. I do *not* voluntarily give up my command."

"If you don't reconsider your decision, Commodore, than this is no longer a request—you are fired and I must order you off this ship."

"That's better. Now you might as well call the port engineer and agent in."

"Yes...thank you. I'd appreciate your starting with the agent. He'll need an accounting of the ship's funds. I'll be back shortly to go over the other paper work with you."

"Mate!" The port captain waited a moment and knocked. "MATE!" he called again and tried the door—it was locked.

The port captain walked to the companionway leading down to the next deck. Hearing conversation as he approached the officer's lounge, he looked in—all three of the *Alaskan Seas'* mates were there.

"Mate," the captain caught the man's attention, "can I have a word with you?" He didn't enter the lounge.

"Come on in."

"Thanks...but I have to see you in private."

The mate glanced at his fellow officers a moment, got up from the couch and walked towards the doorway.

"I'd like to use your office."

"Aye." The chief mate led the way back up to his quarters; he entered his office and went over to the desk. The young captain pulled up a chair facing him.

"Captain Stacey is leaving the company," the port captain announced as soon as they were seated. "I'm certain his decision was made with retirement in mind... You've sailed relief captain for ten years with an exemplary record. With the commodore's leaving we feel the permanent captaincy of the *Alaskan Seas* is rightly yours."

The mate was hunched over his desk, left forearm flat on the surface, the right one, upright, thumb and forefinger tugging slowly at his bearded chin. "Master of the *Alaskan Seas!*" he thought. *"Motherfucker!"* It was all he could do to control his inner rage—he finally understood the parochial school's priest and his sermon on 'Christ's Temptation.'

"Yes, Sir." The port captain reached into his jacket and laid a long envelope on the desk. "Signed sealed and delivered, *Captain* —I think you'll be surprised."

"'*Get thee behind me, Satan!*'" The words, barely whispered, resounded throughout the room.

"Wha—"

"GET OUT OF MY OFFICE!" The mate shoved the envelope off the desk as he rose menacingly.

"I... You...you don't under..." The young captain was white-faced as he hurriedly got up.

"Take *that* with you!"

"Mate, I...I hope you appreciate my difficult situation." Fairly confident now that the 'pirate' wasn't coming for him, he was trying to regain his composure.

"Pick it up and say what you have to. Then get out of my sight!"

"Mate, I'm really sorry that we—"

"NO SPEECHES, DAMN IT!"

"Very well, Mate. I'm asking that this vessel be deballasted." He picked up the envelope.

"No!"

"Then as port captain I request that you voluntarily leave this ship."

"*No!*"

"Then I have no alternative but to fire you, Mate!"

"If that's all, get out of here!"

The young port captain was still too shaken to confront the other two deck officers alone. He went back to the captain's office and called the lounge on the telephone requesting they come up one at a time. Both men refused his orders to deballast—both were fired.

*   *   *

"That's about it. We'll let you know if there's going to be any changes." The patrolman stood up in the messroom to signal the end of the discussion.

He was an imposing black in his early fifties, 6' 4", 295 lbs. One of the first of his race to become a seamen's union official. Arriving alone about fifteen minutes after the company officials, he had had the bosun round up the crew for the special meeting.

"Boats, better tell your gang to take down that sign," he advised as the crew members started out of the messroom.

Tommy sat where he was and said nothing.

A few of the deck gang held back waiting to hear the bosun's orders. No one spoke and the silence became palpable.

"Go on like I say." The big black looked at the few people still in the room. "You've got new officers coming aboard and the union is abiding by the agreement."

"What agreement, Big Frank?" Tommy looked at the patrolman. "Company ain't seen fit to sign our contract."

"You know we're still negotiating." The big man broke eye contact with the bosun and looked at the few deckhands near the door. "Go on now... I want to speak to the chairman here—alone!"

"What do *you* want us to do, Boats?" the old AB challenged the patrolman's authority.

"Jus' look after things awhile for me, Henry. See someone relieves the gangway watchman." Tommy looked over at the clock. "It's about that time."

"Now, what the hell's this all about, Tommy?" the patrolman asked as soon as the room emptied out. "You got a beer or something?"

"Sure, Frank. In my fo'c'sle."

The two men sat opposite each other sharing the bosun's desk as a table. The patrolman popped a second can of beer and took a long drink.

"Boats... You know I don't call the shots. If the union isn't backing these LDO's there's fuck all I got to say about it... Headquarters knows about the sign—they told me to see it was taken down."

"I ain't takin' it down, Frank."

"Goddamit, Tommy, we been good friends a long time. What the hell's eating you?"

"Nothing and everythin', Frank... But if you want that sign down you'll hafta take it down yo'self—I quit!"

"*Quit!* Man are you crazy? What you doing? Wildcatting?"

"Call it anyway you wants—I ain't agitating the crew. But I ain't sailing with finks and scabs no matter what the union say. And that's it, Frank!"

"Christ, man! This union been damn good to us! Look how far we come!"

"That's true—a black patrolman and a black bosun. We both a long ways from the galley. Thing you forgets, Frank, we didn't get outta that galley by goin' along with the flow. It took standin' up to the union—for that matter it took breaking the laws of the country itself to do it."

"Goddam, you're one hard-headed nigger!" The patrolman finished his beer. "Tommy, the Valdez Oil Terminal people have restricted the crew to the ship. And if you managed to get off, all you going to accomplish is getting thrown out of the union—like it or not man, there's rules. You want to lose everything you got coming—how about Ellen?"

"You still don't understand, Frank, or you wanta act like you don't 'cause it's easier. Couple of years back we had laws and rules 'bout where you sat in a bus. And, shit, like Golden told me, in Germany it become *the law* to kill Jews."

"Boats...Boats you blowing this 'beef' up all out of proportion."

"No, I ain't , Frank. I ain't tellin' you what to think. You got to follow your own feelings. But I ain't buyin' no one's rule and law as substitutes for right and justice!"

"Leave the fuckin' sign, then. Let the new captain take it down or eat the motherfucker for all I care!" The patrolman got up and shook the bosun's hand. "Good luck, Tommy."

*   *   *

"That about wraps it up. Thank you, Captain Stacey." The company's port captain looked at his watch. "We have some security guards coming down to insure the safety of all personnel during this transition period."

Stacey picked up two of his pieces of luggage and started out of the office.

"Here, we'll get those taken down for you, Sir." The young officer got up from the desk.

"No trouble." Stacey walked down the passageway and put his bags down next to the elevator door. He turned to start back for the others, but the captain and agent were already carrying them towards him.

"Well, Sir," the port captain extended his hand, "we're going to miss you. Best of luck!"

Stacey shook hands with the man. "I'll wait in the saloon with the mates."

At 7:30 P.M. fifteen uniformed security guards clambered aboard the *Alaskan Seas*. At their lieutenant's order they spread out across the ship taking up posts a hundred feet apart starting from the bow. The lieutenant and three guards proceeded into the house and made their way up to the ship's office.

A few minutes later Captain Stacey and the mates came out on deck followed by the guards and the company agent. A number of crew members gathered around to say their good-byes and several deckhands carried the officers' gear to the side of the ship, lowering it to the dock in a cargo net with the tanker's inboard crane.

The bosun was not there. But the sign still hung over the side.

Two vans transported the officers, two to a van with two guards in each, the company agent accompanying Captain Stacey and the chief mate.

At the main gate everyone got out of the vehicles. The guards, under order of the Valdez Oil Terminal's authorities, searched every piece of luggage before loading them into the two waiting taxis. The officers, guards and company agent drove into the city and parked at a motel that had a good restaurant. The agent paid the taxi fares and gave the cab drivers instructions where to pick up several men at a different motel who awaited transportation to the *Alaskan Seas*. The guards left with them.

The agent was a friendly sort. He worked for several tanker outfits whose ships called at the oil terminal. His involvement was limited to fiscal matters, arranging air transportation to and from Valdez, and seeing that ship's personnel received medical attention when necessary.

When they had registered and dropped their gear off in their rooms, the four officers and the agent went into the restaurant.

"Eat hearty, Gentlemen, the company is picking up your tabs here," the agent advised the four men, "and in the morning I'll be back with your airline tickets, also compliments of management. Let me have your final destinations." He got out his note pad and began writing it all down. When he finished he got up and pulled on his heavy jacket. "I'll leave you people here then and see you in the morning."

The same guards that escorted Stacey and the mates to town waited for the agent at the motel where he had earlier left the *Alaskan Seas'* new deck officers. As soon as the taxis got there the four security men paired off with two officers in each taxi. The company agent got in with the new captain and chief mate.

"God!" the agent thought, "these two are dead drunk!" It wasn't his business. It was the port captain's worry. "And the two in the other cab didn't look old enough to *drive* a car!"

—FORTY-TWO—

The three days had been a nightmare. Off-loading the *Alaskan Seas'* 200,000 barrels of oily sea ballast, a job that usually took two hours had taken over eight, and then they hadn't gotten all of it out. And if the chief pumpman who missed the ship in Long Beach hadn't arrived the next night, the tanker would probably still be at the dock, or belly up alongside it.

The drunken mate's staggering trips between control room and well deck were pure slapstick, but the crew members were not in a light mood—their three-day restriction to the ship saw to that.

Few people knew what the new captain looked like. From the moment he came aboard he disappeared into his stateroom and never appeared on deck or in the saloon. The steward's department took his meal orders by phone, leaving them as instructed on his desk and retrieving the empty dishes and trays. He was never in the office when the exchange was made and the door to his adjoining stateroom was closed.

The invisible captain's instructions to the rest of the ship's personnel were transmitted through the second and third mate, two pleasant, unassuming and very upset young men who had unwittingly stepped into the middle of a labor dispute. Neither one even knew the word "scab."

The second mate had graduated from a back east maritime academy and sailed for a year on a nonunion oil tanker. Having been laid off due to a reduction in the company's fleet, he studied and successfully sat for his second's license while waiting to get on again.

The slightly younger third mate had just graduated from the same college. They knew each other and were surprised to meet again at the airport in Seattle.

Both officers had had their applications in at every dry cargo, passenger and oil company in the country—the usual procedure for those seeking work in an industry with so few opportunities. And both had received the joyous news a few days ago to report to the tanker company's office ready to fly out to Valdez. Now they were apprehensive, if not downright frightened. The third mate had happily extended his hand to the seaman on gangway watch as he came aboard only to have the burly figure stare him down, spitting a glob of tobacco juice at his feet before turning away.

Speculation about the whereabouts of the bosun ran from being fired by the company, taken off by the union, ashore drunk, jailed in Valdez, in a hospital, to being murdered. The only hard facts were that his gear was found neatly packed in his room and he was gone.

*   *   *

At 2:30 in the afternoon on Friday, October 10, the deck gang turned to for undocking. The old AB, as acting bosun, along with the chief pumpman saw to it that the tanker was secured for sea. An hour and twenty-five minutes later, with a drunken mate forward, a boy scout (as the young third mate was immediately dubbed) aft, and a very nervous second mate in the wheelhouse, the last mooring wire's eye blinked closed as it squeezed through the chocks and the *Alaskan Seas* swung away from the dock.

"Well, Sir," the pilot turned to the second mate as the two tugs veered away, "you can put her on full ahead now."

"Yes, Sir. Full ahead." The young officer levered the telegraph to 'full sea speed' and started to move the throttle forward.

"BELAY THAT!"

Even the man on the wheel jumped.

"I said, 'Full ahead'! *Not* full sea speed! 55 rpm's, Mister!" The old pilot's voice was lower but just as cutting.

"Ye...YES, Sir! Full ahead—I'm sorry, Captain."

"Ten degrees right rudder, Helmsman."

"Ten degrees right rudder, Sir," the man at the wheel repeated.

A few moments of strained silence pervaded the wheelhouse.

"Well, who was it replaced the commodore?"

"Ah...a Captain Barker... Captain John Barker, Sir," the second mate answered.

"Don't think I know him," the old oil company ex-skipper mused aloud. "What's your compass reading now, Quartermaster?"

"252, 53, 53, 254—"

"Ease to five and steady up on 269."

The man on the wheel repeated the instructions as he took off five degrees rudder angle.

"Surprised he isn't up on the bridge here with a brand new command."

The young officer of the watch didn't respond.

The pilot picked up his binoculars and scanned the sea ahead. He understood the mixture of loyalty and fear. And he *knew* why the captain wasn't on the bridge—his friend, the company's agent, had breakfasted with him this morning.

"Steady on 269, Cap'n," the quartermaster's voice broke the awkward silence.

"Steady on 269—very well!"

Except for an occasional wheel order there was no more conversation as the tanker covered the six miles to the Valdez Narrows, her escort tug following close astern. The pilot called for slow ahead as they approached the entrance, and they moved at just over 6 knots for the three-and-a-half miles remaining.

"What're you heading, Quartermaster?" the pilot broke the

silence as the tanker approached the end of the ship channel.

"Steady on 224, Sir."

"Bring her left easy to 218."

"Left easy to 218."

"Kick her back up to full ahead, Second, and you best give the Old Man a call. We'll be off Rocky Point in about 30 minutes."

"Aye, Sir. Full ahead," the second repeated and executed the order but didn't ring the captain. "Captain Barker left orders not to call him till we were at the pilot station, Sir," he explained.

"Hmm... I see..."

As the tanker left the shelter of the narrows behind spray began whipping across the well deck.

"Getting choppy already—think you're in for a bit of weather this trip," the pilot prophesied.

"Yes, Sir. Looks like it."

For the next 15 minutes the only sounds in the wheelhouse were the ship's vibrations and the howl of the wind through the open door.

"Dead slow ahead, Second. I'll be getting off in ten minutes."

"Aye, Sir. Dead slow ahead." The young officer complied with the order, then pressed the telephone button to the captain's stateroom.

The telephone rang for almost a minute before it was answered.

"Yes?"

"10 minutes to the pilot station, Sir."

"10 minutes?"

"Yes, Sir."

"Okay."

The second mate put down the receiver and went back to the radar console.

The old pilot turned away from the porthole, got up from his chair and walked over to where his coat hung. He came back with it to the porthole and struggled into it. "Stop her!" he ordered.

"Stop her!"

For the next five minutes the tanker continued to lose way and the sea's effect on her became more pronounced.

"Hard left your rudder!"

The quartermaster echoed the pilot's wheel order.

Almost imperceptibly, the ship's bows began turning to the left, providing a lee for the escort tug.

A shaft of light flooded the wheelhouse for a second as the captain entered from the chartroom.

"Good evenin', Captain—Baker, isn't it?" The pilot only got a momentary glimpse of the man before the wheelhouse was blacked out again.

The man's response was mostly unintelligible to him. He only heard clearly, "Barker."

"Yes, excuse me—*Barker*... Well, the tug's comin' up. The wheel's hard left, Captain Barker. Have a good trip."

"Wheel is at hard left," the second mate repeated the pilot's words.

The third mate came into the wheelhouse from the starboard wing to relieve the second mate for supper. "Good evening," he greeted everyone. "Pretty good chow tonight," he said to the second. "Take your time getting back."

"Thanks—I won't be long." The second mate picked up the pilot's attache case. "I'll go on down with you, Sir."

"Very well—thank you." The pilot passed the captain as he opened the door into the chartroom and was assailed by a foul smell. It wasn't just whiskey; the man smelled like a bowery tramp. In the momentary flash of light from the chartroom he could see why. Commodore Stacey's replacement was unshaven, still wearing slippers and dressed in clothes that looked like he'd slept in them for a week.

The tug was alongside, her bows bumping against the *Alaskan Seas'* hull as she kept pace. The waves were already running eight feet high and despite the tanker's lee she pitched heavily.

"Thanks!" The pilot shook hands with the second officer before starting down the ladder.

As he reached the safety of the tug's deck he called out over the wind, "Good luck all of you!" To himself he thought—*you'll need it.*

A few minutes after the pilot got off the only officer on the bridge was the young third mate.

"We still comin' right easy to 218," the 4 to 8 AB at the wheel announced as the *Alaskan Seas'* bows swung slowly around.

The third mate glanced up from the radar and looked at the rudder indicator. "Midships!" he called out.

"Midships!" The quartermaster spun the wheel back from hard right.

It took several minutes for the tanker to come back on course.

The wind and waves were increasing and heavy spray slashed across the fo'c'slehead.

"218. Right on, Third. Startin' to take heavy spray for'd—you got a lookout up there on the bow!"

"218. Thank you." The third went to the phone and rang the bow.

"Lookout!" The man's voice was loud enough for all three in the wheelhouse to hear.

"Sorry. Better come stand lookout on the wing." The young officer was embarrassed at not remembering.

"Yes, Sir."

The third went to the console and put the telegraph on "full sea speed" as the captain had instructed him to before leaving the wheelhouse, then eased the throttle all the way forward.

For the next ten minutes the vibrations steadily increased as the huge propellor worked to bring the fully laden vessel up to her maximum of 16 knots at 84 rpm's.

The lookout opened the door from the port wing. It was the weather side and the wind howled as it swept through the wheel-house, exiting through the open door on the starboard side.

"Where you want me to stay?" he called out as he entered and secured the door.

"Port wing." The third looked up from the radar screen. "Bligh Reef is about nine miles off the port bow—if you spot the light through this haze let me know."

"Okay, Sir." The man started towards the open door on the starboard wing.

"I said the *port* wing!"

"Yes, Sir...didn't want to—"

"Excuse me." The nervous young officer realized the lookout intended going around the house to avoid opening the weather door.

The seaman left the wheelhouse just as the second mate came back from supper.

"You're back soon."

"Yeah, just don't have much of an appetite tonight—I'm ex-hausted."

"Well, you shouldn't have agreed to stand the mate's watch—you could have slept till midnight."

"Christ, you'll be lucky if he relieves *you* at midnight. I don't know what he's on...but he looked like a zombie," observed the second.

"Speaking of zombies, the captain sure disappeared in a hurry. I thought for sure he'd stay up here awhile. He left orders to put her on full sea speed and not to call him unless it was *absolutely* necessary; then cut out of here as soon as you left the bridge with the pilot."

"Well, you might as well go below and get a couple of hours' sleep."

"Hope I can—anyhow she's on 218."

"Okay, I've got her—218—see you at 8 o'clock."

The ship was handling well enough. More speed meant faster response to the wheel. But the seas were building steadily, you could feel the tanker shuddering as she plowed into the 10 to 12 foot waves. The second mate checked the radar and then went back to the chartroom to confirm their position.

The helm was relieved and the officer watched the rudder indicator for awhile to see how the new man handled the ship. He was nervous being on watch alone on a monstrous crude carrier. The second was confident he could navigate well enough, but it was his first time alone without a pilot or another officer with pilot's papers for the sound. He knew he had to change course to 184 when he had Bligh Reef's light on his port beam, about 30 minutes away—it seemed an eternity.

When that crisis passed without incident and the new helmsman called out "steady on 184," the second was a bit more relaxed. He went back into the chartroom and walked his dividers down the chart—16 miles on this course, an hour at most, then left to 156—25 miles more down the Southbound Traffic Lane, a hard left around Cape Hinchinbrook to avoid Seal Rocks, bring her over to 110 and they'd be out of Prince William Sound and in the "safety fairway" of the Gulf of Alaska. The second mate looked at his watch, he'd be relieved by the third about a half hour before they rounded Cape Hinchinbrook.

The tanker was pitching strongly and the wind was bitter as Angela made her way up the port side of the house. The ordinary followed her up the ladder on his way out to the wing to relieve the lookout. He was bundled warmly in his new parka.

"See you, Mike!" Angela called after him as she started into the wheelhouse.

"Going 156." The man Angela was relieving brought the wheel back to midships as she hung up her coat and came over to the steering station. "Watch her," he cautioned, "she wants to run to starboard and that's Schooner Rock's light up ahead."

The third looked up from the radar as the pretty girl took the wheel—he had relieved the second mate only moments before.

"Thanks, 156. I've got her," said Angela.

"Wheel's relieved—going 156, Mr. Mate." The AB pulled on his jacket and started out of the wheelhouse.

"Very well, 156."

They were getting closer to Cape Hinchinbrook and the sea was getting rougher by the minute. Heavy spray flew half the way aft on the well deck as the tanker plowed ahead at full sea speed.

Angela was getting nervous. She kept the course as well as anyone could, but felt someone more experienced should be on the bridge—especially rounding Cape Hinchinbrook. And underfoot, the hull's vibrations were increasing. The ship was going too damn fast!

The third mate came back out of the chartroom and glanced again at the radar. They were half way between Zaicof Point and Seal Rocks on the starboard. He looked at his watch. Another ten minutes he'd begin his left turn around Cape Hinchinbrook, steady her up on 110 in the Safety Fairway and they'd finally be in the gulf.

As the tanker started to come out of the lee of Hinchinbrook Island, what had been 15 to 20 foot waves a few minutes ago were rapidly being replaced by ponderous storm swells kicked up south of them in the Gulf of Alaska. The third positioned himself at the midship porthole and raised his binoculars. Angela knew they were about to make the course change. The ship was beginning to pitch heavily into the swells and the unencumbered wind whipped the heavy spray all the way to the bridge and against the portholes.

"Hard left." The young officer gave the order just as the tanker reared upwards. She hovered for what seemed minutes then buried her bows in the sea.

"HARD LEFT! *JESUS!*" Angela yelled as the ship lurched violently. She was almost thrown from the steering station.

The third mate staggered backwards—just managing to keep his feet under him. His binoculars had gotten away; they smashed to the deck and skidded across the room.

"HOLD IT!" he yelled. He didn't know what he meant by it— neither did the terrified girl.

"WHAT DO YOU WANT!" she screamed. "THE WHEEL'S

HARD LEFT!"

The third tried to regain his composure. "What are you on now?"

"138, 136—133 coming left fast!" Angela was trying to stay calm, but she knew things were getting out of control. She was praying someone who knew something was awake—*the damn captain—where in the hell was he?*

"Ease to 20—steady up on 110!"

"Ease to 20 and steady on 110." She felt the ship beginning to climb another mountain of water and braced herself. "Oh Christ," she agonized in silence, *"and I bitched about a captain like Old Man Stacey!"*

"WHAT THE FUCK!" Henry grabbed hold of the table top as everything in the messroom seemed to hang suspended. His coffee cup and the plate with his half-eaten sandwich and cookies landed with a crash on the messroom deck.

"SONOFABITCH!" He regained his balance and picked up his heavy jacket. It wasn't time to relieve the wheel or the lookout but he had to get up and see what the hell was happening.

The hull was still vibrating so strongly that the steel ladders leading up to the bridge felt like they were being hammered at with chipping guns.

On lookout, the ordinary had lost his footing as well. He went sliding down the slippery wing as the ship plunged over the crest and rolled down to port. Luckily, his headlong flight was stopped as his shoulder smashed into the gyro-repeater. If he hadn't grabbed hold of it he would have gone over the side. As he hung there he heard something distinct from the wind and the rush of water as the tanker voided her decks. Letting go of the repeater stanchion, he grasped the rail and looked over the wind screen. Two huge pieces of the new aluminum gangway were smashing against the tank tops. He struggled towards the wheelhouse to report.

The *Alaskan Seas* had made her turn through the Hinchin-brook Entrance and was safely away from Seal Rocks. But 50 foot swells were boring down on her from just forward of the starboard beam. She was in danger of broaching.

"110! RIGHT ON!" Angela called out just as the first one hit.

The bows rose high out of the sea as the tanker rolled up over the mountainous crest. The force of her re-entry was tremendous —the hull shuddered ominously. Green seas closed over her fo'c'slehead as it plunged into the trough, roaring down the well deck like a giant cataract. It smothered the tank tops and smashed against the house.

"GOOD CHRIST!" Angela was white with fear and anger. *"YOU—"*

She never got the rest of it out as Henry slammed back the sliding door. "CAPTAIN!" he shouted.

The third mate was frightened, very frightened, and he reacted stupidly. "I'M IN COMMAND HERE!"

The ship had recovered, but the vibrations, though less pronounced, still persisted.

"YOU... YOU IN COMMAND!"

"GET BACK ON LOOKOUT!" The third assumed that's where the old AB had been. Three sleepless days under the abrasive animosity of the crew, scared and embarrassed in front of the girl, the young officer was cracking.

"Oh, Christ," Angela moaned, "I need to be relieved. HEN-RY— Take the wheel—*PLEASE, HENRY!!"*

"GET BACK ON LOOKOUT!"

"DAMN YOU!" Henry shouted. "SLOW HER DOWN! *You'll split her in two!"*

"The captain left orders to keep her at full sea speed!" the third spoke in a tight, controlled voice. He was in a state of emotional collapse.

"THE CAPTAIN! That asshole and the mate both—they're stoned outa their minds and you know it!" he lowered his voice. "Call the second mate—*now!"*

"GANGWAY'S TEARIN' AWAY!" Mike shouted as he opened the door.

"It's okay, Mike!" Henry's voice was calm. "Stay on lookout!" He pushed past the third mate and grabbed the wheel. "What's the course?"

"110." The girl's voice was barely a whisper.

"Go below!"

The ship rolled sharply to starboard as it started up another crest. Angela fell against the main console and grabbed hold of the railing.

"Mate! You've gotta slow her down and change course! Sayin' it's captain's orders wont save your license *or your life."*

"FOR *GOD'S* SAKE *LISTEN* TO HIM, THIRD!" Angela's

teary voice resounded in the wheelhouse. "HE'S BEEN OUT HERE ALL HIS LIFE!"

The pounding of footsteps coming rapidly up the companionway echoed throughout the bridge.

"WHAT THE HELL—" The chief engineer lost his footing as he raced into the wheelhouse. He swung around grabbing at air as the ship lunged over the crest. *"CHRIST ALMIGHTY!"* he rasped.

The second mate slipped and fell in the chartroom, striking his head on the table—it was several minutes before he came to.

Only the old AB retained his footing. He had the rudder hard right to bring the tanker about before she broached. "CHIEF!" he shouted. *"SLOW AHEAD!"*

The burly heavy-set engineer pulled himself to his feet. He grasped the throttle and eased it back. *"I don't believe this!"* he croaked.

Angela was sitting where she landed on the deck crying uncontrollably—more in relief than in fear.

The third mate got to his feet holding fast to the radar console. In a way he was relieved that the nightmare was over. He wanted to crawl away and hide till he could get off the ship.

*   *   *

On October 25 the crew of the *Alaskan Seas* and some sixty other tankers around the world received a telex from the head of the Licensed Deck Officers Union in which he quoted the Labor Federation's President:

"THE UNJUSTIFIABLE REFUSAL OF TANKER COMPANIES TO NEGOTIATE IN GOOD FAITH AND DEAL FAIRLY WITH THE LICENSED DECK OFFICERS' UNION IS A SAD CHAPTER IN MARITIME HISTORY. THESE EMPLOYERS ARE ENGAGED IN A FLAGRANT ATTEMPT TO BUST YOUR UNION AND DESTROY THE CONDITIONS OF EMPLOYMENT WHICH HAVE BEEN BUILT UP OVER THE PAST 50 YEARS. BY REPLACING QUALIFIED DECK OFFICERS WITH SCABS, THEY ARE PUTTING AT RISK THE SAFTEY OF THESE SHIPS AND CREWS."

PRESIDENT
LABOR FEDERATION

Some of the tanker officers found employment on American flagged freighters belonging to their affiliated union, some sought work in related industries, many left the sea for good, seeking different careers, and some, like Captain Stacey, retired.

Tommy Deel, adamant at what he felt was a flagrant betrayal of all a union should stand for, paid his fine for missing ship, retired his book, and put in for his pension.

Well liked and popular around the hall, he was advised, lectured, and cajoled by union officials and friends alike to rethink his decision. But he went home to Ellen.

Like Big Frank said, he was "one hard-headed nigger."

—EPILOGUE—

The S/T Voyager's bow-wave cut a perfect furrow which stretched back like a great silver chevron on the turquoise colored water. Overhead, the light blue of a completely cloudless sky arched flawlessly down to an unbroken horizon, empty save for the low afternoon sun. The tight intense ball of it's midday incandescence had mellowed into a great golden orb whose rays, reflecting from the smooth surface of the sea, softened the stark white superstructure of the ship. One had to look closely to see the damage to the house. It was an ugly scar against the white.

The Voyager was the flagship of Cosmos Carriers, Ltd. and the first Ultra Large Crude Carrier which the British-owned tanker company had contracted to have built for them. She was ten years old, and on the final trip of her two-year charter with Global Oil Transport Ltd., carrying Kuwaiti crude to Japan.

She was 1,242 feet in length with a 240 foot beam. Fully laden, 92 feet of her enormous hull rode beneath the surface of the sea with 22 feet of freeboard above the waterline to her well deck. The 42,500 horsepower steam turbine which moved this 486,000 dwt behemoth at 16.8 knots rose level after level till it attained the equivalent height of a fifteen story building. Her cargo of 3,428,570 barrels (143,999,940 gallons) of crude at $15.00 a barrel represented a value of over $50,000,000 each trip, and would require a fleet of 29 standard T-2 tankers to haul it.

*   *   *

The chief mate hesitated in front of the captain's office and looked at his watch. "Sir... it's almost 6 o'clock." He rapped on the door as he spoke.

"Come in." The captain turned in his chair as the mate entered, "I'm about ready."

"Do you want me to have everyone off watch turn to on the fantail?"

"Aye, Mate. I'll be along shortly."

Stacey turned back to the letter in front of him as the chief mate quietly closed the door.

July 21, 1988
At Sea

Dear Ellen,

This letter won't reach you for several weeks but my cable to you was far too brief. I still can't believe Tommy's gone.

It's over two years since Keiko was thrown and killed, yet a part of my mind is so certain she'll be there in the front of the crowd, waiting as always, when I get off the plane. I don't wear a St. Christopher medal when I fly now—it lies buried with my heart on the hill overlooking the stables.

She was my life, my only line to shore. When it parted I could escape nowhere but to the sea. How easy it was to be generous with my grief! If I had not been, Tommy would never have asked to join me on this ship.

It seems an eternity, yet it's only 48 hours since we were hit. The plane that fired its missile at us made only one pass. We still don't even know whose it was. It's ironic that this was our last trip out of the gulf and only days after the announced cease-fire in this insane war.

Tragedies like the one two weeks ago when the Iranian Airliner was shot down killing 290 people make headlines. Who will look twice at the small blurb in the paper about the loss of only two men on a tanker?

In an hour, I'll be standing in front of our shipmates—a group representing a broad spectrum of intelligence, compassion and belief—quoting as usual from various religions and philosophers.

I never felt wrong or hypocritical conducting the service for the dead as I support any moral concept aimed at alleviating the anguish for which the human soul seems so eminently suited. The fact I didn't believe any of it never fazed me. What bothered me was that I envied those who did.

In contrast, Tommy had a philosophy he believed in and lived by. That's why he was able to see through me.

One night—about a year ago—we were out on the wing of the bridge talking. He said I was not an honest man—a "good" man, he added, but not an honest one. He asked me then how I could preach what I didn't believe.

I gave him my pet argument about our need for a "God" even though I thought there wasn't one. I added that we had a great responsibility to try and set things right in the world—man being the only creature with a developed sense of morality—that we had a duty to try even if it <u>was</u> accidental.

Tommy said I was not only dishonest, but a hypocrite and an unhappy one at that—evidenced by my statement that Keiko and I never wanted children in a world as senseless and cruel as this. Boats had a unique way of sorting through the piles of bullshit and getting to the crux of a problem. I had seen him demonstrate it time and time again with the men he supervised—but now he was doing it to <u>me</u>!

"I've watched you stick your neck out for one cause or another and you can't pass a beggar ashore without emptying your pockets. Are you trying to tell me this all comes from your belief in the 'survival of the fittest'?" he scoffed. "You may feel superior to people who believe the words you only mouth, but you are the one to be pitied—because you lack the one thing they all have—<u>hope</u>!

"It's really sad," he continued, "that you spend so much time, effort and money trying to give others what you deny yourself." He shook his head.

"Your actions show you really believe hope is what it's all about in the end, so how come you buy a 'religion' that doesn't hold out a glimmer of it?"

My "religion"—as he was fond of calling it—was nothing much more than the "big bang" theory. I thought it provided a neat explanation of the beginnings of the universe. He showed me no mercy!

"That bullshit with the whole universe starting from a tiny point a quadrillionth of a q—of a q—of a q—of an inch and reaching such a critical state of density that it finally went bang is nothing but a numbers racket. And, those four forces you told me about—the weak and strong bonding, electromagnetic and gravitational forces—they had to come into being a trillionth of a t—of a t—of a second after the bang yet they wouldn't be needed for billions more years while all this energy was forming into atoms and gas and dust and finally into stars. It may sound more sophisticated than 'the old man up there with a beard'—but man—if you can buy that as an accident—you can buy anything!"

Ellen, you know Tommy wasn't tied to any particular "gospel" of his own, but he sure was a believing man. He believed in the Creator, that man was formed in His image—not physically, but in having the capacity to reason and exercise free will in choosing between right and wrong. He always said that—even though we never asked to get here—we can control how we live while we are here—and sometimes how we leave here.

He said, "Face it... Every time we talk about this, the discussion is the same. You always say you can't believe in a Creator 'cause then you'd have to ask who created the Creator? In the same breath, you say you can't accept that the universe just is—that it wasn't created. So, instead of being just a little bit humble and realizing maybe there are things beyond our understanding, you adopt a dingbat idea like that!"

He took a gulp of beer and looked at my desk, spotting the big agate marble I'd bought several years ago in India. "Here," he said, plucking it out of the pencil tray and waving it in my face. "Here—let the professors of this 'religion' begin their 'BIG BANG' with something this size and then see how long it takes you to pop the question where did it come from?"

You know, Ellen, I suddenly began to chuckle and then to laugh out loud. "Go ahead, laugh damn it!" Tommy had his back up. When I could speak, I told him I wasn't laughing at him, but at myself. He was right. The wonderful theory didn't hold up in the light of common sense.

I was suddenly liberated. My dismal view of a mindless and meaningless universe wasn't a proven fact. I could entertain hope again.

It was around 7:00 P.M. when the missile struck us. It penetrated the bulkhead at well deck level and exploded into the pumproom. The man who was painting down in the lower section was trapped. He was a young fellow, nineteen, only a boy. An orphan to begin with, he was a hard case who grew up in miserable circumstances; kicked around from one foster home to another, under-privileged, abused, into the drug scene, in and out of jail. He was a terribly hurt and hostile young animal when he joined this vessel almost a year ago. He was handicapped by bigotry as well, proud of only one thing—that he was white. It was the only thing he had going for him, the last refuge sheltering what little was left of his ego.

Poor Tommy. He was forced to take even that away before he had a clear platform to build something on. After he put the boy down verbally many times, and with his fists on two occasions I know of, Boats saw that our misfit actually started to learn the trade. The change was astonishing. He became enthusiastic about life in general, took pride in his person, and even learned civilized table manners. He became a good shipmate.

Really, Ellen, none of us held out any hope, but the two of them fooled us. After awhile this kid got to caring about "Old Boats" so much he'd have given his life for him—well, you can imagine the rest.

Going below to try and save the ordinary—as he knew the kid would have done if their positions were reversed—was just Tommy's way.

I'm certain you remember that trip Boats and I sometimes spoke about together. It was when a tough, hard, old loner named Bill Evers—who never had any use for "jews or niggers"—gave his life trying to save "one" from a sinking hulk some 38 years ago.

I was the first man Evers went back for. Tommy wanted to do two things at the same time, look after me and help with the others. The big AB made the decision for him. "LOOK AFTER YOUR BUDDY!" he shouted. "WE'LL GET THEM ALL!"

—The chief mate just knocked at my door—but I'm almost through—

Everyone expected Captain Finney to be the last man taken off, and when Evers and Hansen finally appeared at the rail with him, we all cheered, thinking he was.

The men were yelling for them to hurry. They wanted to pull away from the sinking stern. It was starting to slip under.

Bill heard the warning, but it was Tommy's shout that they'd forgotten Sam Diamond, the chief cook, that he listened to. Telling Hansen to get the injured captain into the lifeboat, the big AB went back alone.

Funny thing is I don't think Evers had even noticed old Sam before then. Tommy was the first black man he'd gotten to know. See, it was Tommy he had grown to admire and respect. Going back to try and save the cook was his way of showing it.

Ellen, some things never change.

My love to all of you,
Al Stacey

* * * AFTERWORD * * *

Just prior to the Second World War, the U.S. Maritime Commission authorized the construction of ninety-five new single-screw (one propeller) bulk-oil carriers to be designated as T-2s. They were designed for speed in hope that they might elude their pursuers.

A number of these hastily constructed vessels foundered without the aid of the enemy: in freezing and stormy seas some of their hulls broke up. Disproportionate to all other shipping, the losses suffered by these T-2s and those who served on them has been documented, but the story of the survivors, both men and ships, destined to haul the oil of the needy post-war world is largely unknown.

After the war, many maritime fortunes were amassed by people who purchased these remaining "Kaiser's Coffins," as they came to be named, for less than the price of scrap.

They were not easy to crew. The contracts (called "Foreign Articles") committed men for up to 24 months shuttling between barren deserts or primitive jungles to load; then back to refineries, located far from the urban centers which they served, to off-load. There were only short stays in port and little or no time off; tank cleaning with its demanding round-the-clock work in filth and fumes (always noxious and sometimes deadly) and finally, their reputation for breaking up and blowing up was known to most seamen.

The end of the war also marked an end to the wartime truce between the shipowners and the seamen's unions for control of the American maritime industry—the bitter struggle resumed with the 1946 "General Strike" and persisted on through the early 1950's.

The fiery rhetoric of union and company bosses incited rank and file supporters (usually innocent pawns) into committing acts of psychological and physical violence on one another.

Ashore, the boycotts, picketing, and the more violent strikes and police confrontations made the headlines. But only those seamen, union and nonunion alike, caught up in the resulting webs of shipboard intrigues ever really knew what it was like to live with the coercions, beatings, and constant threats of becoming another of those "mysterious disappearances at sea."

During these trying times of labor unrest in the early ' 50's, the outbreak of the Korean War ushered in a considerable expansion of the American Merchant Marine. Vessels from the "mothball" fleet were hurriedly outfitted and recommissioned, making the spoils that much more enticing to those who sought to control the waterfront.

At sea, the 1960's marked the beginning of the end for the traditional dry cargo freighters—"stick ships"—rigged with up to two dozen booms to work the cargo. The Liberty ships, Victory ships, C-2s, C-3s, C-4s, and Mariners were all made obsolete by a completely new breed of vessel—the container ship.

In the tanker trade, the old T-2s' hulls were extended to increase their tonnage—a stopgap measure till the new class of "Supertankers" made their debut, ratcheting the oil carrying capacity of a single vessel to three, four, and five times the approximate 5 million gallons of oil a standard T-2 tanker could carry.

And as the ships grew bigger and bigger—the crews grew smaller and smaller.

Also during the '60's, aboard both union and nonunion ships, the "checkerboard crew" issue (Blacks allowed to sail in any department) paralleled the civil rights movement ashore with men putting their lives on the line for their beliefs.

The war in Vietnam sparked another revival in the U.S. Merchant Marine, but by the early 1970's the number of "Runaway Flag" vessels (American-owned ships registered in foreign countries and manned by foreign seamen in order to maximize profits) far exceeded any additional tonnage the war accounted for.

The phenomenal scientific advances realized in the half-century since the outbreak of the Second World War can be easily identified aboard any modern vessel. Navigation and cargo handling have become largely automated and carrying capacities increased to limits undreamed of in the recent past. Unfortunately, concern and provision for "Safety at Sea" and the safety of the sea have not kept pace.

It wasn't until the early 1980's that seamen sailing in frigid waters were issued "Survival Suits." Yet the effects of hypothermia and the means of producing the suits were common knowledge for decades.

The disgraceful sight of ultra-modern vessels outfitted with antiquated lifeboats still persists. [In 1989 the U.S. Coast Guard finally proposed that large cargo and tank ships be required to carry "totally enclosed lifeboats, self-righting or provided with a means of escape." This and other measures will at long last bring the United States into compliance with the international treaty known as SOLAS (Safety Of Life At Sea).]

Sailing ships carried spare sails. As sail gave way to steam, turbines powered by multiple boilers became the norm. The perfecting of Diesel engines saw the design of twin and quadruple engines electrically-coupled to the main shafts with provisions for rapid conversion to mechanical drive should the electric coupling fail.

The state of the art in marine propulsion (with the common sense provisions of "back-ups" in the case of emergencies that served this country so well during W.W. II) soon gave way to new designs that stressed economy over safety—1 ship = 1 boiler or 1 Diesel.

The same "bottom-line myopia" saw to it that shipboard personnel be reduced as well to "zero redundancy" with total disregard to the resulting stress and danger to the ship and crew when one or more men became incapacitated.

In 1988 the decade-long, Iran/Iraq "Tanker War,"in which over 300 merchant mariners lost their lives, came to an end. The material losses to some 500 vessels and their cargoes (mainly tankers and oil) were so enormous that as of this writing they were still not fully tallied. With our dependency on oil from this region in excess of 35 percent, it is difficult to understand why the price of crude did not soar during those years. Especially in light of the 1989 grounding of the Exxon Valdez where the loss of only 12 million gallons and a several-day slowdown in shipping resulted in immediate price increases of 30 to 40 percent.

Another incident during this past decade, one receiving practically no news media coverage at all, was the removal of the highly qualified M.M.&P. (Master, Mates and Pilots Union) licensed deck officers from some 60 tankers.

Several of the largest independent American oil transporting companies gambled the safety of their crews and vessels by hiring nonunion officers rather than continue to provide union scale wages and benefits to masters and mates who had served them well and faithfully for years.

The loss of the Titanic and 1,635 souls in the icy North Atlantic shocked the world of 1912 into realizing that inlaid wood panelling and silk drapes were no substitute for lifeboats. And watertight compartments no excuse for excessive speed in the vicinity of icebergs. The Titanic set sail with lifeboats for only half her passengers and maintained a speed of 21 knots through the ice fields because the thought of her foundering was inconceivable.

How many more disasters like the Exxon Valdez must there be before we discard our philosophy of "profits first?"

Entering the last decade of this century, the United States merchant marine is in a state of almost total collapse:

Foreign ships carry over 95 percent of our exports.
Our ships grow old and are not replaced.
Most shipyards are idle—many are bankrupt.
The seamen's unions, licensed and unlicensed alike, are weak and quarrelsome; fighting each other for an ever diminishing piece of the pie—all the while under the shipowners' threats of their having no jobs at all if they don't accede to even more drastic cuts in shipboard personnel.
The crews that are left are overworked. The industry's creed of "PROFITS FIRST" with the demand for 15 to 25 hour "TURN-AROUNDS" (getting a vessel in and out of port) have wiped out even that brief respite ashore seamen once had between trips—to unwind, drink, relax and still have time to sober up before coming back aboard to resume their far-from-easy lives.
New men are not coming into the industry.
The day of the skilled, non-licensed deckhand is obviously coming to an end—you can't have ABLE-BODIED SEAMEN when you no longer hire ORDINARY SEAMEN to learn the trade!
Crews of 20 men work tankers hauling as much as 30 times the oil that T-2s carried with crews of 40.

GREED, like tonnage, seems to know no upper limit.

Larry Reiner
February 9, 1990

About the author . . .

That old adage, "write what you know about," was taken to heart by Larry Reiner in committing **Minute of Silence** to paper.

Born during "Great Depression" year 1930 in New York City, Reiner began sailing on inland tugs and barges as a 19-year-old in 1949. He made the jump to deep-sea tankers in 1950.

Drafted in August, 1951, he served two years in the Army during the Korean Conflict.

During the next four decades, when not at sea, Reiner used his GI Bill to complete his education as a geologist and mined and prospected in the American Southwest and Mexico.

Always an avid reader, Reiner was amazed that there were so few books written about the lives of merchant seamen in the modern era. His determination to help remedy this situation led him to write **Minute of Silence**.